Path

of

Injustice

BEVERLEY HANSFORD

Matador
9 Priory Business Park,
Wistow Road, Kibworth Beauchamp,
Leicestershire. LE8 0RX
Tel: 0116 279 2299
Email: books@troubador.co.uk
Web: www.troubador.co.uk/matador
Twitter: @matadorbooks

ISBN 978 1789016 741

British Library Cataloguing in Publication Data.
A catalogue record for this book is available from the British Library.

Printed and bound in the UK by TJ International, Padstow, Cornwall
Typeset in 11pt Bembo by Troubador Publishing Ltd, Leicester, UK

Matador is an imprint of Troubador Publishing Ltd

To all those innocent people – past and present
who have suffered injustice.

Chapter 1

Finn Yago paddled his boat slowly down the river. The August day was hot and did not invite strenuous exercise, so occasionally he would rest his oars and allow the boat to drift idly along. It was a pleasant and tranquil scene, but for Finn the beauty around him only held passing interest: his focus was on the livelihood the river could provide him with. His earlier catch of fish had been excellent, and after making his usual trek to the nearby town of Toomer he had been fortunate to sell all the spoils of his labour quickly in the market there. Now two silver coins nestled safely in the pouch at his belt. It had been a particularly good day, he reflected, and on his way home he would likely quaff a jug of ale at his local hostelry before returning to his wife and six children.

It was the sound of young people's laughter that roused him from his musing. Rounding a bend in the river, he spied the source of the merriment. Here the river was shallow, and a spit of sand ran alongside its bank and jutted out into the water. Two teenage girls and two boys of a similar age were enjoying walking in the cool water. The boys waded up to their knees, but the girls modestly only held their dresses up sufficiently to allow their ankles to be immersed. All were enjoying the unusual freedom of being closer to nature and feeling the water lapping against them.

Finn smiled to himself. As a boy he had done the very same thing at the same spot. He recognised the group of revellers: Daintry and Mela were the daughters of Anton Brouka, the grain merchant and miller of Toomer. Conrad was the son of the

1

mayor of Toomer, and Miklo was the doctor's son. Finn allowed his boat to drift past the group.

'Girls! Out of there this minute!' The peaceful interlude was broken by the harsh tone of a woman's voice.

A middle-aged, rather plump woman hurried along the river bank towards the group. She was red-faced from her exertion.

'Out of there, I say!' she ordered.

The two girls had already heeded the first instruction and were heading back to the spot where they had abandoned their belongings.

The two boys were also leaving the water, but they were not to escape reprimand.

The woman turned her attention to them. 'And you two boys should not be enticing young ladies to behave in such a shocking manner.'

Finn smiled to himself. He knew the woman quite well, for he had almost grown up with her. Their families had lived in the same street when they were children. She was Mogo Parr, Anton Brouka's faithful housekeeper. She had served in the Brouka household ever since Anton's wife had died birthing their last daughter, and had subsequently brought up the two girls. He also knew that Mogo's bark was worse than her bite.

Finn stood up in his boat and greeted Mogo. 'Good day, Mistress Parr.'

His action calmed Mogo's wrath. She composed herself before turning her attention to him and returning the greeting. 'Good day, Master Yago.'

Finn rowed slowly on down the river, still observing the unfolding scene on the river bank. By now the two boys had retreated to a safe distance, away from Mogo's sharp tongue, and the two girls were replacing their stockings and shoes under the watchful and disapproving eyes of their guardian, both conscious that they were not yet free from her admonishment.

'You should both know better at your age than do such things,' she remarked sternly.

'It was so hot, and we only paddled in the river,' retorted Mela, who was the older and more rebellious of the two.

'We picked lots of berries,' pleaded her sister, faintly hoping that their labours prior to their escapade might appease Mogo.

The remark distracted Mogo from her chastisement. She glanced at the basket full to the top with the wild berries that grew in profusion along the banks of the river.

'That's good. We'll have some for supper and I'll preserve the rest.' She was calming down now.

Before the girls could respond she spoke again. 'Hurry! We'll be late.'

'But it's hours and hours to suppertime,' protested Mela.

'Never mind that. I want you both home well before then.'

The two girls did not argue any further. They knew Mogo of old and were well aware that as soon as she felt she had control of them again her anger would subside. They were not to know that her apparent displeasure with them was partly caused by an incident that did not concern them. On her way to the river, Mogo had encountered her old friend Arlee and had spent more time chatting and gossiping than she had intended. On top of that, she feared that Arlee might still be somewhere in the vicinity, and she was anxious that she might have seen Daintry and Mela acting in a most unsuitable manner for two young ladies of thirteen and fifteen. Mogo knew that if that had been the case, Arlee would have quickly spread the news around the town and her supervision of the girls would have quickly become another item of gossip among certain residents.

Urged on by Mogo, the girls made their way the short distance to the rough and dusty road that led uphill for about a mile to the small town of Toomer. Mogo immediately set a quick pace, much to Mela's disgust.

'Why do we have to walk so fast?' she asked.

3

'It's so hot,' complained Daintry, who was carrying the basket of berries.

Mogo relaxed the pace a little, but her action was accompanied with the repeated remark, 'We have to hurry.'

'But why?' repeated Mela.

Mogo did not reply, and the little party continued their trek, conscious of the afternoon heat. The road was open and there was no shade from the sun.

Hot and dusty, they eventually entered the town. It seemed to be busier than usual, and in the square people were beginning to gather in small groups around a piled-up heap of logs.

'Why are there so many people about, and what is that pile of logs for?' asked Daintry.

'I know why,' announced Mela.

'Why?'

Mogo butted in before Mela could reply. 'Never mind that. We've got to get home,' she snapped, grasping Daintry's arm and hurrying her forward.

Mogo's efforts were of no avail. As they left the square and hastened towards the street where they lived, the murmuring of the crowd increased. The source of the spectators' interest soon became apparent. Four men on horseback came into view, stern-faced and intent on their task. In their midst stumbled a young woman. Her hands were bound, and one of the horsemen held the loose end of the rope. Wherever the horsemen went, the woman was forced to go. The noise of the crowd ceased as the party drew near.

'Where are they taking that lady?' Daintry whispered.

'She's a witch. They're going to burn her in the square,' replied Mela, adding for good measure, 'Peena told me.' Peena was the servant employed by Anton's household.

'Hush. Don't talk of such things,' snapped Mogo. Then she issued her next instruction. 'Daintry, Mela, turn your faces to the wall.'

4

The two sisters recognised the tone of Mogo's command and meekly complied.

Mogo had desperately wanted to get them home and safe before the much talked-about event was to take place. Now, thanks to her own indulgence in gossiping with Arlee, her worst fear had materialised. No doubt her neighbours would have something to say about her allowing Anton Brouka's two daughters to witness such a thing. At least she would make sure that her charges saw as little as possible.

Mogo's intention was not entirely honoured. After a few minutes of staring at a blank wall, the girls could not resist peeping at what was happening. Their efforts were facilitated by Mogo, whose focus was now fixed elsewhere. For Mela the event was a subject of curiosity. Her younger sister was more deeply affected. Once she had observed that Mogo's attention was distracted, Daintry looked at the unfolding scene with a mixture of horror and disbelief.

The dismal procession moved slowly at the pace of the prisoner. The woman was dressed in rags and walked barefoot over the rough cobbles of the street. Her shoulders were bent over, her eyes cast down. All hope was gone. Now only despair enveloped her. The local priest, Pastor Kartov, followed behind, uttering prayers of comfort.

Once they had passed, Mogo urged the two girls to continue the journey home.

Daintry was still puzzled and concerned over what she had just witnessed. 'Why are they doing that to that lady?' she asked.

'Because she's a witch,' retorted Mela.

'But what's she done?' Daintry pleaded.

'She's done bad things to someone,' Mogo replied, in a bid to end the conversation.

'What things?'

'It's best not to talk about it. She's a bad lady and must now pay the penalty for her wickedness,' explained Mogo, hoping her answer might appease Daintry's curiosity. She was well aware of the alleged crimes the poor woman had been accused of. She and Arlee had talked about it all, and Arlee had been a mass of information.

'Peena told me she could cast spells on people,' announced Mela.

Mela's contribution to the conversation fuelled Daintry's search for an answer. 'What sort of spells?' she asked.

'She cast a spell on her husband and he fell down dead,' whispered Mela.

'Hush! You must not talk about things like that,' Mogo intervened sternly.

Daintry would still have asked another question, but now they had arrived home. Anton Brouka's was in a row of houses standing in one of the better streets of Toomer. The mayor of Toomer occupied the house next door, an imposing building reflecting the prosperity of its owner.

Once indoors, Mela quickly forgot the incident she had just witnessed. Daintry was more gentle and sensitive and could not dismiss the frightening scene of the young woman, who had looked barely older than Mela, being led publicly to such a horrible fate. That night she would suffer from nightmares, much to her sister's annoyance.

In the early evening, Anton Brouka arrived home. He had travelled many miles that day, buying grain for the two mills he owned and operated. He was now tired and dusty. After returning his horse to the stables at the end of the street, he made his way to his house. As usual his two daughters were there to greet him.

'Good evening, Father,' they uttered, almost in unison.

Anton smiled. He was very fond of his daughters, though like many other fathers in the 18th century he did not always show it.

'And what have my two girls been doing today?' he asked kindly.

'We went down by the river and picked lots of berries,' announced Daintry.

'We saw the witch being taken to be burned when we were coming home with Mogo,' Mela remarked casually, as if it were an everyday event.

This statement caused Anton some concern. Why, he wondered, had Mogo allowed his two daughters to witness such a spectacle? He had been all too aware that it was to take place. Leaving the town earlier in the day, he had passed through the square and observed men piling logs around a stake. He did not agree with the justice meted out. As town elders, both he and the mayor had fought hard to spare the woman's life, but they had been overruled by the Witch Prosecutor and church dignitaries. He was thinking of a suitable reply when Daintry chipped in again. 'Mogo was angry with us,' she said in a hushed voice.

'And what were you doing to arouse Mogo's displeasure?' asked Anton sternly.

'We paddled in the river with Miklo and Conrad,' replied Mela.

'It was so hot,' pleaded Daintry. It was the best defence she could muster.

Anton hid his humour at his daughters' confessions. He had done the same as them when he was a boy, but the situation demanded his disapproval. Young girls in their teens did not expose any part of their bodies to boys and young men. 'Don't you think it was unbecoming for young ladies of your age to do that?' he asked.

'We won't do it again.' Daintry was almost in tears now. She prayed that her father would not hand out some form of punishment to suit the occasion.

'We really are sorry.' Even Mela was more subdued now.

'Very well. Don't do it again.'

With that remark Anton was glad to finish the incident. He was tired and the events of the day weighed heavily on his mind.

First had been the burning of the witch, and then on his return to the town he had heard the unmistakable sound of the town crier's bell. He knew that this must be something important so late in the day. He stopped to hear the news.

The town crier waited until a crowd had assembled and then cleared his throat as he consulted the sheet of parchment he held.

'Now hear this. King Oliff is dead. Prince Henri will be the new king. Long live the king.'

The news concerned Anton greatly. King Oliff had been dearly loved by the people of Altaria for his wise and peaceful rule. Now an unknown and inexperienced young prince would take on the role his father had held for sixty years.

Anton had lingered and discussed the news with several other notable townspeople of Toomer. All agreed that the information they had just received was deeply alarming. The situation did not bode well for the future for the kingdom of Altaria.

Chapter 2

Two years had passed since King Oliff had died and Prince Henri had become king. After a hard winter, spring had returned to the kingdom of Altaria.

Anton Brouka chose a bright March morning to venture out and call at the two mills he owned close to the town. He was also anxious to make a visit to the new watermill he was building an hour's ride away. Bad weather during the winter had held up its construction considerably.

As he rode along the rough road, he was deep in thought about past times and the future. Since taking over his father's windmill he had been successful in his ventures. One mill had soon become two, and now he was one of the most respected mill owners in the country. Producers of grain were keen to sell their produce to Anton, for he had a reputation for being an honest man and paying a fair price. The new watermill would enable him to greatly increase his production of flour, for it would be able to operate continuously, unlike his other two mills, which required the wind to blow. In Toomer he was a respected and popular figure; it was even rumoured that he would be the next mayor of the small town.

While his business ventures were going well at present, there was one thing that worried Anton, and that was the lack of a son and heir to run the mills when he could no longer do so. Only this last winter he had been laid up for several weeks with rheumatics, which seemed to get worse as the years passed.

Sometimes he wondered whether the solution to the problem might lie with his two daughters. If one of them could marry a young man able and willing to take over the mills, the problem would be solved. His thoughts turned to Mela. She was now seventeen, the same age as his wife when he had married. As far as Anton was concerned there were two likely young men in the offing: Miklo, the doctor's son, and Conrad, the son of Anton's very good friend and neighbour the mayor. Both boys had enjoyed frequent contact with his two girls when they were growing up. Miklo was now studying in Taslar, and tomorrow Conrad, the younger of the two, would also leave for the university. Anton had always considered Conrad the more likely candidate for his business affairs, particularly since, having left Toomer, Miklo appeared to have bigger ideas than settling down in his home town. Conrad was the quieter of the two boys, and a bit of an unknown quantity, but Anton was aware that Mela admired him, and he felt that this would aid his cause. This very evening he had invited Conrad to have supper with the family. He would, he decided, before Conrad departed, outline his plans and sound him out as a potential son-in-law.

The sound of an approaching horse and cart aroused him from his thoughts. It was Adler, the town carrier. Twice a week he made the day's journey to the distant city of Taslar and brought back goods for the townspeople of Toomer. His undertakings were varied: anything from a new cooking pot to material for a wedding dress. He regularly carried passengers to and from Taslar for a few coins. Anton had a particular interest in the carrier and his activities. Several years previously Adler had needed a new horse and had not had the money to buy one; it had looked as if he would be unable to work and his family would starve, but Anton had stepped in and provided him with a new horse and a covered cart. Anton received a few coins each week from Adler to recoup his outlay and enable him to make a small profit on the deal.

Adler brought his cart to a halt and waited for Anton to draw alongside. As the merchant approached, he raised his hand in greeting.

'Good day, Master Brouka.'

'Greetings, Adler. What news from Taslar?'

The carrier thought for a second. 'They say the king becomes more arrogant every day,' he recounted gloomily.

Anton sighed. 'That seems to be an ongoing story,' he remarked.

The carrier's remark saddened Anton. His original fears had been proved correct. The young king appeared to have little regard for his subjects and spent much of his time indulging his personal interests.

'There is more news as well.' Adler waited a few seconds, observing Anton as if to ensure his attention. He continued. 'Princess Aleena has been accused of treason.'

'What?' Anton was shocked. 'She is the king's sister!'

'That counts for nothing, it seems,' Adler replied.

'But what are the charges?'

'Plotting to overthrow the king is what I've been told.'

'What has happened to her? What about a trial?'

Adler thought for a moment. He nodded. 'There was a trial, but people say the court was afraid to go against the king and found her guilty.'

'But the crime of treason carries a death penalty. Where is she now?'

'After the trial she was paraded through the streets of Taslar and then taken somewhere. It is thought that she is held in Geeva castle. Nobody is certain,' explained Adler, recalling the gossip he had heard during his recent visit to the city.

Anton was shocked and stunned by the news. 'But Geeva castle hasn't been occupied for years. It's practically derelict,' he said, almost to himself.

Adler nodded in agreement, but he had no more information to give.

The two men talked about other matters for a short while and then each went on his way.

The news that he had just heard worried and depressed Anton. Since coming to the throne of Altaria two years previously, Henri had proved to be a poor replacement for his much-loved father. Arrogant, ruthless and with a taste for extravagance, he had not endeared himself to his subjects. Barely twenty-four, he had little experience of running a country and often relied on poor advice. Though Princess Aleena was two years older, Altaria's law of succession did not allow a woman to ascend the throne. Like many people, Anton believed that this law should be changed.

Still deep in thought, he reached his destination. Already the walls of the new mill were standing proud, and men were busy digging out the millrace to feed the giant waterwheel that would complete the job.

Brodvic the master builder saw Anton coming, walked over to meet him, and held the horse's head while Anton dismounted. He gave him a broad grin from his red and weathered face.

'Good day, Master Brouka.'

'Good day, Master Brodvic. How is work going?'

'It is going well, now that the worst of the winter is over. The walls are now complete and soon we shall start on the roof.' Brodvic smiled again. He was pleased with the progress he could report.

'And the millstones, are they in place?' Anton enquired.

'They are,' Brodvic replied confidently. 'It took two teams of horses and two days to bring them from the quarry,' he added.

'That is indeed good progress.'

'I have the best craftsmen in Taslar making the wheel, a strong one of iron and wood. It will be transported and in place before two months have passed,' the builder announced proudly.

'You have done well. You have made excellent progress after the delays of winter,' Anton replied enthusiastically.

Anton was well pleased with the way the building of the mill had progressed. So far things had not been easy. Getting permission from the owners of the land had been slow and protracted, and he had ended up having to buy a large parcel of the land to site the mill and have access to it. It had stretched his resources a little, but now that he could see everything taking shape his enthusiasm for this new venture was renewed. He would reimburse Brodvic for the recent expenses and had some gold coins in his pouch for the purpose.

Anton spent several hours at the site, being shown every detail by Brodvic and discussing the plans. The afternoon was well advanced when he at last made his way to his horse.

Brodvic accompanied Anton and waited until he had mounted. He looked up at him. 'Have you heard the news from Taslar?' he enquired.

Anton nodded. 'I met Adler the carrier on the road here, and he told me about Princess Aleena.'

Brodvic spoke gravely. 'Who would have thought such a thing would happen? Treason! And by all accounts she is such a gentle and kind maiden.'

'It is hard to contemplate,' replied Anton, 'and I have to confess I have little regard for King Henri.'

'I too,' agreed Brodvic.

After a few more minutes' conversation, Anton took his leave. Brodvic watched him disappear from sight and then returned to supervising the construction of the millrace.

The garden at the rear of Anton Brouka's house was large and secluded. Paths darted here and there, with tall hedges obscuring them. Here and there seats were placed in alcoves for people to linger.

This evening one of the alcoves was occupied by Daintry and Conrad. The garden had been a favourite place where Anton's two daughters would play with Miklo and Conrad as children, but this evening Daintry had scorned convention and contrived to get Conrad alone in the garden. She sat on a bench dressed in her best frock; Conrad sat at a respectful distance from her, as propriety dictated.

Daintry looked at Conrad. There was sadness in her voice. 'Tomorrow you are leaving us, and you won't come back.'

'Of course I'll come back,' replied Conrad.

Daintry was not so sure. 'Miklo said he would, but now he's going to stay away,' she replied, somewhat crestfallen.

'I will come back,' Conrad said emphatically.

Daintry was still not convinced. 'You'll meet one of those fine ladies who live in Taslar, marry her and never come back.'

'I'll come back when I have finished university, and then I will marry you,' Conrad announced, 'and we'll have the finest house in Toomer to live in.'

Daintry was overwhelmed. Her secret longing was materialising. She would have kissed Conrad there and then, but her strict upbringing by Mogo forbade that. She blushed. 'Do you really mean it?' she whispered.

'Of course I do,' Conrad assured her quietly.

There was an awkward silence, and then Conrad spoke.

'I have a present for you,' he announced.

'What is it?' asked Daintry, intrigued.

Conrad rummaged in his pocket and pulled out a small object. Handing it to Daintry, he declared, 'I found it in the river. I polished it and made a hole through it. You can wear it round your neck.'

Daintry was thrilled. No boy had ever given her a present like that before. It was a round stone of many colours, threaded onto a leather cord.

'Do you like it?' Conrad asked anxiously. He had worked hard on the stone for several months. His stirrings of admiration for Daintry had been growing. Now he had overcome his natural shyness to express them and he was pleased he had.

'It's beautiful. Thank you. I will keep it always.'

'Will you wear it?'

Daintry smiled at him. 'Of course I will. I will wear it under my shift, close to my heart, to remind me of you,' she whispered.

Suddenly the longing that had been building in Conrad burst forth. He leaned towards Daintry and kissed her softly on the cheek.

He would have kissed her again, but Daintry remembered her position. She pulled away slightly, and then gently took hold of his hand. She looked at him lovingly. 'Now you've kissed me, you'll have to marry me,' she announced, laughing. Then she asked softly, 'Will you write to me?'

'Of course I will. I will send a letter with Adler,' Conrad assured her. It was fortunate that, rather unusually for the time, Anton had provided a good education for his two daughters. Both were well versed in the skills of reading and writing.

'Daintry, Mela, Conrad! Supper!' The stillness of the evening was broken.

The sound stirred Daintry and Conrad from their indulgence and they hurried in the direction of Mogo's voice.

Mela emerged from her place of concealment. Anger and jealousy raged within her, intensified by what she had just witnessed. How dare Daintry take from her what she had always believed to be hers! Had she not always given Conrad full indication of her feelings? Now he had spurned her and turned his attentions towards her sister. He had even promised to marry her! Never. Never would it happen, she vowed. She would do everything in her power to prevent it. She turned to hurry to the house before anyone discovered where she was. She would not stand for it. Conrad was rightfully hers, and she would make sure things remained that way.

Chapter 3

Anton Brouka was not anticipating a good day. The tax collector from the King's Purse was in town, making his yearly visit to notable citizens like Anton. Anton hoped there had not been any increase in taxes since the collector's last visit. Since the accession of King Henri to the throne of Altaria, taxes had risen continually. Many people believed this was to fund the extravagant spending habits of the king, making the visits of the tax collector even more unpopular.

A violent knocking at the door roused Anton from his musing. The tax collector, a sombre-looking individual, stood on the doorstep, his secretary close at hand. Behind them in the street was a covered horse-drawn wagon accompanied by six mounted soldiers in the livery of the King's Guard. Two more horses stood by.

'Anton Brouka, grain merchant and miller?' the collector asked, regarding Anton gravely.

Anton nodded and bade the two men enter. Their boots loud on the wooden floor, they followed Anton into his workroom.

'Would you like some refreshment?' Anton asked. 'The day is warm.'

'Nay, but I thank you for the offer,' replied the collector brusquely.

There was a brief silence. The secretary reached into his bag and handed the collector a sheet of paper.

The collector studied it for a few seconds, and then

announced: 'Tax on three mills and estimated profits, fifty gold pieces.'

Anton was shocked. He protested calmly. 'But the third mill is not yet completed, and last year the tax was only thirty-five gold pieces.'

There was no sympathy from the collector. 'The first is not my problem,' he replied curtly, 'and on the second the High Council has deemed it necessary to increase taxes.'

Anton hid his anger. He knew it was of little use to try to oppose or even reason with the tax collector. Only a few months ago a baker in a nearby village who had protested about his tax had been accused of cheating on his payments and placed in the stocks for a day.

Anton went to the chest where he kept his money, drew out the canvas bag containing gold pieces and counted out the required sum. The tax collector's secretary counted the coins again and made an entry in a book. With that the visit was over, and after a brief exchange of words the two men left.

Anton saw them to the door of his house and watched as they mounted their horses and the party moved off with a clattering of hoofs to their next unfortunate client.

Anton returned to his workroom and slumped into his chair. Like many citizens of Altaria, he was beginning to wonder where the small country was heading. As the taxes continued to rise, the population became poorer and suffered as a result. New laws were being introduced by an unseen administration, and in some parts of the country protests against the changes being imposed were being put down with brutality by soldiers from the King's Guard.

There was a tap at the door. 'Enter,' Anton invited.

The door was pushed open, and Mela came in.

'Father, has the tax collector left?' she asked hopefully.

Anton smiled at his daughter. 'Indeed he has, and now we are fifty gold pieces poorer,' he remarked dryly.

'Will we be very poor? Will there be some money for my wedding gown?' Mela asked anxiously.

Anton smiled again. 'I am sure there will be sufficient for that,' he replied, adding quickly, 'Besides, that event is some distance off.'

'Conrad's studies will be completed soon,' Mela stressed.

'True,' her father replied. He could tell that something was bothering his eldest daughter, and he thought he knew what it was. 'But you wish to talk about other things, do you not?' he asked, as kindly as he could. 'Please sit down.'

Mela took a seat on a nearby chair and thought for a few seconds. Anger still burned in her heart. A few days previously she had caught Daintry wearing only her shift. She had immediately noticed the stone Conrad had given her sister. The sight of it had made anger well up in her.

'What's that?' she had demanded, pointing to the offending item.

'Conrad gave it to me before he left for the university,' Daintry had replied innocently.

'Why did he give it to you? You know very well that we have been promised in marriage for a long time now.'

'But he wants to marry me,' Daintry had protested meekly.

The revelation had infuriated Mela even more. 'How can you say that? You have no right to take Conrad away from me,' she had retorted. She had stormed out of the room, calling over her shoulder, 'I shall speak with Father about this.'

Now as Mela sat with her father her encounter with her sister was fresh in her mind.

'Daintry wants to marry Conrad. She told me so, and she is wearing a stone he gave her.'

Anton did not reply immediately. Conrad and Mela had more or less grown up together and it had been an unwritten agreement that they would be married eventually. Such an event would suit Anton's business plans admirably. Now it seemed that

Cupid had shot an arrow and threatened to disrupt everything.

Before Conrad had left for university, Anton had spoken to him about an ideal marriage to Mela. He had been concerned and a little irritated to learn that Conrad's affections lay not with Mela, but with Daintry. He had remonstrated with the young man, stressing the importance of selecting a suitable wife and outlining his plans for a capable son-in-law to help him run and expand his business. He had made it clear that he would oppose a marriage between Conrad and Daintry and had even hinted that in the event of such a union going ahead he would consider disinheriting his younger daughter. He had been reluctant to speak with Daintry about the matter, relying instead on the hope that the attraction between the two young people was merely the infatuation of youth and that eventually with the absence of Conrad the whole thing would die out. Now he knew he would have to speak with her, but in the meantime he had to deal with Mela's concerns. He chose his words carefully.

'I have spoken with Conrad. He is a sensible fellow and I am confident that he will see the error of his ways and realise that the infatuation with Daintry is a passing phase.'

'But Daintry really believes he will marry her,' persisted Mela.

Anton thought for a second. He did not really want to say what was in his mind, but it seemed necessary. 'Conrad will not marry Daintry,' he announced firmly.

'But suppose he insists on marrying her?' pleaded Mela.

Anton smiled briefly. 'I doubt if Conrad would turn down the opportunity to inherit a prosperous business in order to marry a wife who is destitute and without a dowry,' he replied.

The remark consoled Mela, but it also surprised her. 'You mean you would disinherit Daintry?' she asked, slightly aghast.

Anton nodded. 'If necessary,' he replied quietly. Then he added, 'But I don't think it will come to that.'

Her father's words were magical to Mela. They justified her jealousy of Daintry. She and her sister had never been close, and

Daintry's wooing of Conrad was the last straw. It had driven her anger to the point where she had had to consult her father. Now he was on her side. This would teach that little upstart Daintry to know her place. For now Mela was satisfied, but there was just one last thing.

'Father, there is something else you should know,' she ventured, pausing for a response.

Anton looked at her gravely. 'What do you wish to tell me?'

'Daintry and Conrad send each other letters. I have seen Daintry give them to Adler the carrier.'

This revelation irked Anton. He was beginning to realise that what he was dealing with was not as easy as he had first thought. He knew that he would have to put a stop to this. He was sure that he could persuade Conrad, but dealing with Daintry would be more difficult.

'Very well. Leave everything to me.'

Mela saw that she had achieved all she could for now. She gave her father a sweet smile. 'Thank you, Father.'

As she prepared to leave, Anton made the decision he had been putting off for a long time. 'Send Daintry to me,' he instructed.

Mela made her way to the kitchen, where she could hear Daintry and Mogo talking. She was pleased with her visit to her father. She knew now that his intended intervention would secure for her the one thing that mattered in her life: marriage to Conrad. The anger that had smarted inside her ever since the night before Conrad's departure was now dissipating, thanks to her confession to her father. She had been jealous of her younger sister for as long as she could remember. She had always been obliged to share with her, and this had been a constant barrier between them. Many times she had run to Mogo complaining about some misdemeanour her sister had committed, and Mogo had tried to pacify both girls instead of siding with her. This had been another source of division between them.

Daintry had her hands in a bowl of flour, and Mogo was busy plucking a fowl. They looked up as Mela entered the kitchen.

Mela regarded her sister with a cold stare. 'Father wants to see you,' she announced.

Daintry was surprised. 'What does he want to see me about?' she enquired.

'How should I know? Go and see him, and then you'll find out,' retorted Mela.

Daintry removed her hands from the flour and looked anxiously at Mogo.

Mogo smiled at her. 'You go and see what's what,' she suggested kindly. 'That can wait,' she added, indicating the bowl of flour.

Daintry washed and dried her hands and smoothed her dress and apron. It was unusual for her father to summon her, but she thought she knew why he wanted her. She could see that Mela was already gloating. Trepidation flowed through her body as she tapped at the workroom door.

'Enter.' The voice sounded stern.

Daintry opened the door. 'You wanted me, Father?' she enquired meekly.

'Yes. Sit down.'

Daintry perched on the edge of a chair and waited for the judgement she knew would follow.

Her father looked at her gravely. 'Adler the carrier has been taking letters to Conrad from you.' It was both question and statement.

'Yes, Father.' Daintry's voice was soft, almost a whisper.

'What is the nature of these letters?'

Daintry spoke softly again. 'Conrad and I are in love.'

Her father declared firmly, 'You will stop sending these letters immediately.'

'But we love each other,' protested Daintry feebly. She was close to tears now.

Her father leaned forward to her across his desk. 'It will stop,' he announced, as if that was the end of the matter.

'But—' Daintry got no further. Her father interrupted her.

'Are you not aware that your sister Mela and Conrad have been promised to each other in marriage for several years now? What you consider to be love is merely a young girl's infatuation. It will cease immediately. Is that clear?'

'Yes, Father.' Daintry's world was falling apart.

Anton had more to add. He looked at his daughter, trying to appear less severe. When he spoke again, his voice was deliberately softer. 'You are not yet seventeen. Mela is almost nineteen, more than ready for marriage. Once she and Conrad are married, I will find a nice and suitable husband for you.'

His words were little comfort to Daintry. She made no reply. The tears she had fought against started to flow.

Anton felt a degree of sorrow for his younger daughter. She had always been the more sensitive of his two girls, but he could not allow her to jeopardise the match between Mela and Conrad and his own future plans.

'All is for the best. You will learn that eventually. Now dry your tears and go and help Mogo.'

Daintry rose from the chair and made for the door, unable to speak.

Anton was satisfied with his intervention. He knew that Daintry would obey him. He would speak to Adler and instruct him not to carry any more mail between the two alleged lovers. He would also send a letter to Conrad, once again making the situation clear.

Chapter 4

Conrad Accker looked out of his workroom window: everything was covered in a blanket of snow. Far below him he could see the citizens of Taslar hurrying about their business, preparing for the festival of Christmas that would take place two days later. He gazed at the scene for a few minutes and then, losing interest, turned to resume his work. The small room had been his home for three years. It was sparsely furnished, containing little more than a bed and a desk. In winter a fire burned in the grate, but it had little effect on the chill of the room. From time to time he would warm his hands on the meagre heat it provided.

Conrad's studies were almost completed. Several certificates lay on the desk, evidence of hard work during his time at the university. He knew he had done well, and soon it would be time to consider what profession he would apply himself to. This occupied a great deal of his thinking.

The situation was complicated by events in his home town. His father, the mayor of Toomer, was ailing and would soon have to surrender his position. It was considered likely that Anton Brouka would succeed him. The Brouka family often featured in Conrad's thoughts. He had grown up with Anton Brouka's two daughters, and they had been constant companions, playing together as children. As they entered adolescence, his interest had centred on Mela, the assumption of their parents being that, when they reached an appropriate age, he and Mela would marry. He had meekly accepted the suggestion and gone along with the idea. It had been part of his life. Gradually, however, as the time approached for him to depart for university, he had begun to see Mela as manipulative and domineering, with at times a temper to match. His attention had transferred to Daintry. Her sweet nature was a direct contrast to Mela's temperament, and he could see that she would be a loyal and loving companion. On the evening before his departure for university he had taken the plunge and declared his love for her. Daintry's acceptance had made him feel on top of the world, particularly when she had told him she would wear the little stone he had laboured on for hours.

His elation had been short-lived. Later that evening, after he had said goodbye to Daintry and Mela, Anton Brouka had called him into his workroom. The conversation had centred around Anton's plans for the future, in which Conrad would have a prominent role. On completion of Conrad's studies, asserted Anton, Conrad and Mela would marry, and Conrad would become his assistant. Anton's plans had been thrown awry when Conrad explained that his interest lay with Daintry, not Mela. Anton had remonstrated with him, stressing the importance and need to secure a wife who would be a suitable partner for the future. It was clear that Anton favoured Mela for this role. While the idea of becoming Anton Brouka's assistant was vaguely attractive, Conrad was unhappy about Anton's choice of marriage partner for him. Anton was determined to have his way, but Conrad could see no reason why Daintry should be excluded from the role.

Once at university, Conrad had become immersed in his studies and university life. He and Daintry had kept in touch with a prearranged mail service via the carrier. He had told her about life at the university and she had related snippets of news from the Brouka family and his home town. While they were not love letters, there seemed to be a silent agreement between Conrad and Daintry concerning their future. Only the meeting with Anton hung over Conrad. He did not mention it to Daintry.

Conrad had been shocked to receive a letter from Daintry telling him that she could no longer write to him and that she wanted to withdraw from their unwritten plans for the future. Bewildered and upset, he felt somehow that she was not being truthful. His suspicions had been confirmed when the carrier announced that he had been instructed by Anton Brouka not to carry any more letters between them.

As soon as he could, he had made his way back to Toomer to learn the true state of affairs. It was clear that all was not well within the Brouka family. Anton seemed to want to spend a lot of time introducing various aspects of his business to Conrad, Mela was clearly trying to attract his attention, and Daintry appeared subdued and sad. It had taken a great deal of effort for Conrad to get time alone with Daintry. Eventually he had managed to talk to her unobserved in the garden as she was picking fruit. As he approached her she stood up.

'Conrad, you must hate me,' she whispered, turning her face away.

Conrad shook his head. 'No. I do not hate you. But I am puzzled by the letter I received from you.' He looked at her intently.

Daintry turned to face him again. There were tears in her eyes. 'Father made me write it. He wants you to marry Mela.'

'I know that, but I have told him that my love is for you, not Mela,' Conrad replied, gently taking hold of one of her hands.

'I cannot disobey my father. You must marry Mela.' She looked up at him. She was close to weeping.

Conrad shook his head. 'Never,' he replied firmly. He held her hand close to his lips.

Daintry pulled away with a little cry. 'No. it would not be right. You must marry Mela and do as my father wishes.'

'I will never marry Mela,' Conrad announced firmly. He thought for a few seconds. 'I care little for your father's plans, unless you are part of them. If they do not come to pass, then so be it. We will marry and leave Toomer.'

Daintry looked at him miserably, 'No. We cannot do that. If we did my father would disinherit me. You would be marrying a pauper.'

'Then so it must be,' Conrad announced firmly, still holding her hand. 'When I have finished university and qualified, I will obtain a position and we will be married.'

Again Daintry shook her head. 'No, it cannot be. My father would be angry. He—'

'DAINTRY! Are you there?' The shrill tone of Mogo's voice carried across the garden.

Daintry stiffened and snatched her hand away from Conrad. 'I must go,' she exclaimed hoarsely.

With that she turned away and hurried in the direction of the house.

Conrad watched her go and then retreated sadly to another part of the garden from where he knew he could disappear to his father's house unseen.

Since that meeting with Daintry he had only seen her a couple of times, in similar circumstances, and each time the outcome had been much the same. Daintry steadfastly refused to disobey her father. Conrad's resolve for the future remained undiminished.

'Master, are you there?' The voice of Alvin, the students' servant, aroused Conrad from his contemplation.

'I am here,' he called out.

Alvin entered the room. His face was flushed with excitement.

'Professor Komas wants to see you urgently,' he announced. He grinned at Conrad. 'I think he has some good news for you.'

'I'll go straight away,' said Conrad, rising from his chair. Professor Komas had been his principal tutor at the university. With his studies almost completed, this summons must be important and could be interesting.

Five minutes later he was outside the professor's room. He knocked at the door. A muffled voice bade him enter.

The room was dim and dusty. Books were everywhere from the floor to the ceiling. A single candle did its best to alleviate the gloom. The professor was sitting on a stool concentrating on a book he was holding close to his face. He was old now, but almost a legend at the university for the quality of learning the students received from him. His clothes were worn and patched.

As Conrad entered, the professor put down the book and peered at him with half-closed eyes.

'Good. You are here, Conrad.' His voice was quiet and precise. He motioned to his student to sit down on a convenient chair. He regarded Conrad for a few seconds. When he spoke his words were accompanied with a pleasant smile. He cleared his throat.

'Conrad, you have been an admirable student and have done well in your studies. I would like to know what plans you have for when you leave the university.'

Conrad had been half expecting the question, but it was not an easy task to answer. He felt obliged to explain the dilemma that faced him in Toomer.

The aged professor listened intently, nodding occasionally as if in agreement. When Conrad had finished, he gave a little sigh as he responded. 'Ah, yes. The path of matrimony is not always easy to follow.'

Conrad made no reply. There was silence for a few seconds and then the professor spoke again. 'And will you marry this young woman?' he asked kindly.

Conrad nodded. 'That is my intention.'

'And go against her father and family?'

'Yes, if need be,' Conrad replied.

'Such a decision would be fraught with problems. The young lady would be penniless,' the professor pointed out. There was a trace of humour in his reply.

It was a situation that Conrad had thought of many times, but it did not make the decision any easier. 'I will find a means of supporting my wife,' he announced thoughtfully.

'Without recommendations such a move would not be easy,' his mentor suggested.

'I see no other way,' Conrad replied sadly.

The professor smiled. 'You are a determined young man,' he agreed. 'You would give up the chance of marrying into a good family and an established business career for love and an unknown future.'

'Yes,' Conrad replied in a low voice.

The professor cleared his throat again and picked up a sheet of paper from his cluttered desk. He regarded Conrad with a look of compassion. 'You need to use the skills you have learnt here. The task of running flour mills in a small town is not for you. You must strive for greater things.'

Conrad struggled to find the words to reply. The professor's confidence in him was unexpected, though he knew that he had done well in his studies. Before he could say anything the professor continued, first glancing at the paper he held.

'I wrote to my very good friend Assem Rokar about you. He is most impressed with the results of your studies and has offered to take you on as his assistant.' Professor Komas regarded his student, intent on discovering how this proposition was being received.

Conrad suddenly felt overwhelmed. He had not expected such a suggestion. He knew that there must be more. He looked at the professor enquiringly.

He was not kept in suspense for long. In a quiet voice the old professor announced, 'As I expect you know, Assem Rokar is Keeper of the King's Purse, one of the most important people in the king's palace.'

Conrad struggled to reply. 'But do you think I am worthy of such an offer and position?' he managed.

The professor half frowned at his student. 'If I did not think you were, I would not have taken the step of recommending you for the post,' he replied. His face suddenly lit up, 'Of course, the position of assistant to the Keeper of the King's Purse will carry a remuneration of five or six hundred gold pieces a year.' He gave a little smile. 'More than enough to keep a wife and family.'

He did not wait for Conrad to respond to his suggestion. Almost immediately he followed up with, 'What say you? Do I write to Assem Rokar and tell him you will be his assistant?'

Conrad replied straight away. 'I shall be honoured and humbled to accept the post.'

The professor could not hide his delight. 'Splendid!' he announced. 'I will write to Assem at once and tell him to expect you.' He chuckled. 'Who knows? You could become the next Keeper of the King's Purse.'

Conrad had no problem in accepting the offer his professor had arranged. If he refused, he would be a penniless scribe scratching a living as best he could, with perhaps even a penniless wife into the bargain. Accepting the position raised his status far beyond what he had envisaged. If everything went well, once he had settled in he would be able to take Daintry as his wife and have a comfortable lifestyle.

Chapter 5

Assem Rokar, Keeper of the King's Purse, sighed to himself as he dipped his quill in the ink. It was always the same these days: difficulty finding sufficient funds to meet expenses. It had not always been like this. In the days of King Oliff the Court's spending had been extremely moderate, but since his son had succeeded to the throne things had changed for the worse. Always, it seemed, the king wanted more money to finance his extravagant lifestyle.

Assem had served the Court for a long time and had always enjoyed his position of trust. However, recently things had changed and his daily meetings with the king had become a constant source of disagreement and disquiet, for the young king was headstrong and not inclined to listen to advice.

A tap at the door of his workroom alerted Assem from his work. 'Enter,' he called out. The door opened and Rogo, the king's page, entered the room. He bowed briefly. 'Master, His Majesty the King has instructed me to request your presence in his day room as soon as possible.'

Assem knew what was expected of him. 'Of course. Tell the king that I will attend him directly,' he replied.

Rogo bowed again and disappeared quickly with Assem's message.

Assem rose from his table and prepared himself for the interview. He tidied his clothing and with the huge ledger under his arm made his way through the rambling building. By the time he reached the king's apartment a good twenty minutes had passed. Rogo led him to the king.

King Henri was busy looking at some large drawings on a table. He glanced up briefly as Assem entered and then returned his attention to the table. Assem approached, cleared his throat, bowed briefly and announced his presence. 'Your Majesty sent for me.'

There was silence for several seconds, as if the king were thinking what to say. When he eventually spoke, his voice was tinged with excitement. 'Yes, Assem.' After another pause, he announced, 'I have decided that we need a new royal palace. This one is old and crumbling.' Without waiting for a response, he indicated the drawings in front of him. 'Kannoc the architect has already produced an excellent plan under my supervision.'

Assem tried to hide his shock and concern by asking a question. 'Where will the new palace be built?'

Mistaking Assem's response for enthusiasm, the king immediately pulled a map from under the drawings. He pointed to an area on it. 'Here,' he exclaimed, adding excitedly, 'in the Doocan Valley.'

Assem's heart sank. The Doocan Valley had some of the best grain-growing land in the kingdom of Altaria. What could the king be thinking, choosing this area?

The young king continued to outline his proposal. 'We will build the palace here,' he explained, again pointing a finger at the map. 'I also intend to build an artificial lake and plant an area of forest around the palace.'

Assem could stand no more. 'But, Your Majesty, the Doocan Valley is a prime grain-growing area, and such a project would take up a great deal of land.'

This remark appeared to make little impression on the king. 'Oh, there are many other places where grain can grow in Altaria,' he said, with a wave of his hand as if to dismiss the problem.

'But what of the people who live in the Doocan Valley? Many would have to leave,' Assem pointed out.

'They can go somewhere else,' replied the king curtly.

Assem knew he was obliged to object from another angle: that of finance.

'Your Majesty, such a project would require a considerable amount of money. At present the Purse would not be able to fund such an enterprise.'

'You're always grumbling about money,' growled the king. Then he announced calmly, 'We can raise taxes.'

Assem was horrified. 'Your Majesty, I urge you not to do that. The people will only stand for so much taxation, and this year's increase was quite heavy.'

The king scowled. He did not like interference in his wishes. 'We can sell some grain,' he announced, adding thoughtfully, 'Forancer wants to buy grain from us.'

Assem was becoming completely downhearted. The idea of selling precious grain to a neighbouring country alarmed him. 'But, Your Majesty,' he protested, 'Altaria needs all the grain it grows.'

'Nonsense,' retorted the king. 'The granaries are full of grain.'

'But we need that grain for our own people,' Assem persisted. 'We are only just self-sufficient.'

This remark clearly displeased the king. 'You're an old fool, Assem. Go back to your books and leave obtaining money and decisions about it to me,' he bellowed.

Assem knew that it was time to take his leave. 'Very well, Your Majesty.' He bowed slightly and left the room.

King Henri watched him disappear without a word. Only slender loyalty to his father made him retain Assem Rokar in the position of Keeper of the King's Purse. As soon he could he would replace him with somebody more amenable to his plans. Within days an assistant to the Keeper would arrive at the palace. Perhaps he could be trained to be more in tune with the king's way of thinking and ultimately replace Assem. Until then the king would have to put up with the objectionable old fool, unless something unforeseen happened.

Conrad trudged through the snow. It was hard work walking uphill to the Royal Palace of Taslar, which stood majestically overlooking the city. He carried a bag containing all his worldly possessions, including a new suit of clothes that he had purchased for his new role as assistant to the Keeper of the King's Purse. He was feeling tired and a little the worse for wear. The previous night had been his last at the university, and a crowd of departing students had made the rounds of the taverns and drinking houses of Taslar. It had been a boisterous night out, and this morning he was suffering the after-effects.

As he drew nearer to the palace, little tremors of trepidation swept through his body. How would he fit in as assistant to such an important man as Assem Rokar? Would he be able to fulfil the role allocated to him? He clutched his pocket to ensure that the letter of introduction from Professor Komas still nestled there. It was a degree of comfort to feel it still securely in position.

Crossing the drawbridge to the main gate of the palace, sunk into the high walls of the fortified building, he was halted by a guard.

'What is your business?' demanded the soldier, scrutinising him.

'I am expected by Assem Rokar, Keeper of the King's Purse. I have a letter of Introduction.' He held out the document.

The guard glanced at it briefly, but it was clear that he could not read. He motioned Conrad to wait and called the Guard Commander.

It was a good ten minutes before Conrad was allowed to continue. By that time he was cold from waiting in the snow, surrounded by equally cold and miserable guards. After a while a page appeared, resplendent in a fine suit of clothes bearing the king's crest. He bade Conrad follow him and led him into the palace. They walked a long way up and down stairs and along corridors opulent with fine furniture, their progress made silent by finely worked carpets. Eventually they arrived at a closed door.

The page knocked, and a voice from within bade them proceed. The page threw open the door and motioned Conrad to enter.

Conrad entered a spacious room. It was light and airy, and the walls were covered with colourful tapestries. A fire burned brightly in a grate and provided welcome heat. The main feature of the room was a tall desk, where a figure seated on a high chair was bent over a large book, quill in hand. Conrad guessed it was Assem Rokar.

The page departed and closed the door silently behind him. Conrad moved towards the desk at the same time as Assem Rokar rose to greet him, his arms held out.

'Young man, it is my pleasure to welcome you to the palace. You must be cold after your journey.'

Conrad found his voice. 'Indeed I am, Master, but I am pleased to be here.'

Assem embraced his new assistant and smiled kindly at him. 'I too am pleased you are here. You come very well recommended.'

Conrad expressed his anxiety. 'I hope I can fulfil such expectations,' he replied.

Assem smiled again. 'I know Will Komas very well. We were at university together, more years ago than I care to remember. I know that his interest in you is not misplaced. He would not have recommended you had he not been certain you could undertake the task.'

'I will endeavour to do my best,' Conrad replied quickly.

Assem took him by the arm. 'I am confident you will. Come, let us sit by the warmth of the fire. We can talk further and I will send for a tankard of hot refreshment.'

Conrad found himself seated close to the welcome heat of the fire. Assem picked up a bell from his desk and rang it vigorously. The page appeared immediately, and Assem issued his instructions. This gave Conrad an opportunity to study his new superior. There was no doubt that Assem was quite aged. His rather unruly hair was white, and his complexion pale. His suit of clothes was old and worn. He was slightly bent over as he walked.

Conrad's observations were brought to a halt when Assem sat down opposite him. Assem smiled at his new assistant. 'That's done,' he remarked, referring to his encounter with the page. 'After we have taken refreshment and have talked, I will have you shown to your quarters.'

Conrad felt he was growing to like Assem. His feelings of anxiety were slowing beginning to disperse. They chatted lightly until the page reappeared with two tankards of hot toddy. Assem clasped his hands around his tankard to warm them. He turned his attention to Conrad as he spoke again.

'I am so glad you are here, my young friend. I need your help. My eyes tire quickly these days.'

Conrad was about to reply, but Assem spoke again. 'I should have departed long ago, but King Oliff bade me stay.' He paused. 'Sadly, I feel I need to remain at the present time. There is so much more to do.' He studied Conrad for a few seconds, as if trying to gauge his reaction. When he eventually spoke again it was in a lowered voice. 'My friend, I wish to divulge something to you that is for your ears only.'

Wondering what he was about to be told, Conrad was quick to acquiesce. 'I can assure you that you have my complete confidence,' he replied.

Assem nodded. 'I thought so,' he remarked, with a brief smile.

There was a moment of silence while Assem gathered his thoughts. Conrad waited eagerly to hear what he had to say. When Assem spoke there was sadness in his voice. 'My friend, at the present time all is not well in the kingdom of Altaria.'

'In what way?' Conrad asked, though as a student he had been well aware of the changes taking place.

Assem continued in a subdued voice, as if he did not wish to be overheard. 'King Henri's extravagance knows no bounds. When he came to the throne, the King's Purse was full and abundant. Now it is almost empty, and the king continues to want more. Only this day he announced plans for a new palace.'

'Can nothing be done?' asked Conrad. 'What about the High Council? Can they not intervene?'

Assem shook his head, 'Sadly, no. Since King Henri came to the throne, he has replaced many of the members with others who are in agreement with his plans. Though I still have my place on the High Council, I feel my voice is not heard.'

The High Council consisted of sixteen dignitaries chosen by the king who were responsible for day-to-day administration. It was a vulnerable arrangement, because it relied on the wisdom of the monarch to select people with integrity.

Conrad sipped his drink, feeling its warmth filter through his body. 'That is indeed worrying to hear,' he said. 'So what can be done?'

Assem seemed deep in thought for a few seconds. 'I think little can be done at present,' he replied. 'My fear is that eventually the people will have had enough and will rebel against the king. That would be disastrous for Altaria.'

'What has happened to Princess Aleena?' asked Conrad.

The question appeared to rouse passion in Assem, and his calmness dissipated. 'Such a terrible thing. A more sweet and kind lady would be hard to imagine. To have her accused of treason is a crime.'

'Did nobody speak in her favour?'

Assem shook his head. 'I was a member of the jury that found her guilty. Only two of us out of the ten spoke for her.' He paused. 'The rest were cronies and servants of the king, placed there with the sole purpose of condemning the gracious lady.'

'Where is she now?' Conrad asked, alarmed at what he had heard. The princess was popular in Taslar, and news of her arrest had caused concern and questions among the people.

Assem replied glumly, 'She was taken to Geeva castle, but I hear she is no longer there. Nobody I have asked knows where she is, or what has happened to her.'

'Do you think she is still alive?'

Assem shrugged. 'Who knows?' he observed, adding sadly, 'I would not put it past certain people to execute her in secret.'

Conrad was silent, digesting what he had just heard.

After a few moments, Assem spoke more cheerfully. Turning to Conrad with a smile, he said, 'My young friend, you have only just arrived and I am burdening you with these confidences. Come, let us talk no more of such matters. We must discuss your new role here.'

The two men sat for a long time basking in the heat of the fire and talking over their future collaboration. Eventually Assem summoned the page again and bade him conduct Conrad to his quarters. Conrad was pleased and impressed with his new abode: two spacious rooms, furnished elegantly but simply. He felt that despite his concern at the revelations of the past hour, he was going to enjoy his new role as assistant to the Keeper of the King's Purse.

Chapter 6

King Henri was not in a good mood. His regular meetings with Assem Roker were becoming more and more of an irritation to him. As far as he was concerned the services of the current Keeper of the King's Purse could not be terminated soon enough. Their last meeting had incurred his current displeasure and prompted his next action.

He grasped the bell summoning his page. Rogo appeared within a few seconds. The king barely glanced up from his study of the palace plans. 'Instruct Andor Durek to attend me,' he growled. Andor Durek was the First Minister of the High Council, the most important man in the council and at Court. He was also a loyal and devoted supporter of the king.

Ten minutes later Andor Durek was standing in front of him. He was his usual sly and scheming self.

'Your Majesty sent for me?' he enquired, bowing as he did so.

King Henri glanced at him. 'Yes. Sit down, Andor.' He indicated a nearby chair. Andor obediently obliged, adopting an upright pose in eager anticipation of what the king had to say. The king sat down on a chair opposite him and lounged back. He wasted no time in informing his First Minister what was required of him.

'Andor, we need to raise some more money for the King's Purse. That old fool Assem informs me that the Purse is almost empty.'

Andor was immediately ready to do the king's bidding. 'Has Your Majesty any thoughts as to how this might be achieved?' he asked.

King Henri scowled slightly. 'It's your job, Andor, to come up with ideas, but for a start we can raise taxes again.'

Andor nodded enthusiastically. 'That can easily be done, Your Majesty. May I suggest we increase the annual charge by twenty gold coins?'

King Henri nodded. 'That's what I had in mind,' he agreed, pleased that Andor was cooperative. Then he added, 'But we will need more. The new palace will cost more than that will bring in.'

Andor was already thinking of other ways to raise money and please the king. 'Could we not increase our mining output?' he asked. Altaria had rich silver and lead mines.

The king was pleased with the idea. 'That's an excellent suggestion, Andor. Why did I not think of that? The silver mines in particular have not increased production for many years.'

'I will arrange the Royal Command for you to sign,' announced Andor, silently congratulating himself that his suggestion had met with the king's approval.

Henri nodded his assent. 'Good. Please see to it, Andor,' he replied. Then he announced his new plan to raise money.

'We need to establish a Royal Granary here in Taslar. Altaria produces much grain and we can sell some of this. Forancer will be a willing buyer. I have already enquired about that. We need to instruct all the grain producers and grain merchants that one quarter of production will be levied for the Royal Granary.'

Andor was slightly concerned at this suggestion, but he knew it would not be in his best interests to oppose it.

"Very well, Your Majesty. I will attend to it,' he replied obediently.

The king was more than pleased. 'Excellent,' he remarked with a smile.

He paused for a second to gather his thoughts. 'There is one more thing, Andor,' he announced. He studied his First Minister briefly as if wanting to ensure that he had his full attention. 'Has the assistant to Assem Rokar arrived yet?' he asked.

'My understanding is that he is in the palace, Your Majesty.'

'Good. Do you know anything about him?'

'I understand that he is a young man from a good family and comes straight from Taslar University. However, he is well recommended and amply qualified for the job,' Andor asserted, repeating the information he had gleaned from Assem Rokar several days previously.

The king came to the point. 'We need to keep a close eye on him,' he announced. 'Remember, Andor, we will soon need a replacement for that objectionable old fool Assem. We need to have someone who will work with us and not against us. Perhaps this young man can be moulded to our way of thinking.'

The First Minister was ready to please. 'Your Majesty, I will consider it my personal duty to take this young man under my care and instruct him in the ways of the palace,' he announced proudly.

The king smiled. 'Very well, Andor, I will leave his tutelage to you. That will be all for now.'

Andor took his leave. He was pleased that the king had accepted his suggestion that the output of the mines could be increased. As the silver mine was mainly worked by convict labour, it would be a simple matter to send more unfortunate wrongdoers there. Raising taxes on the citizens of Altaria was of little importance to him. The people would initially grumble, but then they would submit. Initiating the establishment of a Royal Granary did concern him, for he knew well enough that Altaria only produced enough grain for its own people. Confiscating one quarter of production would inflict hardship. But Andor Durek was an ambitious man, driven by the need for power. He had secured his position as head of the High Council by cunning and at times devious actions. If his future ambitions could be fuelled by appeasing the king, then as far as Andor was concerned that was all to the good. As for the new assistant to the Keeper of the King's Purse, he would make a point of making friends with the young man and finding out just what he was made of. It was necessary that the new arrival be initiated into appropriate thinking.

Chapter 7

Conrad rode silently along the road to Toomer. He was not alone: two young men in the uniform of the King's Guard accompanied him. The fine horse he rode was from the king's stable. The winter day was cold and each of the riders was consumed in his own thoughts.

As the trio drew closer to his home town, Conrad's thoughts were on what lay ahead. On the one hand, he was exuberant with joy; on the other, he was concerned about how his joy would be received by those he loved most.

Twelve months had passed, and Conrad had settled into the role of assistant to Assem Rokar. They got on well together, and Conrad had quickly developed an admiration and respect for the aged Keeper of the King's Purse. They had spent many hours talking, and Conrad was now well versed in the ways of the Court and the intrigues it generated. Soon after his arrival, Assem had arranged an audience with King Henri. Conrad had not been impressed with the ruler of Altaria. Overweight and bloated from constant indulgence, during Conrad's visit the king had lounged on a couch and merely expressed the hope that Conrad would learn quickly so that he could take over Assem's role, a remark that surprised Conrad. Assem had wisely not warned Conrad what to expect from his audience, instead leaving his young assistant to make up his own mind.

It had been the same with Andor Durek, First Minister of the High Council. Early after Conrad's arrival Andor Durek had made a point of seeking him out and trying to befriend him, presenting himself as a father figure who would always be there to assist him. It was on Andor's insistence that Conrad was riding the horse this day. Andor had also insisted that two guards accompany him: the roads of Altaria were becoming more dangerous to travellers, as villains now roamed the country, intent on mischief.

Conrad had soon realised, without any prompting from Assem, that Andor Durek was a sly and scheming individual intent on grasping power and influence whenever possible. He patronised Conrad by doing his best to indoctrinate him, stressing the importance of the position Conrad now held and pointing out the possibilities, but falling short of suggesting that Conrad might eventually replace Assem Rokar.

Early on in their acquaintance, Andor enquired whether Conrad intended to marry.

'There is a fair maiden in Toomer to whom I have taken my cap off,' Conrad replied.

Andor was quick to give advice. 'I will say, young man, that a person in your position would do well to select a wife from the desirable maidens available here. Such a woman would be advantageous to your situation.' He gave Conrad a sly smile.

'But I already have a woman I love and who is waiting for my hand in marriage,' stressed Conrad, hoping that his reply would satisfy the First Minister.

But Andor shook his head. He lowered his voice as if he did not want to be overheard. 'Take my advice: seek sexual favours where you will, but do not marry a young girl from the country for love. Marry a woman who can benefit your position.'

Conrad tried to assure him that he was intent on his own choice of wife. Turning to leave, Andor remarked with a condescending smile, 'Remember my advice, Conrad.'

Conrad repeated the conversation to Assem, who replied with a rueful smile, 'Be careful, Conrad. Andor Durek has two daughters eligible for marriage.'

Assem's words of wisdom were well voiced. It seemed from then on that Andor Durek made a point of involving Conrad in Court events where there would be young women ready for marriage, including his own daughters. He invited Conrad to his home on several occasions and arranged for him to go riding with the two girls and an escort. Mooka was a year or two older than Conrad, and Zela a few years younger. It soon became clear that Mooka had her eyes on Conrad. She contrived every opportunity to meet him and spend time in his company. Unknown to Conrad, she was assisted in this by her father. Conrad had little interest in her, as she was haughty and domineering, unlike his sweet Daintry.

Conrad handled the situation carefully with extreme politeness, participating in company when necessary but retaining a degree of separation from Court events. Assem Rokar remained in the background, offering advice to Conrad only when asked but allowing his young assistant to find his own level. At the same time he was full of admiration for Conrad's maturity and skill in handling the situation and the scheming of Andor Durek.

The grumbling of one of his escorts aroused Conrad from his thoughts.

'Is it much further?' the man growled.

Conrad assured him that they were close to their destination, and on arriving at the crest of a hill they could indeed see the town of Toomer not far away.

Conrad had not visited the town since leaving university, and now, returning as assistant to the Keeper of the King's Purse, he found himself the object of scrutiny and envy. He was the local boy returning with status, and as he rode through the town he was greeted with admiration by people who knew him.

After depositing the horses at the stables and directing his escorts to a local tavern, Conrad made his way to his family home. His father was sitting at his table dealing with paperwork. He looked up and greeted Conrad with a smile.

'It is good to see you, my boy.'

'It is a pleasure to be here, Father.'

Marius Accker was full of esteem for his only son. 'You have done well, Conrad. Your mother and I are proud of you.'

Conrad accepted the praise humbly. 'I try to do my best, Father.'

Conrad was anxious to know about events in his home town. 'How are things in Toomer since my last visit?' he asked.

Marius's expression changed to one of concern. Looking at his son intently, he spoke with anxiety. 'Conrad, much has changed. The heavy burden on taxes has made the townspeople poor and there is much dissatisfaction with everything.' He paused for a second. 'You should use your influence to lower the burden of taxes imposed. Surely something can be done. The Keeper of the King's Purse must be insane to continue such senseless and crippling taxation.'

Conrad was quick to defend his mentor. 'It is not that easy, Father. The Keeper of the King's Purse has no control over the taxes imposed. It is left to the king and his ministers to decide that.'

Marius received the news with a nod. There was concern in his voice as he replied. 'Most people understand that, but there are a few who disagree and are intent on violence. I pray you go carefully in the town while you are here. Your current position might attract some form of reaction against you from certain quarters.'

The news surprised Conrad, but he was already aware that some people considered that the Keeper of the King's Purse must be to blame for the severe taxation they suffered.

'I will be careful,' he said.

His father nodded approval and then regarded him fondly as he spoke again.

'But, pleased as your mother and I are to see you again, Conrad, I suspect you also have another mission to accomplish while you are here. Am I correct?'

Conrad was eager to agree. 'You are correct, Father. I intend to ask Daintry to be my wife.'

'But her father is opposed to such an arrangement. You would marry her against her father's will?'

Conrad had thought long and hard over such a decision. For him, there was only one path he could travel.

'If necessary, Father,' he replied simply.

'Such a move requires courage. I admire your resolve, but the path will not be smooth. Has not Anton already said that if such a thing were to happen he would cast Daintry out without a dowry?'

'That is correct.'

'And Daintry would disobey her father?'

'I believe so,' replied Conrad, 'but I will talk to both Daintry and her father.'

Marius gave a slight smile. 'And what of Mela?' he asked. 'Has it not always been agreed that you will marry her? She is a fine young woman.'

Conrad shook his head. 'I am in love with Daintry, not Mela,' he stressed, adding thoughtfully, 'I will explain things to Mela as well.'

Marius surveyed his son lovingly. 'I wish you well in your venture, Conrad. Now go and see your mother. She is waiting anxiously to hear your news.'

Anton Brouka was expecting a visit from Conrad. He sat in his workroom, sad and despondent.

Things were not going well for him. The heavy burden of taxation was making its mark on him, as on many of the other people of Altaria. He was becoming poorer by the day. His plans for the watermill had been abandoned, and the unfinished building stood silent and neglected. The huge wheel had never ground any grain. The new law regarding the confiscation of part of the grain harvest had affected Anton perhaps more than most. Now he could barely purchase enough grain to keep his two windmills supplied. His chest was almost empty of money, and unless things improved with the current year's harvest he faced ruin.

He was well aware of the reason for Conrad's visit and he knew that his cherished ambition to secure the young man as his successor was doomed. Conrad's new role at Court had changed everything. He would hardly exchange his position as assistant to the Keeper of the King's Purse for the lowly one of assistant to an impoverished mill owner.

Anton was wise enough to see that Conrad's visit concealed something else: his interest in Daintry. He knew that the pair still felt the same way about each other and that there was little he could do about it. But he was not inflexible. He was ready to change his point of view, and despite the disintegration of his plans he was becoming attuned to the idea of a son-in-law who held a responsible position at Court. It was appealing. He felt he could no longer stand in the way of the couple's desires.

That did of course leave his own future and Mela's aspirations in doubt. However, he was already looking elsewhere for a second son-in-law. Jarek, the baker's son, was slightly younger than Mela, but with adequate training he could, thought Anton, be a suitable candidate for the position of his assistant and successor. However, he had not mentioned the idea to Mela, and here he knew that a major obstacle lay.

The appearance of Peena announcing that Conrad wished to see him interrupted Anton's musing. He bade her ask him to enter.

He greeted his guest. 'Come in, Conrad. It is good to see you again. Pray sit down and tell me your news and the news from Taslar.'

Conrad obediently complied. He went into an account of his recent year as assistant to Assem Rokar. Recalling the reaction from his father and guessing Anton's current financial status, he made a point of saying that the recent rises in taxation did not originate from the Keeper of the King's Purse, but were initiated by the king and his ministers. He touched briefly on the need for more taxes, but was careful not to place blame directly with the king.

Anton listened intently, asking a question here and there. When Conrad had finished he nodded in agreement and made his observations.

'What you have told me, Conrad, I already suspected. I have little respect for King Henri. It is common knowledge that his extravagant spending and lifestyle are the problem.' He smiled at Conrad briefly, and then continued. 'I suspect loyalty and your position dictate that you remain silent on some aspects of your position. I admire your loyalty. It is a noble attribute.'

Conrad nodded his appreciation, but his mind was focused on the real reason for his visit to Anton. He struggled to launch his words. It was Anton who broached the subject.

'But I think you have not come to see me to talk about life at Court. Am I correct?'

It was the opening Conrad wanted. Clearing his throat, he made his announcement. 'Master Brouka, I wish to marry your daughter Daintry.' He waited for the objection he believed would be forthcoming.

Anton appeared to ponder the request. 'Have I not already refused such an arrangement?' he asked eventually, with a stern look in Conrad's direction.

Conrad was prepared for the decision. He felt sad that his mission had failed, but now there was only one thing to do. He spoke quietly and calmly. 'That is true, Master Brouka, but that was a long time ago and I had hoped that you might have changed your mind. I am sorry that is not so, but I still intend to marry your daughter.'

Anton faked surprise. 'You would marry Daintry against my wishes, force me to disown her and marry without a dowry?' he asked.

Conrad had his answer ready. 'If need be, then yes,' he replied.

He knew that this course of action was practically unheard of. It was customary for an affluent father in Altaria to give his daughter away with a dowry, a generous sum of money for the young couple's future needs. Brides without a dowry were virtually unknown, and those who were cast out from their homes penniless ended up paupers or a liability on their new husbands.

Anton had anticipated Conrad's answer, but he was determined not to appear to concede defeat quickly and wanted to appear to be in command of the situation. He tried another move. 'And what of Mela?' he asked. 'Has there not always been an unwritten agreement that you and she will be partners for life?'

Conrad shook his head. 'Such an agreement was not endorsed or encouraged by me, but by those close to us,' he replied, hinting at the truth.

'How do you think Mela would react to your decision?' asked Anton.

Conrad was emphatic. 'I am aware that she still feels that I should marry her instead of Daintry, but my love is for Daintry.'

'Mela would be very upset,' observed Anton.

'I understand that. I will talk to her,' Conrad replied.

Anton stared down at his table, seemingly deep in thought. When he looked up, he fixed his gaze on Conrad. He spoke slowly. 'I am aware that, despite my forbidding it, you and Daintry have been communicating with each other.' He paused and remarked with a wry smile, 'Adler is not as loyal as I deemed him to be.' He continued with his original discourse. 'Despite my displeasure you have continued to encourage Daintry to disobey me.'

Conrad hid his surprise that the communication between him and Daintry was known to Anton. He had eventually persuaded Daintry to renew their correspondence and had been sure that the letters passed between them were a secure secret. He wondered how Anton had found out and why he had not stopped them as he had in the early stages of Conrad's absence. His reaction to Anton was simple. 'I am sorry that I had to encourage Daintry to disobey you,' he replied.

'She could be whipped for this,' remarked Anton, but now there was a hint of a smile on his face.

Conrad was aghast at the suggestion. 'No!' he exclaimed, alarmed that Anton should suggest such a thing.

'And you would still marry her, even if I did that?' Anton asked, his smile showing more now.

'Yes. Most certainly,' asserted Conrad.

Anton knew that it was time to relieve Conrad of his misery. He had played with him sufficiently.

'You are a determined young man. Determination is a good thing, but it needs to be tempered with wisdom. Have you wisdom as well, Conrad?' he asked, looking at the young man enquiringly.

'I believe so.'

Anton smiled broadly as he stood up and held out his hand.

'Very well, Conrad. You have my consent to marry Daintry. Keep her safe and happy.'

Conrad was suddenly overwhelmed. He had not expected such an outcome.

'Th–thank you,' he stammered. 'I will guard her with my life.'

'I have one condition, though,' remarked Anton. 'I ask you to wait at least a year before you carry off Daintry.'

Conrad was puzzled, but happy to agree. 'I accept,' he replied simply.

'You must also pacify Mela and explain the situation to her.'

'I intend to do that.'

Anton smiled again. 'Now go and make my younger daughter happy.'

Conrad needed no bidding. He still could not comprehend

what he had achieved, but it had been more than he could ever have hoped for. Now he could not wait to tell Daintry the good news. And then eventually he would have to explain things to Mela. The first would be a rapturous joy; the second, a stressful encounter.

Chapter 8

Conrad and his two companions rode under a dark and threatening sky. Already the odd snowflake fluttered in the bitter wind. Conrad occasionally responded to a question or a remark, but for the most part he was silent, listening to the others talking about their brief stay in Toomer. It seemed that they had enjoyed the hospitality of a local tavern and in particular the services of the prostitutes who frequented it.

Conrad was also pleased with his visit to his home town, but for an entirely different reason. It had been a few days of mixed emotions. First had been his surprise at Daintry's father's apparent change of mind. Conrad had expected to receive a rebuff from Anton; instead it appeared that Anton had given in to his plans. Anton gave no explanation for this, or of why he had insisted that the happy couple wait a while to get married, but whatever his reasons, things were certainly going well for Conrad.

After his meeting with Anton, it had not been easy for Conrad to secure time alone with Daintry and tell her the good news, but eventually the couple had managed to meet in their favourite place: the arbour in the large garden of Anton's house. They sat close together on the seat, and Conrad took one of Daintry's hands in his own.

'My love,' he said softly, 'at last I have you alone with me.'

Daintry leaned her head on his shoulder. 'I have counted the days until this moment,' she murmured.

'I too have found the days long until this time,' Conrad replied, placing his arm around her.

'Was my father angry?' Daintry whispered.

Conrad held her close. 'No, my love. There is much to rejoice over. He has agreed to our marriage.'

Daintry jerked upright, shocked. 'But... but...' she stammered, 'he has always been against it.'

Conrad smiled at her. 'I too thought that, but now he has apparently had a change of heart.'

Daintry leaned her head against Conrad's shoulder again. 'Then happiness has returned to me. It has been a long time coming.'

Suddenly Conrad turned and kissed her on the lips. They embraced each other for a long time, lost in their own intimate world.

Eventually Daintry pulled away gently. She regarded Conrad enquiringly. 'When will it be?' she asked. 'Our marriage, I mean.'

Conrad still had one arm around her, and with the other he held her hand. He looked at her lovingly. 'Your father has asked me to wait until the end of the year,' he replied.

Daintry accepted the news calmly. 'I think I know why,' she said simply.

Conrad looked at her questioningly.

Daintry elaborated. 'The recent tax changes and the loss of some grain for grinding have made Father very poor. At present his money chest is almost empty and he would not be able to provide a dowry for me.'

Conrad thought that this could also account for Anton's change of heart regarding his and Daintry's relationship, and in particular the fact that Anton had been aware that the couple had been communicating in secret but apparently had ignored it.

'That may be so, but it bodes well for us, my love,' he said. Then he added, 'Your father knew about the letters we sent each other.'

His remark stirred Daintry from her bliss. She looked at him with a doleful expression. 'I think I know how he found out,' she remarked sadly. 'I am almost certain Mela followed me one day when I went to collect your letter from Adler.'

'So she most likely told your father.'

Daintry was alarmed at the thought of what might happen. 'Father will probably punish me for disobeying him,' she said. 'He forbade me to contact you.' Another thought occurred to her. 'He could be angry with Adler as well.'

Conrad held her tight. 'Never fear. Nothing will happen. I am sure of it.'

Daintry was not entirely convinced. She knew well enough that though their father loved them both dearly and was kinder to her and Mela than most fathers were, he could also be a strict disciplinarian. She recalled the times she or Mela had been sent to their room for a day, after some misdemeanour, with only a piece of bread and a pitcher of water for sustenance unless Mogo secretly brought them something different. The worst thing that could happen to her now was to be sent to confess her crime to Pastor Kartov and even have to kneel in church for a specified period of time. If that happened she would quickly become the focus of gossip in the town.

'I hope you are right,' she murmured, resting her head on his shoulder again.

'Nothing will happen,' Conrad reassured her.

There was silence again as they became lost in the pleasure of each other's company. After a while Daintry whispered, 'Tell me what life will be like when we are married.'

Conrad needed no urging. He related his plans for their future together, explaining about the house they would occupy within the castle walls, the fine dresses Daintry would wear, and the events at Court they would participate in.

Daintry listened in silence, dreaming of the time when all this would become reality. When Conrad had finished, she said softly, 'May the days pass quickly until it comes to be.'

Conrad did not reply immediately. Daintry was aware that he was removing something from his pouch. 'I have our betrothal ring,' he announced quietly.

Daintry shot upright in wonderment. Conrad took her hand and gently eased a gold ring onto her finger. No words were spoken between them as they drew together again and kissed. After a while Daintry pulled away and looked in admiration at the ring.

'It's so beautiful,' she whispered.

'I had it made by one of the best craftsmen in Taslar,' Conrad announced proudly.

It was a thrilling moment for both of them. It was a custom among the people of Altaria for the man to give his bride-to-be a betrothal ring as soon as the marriage had been agreed.

Daintry suddenly said, 'I will not wear it on my finger yet. I will hang it around my neck next to the beautiful stone you gave me. I fear Mela's anger.'

'I will talk to her,' Conrad assured her.

Daintry was subdued again. 'Sometimes Mela is not very kind to me these days,' she remarked.

'I will explain to her how things are. She will understand,' asserted Conrad.

Daintry was not persuaded. 'Mela can be unreasonable at times. She is convinced that you should marry her.'

'I swear to you that she has no grounds to believe that. Her assumption is the result of childhood folly. Once when we were very young I said playfully that I would marry her when we grew up, and that is how it all began.'

'I wish you had not done that,' Daintry responded sadly.

Conrad touched her lips with his again. 'She will understand after I have talked to her,' he said confidently.

Daintry was still not convinced. 'I hope so,' she whispered.

Daintry's fear was justified. When Conrad eventually managed to see Mela alone, she was furious and spiteful.

'How dare you stand in front of me and say you intend to marry my sister!' she snapped when Conrad broke the news to her.

'Mela, let me explain,' Conrad replied calmly.

Mela spat fury at him. Her eyes blazed anger. 'Explain? EXPLAIN? Don't you think your actions explain enough? I have been wronged, betrayed and used by you.'

Conrad shook his head. 'It is not like that. When I said I would marry you it was part of childhood play. It was never meant to be the real thing. I have never given you any cause to think otherwise. Our supposed relationship was generated by those around us to suit their desires.'

'You lie,' Mela retorted, dabbing at her eye with a handkerchief in the hope of squeezing out a tear.

Conrad was about to reply, but Mela had more venom to spew out. She glared at him, her eyes full of anger and hate. 'I know what has happened to you. Daintry has bewitched you with her good looks and sly ways. But she will pay for her sins.'

For the first time Conrad felt anger towards Mela. 'Do not talk about Daintry that way. It is not true. Daintry does not deserve such condemnation from her own sister.'

Mela sneered at him. 'Does she not? She has bewitched you and she has craftily got around Father. Even he has fallen under her spell.'

Conrad tried again. 'Mela, you are so very wrong. I love Daintry and she loves me. Nothing can change that. I wanted to talk to you to explain how things were. I hoped you would understand and we could remain good friends, as once we were.'

Mela sniffed. 'You deceive me, break my heart and then creep around me and try to ask forgiveness.'

Conrad was silent for a few seconds, thinking how to reply.

Mela seized the opportunity. 'You see, you cannot even deny it.'

Conrad could see he was fighting a losing battle. Speaking softly he addressed a defiant Mela. 'Mela, I have tried to explain, but you refuse to listen. I wish you well and hope that you one day will find the happiness you too deserve.' He reached out, intending to raise her hand to his lips, but she brushed him aside.

'Get away from me!' she hissed.

Conrad left her angrily dabbing at her eyes.

Conrad brooded over his meeting with Mela as he rode back to Taslar. He still could not understand why she had become so obsessed with the idea that they had a commitment to marriage, or why youthful play had taken such a hold of her thinking. True, the idea had been encouraged by the adults close to them, but he had never endorsed the assumption. Now a simple childhood fantasy seemed to have aroused deep passion in Mela. His love for Daintry had grown through watching her develop from a teenager into a desirable young woman. Now she was beautiful with her fair hair falling in curls over her shoulders. He had never been sure whether she felt the same way about him, but at last his passion had driven him to confess his love for her. The sweet joy of kissing her lips had sealed their relationship and commitment. Now he wanted nothing more than to take her as his wife. After his traumatic meeting with Mela he had been concerned about leaving Daintry in such close proximity to her venomous sister, but he had been consoled by the fact that Mogo had always been a reliable mediator between them. He was also comforted by the fact that it seemed now as if Anton had changed his mind and was now in favour of a union between him and Daintry.

It was a long and hard ride. The road was now covered with a fine layer of fresh snow. The short winter day was already drawing to a close when the spire of Taslar's cathedral came into sight.

'At last!' remarked one of Conrad's companions.

'You're lucky,' retorted the second. 'I'm on guard duty when I get back.'

The first man grunted. 'Who'd be in the King's Guard?' he grumbled.

The sound of approaching horses brought their chatter to an abrupt halt.

A group of some twenty or thirty travellers came into sight. Only about six were on horseback.

'Prisoners on the way to the mines at Katangar,' announced one of Conrad's companions.

The three riders stopped to let the group pass. It was clear that the men on horseback were guarding those who trudged on foot through the snow. They were all male, dressed in rags and with pitiful protection against the biting wind. They walked with heads down, hopeless in their misery. Those on horseback wore the uniform of the King's Guard. Conrad's companions appeared to know several of them, and brief words of greeting were exchanged.

Conrad watched in shocked silence as the forlorn column passed by.

One of his companions glanced at him and grinned. 'More money for the King's Purse,' he muttered.

Conrad looked at him curiously.

The man spoke again. 'The poor devils will hew lead and silver for the rest of their miserable lives; then it will be sold and the money will feed the King's Purse.' He chuckled.

'Perhaps the king will give us a pay rise,' laughed the other.

Conrad said nothing. What he had just witnessed depressed and worried him. He knew, as most citizens of Altaria did, that transportation to the mines at Katangar was virtually a death sentence. Only those convicted of serious crimes, such as murder, were sent there, and they did not usually last long in the harsh and cruel conditions. It was rarely talked about, but now Conrad had learnt for himself where some of the money in the King's Purse came from, and it concerned him. He was jolted out of his thoughts by the conversation of his companions.

'I'm glad I didn't get that duty,' remarked one, clearly referring to the sad column's escorts.

'Two days' ride to Katangar,' said the other.

His companion took a different view. 'I doubt if any of those poor wretches will see any of the fair maidens of Taslar again.' He added with a grin, 'It will leave more for us.'

Conrad rode along in silence. He was deeply shocked, knowing that as assistant to the Keeper of the King's Purse he was part of the tragic event he had just witnessed.

Chapter 9

Over a year had passed, and once again the shades of autumn were becoming apparent, heralding the cold and dismal days of winter. To the people of Altaria this brought no cheer and only promised to make their lives even harder.

The previous year had not been an easy one. The continuing process of heavy taxation imposed by a greedy administration was a burden many carried. The most dramatic feature, however, had been the appearance of a debilitating sickness. It had arrived during the hot summer and had slowly spread throughout the kingdom. Some referred to it as 'the fever'; others termed it 'Forancean fever', for it seemed to have spread into Altaria from the neighbouring country. Its effect was devastating. Many suffered its fury, and some died in the process. Even Toomer lost three of its townspeople. It was several months before the pestilence finally expired and the stalwart population could at last breathe a sigh of relief and declare that there was no longer any danger of infection.

For Anton Brouka the past year had gone from bad to worse. The levy of taxes he had to endure was crippling, but worse was the reduction in the grain crop he had managed to buy.

He had made his usual visit to his old friend Victor Drabic, who owned one of the largest farms in Altaria. Normally at this time of year Victor's barn would have been full, but on this occasion it was not so.

Victor welcomed his visitor in his usual cordial way. 'Greetings, Anton. I hope the day finds you well and in good health.'

'Greetings, Victor. It does indeed,' Anton replied cheerfully, grasping his friend's hand.

'Come inside my house and take refreshment,' said Victor.

Anton gladly accepted. He was hot and dusty after his journey. He followed Victor into the house. Victor motioned him to take a seat. Anton removed the two loaded pistols he carried at his belt and placed them on a nearby table. Travel in Altaria had become more dangerous as poverty in the kingdom increased.

Anton's action provoked a comment from Victor. 'It is a sad day when honest citizens of Altaria cannot go about their business without being armed,' he observed.

'It is indeed, and seems to get worse,' Anton replied.

'Only last month a carrier was held up by armed robbers and lost all his goods and possessions,' Victor announced glumly. 'And what is the administration in Taslar doing about it?' He looked at Anton for a second and then added, 'Nothing.'

Anton nodded in agreement. It was industrious people like him and Victor who had borne the brunt of taxation.

Victor's wife appeared, bearing a rabbit pie and two tankards of ale, which she placed on the table.

After the two men had eaten and drunk, Anton brought the conversation around to the purpose of his visit. 'And what of the grain harvest?' he asked. 'I hear it has been good.'

'It has been one of the best years,' remarked the other.

'Can I purchase my usual quantity of grain at a fair price?' Anton asked hopefully.

Victor's face clouded over. He looked embarrassed, and shook his head sadly. 'I wish I could say yes,' he replied, 'but only this week a large part of my stock was set aside for collection by officials from Taslar bearing a requisition from the king.' He looked at Anton intently. 'I am sorry, my friend, but I have only half the normal quantity you buy available.'

Anton was shocked. He was aware of the royal decree that a percentage of the grain harvest was to be made available to stock the new state granary and be sold to Forancer, but he had not understood how drastic the effect would be. His production of flour would be drastically reduced. 'But what is the king thinking?' he asked. 'We need our grain to feed our own people.'

'We face bad times,' Victor agreed gloomily.

Sad and despondent, Anton rode home. He wished his journey could have had a more positive outcome. He wondered how his customers would react when they realised the impact of the grave news he must reluctantly impart to them.

This was, however, only one of his current concerns. Harmony did not reign in his own household. Ever since he had changed his mind and agreed to the betrothal of Daintry and Conrad, there had been noticeable friction between Mela and her younger sister.

Not long after his talk with Conrad, Anton had sent for Mela and tried to explain his change of heart concerning Daintry. This had not been well received. Shock and disbelief had clouded Mela's response.

'Father, how could you do such a thing? You promised me it would never happen. You have broken your word.'

Anton was all too conscious of the fact that his action had gone against his belief in integrity and honesty, two principles he upheld dearly and had instilled in his two daughters. He could understand how Mela felt. He tried his best to explain and adopted his kindest voice.

'Mela, my precious daughter, you and Daintry are very dear to me. I grieve that you feel the way you do. It also pains me to go against my word, but when I made that promise to you I felt very strongly that the affection between Daintry and Conrad was merely youthful infatuation. It has become clear to me that that is not the situation, and I felt that it was necessary to accept that.' He looked closely at Mela, hoping that his words would have the desired effect.

He could not have been more wrong. Mela pressed her handkerchief to her eyes. 'What about me?' she sobbed. 'You never thought about my feelings.'

Anton was sorry for his daughter, but he recognised the futility of her belief in Conrad's feelings for her. He smiled kindly as he formulated a reply. 'Would it not be wrong of me to give my blessing to a relationship that I know to be insecure and would only lead to unhappiness for several people?' he asked.

'But Conrad and I have always been promised to each other,' Mela protested, dabbing her eyes.

'That is true,' Anton agreed. 'But childhood friendships do not always grow into adult attraction.'

'It is Daintry's fault. She has captivated Conrad with her looks and crafty ways,' Mela whimpered.

Anton was aware of the jealousy between his two daughters, which had existed even before the current confrontation. Mela had developed into a rather plain, sombre woman, whereas her sister was petite and vivacious and was endowed with natural beauty. He knew from Mogo that Mela resented Daintry's attractive looks.

'Come now, Mela. You know that is not true,' he remonstrated.

'It is so unjust,' Mela complained. 'I have been humiliated and deceived. Daintry gets what she wants and I am left rejected and abandoned.' She began to weep in earnest.

'You will meet another man who will marry you. We will endeavour to find you a suitable husband,' her father remarked kindly.

Mela continued to sob. Anton felt it might be an appropriate time to sow the seed of another idea.

'There is Jarek, the baker's son, as fine and upright a man as can be found anywhere,' he said. 'He would make an excellent choice.'

Mela was horrified. 'Jarek? No, never! I will not be sold off into marriage while Daintry gets just what she wants.'

Anton tried his best to continue the conversation amicably, but it was of no avail. It seemed that he was fighting a losing battle, at least for the present. He knew that Mela could be selfish and stubborn, but perhaps with time she would come around to his way of thinking.

Mela left him, defiant and in tears. How could she be treated so badly by her own father? He had broken a promise to her just to pacify Daintry. Anger burned in her heart against her sister. She and Daintry had never been close, but now there was a rift between them that would never heal. How dare Daintry steal from her the only thing she had ever wanted? She would get even with the hussy some day – but how? In the meantime she only felt hatred and resentment towards her.

It was unfortunate that the first person Mela saw after the fateful discussion with her father was Daintry. Daintry had been dreading the encounter, knowing full well that she would be on the receiving end of Mela's wrath.

As she was leaving the kitchen, where she had been helping Mogo and Peena, she came face to face with her sister. Mela immediately blocked her way. She glared at Daintry, her eyes blazing with anger.

'So you think you've got your way,' she snarled.

Daintry shook her head. 'No, no. It isn't like that,' she protested.

Mela sneered at her. 'Don't lie to me, you little cat. You've been creeping round Father and got him on your side.'

'But I haven't,' insisted Daintry.

Mela had more venom to release. 'You think you are so clever. You have used your looks and your wily ways to snare Conrad and take him away from me.'

Daintry looked at her sister with pleading eyes. She shook her head as she replied, her voice almost a whisper. 'That's not true.'

'I think it is,' snapped Mela. 'You think your pretty curls can get you what you want.' She hesitated for a second, glowering at her sister. 'But let me tell you this, young lady. You will not succeed: I intend to see to that. Conrad is mine.'

Daintry was almost in tears by now. She tried to move past Mela, but Mela suddenly made a grab at her, tugging at her hair. Daintry screamed.

'Girls! Stop that this instant!' It was the voice of Mogo, who had suddenly arrived on the scene. 'Girls!' she repeated. 'Behave like the adults you are.' As she spoke, she forcibly pushed the two apart. Daintry was now in tears, and Mela was still defiant.

'What's this all about?' Mogo demanded.

Mela shrugged her shoulders. 'You need to ask her that,' she answered angrily, nodding towards Daintry.

'Both of you, go to your rooms until suppertime,' ordered Mogo. 'I'll talk to you both later when you have calmed down.'

Daintry hurried away, still in tears. Mela followed more slowly. Mogo watched them go. 'Brawling like street women. You both deserve a whipping,' she remarked almost to herself as the sisters disappeared.

Mogo sighed as she returned to the kitchen. She knew well enough what the problem was between Mela and Daintry. Secretly she was one of those who favoured a union between Conrad and Mela, but now it looked as if that would not happen. Conrad had turned his attention to Daintry, and Mogo would now have to mediate often between her two charges.

Chapter 10

The High Council of Altaria was having one of its infrequent meetings. Sixteen members of this exclusive gathering were sitting round a long table, awaiting the arrival of the head of the council – King Henri.

It was common for the king to turn up late for meetings, and today was no exception. Meanwhile the members chatted among themselves, though it was clear that not all of them were engaged in conversation. The more moderate opinions of Assem Rokar and Kasil Lavee tended to isolate the two men from the rest of the council.

The arrival of the king broke up the chatter. The members of the council rose from their seats to greet their ruler. King Henri dispensed with the formalities with a nod as he eased his ample frame into the chair at the head of the table. Immediately he addressed Andor Durek, who was sitting on his right.

'How is the clearing of Doocan Valley proceeding?' he asked. The evacuation of the farmers had being going on for six months.

Andor had been anticipating the question but dreading having to answer it. Progress had been slow. 'Not very well, Your Majesty. Many of the farmers do not want to leave their farms.'

King Henri was irritated. He did not like hold-ups to his plans. 'Then they must be forced to leave. Have they not been given money to assist them?'

Andor nodded. 'That is indeed so, Your Majesty, but many complain that it is a trivial sum, compared to their loss.'

'What impudence!' exclaimed the king. 'They dare to defy a Royal Command?'

There were mutterings of support from around the table, but the king had not finished. 'Send in the King's Guard,' he ordered.

This caused some concern among certain members of the council, but they knew well enough not to oppose the king. Only Assem Rokar dared to speak. 'Such a move might cause problems elsewhere, Your Majesty. It will be moving the military against the people.'

Assem's observation was received with displeasure by the king. 'Stick to your paperwork, Assem, and leave these matters to those who are better versed in them,' he snapped.

Assem knew there was little he could do, but his plain speaking prompted another member of the council to voice his concern. Kasil Lavee cleared his throat and addressed the king. 'Your Majesty, such an action will put pressure on the King's Guard. It is but five hundred strong and many of them are employed on duties here in the castle and elsewhere. '

The little landlocked kingdom of Altaria got on well with its neighbours and in recent times had had no need for a large standing army. The King's Guard were well trained in weaponry and were ready to act as a militia, but this had not been required of them for many years, and these days they were mainly employed to guard the castle and maintain law and order.

The king did not see Kasil Lavee's remark as a problem. 'We need to recruit more men to serve in the King's Guard,' he replied simply. 'Do so as a temporary measure if you wish.'

'That will take a little time,' observed Pagar Yarrow, who was in charge of the King's Guard. He added thoughtfully, 'Could we not recruit some guards from the royal household?'

There were murmurs of agreement from around the table. The king's household had a large staff.

'An excellent idea,' applauded King Henri. He thought for a second or so and then turned to Assem. 'Did I not hear that the young man you have helping you was one of the best swordsmen at university?'

'I believe so, Your Majesty,' replied Assem, wondering where the conversation might lead.

'Then he would be an excellent candidate to be a troop commander,' the king replied.

Assem was alarmed. 'Your Majesty, he is of good birth and ill suited to the rigours of a guard's life,' he protested.

The king laughed. 'Then he will learn much from the experience.'

Assem could see that as far as the king was concerned that was the end of the matter. The king was already moving on to what he considered more important questions. He addressed Pagar Yarrow.

'We need to have at least five hundred more guards,' he announced calmly.

This suggestion caused more concern for Assem Rokar. 'Your Majesty, that will put strain on the King's Purse. The current members of the guard have not been paid for two months.'

The king was not prepared for such a remark. He thought for a few seconds. 'What about the income from selling part of the grain crop?' he asked.

'That has practically all gone, Your Majesty.'

'We need to get more income,' growled the king.

'Can we not increase the taxes?' asked a member of the council.

Assem was shocked at the suggestion. Addressing the king, he quickly protested. 'Your Majesty, that would be a drastic mistake. The taxes have risen four times in as many years. The people will not accept any more direct taxation.'

For once the king saw eye to eye with the Keeper of the King's Purse. 'I agree. We cannot increase taxes any more this year,' he grumbled.

'What about selling more lead and silver from the mines at Katangar?' suggested another member of the council.

The king beamed at him. 'Just what I was going to propose,' he announced.

'The mine commander has already been instructed to increase production by a fifth this year,' another member pointed out.

'We will instruct the mine commander that this figure must be improved on. Instead of a fifth it should be a quarter,' replied the king.

'He will need more prisoners to extract the ore,' Kasil pointed out.

King Henri had an instant reply to Kasil's concern. 'We will instruct the courts to impose harsher sentences,' he announced casually. 'Prisoners need no longer languish in prison. Women due for execution can be sent as well.'

Some of the members of the council were not happy with the king's decision. The suggestion that women be sent to Katangar was disturbing to them, but they knew better than to obstruct the king's wishes.

The king turned to his First Minister. 'Andor, prepare a Royal Command for me to sign,' he instructed.

Always eager to please the king, Andor Durek nodded and uttered his agreement.

The meeting quickly passed to other matters the king considered important, and rumbled on for over two hours, largely dominated by the king, who was intent on indoctrinating the council with his ideas. At last he rose to leave, a signal that the meeting was over.

Assem Rokar left the room with a heavy heart. He had felt isolated in the meeting, with perhaps only a couple of the members sharing his views and concerns. There was also a new worry: how was he going to inform Conrad that he was liable to serve some time in the King's Guard?

Outside the council chamber, he encountered Kasil Lavee, who was also concerned at the day's events. His face was grim as he voiced his thoughts. 'Things did not go well today, Assem.'

Assem nodded. He knew he could confide in Kasil, 'Indeed. Things go from bad to worse. Now the king is prepared to turn the guard on the citizens of Altaria.'

'Agreed,' replied the other.

'I fear this situation will escalate,' remarked Assem. 'The people will only stand for so much.'

Kasil moved closer to Assem. He spoke almost in a whisper. 'Andor Durek is a cunning man, and Pagar Yarrow is foolish. They do not tell the king that there is unrest in other parts of the kingdom.'

'What? Is this true?' Assem was shocked at the revelation.

'I have it on good information. There have been clashes between the people of Raker and the King's Guard. A guardsman was injured. A captain in the King's Guard, just returned from Raker, told me himself.'

'Then I fear it will spread,' replied Assem. 'The people have had enough.'

Kasil was thoughtful. 'And the king thinks that by increasing the numbers in the King's Guard he can control the people.'

'I don't know where the money is coming from to pay them,' replied Assem gloomily.

The conversation was brought to a halt as another member of the council appeared and stopped to chat. Assem took his leave and made his way back to his room.

Conrad was busy leaning over the account book, quill in hand. He looked up as Assem entered. 'Did the meeting go well?' he asked.

Assem shook his head. 'I wish I could say yes, but I fear not,' he replied sadly.

'And what news?' Conrad enquired.

He listened intently as Assem related the events of the meeting, deliberately leaving the news that would affect Conrad until the end. Assem looked sadly at his assistant when he had finished, waiting for a response.

Conrad had taken everything in calmly. He knew that what Assem had told him was serious and a threat to the stability of the kingdom, but his youth made him accept changes more readily than the older man. He felt only mild concern at the possible threat to himself.

Assem was worried for his young assistant. It was with a heavy heart that he made a suggestion. 'My boy, listen to the advice of an old man. You are ill equipped to serve as a guardsman. Leave here now. Go back to your town and marry the maiden who waits for you there.'

The idea had only a fleeting consideration for Conrad. He wanted more than anything else to take Daintry as his wife, but not if that meant running away from the situation he now found himself in. He turned to Assem with a slight smile.

'No, Master Assem, I will not run away.'

Assem nodded. 'You are a fine young man, Conrad, and you hold principles dear to my heart, but I fear for your safety. I pray you, take heed and leave while there is still time.'

Conrad shook his head. 'No, I will stay. What will be will be.'

Chapter 11

Daintry hurried through the streets of Toomer. Word had just arrived in the Brouka household that Adler the carrier had arrived back in town, and she was desperate to know if he had a letter for her. She had not heard anything from Conrad since he had told her three months previously that he had been forced to enlist in the King's Guard.

There were few smiles on the faces of the people she passed. These days most of the citizens of Altaria were bowed down with the problems of living and in particular the constant shortage of food. As she entered the market square, once a thriving community, Daintry was only too aware of the absence of stalls and the meagre selection of food on display. Even Finn Yago, the fisherman, no longer appeared. After twice being robbed by vandals of all his catch and money, he now only fished to feed his family.

Daintry knew well how the situation was affecting her father. The shortage of grain meant that he could no longer produce enough flour for his customers. There had been angry scenes at the bakery when the usual amount of bread was not available. Many people accepted the situation bravely, knowing that it was not the baker or Anton who was to blame, but the cruel and greedy administration of King Henri. However, there were a few hot-headed citizens who did not see it that way and accused the baker of trying to exploit them and make more money. Even Anton had not been spared the accusations. On one occasion stones had been thrown through the windows of his house. He now travelled about with one of his men, both of them armed with pistols.

Adler saw Daintry approaching. These days his trips to Taslar were less frequent, as a shortage of money among the population of Toomer meant that his business had suffered. People were not inclined to ask him to purchase or carry items on their behalf. He knew Daintry would be there to meet him as she always did. He felt sad for her. It grieved him to have no news for her. As she drew close he shook his head to prepare her.

'Have you nothing for me?' she asked sadly.

'I'm afraid not, Mistress Brouka,' he replied as kindly as he could.

'And news of Conrad?' she asked hopefully.

'I made as many enquiries as I could, but it seems he is not in Taslar. It would appear he has been dispatched to keep law and order somewhere else.'

'And Taslar – what news from there?'

'There have been clashes between those loyal to the king, and others on the side of the people,' replied Adler gloomily. 'Members of the King's Guard are keeping order on the streets.'

Daintry thanked him and took her leave. Once again she was disappointed. She wondered where Conrad was. She hoped he was safe and not in any danger. With the situation deteriorating in the country, the King's Guard had been increased in numbers and was now employed to keep the peace. This was not a popular decision, as in most cases the people were not on the side of the king. The situation was fast developing into an armed struggle.

Daintry arrived home to be greeted by a defiant Mela. These days there was no friendship between the two sisters.

Mela could see from Daintry's face that she had received no word from Conrad. She almost glared at her. 'So, what news have you got?' she asked.

Daintry shook her head. 'Nothing,' she replied quietly.

'Does it ever occur to you that your strategy has failed?' asked Mela smugly. 'It is clear that Conrad no longer loves you.'

'No, no! It's not true!' cried Daintry in anguish.

She attempted to escape, but Mela was set on causing her as much hurt as possible. She grabbed Daintry by the arm and held her fast. Spitting fire, she addressed her captive.

'Listen, can't you accept that Conrad doesn't love you? He is mine and always has been. Your sly ways of trying to entice him from me have failed.'

'It's not true!' Daintry almost screamed.

'Mela, Daintry, please come in here.' The stern voice of their father ended the confrontation. He was standing in the doorway of his workroom and had clearly heard everything.

The two girls obeyed him, Mela defiant and Daintry tearful and distressed.

'Sit down.' Anton gestured towards two chairs.

There was a brief silence. Anton summoned up his best admonishment voice while Daintry dabbed her eyes with her handkerchief and Mela fumed inwardly at being caught bullying her sister.

Anton cleared his throat. He looked at his daughters severely as he spoke.

'Mela, Daintry, this brawling has to stop. Mogo tells me it is always going on.' He paused for a second, to give importance to his words. 'It is time you tried to get on better with each other instead of continuing this hostility.'

There was silence from both of them.

'Do you understand?'

'Yes, Father,' Daintry replied meekly, though she found it hard, considering that she was always the victim.

'And you, Mela?' Anton asked, slightly irritated at not receiving a quick reply.

'Yes, Father.' Mela's voice did not convey a great deal of agreement.

Anton had not finished. 'One other thing. Mela, you have to accept, as I have done, that Conrad has chosen Daintry as his future wife.'

Mela pouted, clearly not pleased with the request, as her next outburst made clear. 'Father, Conrad and I have always been promised for each other. For years and years, ever since we were children.'

Anton knew this to be the case, but it was also clear now that such an arrangement would not happen. He addressed his daughter as kindly as he could. 'That is quite true, but Conrad has now made his choice, and we must respect that.'

'But he promised he would marry me,' protested Mela.

Anton nodded. 'That is also apparently true, but remember you were just children at the time. It can be dismissed as innocent childish play, best forgotten.'

Mela was not convinced. 'Everything was going fine until Daintry enticed Conrad away from me,' she complained.

Daintry was upset at the accusation. 'It's not true. I swear it. I never did anything to encourage Conrad to say he loved me,' she whispered.

'And I say it's true,' snapped Mela.

Anton stepped in. 'Girls! I have had enough of this. There will be no more disagreement over the whole affair. I want you to promise me that.'

Daintry was the first to react. 'Very well, Father. I promise.'

'And you, Mela?' Anton prompted.

'Very well, Father.'

To Daintry, Mela's reply was not convincing. She wondered how long it would be before she was once again the object of her disapproval.

Anton appeared to be satisfied with the result. 'Very well, then. It is agreed,' he announced. Inwardly he breathed a sigh of relief. He had enough problems on his hands at present without having to lecture squabbling daughters. Something else also concerned him. He paused for a few seconds. When he spoke again his gaze was fixed on Daintry.

'Daintry, you went out alone today to meet Adler?' he asked.

Daintry was puzzled, and this was reflected in her tone of voice. 'Yes, Father.'

'I do not wish you to do it again. In future you must be accompanied. The streets of Toomer are no longer safe for a maiden alone.'

Both his daughters were shocked by the request. Normally they wandered where they wished.

'But why?' whispered Daintry, concerned how she might receive any letter from Conrad.

Anton was reluctant to elaborate, but he knew he would have to do so.

'Yesterday a woman was attacked by a band of marauding vandals. The mayor has requested that the King's Guard come to offer protection.'

Anton could see that his dictate was causing Daintry some distress. He smiled at her kindly. 'Do not worry, Daintry. I will instruct Adler to bring any letters from Conrad to the house.'

It was a despondent Daintry who eventually left her father. She would be unable to go out at will. Her once quiet and peaceful environment no longer felt secure. It was another symptom of the worsening situation in the country. On top of that she was worried about Conrad. Where was he? Why did he not write to her?

Mela was less concerned than her sister about being confined to the house. These days she rarely ventured out, spending most of her time in her room or helping Mogo. Trips to fetch provisions from the market she left to Mogo, Daintry and Peena. But Anton's ruling concerning Conrad had intensified her anger. Why was everybody, including her own father, against her? She was the innocent party, forced into humiliation, while Daintry was the aggressor who had stolen Conrad from her. Somehow she would get even with Daintry, and Conrad would see her sister in a different light.

In the middle of that night a loud hammering at the door woke the whole household. Anton quickly went to his window, which overlooked the street, and opened it. As he looked down, he knew that all was not well. Andrei the miller and another man from one of his mills stood looking up at him.

'What is wrong?' Anton shouted down.

Two anxious faces looked up at him.

'Master, the big mill is on fire,' one called up to him.

Anton sprang into action, pulling on his clothes. Five minutes later he joined his men, and in silence they made their way to the stable to find him a horse.

During the journey Anton asked what had happened. It seemed that one of the men who lived close to the mill had heard some commotion, and the next instant flames were seen rising to the sky. By all accounts the building was gutted. Anton's heart sank. This was the more productive of his two mills, and on top of that it had been storing some of the grain he had purchased.

'What of the grain store?' he asked anxiously.

The miller was close to tears as he answered. 'Master, we were only able to save a little.' He knew well the significance of the statement. Without grain, there could be no work.

The three rode in deepening silence through the night. Dawn was approaching when they reached the site of the mill. It did not take Anton long to comprehend that it was a total loss. The mill was now only a smouldering shell. Everything inside the building had collapsed. Only the majestic sails remained, standing out defiantly against the lightening sky.

A number of men from the nearby village stood by. Some of them came forward to offer Anton their condolences. One of them addressed him in a lowered voice. 'Master Anton, it was set on fire deliberately. I saw and heard a group of men riding away. They were laughing and shouting your name.'

Anton received the news without displaying any emotion. He knew there were some who thought he had created the shortage of bread to exploit the situation and fill his own money chest. It mattered not. He now faced ruin.

He did not stay long at the depressing scene. After commiserating with the workers who had lost their livelihood, he rode home alone, disregarding his safety.

When he arrived at the house, he retired to his room. He sat at his table, saddened and trying to see a way out of his troubles. He did not have the money to renovate the mill, and even if he did, where would the grain come from?

There was a tap at the door.

'Come,' he instructed.

The door opened and Daintry entered carrying a tray with some bouillon and a morsel of bread.

'Father, I have brought you some food. You have not eaten so far this day.'

Anton smiled sadly at her. His youngest daughter was always kind and thoughtful. The sight and smell of food reminded him of his hunger.

'Thank you, Daintry. I cannot say that it is not welcome.'

Daintry knew what had happened. She felt she needed to linger with her father a while. He looked so sad and despondent.

'Father, is the mill totally destroyed? Can it be repaired?' she asked softly.

Anton tried to smile at her. She was the only one of his household who had come near him since his return. 'The mill is a shell. It could be repaired if I had the money,' he replied.

Daintry voiced a solution that had come to her. 'I can manage without a dowry,' she suggested hopefully. 'Conrad will understand.'

Anton smiled at her again. He knew what a sacrifice she was making. 'It is true that at present there is scarcely enough in the chest for that,' he observed.

Daintry had another idea. 'Mela and I could try to find employment. We can cook and clean, and I can sew a little.'

Anton knew he could never allow such a thing. 'That must not happen,' he announced firmly.

Daintry had another question. 'Will the other mill be able to provide enough flour?'

Anton was impressed with his daughter's interest and her logical questions. He felt he was almost talking to a man. His reply reflected this. 'It could do. But where would the grain come from?'

Daintry was quick to answer. 'What about Victor Drabic? He might have some left,' she suggested.

The thought had occurred to Anton, but here was his daughter, who knew nothing about such matters, suggesting the same thing. It was a degree of comfort to him. 'I'll ride over to see him tomorrow,' he announced, aware, however, that given the current situation in Altaria his mission might well prove fruitless.

Daintry quickly left her father. Her mission was completed and she knew he now wanted to be alone. Anton watched her go with some pride. She had suddenly displayed talents and qualities unobserved by him previously. She had provided light in the darkness for him. She would, he thought, make an admirable wife for Conrad. In a way he was now glad that Conrad had chosen the sweet and gentle Daintry over the haughty and arrogant Mela, but as their father he could not show that.

The next day, accompanied by one of his men, the two of them armed with pistols for protection, Anton rode to see Victor Drabic. It was approaching midday when they arrived at the farmhouse. Victor greeted Anton with his usual courtesy, tinged this time with a degree of sympathy.

'Greetings, Anton. It is a sad day.'

Anton clasped his hand. 'Greetings, Victor. It is indeed.'

Victor regarded his guest thoughtfully for a second. He had anticipated the visit. 'Come,' he suggested calmly. 'Let us partake of refreshment, and we can talk.'

Anton accepted gratefully. The day was warm, and he was hot and sweaty. As Victor made a move towards his house, Anton hesitated, turning to look at his man, who was patiently attending to the horses. Victor reassured him. 'Fear not. My wife will attend to his needs.'

After the two men had partaken of a meal and were relaxing with their pipes, their conversation returned to Anton's problems.

Victor regarded his visitor thoughtfully. 'The mill is completely wrecked?' he asked.

'I fear so. All has crashed in.'

'And the second mill, will that make up for the loss?'

'It could do. With the current reduced production, one mill is enough. But I have no grain to grind,' explained Anton sadly.

Victor gave a hint of a smile. 'There will be some,' he remarked.

Anton gazed at him, hopeful but puzzled.

Victor remained calm. He placed his arm on Anton's. 'My friend, tomorrow you will send your wagon over to me and I will find you some grain,' he announced, smiling.

'But... But how?'

Victor lowered his voice and moved closer to Anton. 'I will take some grain from the stock awaiting collection by the king's men,' he announced. 'I will tell them some was destroyed by rats.'

An overwhelmed Anton struggled to convey his gratitude. 'I don't know how I can thank you. I—' he began.

Victor cut him short. 'Say no more, my friend. The people must have bread.'

'But will it not be a dangerous move on your part?' Anton asked, concerned for his friend's safety.

Victor laughed. 'Perhaps so, but we live in dangerous times.'

Anton was thoughtful. 'I shall have to use some of the money I have put aside for the tax collector,' he remarked.

He was about to say more, but Victor spoke again. 'It is quite possible that both of us will end up in the stocks or, worse, behind bars,' he remarked light-heartedly. 'But at least the people will have bread to eat.'

The following day, Anton went with his wagon to collect the grain. He rode alongside, feeling more optimistic for the first time since gazing at his burnt-out mill. He was thankful that the wagon was a covered one, for on the return journey there was a steady downpour of rain. Though the grain was protected, Anton and his two men were soaked.

When he eventually arrived home, Anton was feeling unwell. He retired early to bed. The next day he was racked with fever.

Chapter 12

The Brouka household was in a subdued state, with Anton lying in a fever that refused to abate. Doctor Janack, Miklo's father, was called to attend to the patient. At first it was feared that Anton had succumbed to a possible return of the fever that had ravaged the country a few months previously, but when none of the other symptoms appeared a sense of relief prevailed. Anton was, however, still very ill. Mogo, Mela and Daintry took turns sitting with him. The doctor appeared to be perplexed by Anton's condition. He prescribed various medicines and even bled the patient, but none of his remedies appeared to work. After a few days he sadly informed Anton's three nurses that unless the fever ceased, Anton would probably die.

The news was greeted with dismay by Mogo and Mela. Daintry was more positive in her response. 'There must be something we can do,' she insisted. 'Father cannot just die.'

The aged doctor regarded her with some disapproval. 'I have done my best,' he replied curtly. And that appeared to be the end of the matter as far as he was concerned.

Daintry was not convinced. She realised that the doctor was old and weary and perhaps not the best person to treat her father, but where was an alternative?

A glimmer of hope came from Peena. The following day, when she and Daintry were alone in the kitchen, their conversation provided a possible solution.

'How is the master?' asked Peena.

'He is not good,' replied Daintry. 'The fever will not leave him.'

'When Pa was ill with the fever, Ma got a potion from Saltima for him and he got better.' Peena spoke quietly, almost to herself.

'Who is Saltima?' asked Daintry.

Peena shook her head. 'I said nowt,' she replied. Fear was in her eyes.

Daintry was not going to let the conversation end there. She grasped Peena's arm. 'Tell me,' she demanded.

Peena shook her head violently and tried to pull away from Daintry. 'Nay. I cannot. It would be wrong,' she almost wailed.

Daintry adopted a calmer approach. 'You must tell me,' she insisted. When Peena still refused, Daintry felt she had to add a threat as an extra incentive, although it was not in her nature to do so. She took a deep breath. 'If you don't tell me, I'll have you dismissed,' she announced.

Alarm appeared on Peena's face. 'No, no. Please, not that, Mistress,' she pleaded. 'I have an ailing mother to keep.'

'Then tell me about this Saltima,' Daintry replied firmly. She hated bullying Peena, but desperation drove her on.

Peena's face was a picture of misery. She crossed herself and muttered, 'May God forgive me.' Then, realising that Daintry would not give up, she whimpered, 'She lives on her own in the cottage up Hangman's Hill. She makes potions with herbs and things.' She stopped and looked around, fearful of being overheard. She spoke next in almost a whisper. 'They do say as how she is a witch and casts spells on people and turns them into creatures.'

'Nonsense!' Daintry replied. 'If she does good things by providing healing potions, she's not likely to do bad things.'

'Well, that's what people say,' Peena grumbled.

Daintry's mind was made up. 'Do you know how to get there?'

Peena was full of fear. 'Yes, but I ain't going.'

Daintry had other ideas. 'Yes, you are,' she announced firmly. 'You are going to take me there this afternoon.'

'No,' Peena wailed.

But Daintry was insistent, and eventually Peena reluctantly agreed to accompany her on her mission.

Leaving the town behind them, it was a good hour's walk before they arrived at Hangman's Hill, so named because of the gibbet that graced its lower slope. Peena had been silent for most of their trek, but when they came to the rough path leading up the hill, she stopped, pointed and muttered, 'She lives up there.'

'You're coming with me, to show me the way,' Daintry announced firmly.

'The demons will get us up there,' whimpered Peena.

'Nonsense,' Daintry retorted.

They made their way up the steep path, Daintry determined on her mission, and Peena clearly distressed. When they came to the gibbet, Peena turned her head away, shielding her eyes. She was fortunate. No criminal hung from its arm.

The path became narrower and more precipitous, with rocks on either side. Suddenly Peena wailed, 'I ain't goin' no further, Mistress.' She sat down on a rock to emphasise her resolve.

'Wait there for me, then. Don't you dare go away,' Daintry commanded.

Leaving the terrified Peena, she continued up the path. She did not have to go much further. Suddenly a cottage appeared before her. It had all the signs of being occupied. Smoke rose from the chimney, and the door was open. A goat viewed Daintry curiously, and hens clucked here and there. This must be it, thought Daintry. She moved towards the door of the cottage.

'What do you want?'

Daintry spun round to find out where the voice came from. A woman carrying a pail of water stood looking at her. She was accompanied by a dog, which rushed up to Daintry to investigate her.

'Are you Saltima?' Daintry asked.

'What if I am? Who are you?'

'I am Daintry, daughter of Anton Brouka, the miller and merchant. I seek a potion for my father, who is sick with the fever.'

The woman grunted. 'Have you a silver coin?' she asked.

'Yes, I have,' replied Daintry. She opened the pouch she carried at her waist and produced the required item. The woman put down the pail, moved towards Daintry and took the coin. She scrutinised it carefully and then put it in the pocket of her apron. 'Come with me,' she instructed.

She picked up the pail and led the way to the cottage. This gave Daintry the opportunity to regard her more closely. She appeared to be a little older than Daintry, but not nearly as old as Mogo. She was slightly taller than Daintry and had a mass of unkempt hair. Her dress, though old and patched, was clean.

They entered the gloom of the cottage. The shelves that covered the walls were lined with bottles, each containing a coloured liquid. Daintry was intrigued, but unafraid.

'Are you really a witch?' she asked.

Saltima laughed. 'Some what's got no more sense do say so,' she retorted.

Daintry wanted to ask more, but Saltima started to question her in detail about Anton's illness.

Daintry answered as best she could. Then she looked up at the shelves, and back at Saltima. 'Did you make all of those?' she asked.

Saltima smiled as she reached for one of the bottles. 'That I did,' she replied. 'I have something for every ill.' Turning to Daintry, she handed her the bottle, which contained a green liquid. 'You must give your father a spoonful every morning and night until the third day after the fever has gone,' she instructed.

Daintry took the bottle, regarding with uncertainty the evil-looking liquid it contained. She looked at Saltima, a concerned expression on her face. 'I would not want to harm my father,' she ventured anxiously.

Saltima laughed. 'It is but a brew of herbs from the fields. If it does not cure your father's fever, it will do him no harm.'

Reassured, Daintry took her leave. She rather liked this strange young woman, and she wondered why people branded her a witch. Clutching the bottle, she thanked Saltima and returned to the frightened Peena. Would the potion work? she wondered. She prayed that it would.

Daintry's plan had so far worked well. Now it was necessary to give her father the potion. Reassured by Saltima's claim that it could do no harm, she resolved to carry out the next stage of her plan, but she would have to do it unobserved. Desperation drove her on. She had already extracted a promise of secrecy from Peena. It was not until later that evening, when Mogo and Mela were in the kitchen, that she managed to give her father a spoonful of the liquid. Afterwards she carefully hid the bottle in her cupboard.

At first the potion appeared to make little difference, but on the evening of the second day Anton seemed to be less feverish. The day after that, the fever had gone. The doctor announced that Anton was responding to the treatment he had prescribed and was no longer at death's door.

Though her father was still weak and would take a while to recover fully, Daintry was heartily relieved. Happiness flooded back into her world. Her father was on the mend. On the third day of his improvement she stopped giving him the potion, as Saltima had instructed.

When Daintry and Mogo had departed to the market to purchase what provisions they could obtain, Mela carried out the first part of her plan to discredit her sister and reclaim Conrad for herself. Except for her sick father, she was now alone in the house with Peena. She cornered her in the kitchen.

'Peena, I want to talk to you,' she commanded.

Alarm clouded over Peena's face. She knew she was not going to enjoy the conversation. 'Yes, Mistress,' she replied meekly.

Mela grabbed her by the arm. Suspicious of her father's sudden recovery, she was determined to get to the bottom of the situation. Looking Peena full in the face, she demanded, 'Where did you and Daintry go the other day?'

Peena was the picture of misery. 'Why, Mistress, w–we went to the market,' she stammered.

The next instant, she recoiled from the blow Mela delivered to her face. Mela was furious. 'Don't lie to me!' she shouted. 'I want to know where you went with Daintry.'

'No, please, Mistress. I promised I wouldn't tell anybody,' Peena wailed.

Mela was not going to take no for an answer. 'You can either tell me, or when my father has recovered I will get him to dismiss you.'

'No, no, please. Not that,' sobbed Peena. 'My mother…'

'Tell me, then,' snapped Mela.

Trapped and miserable, Peena crossed herself and whispered, 'Please, God, forgive me for what I am doing.' She looked up at Mela with an appeal in her eyes, hoping in vain for a reprieve.

Mela was relentless in her interrogation. 'Tell me where you went,' she demanded.

Peena knew there was no way out. 'We went to Saltima, the witch. Mistress Daintry wanted to get a potion for the master,' she sobbed.

'Did she get one?'

Peena's face brightened up. 'Yes, Mistress, she did. She's been giving it to the master. That's how he got better.'

Mela had the information she wanted. Her approach to Peena changed instantly. She made Peena look at her as she spoke. 'Peena, you are a good girl. I just wanted to know what had happened. It was good that you thought of taking my sister to the witch. Look what it has achieved. The master has improved immensely.'

Peena looked puzzled at Mela's change of tone.

Mela had not quite finished. 'Now, dry your eyes and get on with your work. Say nothing about our talk to anybody, and if you are good I will ask the master when he recovers to give you a coin.'

With that, Mela left the kitchen. She was pleased with her handling of Peena. Now she had the information she needed to teach Daintry a sound lesson and no doubt end her relationship with Conrad. She had waited long and patiently to get even with her sister, and now that was closer than she could ever have hoped. Already she had a plan in mind: it just needed the final preparation.

When Mogo and Daintry returned, Peena still had red eyes from her tears. Mogo noticed immediately. 'Peena, why have you been crying?' she asked.

Peena shrugged. 'It was the onions,' she muttered. And that was all she ever said about the matter.

Chapter 13

A violent knocking at the door shocked the women of Anton's household from their routine. It was several days since Anton had begun to show signs of recovery. Though free of the high temperature, he was still very weak and remained confined to his bed, patiently cared for by Mogo and his two daughters.

It was early morning when the disturbance came, and all four women of Anton's household were busy in the kitchen. Hardly had the knocking ceased than it was repeated, this time sounding even louder, as if some metal object were attacking the door, accompanied by a voice shouting, 'Open up!'

'Goodness, what is happening?' exclaimed Mogo as she hurried out of the kitchen in alarm. She opened the door to find three men standing on the doorstep. One of them was the constable of Toomer. He stared at her briefly and then demanded, 'Where is the witch?'

Mogo was aghast at the question. 'There is no witch here,' she answered. 'We are a God-fearing household.'

The constable scowled at her. 'Do not dally with me, woman. We seek the witch Daintry Brouka,' he replied brusquely.

Daintry, who had heard the conversation, pushed past Mogo. 'I am Daintry Brouka, but I am not a witch,' she said calmly. As she looked at the three men and their grim faces, she felt a tremor of fear sweep through her body.

The constable eyed Daintry for an instant and then addressed the other men. 'Seize her,' he commanded. To Daintry he retorted, 'You are under arrest.'

The two men grabbed Daintry and pulled her away from the door. The reaction from Mogo was instant. 'No, no!' she cried. 'There is a mistake. You cannot arrest this child. She has done nothing wrong.'

One of the men reacted quickly. His hand reached for the sword he wore. 'Do you dare oppose an official in the course of his duty?' he asked angrily.

Daintry meanwhile was struggling in the hands of her captors. 'Keep still, witch, or it will be worse for you,' snarled the second man.

'Please, I am not a witch. Let me go,' Daintry pleaded, still trying to escape.

'Bind her fast,' ordered the constable.

'No. This will not happen. Let her be.' Mogo tried to push past the men to reach Daintry.

It was an ill-judged move. One of the men gave Mogo a violent shove, which sent her reeling back into the kitchen. She fell heavily onto the stone floor, hit her head on the wall, and lay silent and unmoving. Mela and Peena stood watching the events in horror. Peena gave a piercing scream.

'You've killed her!' shrieked Daintry.

Mela made to grab her sister, but her efforts were useless.

'Stay away, girl, or I will run you through with my sword,' growled one of the men.

Mela recoiled in fear. She backed into the kitchen and then rushed to assist Peena, who was attending to Mogo.

One of the men produced a length of rope and bound Daintry's hands behind her back. No one had ever done that to her before. Fear gripped her whole body. The events of the last few minutes had turned her world upside down. One minute she had been happily helping prepare breakfast, and the next she was a prisoner. The violence of the situation frightened her. What had happened to Mogo? Had they killed her?

The three men turned to leave, dragging Daintry, struggling and protesting, between them. The constable's job was to ensure law and order. Only citizens who had committed a crime were arrested. As far as Daintry was concerned, she had not committed any crime.

'Please, where are you taking me?' she pleaded, stumbling as she tried to keep up with her captors.

'You'll find out,' the man on one side of her grunted.

'Quiet, witch,' warned the man on the other side.

'You've made a mistake. I am not a witch,' Daintry protested.

'Can't you keep that witch quiet?' grumbled the constable, who was marching slightly ahead. He turned to look back at Daintry and her minders.

The next instant a cloth was forced between Daintry's teeth. She struggled violently, shaking her head from side to side and making sounds of protest as best she could. It was of little use. She was effectively deprived of speech.

One of the men looked at her and laughed. 'That's silenced you, witch.'

As she staggered along between her captors, Daintry found herself shivering, from both fear and cold. Though it was the month of May and a fine day was looming, the early-morning air was chill, and she was without a cloak. The suddenness and violence of her arrest seemed to belong to another world. It felt like a nightmare from which she would soon wake up, but the pain from her bound arms and the rough handling by the men were real enough. She struggled to comprehend why she had been arrested as a witch. What had she done to deserve that?

As she was led through the streets, she was aware of people looking at her. It was an unusual sight for the townspeople of Toomer, a pretty young woman clearly under arrest for some crime. They stared in silent curiosity. Daintry knew that some would recognise her as the daughter of one of the town's most noble citizens and would try to find out what she had done, but she knew that no help would come from them. She would just become a conversation piece.

Eventually she found herself walking in a less familiar part of the town. Realising where she was brought a new fear. She knew what was situated there – the town prison. Surely she was not going to be shut up there. Horror stories about it were town gossip. Her worst fear soon materialised. In front of them stood the Round Tower, a gaunt, circular building, tall and with few windows, the town lock-up for years. Two cottages stood next to it.

As she was led across the open ground in front of the building, Daintry saw that the door was open and the gaoler stood waiting for them. He was a tall, lean man with a sad look on his face. A large bunch of keys hanging from his waist advertised his profession.

The constable hailed him as they drew close. 'Good day, Master Ratner. I have another prisoner for your care.'

The gaoler did not seem too pleased to see them. 'And where will the money come from to keep her?' he grumbled. To emphasise his question, he added, 'I have not been paid for two months.'

The constable laughed. 'I sympathise. I too have not been paid for a month.' He turned and nodded towards Daintry. 'Guard this vixen well. She is a witch.'

The gaoler grunted something and then turned to enter the doorway behind him. 'This way,' he muttered.

Daintry was forced roughly into movement again, the two men holding her upright as they took her down some uneven steps. The gaoler stopped in front of a solid door with a grille in it. He produced a key and fitted it into the lock. With a horrendous creaking sound the door was flung open. Daintry felt her hands being released and the next instant the gag was removed from her mouth. She was propelled forward with a shove through the doorway. She heard the door slam shut behind her, and the key being turned in the lock.

It took her some time to get used to the gloom of where she was, but it did not take her long to comprehend the horror of her situation. She was in a small cell, dimly lit by a small barred window high up in one of the stone walls. The place had a stench about it that made her want to vomit. It was several minutes before she realised that she was not alone. A young girl, perhaps a little older than she was, sat hunched up, her back against the wall and her feet resting on her hands. She was incredibly filthy and she regarded Daintry with curiosity. She was the first to speak. 'I am Meeka. What are you here for?'

'I am Daintry, daughter of Anton Brouka. They try to say I am a witch, but I have done nothing. I am innocent of the accusation.'

Meeka nodded in agreement. 'That's what happened to me. I am a simple seamstress. They said I cast spells on people.'

'How long have you been here?' Daintry asked, looking round her miserable surroundings.

'Over a month,' Meeka replied.

'What will happen to us?'

'We will most likely face the Witch Prosecutor in time, and then we will be hanged or burnt as witches.'

For the first time the gravity of the situation she was in struck Daintry. Up until that instant she had been certain that the mistake would be acknowledged; that someone would come to her aid and end the ordeal. Seeing and hearing Meeka's remark made a new fear seep into her body. She recalled witnessing the poor witch being led to her execution a few years previously. Surely that could not happen to her? She still clung on to a glimmer of hope.

'Perhaps the Witch Prosecutor will release us,' she suggested.

Meeka laughed. 'Believe that if you will. But they say he has a reputation of convicting all who face him.'

'But if we plead innocence, surely we have to be released?'

Meeka grinned at Daintry's naivety. 'Think so?' she asked. Then she sniffed in disgust. 'Confess, and you're convicted, and if you plead innocent they put you to the question and you are forced to confess anyway. It's all the same in the end.'

Meeka's words depressed and alarmed Daintry. It seemed as if she were going through a nightmare. She was quiet for a few minutes, absorbed in the horror of everything and trying to block out the reality of how it might end. She found it hard to understand Meeka's acceptance of everything.

It was Meeka who broke the silence. Studying Daintry, she asked, 'Do you have anything valuable on you?'

'My betrothal ring,' Daintry exclaimed, her hand clutching the area where it rested round her neck.

'Hide it. They take everything of value off you here. The wife of the gaoler is a cow. She'll be here any minute.'

Alarm struck Daintry. 'But where?' she asked, looking at her miserable surroundings.

Before she could do anything, there was the rattle of keys in the cell door. It swung open and two women entered. One carried a bunch of keys and was clearly the gaoler's wife. The other held a bag in one hand and was smoking a vile pipe.

The gaoler's wife regarded Daintry with a look of contempt. She snarled at her. 'You, girl. If you want to eat tonight, get that dress off.'

'M—my dress?' Daintry stammered.

'Yes. Where do you think the money comes from to feed you?'

'But…' Daintry tried to protest.

She was interrupted by the other woman. 'Quickly, girl. We haven't time to waste on you.'

Daintry could see that she had little choice other than to obey. The two women were much bigger than she was. Silently she divested herself of her dress. It was immediately snatched out of her hand by the woman with the pipe. She held it up and looked at it with pleasure. 'Fetch a silver coin, this will,' she exclaimed with glee.

'The shoes and stockings as well, girl. They're all part of the deal,' snapped the gaoler's wife.

Daintry removed her shoes and slid her stockings off. They too were grabbed out of her hand. Daintry stood shivering, partly from the cold and partly from fear. 'Please,' she pleaded. 'I must have something to wear.'

The woman with the pipe was staring at her. Suddenly she lunged for the betrothal ring. Daintry screamed in shock and alarm. 'No, NO. Not my betrothal ring,' she pleaded.

The woman sneered at her. 'You won't need that now,' she snarled, as she ripped it off. She laughed as she added, 'Not where you're going, witch.'

The gaoler's wife spied Conrad's stone hanging round Daintry's neck. She examined it and then spat on the floor in disgust. 'Rubbish,' she growled.

Daintry collapsed, sobbing. It was all too much to bear. The other woman reached into the bag and pulled out a ragged dress, which she threw at her, muttering as she did so, 'Think yourself lucky.'

The two women turned to leave. The woman with the pipe looked down at Daintry, who sat there petrified and in shock clutching the soiled garment. With a sneer she remarked casually, 'The last one who wore that died of the fever and cheated the hangman. Like as not you'll catch it and do the same.'

Enjoying their warped humour, the two women left, slamming the cell door. The key turned in the lock again.

Daintry remained crouched on the floor, defeated and dejected. 'My betrothal ring,' she sobbed, almost to herself. It was all too much to bear.

She received little sympathy from Meeka. 'I told you. You should have hidden it.' She thought for a few moments and then added, 'If you'd had it when you were taken to be burned, you could have used it as a bribe. They would have strangled you beforehand and made it easier for you.'

The words were of no comfort to Daintry. She sat for a long time, miserable and dejected. Eventually the chill of her surroundings made her examine the dress she still clutched to her bosom. In desperation she tried it on. It fitted well enough. It was torn and filthy, but it was better than nothing.

Towards evening the gaoler's wife came and left some food. The smell from it made Daintry retch, but Meeka gulped it all down ravenously, with the remark, 'Pig swill.' Hunger made Daintry try it, but her stomach objected violently.

Afterwards both girls sat in silence, each lost in her own misery. Daintry followed Meeka's example and sat with her feet resting on her hands. It separated her extremities from the cold floor.

As night fell the girls slept, clinging to each other in an attempt to overcome the cold conditions in the cell.

Daintry fell asleep feeling bewildered and abandoned. Surely somebody must come to her aid soon. If only her father were not sick in bed. Perhaps Pastor Kartov would help her. She was not to know that he was the very person who had greatly assisted in initiating her present predicament.

It suddenly seemed as if she had been plunged into hell: into a nightmare with no end.

Chapter 14

For three days Daintry languished in the foul cell. Somehow she grew accustomed to the awful place: the stench, the cold nights and the constant gloom. For the most part she was alone with her thoughts, her melancholy only occasionally broken by short breaks of conversation with Meeka, who seemed to possess a fatalistic attitude to her situation.

Initially Daintry had been convinced that help would come from somewhere. Her father, ill as he was, would not let her remain in such circumstances and would find a way of rescuing her. Mogo, she felt sure, would be concerned for her welfare and would appear sooner or later. Even Mela would feel sorry for her. But as each day passed, nothing happened to break the monotony of her ordeal, and she grew more anxious and worried.

On the fourth day of her imprisonment she learned why she had apparently been abandoned by her family. The cell door was opened by the gaoler, Master Ratner. Following him was the familiar figure of Pastor Kartov. Daintry gave a cry of surprise and expectation as he entered the cell, holding a handkerchief to his nose against the smell.

'Pastor Kartov!' exclaimed Daintry, thankful to see him and hopeful of relief from her ordeal. Sadly she was to be disappointed.

The pastor regarded her sternly. 'Child, it grieves me to see you here in such circumstances,' he responded, not unkindly.

'Pastor Kartov, can you help me get out of here? I have done nothing. I am innocent,' Daintry pleaded.

The pastor looked at her sadly. 'Child, you have yielded to the temptation of Satan and must now repent and seek salvation.'

'But I have done nothing,' implored Daintry.

Pastor Kartov shook his head. 'When your sister Mela came to me and told me of your crime, I was saddened that one so fair and pure should have succumbed to the evil of Satan.'

Daintry was aghast. 'Mela?'

Pastor Kartov nodded. 'Indeed, yes. She was concerned for your soul and came to me for help.'

Daintry was overcome with disbelief. Her own sister had condemned her to this ordeal? But why? 'What did Mela say I did?' she asked.

The pastor raised his hand as if to silence her. 'You visited the witch Saltima and that propelled you onto the first step towards damnation in Hell.' His voice was authoritative and his words decisive.

'But I only went to her to obtain a potion for my father. It helped him and ended his fever.'

'Your father is an honest, God-fearing man,' the pastor replied sadly.

'What has happened to my family?' asked Daintry. 'I have heard nothing from them and nobody has been near me.'

'You have brought a heavy burden on your family.'

'How is my father?'

A sad countenance came over the pastor. 'All is not well. Your father is still a very sick man and is confined to his bed.'

'And Mogo?'

Pastor Kartov sighed audibly. 'She was pushed by one of the men sent to arrest you. She fell and broke her leg. She also hit her head and was unconscious for two days.'

Daintry was devastated by the news. Her whole world had been turned upside down. She needed to be at home looking after her father and Mogo, but here she was in this stinking cell, accused of something she did not understand.

She appealed to the pastor again. 'Pastor Kartov, please help me.'

The pastor placed his hand on her head. 'Child, pray to God for forgiveness and ask him to free your soul from the trappings of Satan.'

'But I have done nothing!' cried Daintry, now in tears.

The pastor did not reply. Raising his hand and muttering an almost inaudible prayer, he nodded to the gaoler and silently took his leave.

Tears streamed down Daintry's face as the reality of the pastor's visit overwhelmed her. Concern for her father and Mogo equalled that for her own predicament. It was all like a bad dream. The true circumstances of the charge against her had become clearer. She was being accused of witchcraft, and that could have only one outcome. The childhood memory of seeing the witch being led to execution haunted her.

Everything that had happened had been silently observed by Meeka, who had remained sitting hunched up, her back against the cell wall. Now, watching the sobbing Daintry, she remarked casually, 'He wasn't much help, was he?' It was of little comfort to Daintry.

That evening the gaoler's wife seemed almost gleeful when she brought them their meal. 'I won't have to run after you much longer,' she chuckled.

'Why?' demanded Meeka.

'The Witch Prosecutor has arrived in town,' the woman replied simply.

'What will happen to us?' Daintry spoke almost in a whisper.

'Like as not you'll hang or be burnt, though they tell me burning isn't done so much now.'

Daintry was silent. The thought was too much to bear. Seeing that there was no response from the two prisoners, Mistress Ratner left them, with the usual slam of the cell door and rattle of the key turning in the lock.

With a shrug of her shoulders, Meeka turned her attention hungrily to the food, but Daintry only picked at it. The thought of what lay ahead dampened her appetite.

The next morning Daintry and Meeka woke to the sound of the cell door opening. It was unusual for this to happen so early in the day. This time it was Master Ratner who stood in the doorway. He glanced at Meeka and almost growled the command, 'You, come with me.'

Meeka disappeared with the gaoler, leaving Daintry alone with her thoughts. She knew what was happening and why Meeka had been taken. Soon it would be her turn.

After a while the cell door opened again and Meeka was thrust through, almost stumbling into the cell.

The gaoler appeared in the doorway behind her, and before Daintry had time to utter a word, his attention was on her. 'You're next,' he grunted.

As Daintry made her way through the door, the gaoler grasped her arm, almost causing her to shout out with pain. Her discomfort was ignored by her captor. After slamming and locking the cell door he propelled her up the stairway into a well-lit room, which, after the gloom of the cell, was blindingly bright. One of the men who had arrested her stood there, a length of rope in his hand. He lost no time in pulling her hands behind her back and tying them securely with the rope. Next, he pushed her towards another door, all the time watched by Master Ratner. On the other side of the door they were joined by an equally unsavoury man, who grasped Daintry's arm.

Daintry found herself out in the fresh air. After the foul smell of the cell this was a great relief, but she had little time to appreciate it. With a shove her captor set her walking, warning her sternly, 'Don't try any tricks, witch, or it will be the worse for you.'

'But I'm not a witch,' pleaded Daintry.

The man laughed. 'Try telling that to the Witch Prosecutor,' he sneered.

Daintry and her two guards walked through the streets of Toomer. It was a bright sunny May morning and the sunshine had brought more people out. In spite of Daintry's predicament, after the gloom and cold of the cell the sun's warmth felt good to her. Only what lay ahead spoiled the feeling. It was uncomfortable and even painful walking barefoot over the cobbles, but her guards had no sympathy and propelled her along with a push if she did not keep up or hesitated for a second. Several people they passed clearly recognised her but none spoke: she was greeted with blank stares or curiosity. Only when they drew near to the marketplace did someone call out to her.

'Mistress!'

It was Peena. She turned from the stall where she was purchasing food and hurried over.

'Mistress, what has happened?' she cried.

'Peena!' Daintry was overjoyed.

Her delight was short-lived. One of the two men, who carried a stout stick, raised it towards Peena. 'Back off, or you'll feel my cudgel!' he shouted.

Peena immediately recoiled. Daintry was pushed violently forward again. They left Peena standing in stunned silence and staring after them in disbelief.

The incident left Daintry saddened and afraid. Peena belonged to the life she had been so violently removed from and now was denied her.

The church loomed up in front of them, and it became clear that this was their destination. It was familiar territory to Daintry. Perhaps the pastor was going to help her after all.

Daintry was quickly taken to a part of the building she had never visited before. She found herself in a small room, bare except for a long table behind which sat four figures. A sombre-looking man dressed all in black was in the centre. On one side of him sat Pastor Kartov. On the other sat two men of serious demeanour. An ornate cross dominated the table in front of them. Daintry guessed that the man in black could be no other than the Witch Prosecutor. He stared coldly at her as she was led into the room. One of her guards pushed her down to the floor in front of the table, with the command, 'Kneel, witch.'

The Witch Prosecutor glanced at a paper in front of him. 'Name,' he demanded, looking at Daintry.

One of the guards gave her a poke.

'I am Daintry Brouka, daughter of Anton Brouka.'

The Witch Prosecutor glanced at his paper again. 'You are accused of the crime of witchcraft. What do you have to say?'

The shock of having the accusation levelled at her again made Daintry hesitate.

'Answer the question,' her enquirer demanded abruptly.

Daintry recovered. 'I am not guilty of this crime. I have done nothing.'

The Witch Prosecutor appeared to be irritated at her reply. He glanced briefly at his paper again and then pointed a finger at Daintry. 'You deny visiting the known witch Saltima and consorting with her?'

Daintry shook her head. 'No, I do not. I went to obtain a potion for my father, who is ill,' she pleaded.

One of the other men seated at the table suddenly produced a bottle and placed it in front of the Witch Prosecutor. Daintry immediately recognised it as the bottle containing the potion Saltima had given her.

The Witch Prosecutor picked up the bottle and looked at Daintry. 'Do you recognise this?' he asked.

Daintry was quick to answer. 'Yes. It is the potion I obtained from Saltima for my father. It cured his fever.'

The Witch Prosecutor turned to his companions. 'Where was this bottle found?' he asked.

The pastor intervened. 'It was given to me by the sister of the accused,' he explained. 'The poor girl was extremely fearful for the salvation of her younger sister. She knew she had visited the witch known as Saltima and indulged in frightful practices of witchcraft.'

The pastor's remarks distressed and frightened Daintry. How could her sister have done such a thing? It was almost unbelievable. The full impact of her situation was now clear. She would be convicted as a witch. Hope was fading fast.

The Witch Prosecutor, instead of replying to the pastor, again addressed one of his companions. 'Has the witch Saltima been arrested?' he asked.

The man shook his head. 'No, Master. The witch escaped before we could get to her.'

The Witch Prosecutor's stern reply was accompanied with a frown. 'Make sure she is caught.'

There was a brief halt in the proceedings as the four men at the table conferred in whispers. Daintry waited anxiously. Kneeling on the floor with her arms bound was hurting her, but she hardly felt the pain. Instead, trepidation gripped her whole being. What was going to happen to her? The few seconds seemed to last an eternity.

When the Witch Prosecutor addressed her again she was trembling with fear. He gave her a cold stare. 'Witch, on your own admission and the evidence of others you have been convicted of the vile practice of witchcraft. There can only be one punishment for this evil crime. You will be hanged by the neck until you are dead. May God have mercy on your soul.'

His words brought a cry of anguish from Daintry. 'No, no! I am innocent. I have done nothing. Please believe me and have mercy.'

The Witch Prosecutor nodded to the men guarding Daintry. 'Take the witch away,' he ordered.

Daintry was hauled to her feet and dragged, still pleading, from the room. Outside, she fell silent. The full impact of her situation was seeping into every part of her body. Nobody believed her. They would lead her to her execution just like the unfortunate woman she had witnessed all those years ago being led through the town. She would never marry Conrad or see any of her family again.

Her two guards pushed her along at a pace so fast that she was barely able to keep on her feet. Several times she stumbled and they dragged her up again with a curse. They treated her even more roughly than on the outgoing walk.

When they arrived at the Round Tower, Daintry was out of breath and had a cut knee from a fall. She was almost glad to be led down to the cell again, though as soon as the door was opened the foul smell overtook her. Her arms were released and she was given a violent push into the gloom. She stumbled and landed on the floor. The cell door was slammed and locked again.

It took her several minutes to recover. Eventually she adopted a sitting position. All the time she had been silently observed by Meeka. Daintry found her voice. 'What happened to you, Meeka?' she asked.

'They're going to hang me,' Meeka replied. She spoke calmly, resigned, it seemed, to her fate.

'But we are innocent. It's not fair,' Daintry whimpered.

Meeka sniffed. 'It makes no difference. Today was just a farce to justify their actions. Our fate was sealed as soon as we were arrested.'

'When will it be?' whispered Daintry.

Meeka shrugged her shoulders. 'Who knows?' she muttered, almost to herself.

'Perhaps they'll tell us when they bring us the food.'

Meeka shrugged again.

When Master Ratner brought their meal, he seemed to be almost gloating. 'So. They're going to hang you, instead of a burning,' he announced.

Neither Daintry nor Meeka responded.

The gaoler appeared to want to linger. 'I've seen a few hangings in my time, but I prefer a witch burning myself. More to watch,' he smirked.

With tears in her eyes Daintry asked, 'When will it be?'

'Likely tomorrow. Then I'll be free of you.'

With that Master Ratner left, with the usual noise from the door.

The two girls ate in silence, each thinking of their gaoler's parting words.

This would probably be their final meal.

Chapter 15

Nothing happened the next day. Daintry and Meeka waited, their misery now creating a silence between them. Each was alone with her thoughts. When the gaoler's wife brought their meal in the evening, she was silent and would not be provoked into resorting to speech.

The following day, the first glimmer of light was just beginning to filter through the barred window when the girls were aroused from a fitful sleep by the noise of the cell door opening. Master Ratner entered, followed by one of the men who had escorted them to the interrogation by the Witch Prosecutor. He had a length of rope in his hand.

'Both of you. Move.' The command was harsh.

Daintry was suddenly overcome with fear. Her mouth dried up. She could not speak. Almost automatically she struggled to her feet.

'Is it time?' asked Meeka, almost in a whisper.

For the first time, the man holding the rope allowed a smile to cross his face. 'You could say that,' he retorted.

A third man entered the cell. He too carried a rope. 'Hurry up,' he growled. 'We've a long way to go.'

The next instant he was tying Meeka's hands with the rope, while his companion did the same to Daintry.

Daintry found herself trembling. She still could not speak and ask the question that dominated her thoughts: where were they being taken?

Meeka spoke again. 'Where are they going to hang us?' she asked, her voice subdued.

It was the gaoler who answered. He laughed. 'No hanging for you two. You have a special privilege.'

'What do you mean?' Daintry at last found her voice.

'Where are we going?' Meeka insisted.

The gaoler grinned at her. 'Katangar,' he said simply.

Daintry was puzzled by his reply, but the name clearly meant something to Meeka. She reacted with horror. 'But no women are sent to Katangar,' she gasped in alarm.

Master Ratner reacted with a smirk. 'They are now,' he replied, adding casually, 'If you ask me, you'd have been better off being hanged.'

Any further discussion was halted by one of the other men. 'Come on. We're wasting time,' he growled.

With that he gave Daintry a push towards the cell door.

The two girls were once more led up the steps and propelled outside. It was a fine morning, with the hint of a sunny day. The sky was already tinged with blue, and the sun was just beginning to appear. At this early hour there was a chill in the air.

The guards were clearly in a hurry to leave. Three horses stood patiently nearby, and the men lost no time in mounting two of them. Watched in silence by the gaoler and his wife, the small party set off. Daintry and Meeka were forced to walk behind the mounted men alongside the third horse, their hands outstretched, as each man held the free end of one of the ropes.

They made their way through the still silent town and then on into the countryside of Altaria. Occasionally the two men exchanged a few words, but for the most part the journey took place in silence. At first Daintry shivered in the cool morning air, and she was glad when at last the rays of the sun began to warm her. She found walking like this uncomfortable and there was always the danger that she might stumble and be dragged along. This had already happened to Meeka, and the man who was holding the other end of her tether had been obliged to stop his horse, cursing her while he waited for her to struggle to her feet.

Daintry still felt bewildered and afraid of what was going to happen to her. The events of the last few days had moved so fast, and in that short time her life had been changed from cosseted comfort to the hardship of a convicted criminal. The trauma of an early death had been hanging over her for nearly two days; now it seemed that something even more terrible awaited her. When she was arrested, she had at first clung to the hope that everything was a mistake and that soon her father or somebody else would rescue her and take her home. Now she knew that would never happen.

The party had been travelling for over an hour when Daintry was overtaken with fatigue. Suddenly she felt faint from lack of food and the pace of the walk. She cried out in panic, 'Please, I am so tired. I must rest for a bit.'

The two men halted the horses and regarded their two dishevelled and dirty charges. 'We'll never get anywhere if we keep stopping,' grumbled one of them. The other, muttering under his breath, dismounted and walked back to Daintry. With a quick movement he gathered her up and sat her on the spare horse.

It was a pattern that continued. Each of the two girls was given a spell sitting on the horse, enjoying the relief of a break from walking, but at the same time clinging desperately with bound hands to the horse's mane to avoid slipping off the animal's back.

Around midday they came to a small village. The two men seemed to cheer up at the sight of an inn. There appeared to be some discussion with one of the villagers about what to do with the two prisoners. The situation was resolved by the innkeeper, who came forward with a key and unlocked the stocks that stood nearby. In less than a minute Daintry and Meeka were sitting on a bench beneath a tree, their feet secured firmly in the stocks.

The guards released their hands and then lost no time in making their way to the inn.

Daintry and Meeka were glad of the rest. They leaned back against the tree, tired and hungry.

'Do you suppose somebody will feed us?' asked Meeka.

'I don't know. I pray it will happen. I am so hungry,' murmured Daintry.

It seemed as if her prayer was to be answered. A young woman emerged from the inn and came towards them carrying a plate of food and a pitcher of water. Quickly she placed some bread and cheese on the prisoners' laps and left the pitcher within their reach 'Get the food out of sight, quickly,' she urged. 'I have given you more than I am supposed to.' She added, 'They will beat me if they find out.' Without waiting for a reply, she scampered off as fast as she could.

The two girls were ravenous and lost no time in devouring the food and slaking their thirst. In spite of their predicament, it was not unpleasant sitting there in the sunshine. The village was quiet and the few people about seemed to be occupied with their own affairs. Tired after their long walk, they both dozed for a while until they were rudely awoken by the return of their minders. They were released from the stocks, their hands were secured once more, and the guards led them to the horses.

It was at this point that Daintry asked the question that was uppermost in her mind. 'When do we get to Katangar?'

The man holding the other end of her rope regarded her for an instant. 'Tomorrow,' he grunted. Then he grinned at her. 'Eager to get there?' he asked, and then he added, still smirking, 'Don't forget this is a one-way journey. Enjoy it while you can.' With that he mounted his horse.

His remarks held no comfort for Daintry. Earlier in the journey she had asked Meeka, 'Where are we being taken? What is Katangar?'

Meeka had been surprised at her companion's ignorance. 'Don't you know anything?' she had retorted. She had looked glum for a few seconds, and then she had enlightened Daintry. 'It's the lead and silver mines. Nobody ever returns from there. I wish they'd hanged me instead.'

With that Daintry had had to be content. It was impossible to contemplate what was in store for her.

The group continued their journey. It had been clear from the start that the two men were not happy with the task they had been assigned. Once the pleasures of their short break at the inn had faded, they rode in silence, speaking only to grumble about their lot. Sadly, whenever the opportunity arose, they took their bad humour out on their charges, cursing them if they stumbled or did not keep up.

The evening was well advanced when the small party entered another village. In the centre stood the lock-up, a round stone building with a conical roof. Daintry and Meeka were quickly handed over to the village constable, who took charge and escorted them into the building. Their hands were released and they were thrust into the tiny cell. It was a tight squeeze for them, as it was only intended for one person, but they were so exhausted from their journey that they took little heed of the fact that even sitting down was difficult.

Some time later the door was opened again and a plate of food was given to them. Unable to see in the dark interior of their prison, they crammed the food into their mouths and then tried to settle down for the night.

The crowing of a cockerel somewhere close by and the early-morning light coming in through a tiny narrow window high up in one of the walls alerted them to a new day. Daintry and Meeka had both slept despite their awkward position. It was not long before the door was opened and they were greeted gruffly by their two minders. They were dismayed to discover that it was raining, and this had clearly made their two minders even more grumpy. 'Thank goodness this is the last day with you two,' one of them remarked, looking up at the sky and cursing the inclement weather.

The two men tied their prisoners' hands again and hurried them over to the three horses, which stood close by. Daintry was alarmed to see the rope marks on her wrists from the previous day's ordeal, but there was no sympathy from their minders. Seeing Daintry examining her wrists, one of them sneered, 'They'll get worse before they get better.'

It was raining quite steadily, and the men had draped protective capes over their shoulders, but before they departed a woman appeared from a nearby building with two large sacks, each cut down one side and end. She carefully placed one over the head and shoulders of each of the girls. It was a little act of kindness in a harsh world.

The weather made conditions for walking difficult, and occasionally Daintry or Meeka would slip on the muddy surface, only to be growled at or cursed by one of the men. Around late morning the rain stopped and the sun came out, much to everybody's relief.

The sun was high in the sky when they halted where two roads met. The men quickly dismounted and led their horses to graze at the roadside, before untying the hands of their two charges. Relieved to be free of the chafing ropes and already tired from the morning's walk, Daintry and Meeka sank down on the ground. Neither considered trying to escape, because in the wide expanse of the surrounding landscape there was nowhere to run.

The two men took some food out of their pack and commenced to eat it. One of them, observing the pleading eyes of their two prisoners, tossed a couple of crusts of bread to them. It was given grudgingly, but at least it was food.

The rest period was longer than their guards wanted. 'They should be here by now,' one of them grumbled. Clearly they were waiting for somebody, but their charges were not enlightened as to who that was.

It was a good hour before anything happened. All four took the opportunity to doze in the sunshine. Eventually they were stirred by the noise of some kind of activity. Daintry and Meeka stared in the direction of the approaching sound. The sight that met their eyes caused both of them shock and concern. A covered wagon pulled by four horses was flanked by two men in uniform. Behind the wagon walked ten bedraggled women, clearly prisoners of some sort. They walked with their eyes to the ground, overcome with tiredness and despair. At the rear of the party rode two more guards.

The party halted close by.

'You've taken long enough,' one of Daintry and Meeka's guards complained. He added grumpily, 'We were supposed to meet up at midday.'

One of the men in uniform laughed. 'The prisoners can't walk that fast,' he replied.

One of Daintry and Meeka's guards addressed them harshly. 'You two. On your feet.'

The two girls quickly obeyed. One of the men in uniform, who had already dismounted, led Daintry and Meeka, not unkindly, to the group of prisoners and ordered them to walk behind them. 'Walk when the others walk, and don't try any tricks,' he advised, 'or you will be beaten or shot.'

It was a grim warning.

The group slowly moved off, watched by the two guards who had accompanied Daintry and Meeka. 'Enjoy Katangar!' one of them shouted with a laugh.

Throughout the rest of the day the column made slow progress, some of the women limping painfully. Fortunately, the four guards let the group find its own momentum and did not force the pace. Occasionally one of the prisoners would stop, exhausted, and would be allowed to ride in the wagon for a while. There was little talk among the women. Each was lost in her own thoughts and misery.

At one stage they walked through a vast forest area, which gave way to a bleaker landscape. Much to the prisoners' dismay, the road started to climb. The steep incline did not last long, however. Suddenly their destination was in sight.

Daintry's first glimpse of her new environment filled her with horror. That Katangar was a place of hard labour was in no doubt. She could see a large number of what were clearly prisoners, most of them women, moving about their work, dirty and dishevelled, each with a look of fatigue and despair on her face. They did not even seem to notice the new arrivals. Fear and panic overwhelmed Daintry. How could she ever survive this place?

'So this is Katangar.' Meeka spoke softly.

'How will we ever manage?' whispered Daintry.

'Same as the rest, I guess,' Meeka replied, with an air of resignation.

Her words brought no comfort to Daintry. During the short time she had known Meeka, Daintry had come to realise that they came from totally different backgrounds. Meeka had a deep sense of resignation to everything: the attitude that she would just have to accept and endure whatever might happen.

Within minutes the twelve prisoners had been handed over to the camp guards. The four men who had delivered them rapidly vanished. The two who took their place wasted no time in organising the new arrivals. 'Line up!' one of them barked.

The group quickly assembled into a row, assisted in the process with pushes and shoves from the two guards. Daintry stood next to Meeka, wondering what was going to happen next.

She did not have to wait very long. Three more men approached the line of prisoners. It was clear that one of these was somebody of importance. He was dressed better than the others and had an air of superiority about him. He viewed the women with some dismay. Throwing up his hands in disgust he exclaimed, 'Women? I want men and they send me women?' He turned angrily to the two guards. 'Mark them, and put them to work tomorrow.' With that the three newcomers strode off.

The two guards immediately went into action. 'Move,' one instructed, giving Daintry, who was at one end of the line, a push. The twelve women were marched a short distance. They halted in front of a hut, outside which a brazier was glowing brightly. A large man wearing a leather apron emerged from the interior of the building. Several more guards stood by.

Daintry was not expecting the next move. Abruptly she was grabbed by two of the guards, dragged towards a low bench and held down over it. Her clothing was ripped from her shoulder and the next instant she felt a terrible searing pain. She found herself screaming at the top of her voice, her nostrils filled with the smell of her own burning flesh. She felt herself being released from the grip of the two men, but suddenly she fainted away and was overcome by blackness.

She came to as water was poured over her face. Screams were in the air from others suffering the same treatment as she had undergone. She looked up to see an older hag of a woman holding a pitcher of water, which she had used to revive Daintry. The woman grinned. 'That's it, girlie. You're marked the same as the rest of us. You're part of Katangar now.' Daintry's consciousness, blurred as it was by the pain from her shoulder, became alive to alarming thoughts: what had they done to her? Would she ever get out of this awful place?

Chapter 16

King Henri surveyed the model on the table in front of him. It represented the new palace he proposed to build, and alongside it on a second table was a map of the Doocan Valley. The tables took up a large amount of the king's day room, but as he spent a great part of his time studying what was on them, it mattered little to him. Today he was awaiting the arrival of Jacub Kannoc, the architect and master builder. He had some new ideas for his craftsman.

His thoughts were interrupted by the entry of Rogo, the page.

'Your Majesty, Master Kannoc is here to see you,' the page announced.

'Good. Show him in.'

Jacub Kannoc was usually summoned to the king's presence at least once a week, and of late he had been dreading these meetings. Most of the time they were about changes the king wanted to make to the new palace and its surroundings. Many of King Henri's suggestions were wild ideas that were not feasible, and Jacub sometimes had great difficulty in persuading him that it was not possible to implement a particular proposal. On top of that, months had passed and the site for the new palace was still not free. The dispute with the farmers occupying the valley had escalated, and the farmers had organised themselves into bands of armed opposition that caused endless skirmishes with the King's Guard, who seemed powerless to get on top of the situation.

As the aged, white-haired architect entered into the presence of the king, he sensed that this meeting would be the same as many previous ones. The king greeted him. 'Ah, there you are, Jacub. I have something to discuss with you.'

'Good day, Your Majesty. I am at your service,' replied Jacub, feigning enthusiasm.

The king lost no time in outlining his plans. He turned his attention to the model again. 'I think this wing needs to be enlarged and I propose that a ballroom be incorporated.' He indicated on the model where he thought the alteration should be made.

Jacub's heart sank. He knew the suggestion was just not practicable. He pondered for a few seconds, thinking how best to respond. He was well aware that he had to be tactful so as not to risk one of King Henri's rages. He cleared his throat before speaking. 'Your Majesty, it is a good idea, but to enlarge that wing would make the whole look of the new palace out of balance. We don't want to spoil the beauty of the building you have inspired.'

'What can we do, then?' asked the king, showing the first signs of irritation at the architect's rebuff of his plans.

Jacub had already quickly thought of a solution. 'What I suggest is that we extend the rear of the building here.' He pointed to a section of the model. 'That would fit in admirably with the overall design,' he added.

King Henri was silent for a few seconds. He did not like opposition to his ideas, but in this instance he could see that the architect was correct. Suddenly, he nodded agreement. 'Good. Do it that way then.' For once he had conceded defeat without argument.

Jacub was not quite prepared for the king's next question.

'Has the work commenced yet?'

Jacub shook his head. 'Regrettably, no. The soldiers of the Guard have not been able to eliminate the armed rebels from the area.'

'What?' the king was aghast. 'They're just a bunch of farmers!' he exclaimed angrily.

The architect remained silent. He had no wish to extend the king's anger.

The king suddenly ended the meeting with a curt 'That's all, Jacub. We'll work along the lines we have discussed.'

Jacub Kannoc was relieved to be able to be dismissed so quickly. Often meetings with the king went on much longer.

As soon as the architect had left, King Henri summoned Andor Durek. He had not seen his First Minister for several days, and he thought that was rather odd.

It took a little time for Andor to be found. King Henri fumed while he waited, but eventually Andor appeared. The king lost little time in bringing up the subject about which he required information. Barely acknowledging Andor's greeting, he posed his first question. 'Andor, what is happening? I have just had a meeting with Jacub Kannoc and he tells me that he cannot start work on the building yet. The whole thing is at a standstill because some farmers are harassing the Guard.'

It was a question Andor had been fearing. For some days now messengers had continually arrived with bad news from the commanders of the King's Guard still trying to clear the Doocan Valley. The situation had become steadily worse, with more and more of the population supporting the beleaguered residents. He also had even more disturbing news for the king. He thought out his reply to the king's question very carefully. Clearing his throat and taking his time, he began to respond.

'That is true, Your Majesty. Progress has been hampered by more and more armed citizens joining the ranks of the farmers. It seems they are becoming better organised now.'

'What! Are you telling me that the King's Guard cannot clear out and arrest a few troublemakers?'

The king was clearly displeased with his First Minister's report. It did not make a diplomatic reply very easy. Andor tried to keep things as brief as possible.

'It is the vast numbers the guardsmen are up against that is the problem. Pagar Yarrow has assured me that his commanders will resolve the situation.' Pagar Yarrow, the member of the High Council in charge of the King's Guard, was no friend of Andor Durek.

'I should hope so,' retorted the king. 'The Guard numbers were increased by over five hundred.'

Andor knew it was time to deliver his next and most important piece of news. The king's last remark had given him the opportunity he needed.

'That is true, Your Majesty, but at present the numbers of the Guard are stretched.' He paused, expecting a response, but when none came he was forced to continue. 'There are problems in the north of the country. Two hundred members of the Guard have had to be sent there to contain the uprising of the townspeople of Raker.'

'What are you telling me?' the king almost shouted. He fumed, 'This is treason. The conflict must be put down and the culprits brought to trial.'

Andor remained calm. 'I agree. We have to show strength,' he remarked, nodding.

The king did not respond immediately. He appeared to be thinking deeply. Suddenly he spoke again. 'I am not happy with Pagar Yarrow's handling of the situation. I think he should be replaced as head of the Guard immediately.'

The king's words brought joy to Andor. Here was the opportunity to get rid of another opponent who had worked against him.

'I agree entirely, Your Majesty. Pagar Yarrow's attempts to get control of these minor disturbances have been pitiful.'

The king nodded. 'I will send for him and dismiss him immediately and place him under house arrest for a time.'

'Who do you think should replace him?' asked Andor.

'I believe Kurt Lassen would be eminently suitable,' replied the king.

Andor was pleased with the suggestion. Kurt Lassen would deal ruthlessly with those who opposed the government. In addition he knew that Kurt would always bow to his and the king's wishes.

'An excellent choice, if I may say so, Your Majesty. I had similar thoughts myself.'

The king was tiring of the meeting with his First Minister. 'Very well, Andor. Prepare the necessary documents and I will sign them. Arrange Pagar Yarrow's detention and Kurt Lassen's appointment.'

It was clear that the interview was over. Andor was pleased with the outcome. It strengthened his personal power and position. As he took his leave he was surprised to see Assem Rokar, the Keeper of the King's Purse, waiting to enter the room. It always worried him when Assem had a private meeting with the king without his presence, but knowing the king's opinion of Assem gave him comfort. He greeted the older man and went on his way, contented with his efforts.

The king had returned to studying the model of the new palace. He hardly looked up as Assem entered his chamber. He did not respond immediately to Assem's greeting.

Eventually he turned his attention to the old man. 'Good day, Assem. How is the King's Purse?'

Assem had been expecting the question. 'The funds are not as good as I would like, but we can now pay the King's Guard and some other expenses that have been on hold.'

'And funds for the new palace?'

Assem shook his head. 'Accumulating a surplus to fund the building is proving to be slow,' he replied.

The king was not pleased. He had anticipated a more positive answer. 'What about the income from the mines at Katangar?' he asked.

'The sales of silver have increased only slightly,' answered Assem.

'But we are sending more convicts there and we instructed the mine commander that we wanted greater output,' the king pointed out.

'That is true, but I think it will take a little time for the results to appear in the form of actual money.'

The king grunted by way of a reply. His next remark worried Assem.

'Pagar Yarrow is to be replaced as head of the King's Guard. His performance in handling the current situation has been slow and incompetent.'

Before Assem could formulate a reply, the king added further to his concerns.

'Kurt Lassen will replace him.'

Assem was greatly alarmed at this news. Replacing the calm and careful Pagar with Kurt Lassen was a potential disaster. Kurt had no knowledge of military strategy and was well known for his propensity to do little other than agree with what the king wanted. Assem struggled to come up with a suitable reply, knowing full well how the king regarded him.

'Do you think that is wise, Your Majesty? Kurt Lassen is inexperienced in military matters, and what is needed now is an approach to calm the population.'

The king's displeasure showed in his reply.

'And show weakness and appease the demands of a few troublemakers?' he sneered.

Assem knew that, whatever the result was, he had to speak frankly. 'Your Majesty, the present situation could well lead to a civil war between the state and its people.'

'You have been listening to idle gossip, Assem.'

'It is not idle gossip, Your Majesty. It is the reality of the situation.'

The king gave a laugh. 'You are an old fool, Assem.'

'But, I beg to offer, also a wise one, Your Majesty.'

'Stick to your figures and books, Assem,' retorted the king, 'and let your betters run the country. What is needed now is a strong administration to crush this uprising and bring the culprits to justice.'

Assem knew the time had come to tell the king the truth, even if it meant losing his own life.

'Your Majesty, it grieves me to say this, but you are being badly advised.'

'What? Be careful what you say, Assem.' Anger showed on the king's face.

Assem had not finished. 'I am saying this because I love this country and what it has stood for. Now I see it disintegrate by the day, a situation caused by those around you giving you bad advice.'

The king's face was red with fury. At first he seemed unable to speak. After a few moments' silence he bellowed, 'Get out of here!'

Assem bowed. 'Very well, Your Majesty,' he replied, and left the room. He knew that the events of the last few minutes would have repercussions. The king did not like being told that he was wrong.

As soon as Assem had disappeared King Henri summoned his page. His command was shouted. 'Get Andor Durek here, now!'

Andor arrived a few minutes later, out of breath and flustered. 'You sent for me, Your Majesty?'

King Henri looked at his First Minister. 'Yes. That old fool Assem Rokar has got to go. I have had enough of his rambling.'

The statement brought joy to Andor, but he remained calm. 'Very well, Your Majesty. May I ask who you think should replace him?'

The king had not thought that far ahead. 'Who do you think would be suitable for the job?' he asked.

Andor thought for a second. 'What about Conrad Accker, Assem's assistant?

At first the king showed interest in the suggestion. 'Where is the young man now?' he asked.

'I believe he is a troop leader in the King's Guard,' replied Andor.

The king, having reconsidered, shook his head. 'No. Leave him there. He will have learnt the ways of that old fool Assem too well. Who else can you suggest?'

Things were going Andor's way. 'Your Majesty, may I suggest Erik Vasin?'

The king did not respond immediately. Andor decided to add weight to his proposal. 'Erik has served on the council for only a short time, but he is well versed in the use of figures.'

Andor waited as the king considered his idea. Suddenly the king snapped into action. 'Send for him immediately,' he ordered.

Andor was delighted. It had been a most productive morning. Two of his opponents dismissed, and Erik Vasin, who he knew was easily manipulated, to replace Assem Rokar. He could not have hoped for better. Once Erik had taken up the position, Andor's personal influence on the king, and his own status, would be greatly enhanced. He could scarcely contain his pleasure as he replied. 'Very well, Your Majesty. I will attend to it at once.'

Chapter 17

Conrad felt the rain seeping into his clothing. His troops had been marching for two hours in the inclement July weather. As leader, he had little option but to put up with the unpleasant conditions, but behind him he could occasionally hear the grumbles of the rest of the party.

Since his enforced enrolment in the King's Guard, Conrad had quickly established himself as a competent officer and now was a respected leader and commander. At the same time he was saddened with the way things were developing. What had started out as perhaps an adventure, an experience of a different way of life, had now become a time of unease and disillusionment. The months of serving in the Doocan Valley, resisting repeated attacks from the residents of the area, had made an impact on the way he viewed what he was doing. He had lost five men to the rebels' guns, and others had even defected to the rebel side.

The problem Conrad wrestled with was that, though he was expected to condemn the local uprising and maintain the discipline of his men, inwardly he was gaining more and more sympathy for the people resisting the takeover of their land. What he had witnessed in recent months had made him change his view of the king and the administration in Taslar.

Two days previously he had been given the command to march his troops to the sizeable northern town of Raker to help sort out the problems there with the rebel movement. It was now becoming clear to Conrad and the rest of his men sent to quell the uprisings that what had started out as a band of farmers protesting against the takeover of their land had now virtually become a civil war, with the ordinary people of the kingdom fighting against the king and his supporters.

Around midday Conrad's party came to a small village. They were glad of the opportunity for a rest and some refreshment, but it was clear that they were not welcome in the village or at the inn. The men were subjected to sullen and angry stares from the population, and those who ventured into the inn were served in silence.

While they were preparing to leave the village, a woman appeared. She was not young and she was carrying what appeared to be a heavy load on her shoulders. Close to Conrad she suddenly stumbled and fell to the ground, her load scattering. Conrad moved to help her, but she resisted his offer of assistance. Struggling to her feet, she gave him an angry look and spat on the ground. 'I want no help from a member of the King's Guard.'

Conrad felt he had to say something. 'Why are you so angry?' he asked.

The woman glared at him again. Eventually she spoke. 'Why am I angry, you want to know?' She spat on the ground again. 'I'll tell you why. My husband and daughter were arrested by your lot and sent to the mines at Katangar.' She paused for a second, and then moved her face nearer to Conrad's. 'And do you know why?' she demanded.

Conrad was shocked but remained calm. 'Please tell me,' he urged the woman quietly.

She stared at him for an instant, and then started speaking again. 'For stealing a few scraps of food to try and feed us.' She paused, and then tried to strike Conrad.

Two of his men rushed to his aid, grabbed the woman and manhandled her to a safe distance. She stood between them, glowering and cursing.

The two soldiers looked at Conrad, waiting for a punishment to be meted out to the offender.

Conrad issued his instructions. 'Release her and help her to her home with her load.'

With a look of surprise on their faces, the two men obeyed. Conrad was being extremely lenient. Normally the woman would have been at least arrested for attempting to strike an officer of the Guard, and whipped in public.

It was edging towards evening when Conrad and his troops reached their destination, the Guard's recently established tented camp on the outskirts of Raker. After the long march there was relief among the party. Conrad made his way to the commander's tent to report their arrival. He was surprised to recognise the man emerging from the tent. It was his childhood friend.

'Miklo!'

The man stared at him for a second, and then, as recognition dawned, his face broke into a smile as he returned Conrad's salute.

'Conrad, my old friend, it's good to see you.' He was still grinning broadly as he added jokingly, 'I had no idea you had joined our ranks.'

'I didn't actually volunteer,' Conrad replied, smiling politely.

'Nevertheless, you are here now and most welcome,' Miklo enthused. He glanced in the direction of Conrad's men, who were awaiting orders. He spoke again. 'Look, see to your men's welfare and then come back here. You're housed in the tent next to mine. We'll have a drink of wine together and catch up on each other's news.'

Conrad obeyed and took his leave. He had not expected to come across his old friend in such a superior position in the King's Guard. He knew that Miklo had joined the Guard after leaving university, but they had not been in contact for a long time.

It took Conrad over half an hour to arrange quarters for his men and attend to several other necessary tasks. There was the smell of cooking in the air as he returned to Miklo's tent, and two tin plates were already on the table. Miklo was sitting on a chair, his uniform coat and sword abandoned on the nearby bed. He greeted Conrad warmly again.

'Come in and be seated, my dear fellow. You'll dine with me this evening. Take your sword off and make yourself comfortable.'

Conrad was glad to obey and relieved himself of his sword, jacket and pistols. He took a seat opposite Miklo on a trunk that served as a chair. He had hardly sat down before an orderly came with food and ladled some form of stew onto the two plates. Miklo was already producing a flagon of wine and two metal goblets. He poured the wine, laughingly bidding his guest, 'Eat, drink and be merry.'

Conrad was anxious to learn what was happening locally. 'What's the position here?' he asked. 'There are some frightful stories circulating.'

Miklo became more serious and nodded. 'Not without foundation. The rebels hold most of the town. It's our job to clear them out. Now you are here with your troops, we stand a chance.'

'What sort of numbers are we up against?'

Miklo looked grim as he replied. 'The numbers of the enemy grow daily, but once we have got rid of the ringleaders the rest will quickly disperse.'

The news confirmed what Conrad had feared. 'So it is really a situation of civil war,' he responded thoughtfully.

Miklo was aghast at the comment. 'Nonsense. This conflict is caused by a bunch of traitors who don't like what the king wants to do. They are challenging the established law and order of the kingdom and we have to teach them a lesson and eliminate them.'

Conrad was disturbed by Miklo's reply. It rekindled the feeling of discontent he had been experiencing of late. It was quite clear that he and Miklo did not hold the same view of things. He did not respond directly to Miklo's last remark, but instead asked another question. 'Do we have enough men and equipment to combat the rebels?'

Miklo was quick to reassure him. 'Of course we do. We are better trained and equipped than them – and better organised.'

Conrad did not reply immediately. He was silent as Miklo poured more wine into his goblet. It was Miklo who spoke again first. 'A few days here, and you will soon learn what it's all about. You will see some real fighting.'

Miklo's words rang true the next morning. The camp was attacked. A strong group of rebels surprised a patrol returning to the camp from Raker, and the exchange spread to the outskirts of the camp. A volley of shots was fired and then the conflict became one of hand-to-hand fighting. For the first time Conrad witnessed the bloody exchange of battle for the control of Raker. He and his troops were held in reserve, with Miklo commanding the first defence. Conrad had to admire the military skills of his commander. The attack was soon overcome and the rebels were chased away, hotly pursued by Miklo and his men.

It was not long before Miklo's party returned. It had been a resounding victory. A number of the enemy had been killed, with only one casualty amongst the King's Guard. Hot and dusty, Miklo was overjoyed. He laughed as he passed Conrad. 'That taught them a lesson. They won't try that again,' he remarked, wiping the blood from his sword.

Conrad was surprised to see that the party had returned with some prisoners. Three men and two young women with bound hands were pushed along by grinning soldiers. The look on the faces of the prisoners was one of defeat, yet at the same time there was defiance in their eyes.

Conrad stood by as the prisoners were brought before Miklo. The commander merely gave a cursory glance and then nodded, as if to give his consent to the lead soldier who was guarding the pitiful group. The prisoners were immediately marched off.

'What's going to happen to them?' asked Conrad.

Miklo seemed surprised at the question. 'They'll be hanged forthwith, of course, as a lesson to others.'

Conrad was shocked. 'But we are killing our own people,' he protested.

Miklo looked at him for a second and then spoke. 'Look, it is now us or them. If we don't kill them, they will kill us. You will learn soon enough.'

Miklo's remarks only caused Conrad more inner conflict. He did not reply.

The next day he saw evidence of Miklo's justice. He was detailed to lead a patrol south to a village half a day's march away where there had been rumours of rebel activity. As they took to the road leading away from Raker the party came upon a recently erected timber scaffold at the side of the road. The bodies of the five prisoners hung from it, swaying gently in the breeze.

There were a few expressions of glee from some of Conrad's men as they gazed at the scene. The sight sickened Conrad and brought home to him fully the ruthless regime he was an enforced part of and whose barbaric actions he was detailed to carry out.

When they were close to the village, the party came under fire from a house at the side of the road. Conrad immediately gave the order for his men to take cover. The exchange only lasted a few minutes. The advantage of superior firepower from Conrad's troops quickly silenced the firing from the rebels. Conrad despatched some of his men to storm the house from the rear.

They did not take long. They returned a few minutes later, dragging with them a young woman, who bit and struggled as she was propelled along. Her captors flung her at Conrad's feet. One of the men gave his report. 'All the rebels are dead, but we found this vixen. Shall we hang her?'

'Stand her up.' Conrad commanded.

Two of the men hauled the girl to her feet. Conrad could see that she was quite pretty and she reminded him very much of Daintry. He wondered fleetingly how Daintry was and what she was doing. Since his enrolment in the King's Guard he had not been able to have any contact with her, and this had caused him anguish.

'Shall we hang her?' repeated the soldier.

'No. Wait.' Conrad responded curtly.

The young woman was struggling again and attempting to hit everybody around her. Conrad applauded her pitiful resistance. 'Secure her,' he ordered the men.

A length of cord was quickly produced and the prisoner was tied up. She stood in front of Conrad, sullen and defeated, her gaze now directed at the ground as she awaited her fate.

'What is your name?' Conrad asked.

'Zeeta,' the girl replied, without looking up.

'Why were you helping the rebels?' Conrad asked.

The girl looked up at him. 'I wasn't,' she sobbed. 'They took over my house.'

'She tried to attack us,' one of the soldiers interjected.

'I did not!' The girl looked defiantly up at Conrad. 'They tried to rape me,' she cried out in anguish, for the first time glaring angrily at the two men who held her.

Conrad was about to ask a further question, but the gathering was interrupted as a young man pushed his way through the group of villagers who had gathered to watch the scene and were being held back by the soldiers. The intruder was quickly grabbed by two of Conrad's men. He seemed intent on reaching Conrad. He flung himself at Conrad's feet.

'Commander, I beg you, spare the girl,' he pleaded. 'She is my betrothed.'

'Let's hang them both!' yelled one of the soldiers.

'Be silent!' Conrad shouted. 'I'll discipline the next man who interrupts.'

Silence prevailed. Conrad addressed the young man kneeling at his feet.

'Stand up,' he ordered.

The young man rose and stood next to the girl.

'What is your name?' Conrad asked, not unkindly.

'I am known as Elar.'

'And your trade?'

The young man seemed taken aback. 'I am a carpenter,' he replied simply.

Conrad turned to the soldier holding the rope securing the girl. 'Untie her cords,' he instructed.

The soldier looked surprised, but obeyed in silence. As soon as she was freed, the girl clutched the hand of her young man.

Conrad gave his instructions. To the men holding the pair he said, 'Release both of them.' He then turned to the young man. 'Take your girl away from here and return to your work.'

The couple quickly disappeared into the gathered throng. There were cheers from some in the crowd.

Conrad's men did not take kindly to his decision. Some could not understand his leniency towards what they considered to be rebel sympathisers. Others lamented the loss of the relished spectacle of hanging the girl.

From that point on, it was clear that Conrad was beginning to be viewed by a few under his command as a weak and ineffectual officer. He had quickly learnt that many of the King's Guard, like Miklo, were brutal both in their dealings with the population of Altaria and in their suppression of the rebels. They appeared to consider themselves to be endowed with a special privilege of dispensing arrogant and brutal justice. They clearly regarded the current uprising of people as rabble that must be exterminated. Conrad had found himself increasingly at odds with the opinions held by his troops. It was no accident that the way he dealt with the young couple did not go down well and was considered by some to be a failing on his part. The news reached Miklo's ears. He was not pleased with Conrad's action.

'What do you think you are doing, releasing rebels to fight again?' he demanded.

Conrad explained. 'In my opinion they are not rebels.'

'Your opinion?' Miklo's anger showed. 'How long have you been here? Listen to the advice of others who have more experience of fighting rebels.'

Conrad did not reply.

Miklo stood closer to him. He lowered his voice. 'Listen to me, Conrad. Our job is to support the king and destroy his enemies, wherever they are. That includes when they are taken prisoner.'

Again Conrad said nothing. Miklo's remarks revolted him.

Miklo lectured him for a further five minutes, and then dismissed him abruptly. It was clear that a deep rift now existed between the two former friends.

A whole month passed, and it became apparent that, far from clearing the rebel forces from Raker, it was the King's Guard who were now under threat. Spies had reported that more had joined the rebel forces. Miklo considered this to be a minor distraction from his plan. Clashes between the two sides occurred almost daily, as the King's Guard tried to regain the town. Their attempts were often hampered by the townspeople, most of whom sided with the rebels.

The final onslaught happened early one morning without any warning. Suddenly the camp was attacked on all sides. The first volley of shots claimed the lives of many of the unprepared soldiers. Conrad found himself isolated with a group of his men in a corner of the camp. In the end it came down to hand-to-hand fighting, with the defenders on the losing side, due to the vast numbers of the attacking forces.

Sword in hand, Conrad put up a brave fight, but it was obvious that his small party were outnumbered and surrounded. It was only a matter of time before he too would be cut down. Suddenly he received a blow to the head, and everything went black.

Chapter 18

Conrad gradually returned to consciousness. There was the sound of voices and he could detect the smell of burning in the air. It took a few minutes for him to completely regain his senses. He was lying on the ground, but as he attempted to move he found that he was unable to use his arms. They were tied behind his back. His jacket and boots had been taken, and his sword was gone. He suddenly realised that he was not alone. Five other soldiers of the King's Guard were kneeling on the ground close by, their hands also bound and their boots removed.

One of them spoke to Conrad. 'We thought you were dead, commander.'

Conrad replied hoarsely, 'I think I will survive. I seem to have been struck on the head.'

'What are they going to do with us?' asked another man.

Conrad looked around. The whole camp was being sacked. There seemed to be a lot of people removing what was of value to them from the tents and then setting fire to everything. As well as rebel forces, Conrad could now see women helping themselves to goods.

The six soldiers remained on the ground watching and listening to the destruction of their camp. It was abundantly clear that the size and ability of the opposing forces had been grossly underestimated.

'What are they keeping us here like this for?' grumbled one of Conrad's men.

'I guess they want to have the pleasure of seeing us hang,' laughed another.

'Here comes our executioner,' remarked the first man grimly.

A member of the victorious forces was approaching the group. He carried a sword in his hand that Conrad recognised as his. The man stopped and looked down at him. 'Can you walk?' he asked.

'I think so,' Conrad replied, wondering what was going to happen.

The man said nothing, but suddenly reached down and hauled Conrad to his feet. He peered at his prisoner's head. He grinned and spoke again. 'You'll survive. You have a tough skull.'

The man turned his attention to the other five prisoners. 'Get on your feet,' he ordered.

The five men obeyed, albeit with some difficulty because of their bonds.

'Why don't you kill us here and now and have done with it?' one snarled.

Their captor addressed them again. 'We are not barbarians. We do not kill prisoners.' It was obvious he could not help adding, 'Like the King's Guard do.'

None of the six prisoners responded, and the man in charge of them issued another order. 'Walk.'

The group started to move. Conrad still felt weak and dizzy, but he managed to keep up. They were led to another part of the ravaged camp, where wagons were being loaded with the spoils that had been collected. The man in charge of the prisoners shouted for somebody, and the next instant a young woman stood in front of Conrad. He immediately recognised her as the girl whose life he had spared some weeks before. She did not speak or admit recognition. She produced a piece of cloth and wound it round Conrad's head. For the first time he realised that his head had been bleeding. The girl vanished as quickly as she had appeared.

It did not take long for the rebels to assemble the party into some sort of order for a journey.

Groups of men and women marched behind loaded wagons. Conrad and his companions found themselves walking with rope nooses tied around their necks and attached to a wagon. A single guard marched alongside them.

As the party moved off, one of the prisoners asked, 'Where are we being taken?'

The guard grinned at him. 'Raker,' he said simply.

The trek to Raker took a long time. The women tended to walk slowly and some of the wagons were heavily laden. Conrad was relieved when the walls of the town appeared and they walked through the massive gates, now thrown wide open. Many of the local people had turned out to witness the return of the victorious army. The prisoners were subjected to taunts and jeering. Conrad was glad that the journey seemed to be over. His head ached and he felt weak from loss of blood. He was puzzled to see again the girl who had bandaged his head. It was clear to him that he had been mistaken when he set her free, and that she was indeed involved with the rebel movement.

He and the other prisoners were led to the ancient castle. There he was pushed alone into a bare turret room. He was glad to sink down onto the floor and rest. Perhaps an hour later a guard returned and motioned to him to accompany him. Conrad could not help noticing that the man was wearing a pair of King's Guard boots. He wondered who was wearing his.

He was led into a small room nearby. A young man sat behind a table. He looked up as Conrad entered. Conrad was astonished to recognise the same man who had pleaded for the life of his girl. He now had an air of authority.

The man smiled at him. 'We meet again, my friend.'

Conrad suddenly realised that he had made a dreadful mistake. This man was not a carpenter. It was quite clear that he was one of the rebels, and high up at that. Conrad knew he had let down his men, he had let down Miklo and he had let down himself. He had been a failure as an officer and a member of the King's Guard. He could only stammer a reply. 'Who... who are you?'

His host waved to a nearby chair. 'Please sit down. You ask who I am. I am Elgar Rigor, in command of the rebel forces here in Raker.'

Conrad gratefully sank into the chair. 'You told me you were a carpenter,' he replied.

The young man smiled again. 'I was a carpenter. But now I fight for the people of Altaria to overthrow the tyrant who rules them.'

'The army of the King's Guard will defeat you,' Conrad replied. There was no conviction in his voice.

Elgar shook his head. 'I think not. The people of Altaria are not on your side. They are on the side of those who fight for justice and less taxation.'

Conrad knew this was true, but he did not respond.

Elgar continued. 'The rebel movement is going from strength to strength. We have completely destroyed your presence here in Raker. Soon we will be marching south on Taslar itself.'

'What is going to happen to me and the five other members of the King's Guard you hold prisoner?' Conrad asked.

'You are the lucky ones. We will hold you hostage. As for the rest, those of your companions who were not killed fighting were given the option of joining our ranks. Over a quarter of those captured did so. The remainder are scattered without weapons and food. They will find little sympathy from the local people.'

Conrad wondered what had happened to Miklo. 'What about our commander, Miklo Janack?' he asked.

Elgar shrugged his shoulders. 'He was not among those we captured or those who absconded to our ranks. His whereabouts is unknown. It is likely that he escaped with a few others after the battle.'

Conrad wondered vaguely whether Miklo had indeed escaped. He knew that the extent of their defeat would weigh heavily on the commander. It was now evident that Miklo's assessment of the strength of the rebels had been deeply flawed.

There was a few seconds' silence between the two men, Conrad trying to make sense of everything, and Elgar watching him closely. It was Elgar who spoke first. Grinning slightly, he asked. 'And what of you, Conrad Accker?'

'How do you know my name?' asked Conrad in surprise.

'Conrad Accker from the town of Toomer, former assistant to Assem Rokar, Keeper of the King's Purse, and lately drafted into the King's Guard.'

'You know a lot about me.'

'Of course. We have spies everywhere. We are not just a band of rebels fighting a lost cause.'

'I see,' Conrad replied simply. The extent of the rebel movement surprised him. Even Miklo had not seemed to comprehend its size and organisation.

Elgar leaned across the table towards Conrad. He spoke in a soft voice. 'My friend, forget what happened when you made the mistake of accepting me as a simple carpenter. Perhaps it was meant to happen. The defeat of the King's Guard here in Raker was also meant to happen. The people's voice is being heard. There is no stopping us now.'

He paused for a few seconds.

This gave Conrad the opportunity to collect his thoughts. He still had feelings of despair over not recognising Elgar as something more than a carpenter. He had shown weakness and he had failed as a commander in the King's Guard. He also knew that Elgar had touched on the truth when he had spoken about the strength of the rebels and the mood of the population of Altaria.

He was roused from his misery by Elgar speaking again. 'Conrad Accker, I am asking you to join our ranks. Search your heart and ask yourself if you are truly on the side of the king and his extravagant administration, or whether you are with those who fight for justice and fairness.' Elgar studied Conrad as if to let his words sink in. Then he grinned slightly as he spoke again. 'There is an urgent need for a second commander in our group.'

Conrad had a few seconds of inner torment. He had sworn allegiance to the king and his cause, but that oath had been made in ignorance. What he had witnessed in his brief period of service had changed him. Deep down, he knew that his sympathy lay more with the rebels than with the king's ambitions. On top of that, the misery of his own failure here in Raker had produced in him a feeling of indifference to which path his life would take. If his life ended fighting for the rebel movement, then so be it.

He stared straight at Elgar. 'I will join you.'

Chapter 19

Daintry had been incarcerated at Katangar for a month, trying to relate to the misery of her new life.

The first few minutes after she arrived in this strange and cruel environment had changed her life forever. She was now branded with the mark of a criminal. Like the rest of her group of prisoners, after the brutal initiation she lay on the ground sobbing from her ordeal and in a state of shock. The old hag who had doused her with water spoke again, not unkindly. 'On your feet again, girlie. Tomorrow you'll be put to work.' She grabbed Daintry's arm and hauled her to her feet.

Bewildered and in pain, Daintry and the rest of the prisoners, urged on by two burly guards with cudgels, stumbled to a nearby windowless stone building. Straw was strewn over the floor inside. The only light came from several openings high up in the walls. This was to be their home now.

The room was already half full of women. Some of them grumbled at the influx of new contenders for space. Daintry sank gratefully down upon the straw. She was exhausted from the long day's trek and now her back throbbed and burned with the after-effects of the branding. Meeka lay silently beside her, occasionally whimpering in her misery. An older woman stood up and came over to the new prisoners, carrying a clay dish in her hand. 'Let me put some of this on the burn,' she soothed. 'It will ease the pain.' Daintry allowed her to smear some foul-smelling substance on her back. The woman offered the salve to the other victims of the vile treatment.

'They mark us like animals,' one girl sobbed.

'We are all marked the same,' the woman replied, perhaps as some form of comfort for the new arrivals.

A girl close to Daintry who had also just been branded sobbed, 'Now my man will never marry me.'

'Think you'll ever see him again?' retorted another girl.

Daintry thought of Conrad. Would he ever marry her after all this, branded as she was as a criminal? As she clutched his stone, tears came to her eyes.

She spent a restless night. In the past she and Meeka had cuddled up to each other, but now the weather had turned warmer and the temperature in the building with so many occupants was hot and oppressive.

The first shadowy light was beginning to penetrate the building when the prisoners were woken by the noise of the door being opened and someone banging on a metal object, accompanied by the shout, 'Outside!'

Silently the women filed out through the door. Guards armed with cudgels supervised the proceedings. The women were led to an area where food was being prepared in a building with a roof but no walls. Some sort of food was being slopped out into earthenware bowls. Daintry and Meeka followed the example of the other women and queued for their first meal at Katangar. Each was to receive a bowlful of gruel. They had no spoons, so they were forced to eat from the bowl as best they could. In spite of the primitive method of eating and the tasteless contents of the bowl, they both welcomed the food.

They had barely finished when the order to start work was barked out by one of the guards. They were marched to an area close to what was clearly the mine entrance. Here a large platform had been constructed, and at its centre stood a massive capstan from which wooden bars projected. The women were ordered to position themselves in fours behind each bar. Daintry and Meeka stood together, wondering what was to come. They were soon to find out. A bell rang somewhere below them and the order was given to push. Desperately trying to gain some momentum, the panting prisoners struggled to move the bars, their feet often failing to get a grip on the slippery floor. Eventually the huge capstan started to turn. For the first time Daintry noticed a rope disappearing off somewhere under the wooden floor below. At last a shout indicated that the toil was to stop. Daintry flopped against the bar she was holding, exhausted by her efforts.

Daintry lost count of the number of times that day she struggled round at the capstan. She was perplexed at what the group of prisoners might be achieving, until one of the other women explained that, as they walked round turning the centre post, they were lifting huge tubs of ore mined by the male prisoners below. The shout to stop came whenever a tub of ore reached the surface, where it was transported by some other female prisoners to the washing station on the nearby river.

At midday there was a break for some sort of soup, again slopped into earthenware bowls, accompanied by a hunk of stale bread. Then it was back to work again until the evening. When at last the order came to stop for the night, Daintry and the other prisoners who had arrived with her were completely exhausted. Daintry had hardly any interest in the thick soup that was their evening meal. She was glad when the guards ordered all the women to their stone prison for the night and she could lower her aching body onto the straw. In spite of her surroundings, sleep overtook her within minutes. She had spent her first day as a prisoner at Katangar.

The following day a little act of kindness reached Daintry. One of the older women, who was employed in cooking the food, pushed some pieces of sackcloth into her hands. 'Put these on your feet, dearie,' she instructed. Daintry thanked her profusely. She had noticed that some of the women who had been at the camp for some time had their feet wrapped up in any rags they could find. The ground of the mine was littered with sharp bits of stone, which made walking barefoot painful, and she already had several cuts on her feet. The gift of the bits of sackcloth was a blessed relief. She was soon to learn that any rags suitable for foot covering were eagerly sought after and greatly prized in the camp. Her relief was to be short-lived. A few nights later, as she slept the items of comfort were stolen from where she had placed them, by her side. She never saw them again.

The days afterwards followed the same pattern as the first. Each morning the prisoners were noisily woken by one of the guards, and from then on, except for short breaks for insipid food, they laboured at their allotted tasks. Each day, Daintry was assigned to push at the bars of the capstan. It came as a shock to her to learn that among the women prisoners who were already established at the camp this was considered one of the better work options. Those who had to empty the full tubs raised from the depths and transport the ore to the washing beds envied those at the capstan. The worst job was at the washing beds. Here the workers had to stand knee deep in water, washing the ore before it was loaded into carts to be transported away from Katangar. Work at the washing beds did offer a glimmer of hope for escape, however, because it was outside the main camp.

Escape was a frequent topic of conversation among the prisoners.

'How do you get out of this rotten place?' one of the newcomers asked.

One of the established prisoners laughed. 'You don't. And if you do, there is a bounty on your head. They will bring you back and beat you. And you won't get another chance.'

Daintry was to learn what the words meant the following day. She spied a prisoner walking with heavy ankle chains on.

'Why is she chained like that?' Daintry whispered to another prisoner.

'She tried to escape and was recaptured,' the girl replied.

The sight horrified Daintry. She could hardly bear to look as the woman shuffled along in her bonds, a look of resignation on her face.

The cold facts that very few manage to escape and that most of those who did were quickly recaptured did not completely extinguish hope for some. Expectations were always raised when, on a rare occasion, a prisoner did escape and was not recaptured. It was a moment of despair when news circulated that a secure wall was being built around the camp by a group of male prisoners to prevent escapes.

For the most part the women were kept segregated from the men who toiled in the depths of the mine extracting the ore. There was a reason for this. Familiarity between the sexes led to pregnancy, and pregnant women were a loss of labour to the mine. The first time new women prisoners caught sight of any of the male workers, they were stunned by their appearance. Most of the men were dressed in rags. Some were practically naked. Each had a look of hopelessness on his face. Daintry was shocked to observe that some were actually branded on their foreheads with the same mark she now bore on her back, a letter K within a circle. Seeing the state of the male prisoners made her own ordeal seem almost bearable.

As she toiled each day at the wretched capstan, Daintry's hope of redemption gradually faded. Ever since her arrest she had clung to the hope that a miracle would happen and that somehow she would be rescued from her ordeal. Perhaps her father would secure her release; she even dreamed that Conrad might rescue her. As each day passed she knew that neither of these things was going to happen. Nobody had appeared to ease her plight, not even her father. He, Mogo, Mela and even Conrad must have forgotten about her. At first she had been puzzled that none of those she loved came to her aid, but now she reasoned that perhaps, as the pastor had intimated, they really did all believe she was guilty and had left her to her fate. When she thought of Conrad, her heart was full of pain. She would no longer be able to marry him. Even if a miracle happened and she found freedom, he would not want her now that she bore the mark of Katangar. When she looked at her fellow prisoners she knew she must look the same as they did, dirty and dishevelled, her clothing torn and ragged. Even her own family would not recognise her now.

She still kept close to Meeka. They slept beside each other and occasionally if tiredness did not immediately force sleep upon them they would chat about their former lives. Meeka had had a very different life from Daintry's. She had been brought up in a poor family and with a drunken father, and it had been her mother who had worked to hold the family together. The eldest of four children, Meeka had worked as a seamstress from the age of twelve, until evil gossip had had her unjustly accused of witchcraft. Daintry grew to like her companion, who toiled beside her at work each day. It was a blow when Meeka was ordered to the washing beds.

One day Meeka did not return from work. Word soon got about that she had escaped. Daintry waited and prayed, anxious lest her friend be recaptured, but as the guards searching for her returned each day empty-handed, her hopes began to rise. After three days the search was abandoned. Meeka had got away.

Daintry missed her companion terribly. They had shared so much and she had not made a similar friend among the rest of the prisoners. However, her own circumstances were soon to change.

One day, as she and her fellow prisoners were eating their meagre breakfast, one of the guards came up to her.

'Can you read and write, girl?'

Daintry was surprised at the question, but she answered. 'Yes.' Unlike many girls of the time, she and Mela had both been taught to read and write. The guard stared at her for a second or two and then ordered gruffly, 'Come with me.'

He pushed Daintry in the direction of the mine entrance, where each day the heavy tubs of ore she and her fellow prisoners hauled from the depths emerged. A mine official came over. It was unusual for the prisoners to have any contact with the elite group of men who ran the mine, who were easily recognised from their clean and neat appearance. The official scrutinised Daintry. 'Can you read and write?' he asked.

'Yes, Master,' Daintry replied, aware that lack of respect would ensure a beating.

'Can you count as well?'

'Yes, Master.'

The official nodded, muttered something and then pushed a slab of slate and a marker into Daintry's hands. 'Stand here and count the tubs of ore as they come up,' he ordered. As he walked away, he growled, 'Make a mistake, and I'll have you whipped until you can't stand.'

The guard who had accompanied Daintry smirked at her. 'You heard him. Get on with it.' With that he swaggered off.

Daintry positioned herself where she could clearly see the tubs of ore reach the surface. Each time one appeared she carefully made a mark on the slate. At first she was puzzled that she had been selected for this work, but later in the day she learned that the older woman who had preceded her had made numerous mistakes and in the end had been removed and sent to the camp kitchen. It was the practice in the camp for the older women to be employed in cooking or fetching water rather than one of the more strenuous jobs.

At the end of the first day at her new task, Daintry was anxious that her efforts would not meet with the approval of her masters. The same official she had seen that morning came to relieve her of the slate and after briefly viewing her efforts glanced at her, grunted something like 'Good' and marched off with the slate. A relieved Daintry went in search of her evening meal.

From then on, this was Daintry's assignment each day. At the end of the day a mine official came and took away the slate bearing the total number of tubs of ore mined. Daintry was relieved that she no longer had to struggle at the bars lifting the ore to the surface. Her new position gave her a slightly elevated degree of freedom. She was allowed to go to her place of work and turn up for meals unaccompanied. After the first few days, instead of waiting to be relieved of the slate and the day's total of tubs, she was permitted to take it to the mine official in charge of her counting efforts.

However, there were downsides to her new role. During the first few days she became conscious of jealousy from some of the other prisoners in her group, who considered that she had somehow manipulated her way into an easier job. There was also the difficulty that when it rained she was exposed to the elements. Those working on the capstan had a rough covering of a roof over them, but Daintry was standing out in the open, and when it rained she had no shelter. It was impossible to keep dry outside, and there was the danger of the rain erasing her score from the slate. It was a relief when she managed to obtain a sack to put over her shoulders in an attempt to protect herself and the slate from the elements.

But there was a far worse problem attached to her new workplace. She was now in sight of The Beast. This was the name the female prisoners had given to the head guard, Karrick Bruler, a bullish, thickset brute of a man, who carried out his duties with extreme cruelty. He also seemed to have acquired special privileges when it came to the women prisoners. It was well known that each evening he drank heavily, and from time to time he would select one of the hapless females for his pleasure. Though fraternisation between the sexes was frowned upon by the mine overseers, they appeared to turn a blind eye to The Beast's indulgences. It was rumoured that even the mine supervisors were in fear of him. This did not bode well for the unfortunate women who received his attentions. When Daintry first spied him looking at her, fear filtered through her body, and it reappeared whenever he was about.

Oddly it was not The Beast who was Daintry's downfall. One day she was conscious of one of the other guards looking at her. She did her best to remain focused on her work, and the incident passed. As she was finishing her day's work, however, the man appeared in front of her. He did not speak, but suddenly grabbed her arm. She immediately resisted and started to struggle, in the process dropping the slate, which fell to the floor and shattered. She let out a cry of fear and protest. Instead of discouraging her assailant, this only seemed to encourage him. Now he had his arm round her. Daintry hit him in the face with her free hand.

'What's going on here?' Two other guards had suddenly appeared on the scene.

'Did you see that? She struck me,' protested Daintry's attacker indignantly.

'We'll teach her a lesson, then,' replied the guard who had spoken.

'Make sure you make it a good one, then,' retorted the guard who had molested Daintry, holding a hand to his face.

Daintry suddenly found herself being dragged along by the other two guards.

'I have done nothing!' she shouted, already fearful of the guards' intended punishment for her. She knew well enough that striking a guard was a serious offence.

'Please, I was only protecting myself,' she pleaded.

'Shall we whip her now?' one of the guards asked his companion.

'No,' replied the other. 'Save it for tomorrow.'

Daintry's pleas and protestations of innocence were ignored by the guards. She wondered where they were taking her, and she was soon to find out. In an isolated part of the camp stood a circular stone building with a conical roof. It was only about the height of a person and had no windows. She realised at once that this was her destination. She had heard other prisoners talking about 'the tower' where wrongdoers were incarcerated for varying degrees of time.

Daintry was dragged to the building and pushed inside. The door was slammed shut and she heard the bolt securing it being put in place. Her prison was dark and cramped. It was almost impossible to sit down, and the room smelled of filth and urine. Not even a chink of light was allowed in. She stood in the darkness, frightened and apprehensive. The sudden change in her circumstances had shaken her, and the injustice of the guards was barely believable. She knew that tomorrow they would take delight in beating her. After that, what would happen to her? In her first few days at the mine she had witnessed a fellow prisoner being whipped by the guards. The poor woman had been attached to a post by her wrists and the blows had fallen upon her back. When eventually she had been taken down, she had collapsed on the floor, only to been dragged off somewhere. Her recovery had been slow, and when she eventually reappeared she had been sent to the washing beds. The memory of that event came back vividly to Daintry now as she contemplated the ordeal that awaited her.

Time seemed to have no meaning as she waited in the darkness. Perhaps two hours had passed when suddenly she heard the bolt on the door being drawn. The door swung open, and Karrick Bruler, the man known as The Beast, stood before her.

Chapter 20

Desperately trying to adjust her eyes to the light, Daintry shrank back in horror.

'And how's this little chicken?' chuckled The Beast. He reached in and grabbed her arm as she pressed herself against the stone wall. Still laughing, he ignored her feeble attempt to evade him and pulled her roughly out of the prison. He was a huge man and he towered above Daintry. She struggled in his grasp as he held her at arms' length eyeing her up and down.

'You're a nice little chicken, to be sure. Just about ready for plucking.'

Daintry knew what he was about. She made a brave attempt to save herself. 'Please, please,' she begged, 'I am a maiden. I have never known a man.'

Karrick Bruler laughed again. 'Not for much longer,' he sneered.

'Please don't molest me. I'll die if you do,' Daintry cried out in desperation.

Karrick looked at her. 'Tomorrow you'll be whipped to within a whisper of your life. Enjoy this night with a good man and learn the joys of womanhood.'

Suddenly he reached up and grabbed a handful of her hair. He stretched his arm out and propelled her forward. 'Walk, girl,' he ordered.

Holding her hair so tightly that it hurt her, he led Daintry out of the camp and past the washing beds, and headed for a small cottage. When they arrived there, he threw open the door and pushed her inside. She found herself in a sparsely furnished room. A bed occupied one corner, and a table and a few chairs stood nearby. A pot of food simmered on the fire that burned in one wall. The smell tantalised Daintry, who had not eaten for many hours. She hardly had time to take everything in before the door was opened again and two of the older female prisoners stood there.

Karrick glared at the newcomers and then nodded in the direction of Daintry, who stood, tearful and dejected, in the centre of the room. 'Scrub her clean,' he ordered, adding as he made a move to leave, 'She stinks.'

He lumbered out of the cottage, leaving Daintry with the two women. They stared at her for a few seconds, and then they unceremoniously grabbed her by her arms and pushed her out of the door. The women were strong, and Daintry was unable to withstand them.

A tub of water had been placed just outside the door. One of the women addressed Daintry. 'Get your clothes off.'

Daintry shook her head. It was the only resistance she could muster. The two women had clearly expected some reluctance on her part, because she was immediately and without any finesse stripped of her clothing. One of them made a grab for Conrad's stone, which still hung round Daintry's neck, but after a cursory glance she disregarded it with a sniff of disgust. As Daintry stood there naked, one of the women ordered her to get into the tub. Shivering from both fright and the cold water, Daintry found herself being scrubbed none too gently from head to toe. The women even washed her hair after a fashion. They appeared unconcerned as they included the most intimate area of her body, and she blushed with shame and embarrassment. The worst thing was that The Beast sat nearby, drinking from a jug, but he seemed to want the women to complete their task uninterrupted and paid little attention to the proceedings.

When they had finished with her, the two women led Daintry, still naked, back into the cottage and deposited her on the bed. Their task completed, they left. Daintry immediately jumped up from the bed, escape on her mind. She edged open the door a little and peered out through the crack. The Beast was still sitting there quaffing ale. There was no escape in that direction. She closed the door again. There was no back entrance to the cottage, and no window she could use. Suddenly she spied a long knife lying on the table. An idea came to her. She grabbed the knife and retreated back to the bed; she wrapped one of the grubby bed coverings around her body and sat clutching the weapon. Desperation had now driven her to the limit. She would use the knife on her tormentor. She knew they would hang her as a result, but tomorrow she would be whipped and most likely die as a result anyway, so what difference would it make? At least she would die with her honour intact.

She waited in the gathering gloom. Night was already falling. It seemed a long time before Karrick Bruler returned. He entered the cottage slowly. She heard him cursing as he struggled to light a candle from the embers of the fire. Eventually light penetrated the darkness in the room. Karrick was unsteady on his feet as he lifted the pot from the fire and poured some of the prepared food into a bowl. She watched fearfully as he sat down at the table and slurped greedily, taking deep draughts from the pitcher in between mouthfuls. She waited, her heart thumping, all the while holding the knife tightly.

Eventually Karrick rose from his chair and turned his attention to her. He swayed from the effects of the drink as he approached the bed. 'Now, my little chicken,' he leered. He made a grab at the blanket Daintry had around her. The suddenness of the movement caught Daintry off guard. As he pulled the covering off her, she lost her grip on the knife, which clattered to the floor. He laughed as he lunged for one of her breasts. 'My little chicken shows good form.' He heaved himself at her, his hands fondling her breasts. With one last effort of strength, Daintry pushed him away with all her might, using her knee to assist her. Her strategy worked. He staggered, lost his balance and fell backwards, crashing into one of the chairs. He attempted to stand up and then collapsed on the floor and lay still.

Daintry watched in horror. She stood gazing at him, half hoping that he would get up, but he did not move. She did not have the experience to know that he was lying in a drunken stupor. Terrified that she had killed him and knowing what the outcome would be if that were the case, she knew that she had to try to escape.

With one last fearful look at her assailant, she opened the door of the cottage. It was now dark outside, but from time to time the moon appeared from behind clouds, giving a faint light to her surroundings. She knew she was outside the mine complex, for the construction of the perimeter barricade was taking place nearby, but she had no knowledge of the best route of escape. As she stood there feeling the cool night air on her naked body, she saw a light approaching. Panic overtook her. In desperation she crouched behind some bushes, hoping that the darkness would conceal her. Luck was on her side. Two guards, one of them carrying a lantern, passed slowly by, deep in conversation. She waited until they were out of sight and then emerged from her hiding place. As she did so, she spied her clothes hanging on a line. The two women who had washed her had also washed her dirty garments. She quickly removed them from the line and struggled into them. They were still wet, but at least they covered her nakedness.

Uncertain of which direction to take, she started to walk away from the cottage, her back to the mine complex. She passed the now unoccupied washing beds again and followed the course of the river downstream. It seemed to offer the best hope of escape. She knew that Meeka must have got away by using the river, but she was unsure how she might have accomplished this.

She had only been walking for a few minutes when to her horror she heard voices again.

She sought desperately for somewhere to hide, but the reeds on the edge of the river gave no cover. Suddenly she caught sight of a small boat moored a short distance from the reeds. It offered the only means of concealment. Frantically she waded into the river. The water came almost to her knees, but she reached the boat safely. Quickly she climbed into it. It was just big enough for her to stretch out full length on its floor. She prayed that she had not been seen by the approaching guards.

She lay there, frightened to move even a muscle, listening to the voices becoming louder as the men approached. She waited, expecting to hear the shout of discovery at any moment, but it did not come. Instead she heard the voices slowly fade away into the distance. She waited a long time before she dared raise her head and look out. All was quiet. Suddenly an idea came to her. Why not use the boat as a means of escape? The river would take her somewhere. She reasoned that if she tried to get away overland, the chance of recapture was greater. Most of the prisoners who had proceeded in that direction had been caught quickly. And if that happened to her she knew what fate awaited her. Even if she survived the severe beating she would receive, her ankles would be confined in those ghastly manacles for as long as she remained a prisoner at Katangar.

Her mind made up, she set about getting the boat in motion. It took her several minutes to undo the tight knot in the rope that secured it to the bank. After that she had to manoeuvre the boat out into the river where the current flowed. She waded as far as she could, pushing the boat ahead of her. The water came up to her thighs before she detected any voluntary movement in the boat. With some difficulty she managed to resume her place in its interior.

Slowly at first, the boat drifted along. Several times it swung around with the current, making Daintry puzzle at what was happening in the darkness. Gradually the small craft gathered momentum until it was moving at a good pace, caught up in the flow of the river. Occasionally it would come to rest among reeds and Daintry would have to push it away from them to get it moving again. It was cold on the river in the night air, and Daintry found herself shivering in her damp clothes. As she huddled there, she wondered how far the boat would carry her and what would be the outcome of her escape. Would she find somebody to help her?

In spite of her predicament, drowsiness began to overtake Daintry. She found her eyes closing and eventually she fell asleep curled up on the wooden boards. The boat continued its journey, drifting peacefully along.

Chapter 21

Daintry woke up with a shock. How long she had been asleep she did not know, but it was daylight and the boat had come to rest against some reeds. Now that she was awake she felt cold and stiff from lying on the hard boards.

She sat up cautiously and hurriedly looked about her, but everything seemed quiet. All she could hear was the sound of water falling. She quickly discovered how lucky she had been that the boat had stopped when it did. If it had drifted along a bit further it would have reached some rapids and rocks. What might have happened to her then did not bear thinking about.

The river was bounded on both sides by the forest, dark and mysterious. While the dense trees looked forbidding, she knew the forest offered the best chance of escape. She had no way of telling how far she had travelled during the night, but she knew that a search for her would be going on already. The boat would have been missed, and the logical course of action would be to follow the river to find her. The thought of what would happen to her if she was caught drove her to leave her immediate surroundings and plunge into the unknown.

She climbed out of the boat, waded to the shore and set off into the forest. She soon discovered that it was not as frightening as she had imagined. Sunshine filtered through the trees, birds fluttered and sang above her, and occasionally she disturbed a browsing deer, who scampered off hurriedly at her approach.

Daintry had been walking for some hours when hunger and fatigue overcame her. She felt that she had to rest and sank down beneath a tall tree. She had not eaten properly for over twenty-four hours and she was beginning to feel weak from the lack of sustenance. She had found a few berries to eat and also some leaves that she knew were edible, but they did little to quell the pangs of hunger.

She dozed for a short while, and then desperation drove her on. She knew that unless she found food and shelter soon she would die in the forest. Almost in a daze she continued to walk.

It was late in the afternoon when she came to a clearing in the forest. A faint track led across it, perhaps worn by animals. She followed it, thinking that surely she must encounter another human being soon.

Suddenly the ground gave way beneath her. She screamed as she plunged down, landing awkwardly on soft ground. A searing pain shot through her foot. She lay there for a few seconds, nursing her ankle and sobbing from the pain. It took her a while to work out where she was. She seemed to be lying at the bottom of a pit. Way above she could see blue sky through the gap she had made when she fell. The earth walls were so high that she would be unable to get out of this place unassisted. Logic told her that this place must have been constructed by human beings, perhaps to catch wild animals, and that offered a degree of comfort. How often, though, did they return to the pit? With all her might she shouted for help.

She lay there for what seemed a long time, calling out at intervals. Surely she would not die in this place…

Suddenly there was a sound from above.

'What have we caught here?' A man's face was peering down at her.

'Please help me. I have injured my foot.'

At last help was at hand. The man produced a rough ladder

and lowered it into the pit. Slowly and gingerly she climbed up, conscious of the pain in her ankle. When she reached the surface and struggled to her feet, the man was standing grinning at her. He reached out his hand and fondled her curls.

'So... You're a pretty little catch.'

'Please help me,' begged Daintry.

The man continued looking at her. 'And where might you have come from?' he sneered. Suddenly and without warning he grabbed her with one hand and with the other ripped her dress off her shoulder. He looked at the mark on her skin and laughed. 'I thought so. An escaped prisoner from Katangar.'

Fear gripped Daintry. 'Please don't send me back there,' she pleaded. 'I'll die if you do.'

The man laughed. 'Too bad,' he grunted. 'You'll earn me a silver coin tomorrow.'

'Please don't take me back to the mines. If you return me to my father, he will reward you.'

The man had not shaved for days, and he spoke from a toothless mouth. 'And who might your father be?'

Daintry's hopes rose. 'He is Anton Brouka, the grain merchant and miller of Toomer,' she replied.

The man laughed. 'Never heard of him, and Toomer is two days' ride away. Katangar is but one.'

'Please, not Katangar!' cried Daintry.

Her entreaty was in vain. The man grabbed her arm and swung her round. 'Walk, girl.'

Daintry tried, but her injured ankle made it painful and difficult for her to put weight on her foot.

'I cannot walk. I am injured,' she whimpered.

The man reached down and with one movement swept her off her feet and slung her over his shoulder as if she were a bag of flour. He hoisted his gun over his other shoulder and set off through the forest. Daintry was lying face down and was forced to watch the ground moving beneath her.

Her captor walked for a short distance through the trees and then set her down. Daintry looked around. They were in another clearing. A rough shelter had been constructed in the centre and a fire burned close by. A second man emerged from the shelter. He glanced at the first and then stared at Daintry, who was standing dejectedly nearby.

'And what have we caught this time?' he asked.

'A night's entertainment for us, and a silver coin tomorrow.'

The second man moved towards Daintry. He too peered at her mark, and then he addressed Daintry. 'Well, you're a pretty one. You may be worth even more than a silver coin.'

Daintry stood defeated. It was clear that these two men were not going to help her.

She was unprepared for what happened next. One of the men went into the shelter and returned carrying some rope. His intention was immediately clear.

Alarmed, Daintry cried out, 'No, please! Don't tie me up.'

The men laughed as they pushed her towards a tree at the edge of the clearing. Daintry found herself forced into a sitting position, her hands bound together behind the tree. For good measure they wound several coils of rope around her and the tree.

'That'll stop you from wandering off,' remarked one of the men, as they walked away. He added with a smirk, 'You're not the first prisoner we've recaptured, but you're the prettiest by far.'

Daintry felt exhausted and weak from hunger. She could see the men preparing some food. The smell of the cooking tantalised her. Would they feed her? She hoped so. After a short while she either fainted or dozed off. She woke up, alerted to the fact that her bonds were hurting her. She struggled, trying to find a more comfortable position, but it was of little use. Her mouth was dry and her lips parched. She could see the men eating. One of them stood up and walked towards her, carrying a bucket. As he neared her she found the energy to plead with him.

'Please, can I have some water?'

The man grinned at her and nodded. He disappeared somewhere behind her. Several minutes later he reappeared carrying the bucket full of water. He stopped in front of her. 'You want some water?' he asked.

'Please,' Daintry begged.

She was not prepared for what happened next. The man raised the bucket and poured the contents over her. Daintry screamed as the deluge hit her.

'You wanted some water. Here it is,' mocked the man.

Unable to move out of the way, Daintry was soaked to the skin. Her assailant laughed. 'That'll make you want to take your clothes off quicker shortly,' he remarked over his shoulder as he walked away.

Daintry sobbed uncontrollably. She had already suffered so much, and now this. It did not seem fair. Men were so cruel. She wished with all her heart that she had died peacefully in the forest, instead of having to endure all this torment. Wet, hungry and in pain, she closed her eyes and awaited her fate.

She must have briefly lost consciousness, because when she opened her eyes again the two men were drinking from an earthenware pitcher, which they frequently passed to each other. She closed her eyes again, to block out the view and to blot out what might lay ahead at the hands of her tormentors.

Suddenly a soft male voice somewhere behind her alerted her. 'Can you hear me?'

Puzzled, Daintry uttered a faint 'yes' from a dry mouth.

'Don't move. I'm going to cut the rope.'

Daintry felt her bonds being attacked by a knife, and the rope falling away.

The man spoke again. 'Wait quietly now, and when those two scoundrels aren't looking, slide round to the back of the tree.'

Daintry found her heart thumping. Who was he? Was some form of rescue at hand, or was another torment about to start?

As instructed, she sat quietly and waited for a suitable moment. After what seemed to be an age, one of the men went into the rough shelter and the other disappeared into the trees nearby. Carefully, Daintry slid behind the tree, all the time watching and praying that the men would not reappear before she had completed the task. Luck was on her side. She slipped out of sight without being detected. For several seconds she crawled away from the tree. Then she stood up, looking for the owner of the mysterious voice. She spied him a dozen or so steps away: a sandy-haired young man of about her own age. He beckoned her towards him, at the same time putting a finger to his lips for silence.

Daintry complied as best she could. She was soaking wet, her limbs were stiff from being tied up, and it hurt her to put any weight on her foot. On top of that a lack of food was making her weak and light-headed. She limped slowly and painfully towards her rescuer.

The young man smiled at her as she drew near to him. 'We must hurry, or those scoundrels will see you are missing,' he whispered gently.

'I have hurt my ankle. I fear I cannot walk very far,' replied Daintry.

Without a word the young man slung the gun he was carrying over his shoulder and picked her up in his arms as if she was no weight at all.

They had not walked far when there was a shout behind them. Daintry's escape had been discovered. The young man set her down. Her captors were approaching fast. The man who had found Daintry in the pit carried a gun, which he was pointing at the young man. 'Stop, thief!' he shouted. 'You are stealing our property.'

The young man pushed Daintry to one side and took his gun off his shoulder.

'Give us back our property, or I'll shoot,' threatened the man.

Daintry's rescuer stood firm. 'This maiden is not your property,' he responded calmly.

'She's an escaped prisoner. We are taking her back to Katangar,' the other replied.

'I think not this time,' the young man replied.

His opponent cursed, took aim and fired. The young man ducked, and the shot rustled into the trees close to Daintry. She screamed as the young man returned fire. The attacker spun round, crashed to the ground and lay still. His companion, who was unarmed, fled the scene.

The young man turned to Daintry, who stood petrified, her hands over her eyes. 'I am Karl,' he said. 'I'm going to take you somewhere safe.'

Once more he swept her up into his arms. He spoke again. 'Do not fret for those two villains. They are robbers and thieves and have killed many an innocent traveller in the forest.'

Daintry did not reply. She was feeling quite unwell. Karl seemed to have good intentions, but she did not understand what he meant when he declared that he was taking her somewhere safe. Was it to be yet another trauma for her? She felt too weak and ill to care.

They only went a short distance before they came to a horse tethered to a tree. Without a word Karl mounted the horse and hoisted Daintry up in front of him. He gave a command to the horse, and they set off in the evening gloom.

How long they rode, or how far, Daintry could not tell. For most of the journey she leaned against Karl with her eyes closed, conscious of his arms holding her in place.

When the horse eventually came to a halt, Daintry opened her eyes. They seemed to be in some sort of habitation. Karl had stopped in front of a cottage. To Daintry's relief, there were a number of women around.

Karl lifted her down from the horse. She heard him say, 'I rescued her from those two robbers Zarek and Okel. They had her tied to a tree. She is ill and has been injured.'

Daintry, her eyes half-closed, heard a woman's voice say, 'Bring her in here.'

She was helped into the cottage. Several women stood around her, asking questions. 'Has she got the fever?' 'Where is she from?' Another voice answered, 'No. She is just overcome with fatigue and hunger. She has also hurt her foot. Look how swollen it is. We need Saltima. Fetch her.'

Carefully they removed Daintry's wet clothing and laid her in a soft bed. Somebody started to feed her some broth. Her ankle was gently prodded and then bound up. She lay back exhausted, and sleep finally overtook her.

Chapter 22

For two days Daintry lay almost oblivious to what was happening around her. She was fed and cared for and, but she seemed to need to sleep a great deal. Occasionally conversation went on around her, to which she paid little attention. From time to time she was conscious of a woman bending over her with curls similar to hers. Another young woman was feeding her regularly.

It was on the morning of the third day that she began to observe her surroundings. She was lying in a comfortable bed, her injured ankle bound up. The room she was in was small and contained little other than two beds, a table and several chairs. Her gaze focused on a young woman, perhaps a little older than she was, who was sitting at the table engrossed in writing. At once Daintry noticed her hair, which fell in ringlets around her shoulders. She reasoned that the young woman must have been one of her carers for the last few days. Another young woman, who appeared to be some kind of servant, was busy at a task nearby.

When she heard Daintry stir, the woman at the table looked up from her writing. She stood up and walked over to the bed. 'How are you feeling now?' she asked.

'A little better, I think,' Daintry replied, wondering where she was and what was happening.

'You were quite poorly when Karl brought you in.'

'I had a horrible time in the forest. I was captured by two men. They tied me to a tree. They were... They were going to rape me and then take me back to Katangar.' Daintry spoke softly as she recalled the experience, but then panic overtook her, and she blurted out anxiously, 'Please, PLEASE, don't send me back to the mines. They will kill me there if you do.'

The woman smiled at her. 'Do not fear. You are safe here.' Then she asked kindly, 'What is your name, and where do you come from?'

'I am Daintry Brouka, daughter of Anton Brouka, grain merchant and miller of Toomer.'

'I am Aleena and this is Sharla.' Aleena indicated the other young woman present. 'We have been looking after you, with some help from someone I think you know.'

'Someone I know. Here?' Daintry was intrigued.

'You will see,' Aleena replied, giving her a coy little smile.

Daintry did not have to wait long to satisfy her curiosity. Almost before Aleena had finished speaking, the door opened and a woman entered. At first Daintry had difficulty recognising her, because she was dressed in bright, colourful clothes, but suddenly she realised: it was Saltima, the alleged witch who had provided the potion to heal her father.

'Saltima!' Daintry cried out excitedly. 'What are you doing here?'

Saltima grinned at her. 'I sought refuge here after I escaped arrest.'

Daintry was suddenly subdued, remembering. 'They arrested me and sent me to the mines at Katangar.'

Saltima nodded in sympathy. 'I know. There is another here from Katangar whom I think you know.'

Daintry had an inkling who this might be. 'Is it... Is it Meeka?' she asked hopefully.

'It is indeed Meeka,' replied Saltima. 'Now, let's have a look at that ankle of yours.'

Watched by Aleena, she gently removed the bandage from Daintry's foot. After scrutinising it carefully, she announced, 'You didn't break it. It was just a very bad sprain. But you need to try to avoid doing too much walking on it for a few days.'

Saltima fussed over Daintry for a few minutes, rebinding her ankle, and then suggested, 'You should try to get up now. It's a fine day; you can sit outside in the sun for a while.'

Saltima and Sharla helped Daintry to her feet and wrapped a blanket around her to cover the rough nightshirt she was wearing. She was still weak, but she felt much better. Slowly the two women led her outside into the sunshine and helped her sit on a bench against the cottage wall. Somebody called Saltima away, and with a grin and the assurance 'I'll come and see how you are later,' she hurried off.

From her position, Daintry was able to see what was going on around her. The cottage was the only permanent building, standing at the edge of a huge clearing in the forest. What intrigued her was the vast number of gaily painted covered wagons dotted around the site. There were quite a lot of people in the camp. A fire burned in the centre, tended by some of the women, who were clearly engaged in preparing food. There seemed to be more women present than men.

The brightly coloured dress of the women and the painted wagons gave Daintry a clue as to where she was. She realised that she must be in a settlement belonging to the Forest People. They were a community who inhabited the forest areas of Altaria, emerging from time to time to sell the goods they had made. She had seen them selling baskets in the marketplace in Toomer. Mogo had bought several.

As Daintry sat in the welcome sunshine observing the peaceful scene in front of her, a familiar figure approached.

'Meeka!'

Meeka smiled broadly. 'It's good to see you again, Daintry.' She sat down on the bench next to her friend.

Daintry was full of questions. She gazed at Meeka, who was now dressed in the same colourful clothes as the other women in the camp. 'But how did you escape, and how did you find the Forest People?' she asked excitedly.

Meeka grinned at her. 'They found me. When I escaped from Katangar, I followed the river until I came to the forest. The Forest People picked me up, and here I am.'

Daintry was silent for a few seconds, remembering her own ordeal. Meeka must have noticed her anxiety, because she asked, 'What about you?'

Daintry related her experience. 'I was selected by The Beast for his pleasure, but I managed to escape from him.' She paused for a second, recalling the horror of the encounter. 'I pushed him quite hard away from me and he fell backwards onto the stone floor. I don't know if I killed him.'

She stopped talking. Recalling the event brought tears to her eyes.

'And then?' Meeka gently urged.

'I managed to escape down the river in a boat and then I thought I had better go into the forest and look for help.' Daintry paused. A tear trickled down her face as she continued. 'Instead, I was picked up by two horrible characters. I shudder to think what plans they had for me, and then they were going to take me back to Katangar. They boasted about how much money they were going to get for me.'

She hurriedly wiped away another tear.

'But you were picked up by Karl and brought here,' Meeka interrupted.

Daintry nodded. 'Yes. I will be forever grateful.'

Meeka placed her hand on Daintry's. 'The Forest People know everything that happens in the forest. They were on the lookout for you.'

Aleena suddenly reappeared and sat down close by. She looked at Meeka and then at Daintry. 'We need to get you some clothing. We had to throw away the clothes you were wearing when you came,' she remarked with a little smile.

'I'll see to it.' Meeka had already jumped up. 'I'll be back shortly.' She hurried away.

Aleena moved closer to Daintry. 'Has a man spoken for you, Daintry?' she asked kindly.

The question brought instant misery to Daintry. 'I did have a betrothed,' she replied, 'but I fear he will never marry me now.'

'But why not?' Aleena asked, seemingly surprised.

'I have been to Katangar. I have been marked. I am a criminal,' Daintry whispered.

'What trade does your man follow?' Aleena asked softly.

Wondering why Aleena wanted to know, Daintry replied, 'He was assistant to Assem Rokar, The Keeper of the King's Purse, but then he was made a commander in the King's Guard. I have heard nothing from him for a long time. I do not know where he is now.'

'Conrad Accker...' Aleena's remark seemed to be both statement and question.

'Do you know him?' Daintry asked, surprised.

Aleena smiled. 'I know of him,' she replied.

Daintry was quiet, deep in thought. Talking about Conrad and her past hopes and aspirations made her sad. Conrad would never marry her now. No doubt Mela would redouble her efforts to woo him.

Aleena suddenly interrupted her pondering. Removing her scarf, she bared her shoulder and turned it towards Daintry. 'I was at Katangar,' she said simply.

Daintry was astonished at seeing the same mark she bore. 'You were at Katangar also?'

Aleena re-adjusted her clothing. She nodded. 'Yes. Both I and Sharla were there. We both know the horrors of that place.'

Daintry, surprised and intrigued, wanted to ask a lot more questions, but she was interrupted by the arrival of a horseman in the clearing. He was hot and dusty. Clearly he had ridden far and fast. He dismounted and made his way towards them. He was dressed in leather clothing that was old and tatty. Stopping in front of Aleena, the young man doffed his hat, revealing a mass of fair hair, and gave her the Altarian salute.

He bowed as he spoke. 'Greetings, Your Highness. I bring good news.'

Aleena smiled at him. 'Greetings, Tomaz. Tell us what has been happening.'

Tomaz responded eagerly. 'Your Highness, the rebels are prevailing; much of the north of the country is now in their hands. Their command has been split into two and the division marching south under Conrad Accker has been gaining ground rapidly. Everywhere they go they are winning support. They are now but two days' march from Taslar.'

'And the news from Taslar itself?' asked Aleena.

'King Henri and the High Council are adamant that Taslar is secure and that the rebels will soon be defeated.'

'And Assem Rokar?'

'My understanding is that he is confined to his house and under guard,' replied Tomaz.

That seemed to be the end of the report. Aleena addressed the young man again. 'You have done well, Tomaz. Now relax and refresh yourself, and go well on your journey back to Taslar.'

Tomaz bowed again and saluted, and with the words 'Your Highness', he turned and left.

Daintry was overwhelmed by what she had just witnessed. Even having news about Conrad had to take second place to her shock at what she had just worked out. Now she knew why Sharla appeared to treat Aleena as her superior. She knew why Tomaz had saluted. She looked at Aleena, who was watching her as she struggled to speak.

'But… But… You must be Princess Aleena,' she stammered.

Aleena smiled at her. 'Yes. I am Princess Aleena,' she replied.

Daintry was embarrassed that she had not realised earlier.

'But I did not comprehend – and I did not even address you properly,' she replied sadly.

Aleena reached out and took Daintry's hand. She spoke softly. 'Once I was Princess Aleena, living in a grand palace, surrounded by servants and wearing fine clothes, but here I am just plain Aleena, a barefoot Forest Woman.' She laughed and glanced down at her bare feet as she finished speaking.

'But you were at Katangar.' Daintry was still puzzled.

Aleena appeared slightly more subdued. She hesitated as she formulated a reply. When she finally spoke it was in a quiet voice.

'I was falsely accused of treason by my brother, King Henri. I was convicted and publicly humiliated. Then, with Sharla, I was incarcerated in Geeva castle. We were thrown into a ghastly dungeon and then one night four masked men entered our cell. They bound and blindfolded us and took us to Katangar.'

She paused and then added sadly, 'It was all arranged by Henri.'

Daintry had been listening intently. Aleena's explanation had answered a lot of her questions. It seemed that the princess's ordeal had been similar to her own, but one thing still intrigued her.

'But you managed to escape?' she asked.

The question brought Aleena's composure back. She quickly became more cheerful as she answered.

'Yes. One night we were helped by followers loyal to me. They brought us here to the Forest People and we have been hiding here ever since. There is a price on my head for my recapture.'

Daintry would have liked to continue the conversation, but at that moment Meeka reappeared, accompanied by a slightly older Forest Woman. Both carried articles of clothing.

Meeka grinned at Daintry. She nodded towards her companion. 'This is Mantee and we're going to dress you and turn you into a Forest Girl.'

Under the eyes of an approving Aleena, Daintry was ushered into the cottage by the two women. In less than five minutes they had transformed her. She now wore the wide colourful skirt of the Forest Women, and a white top. Mantee produced a bright shawl, which she draped around Daintry's shoulders. They attended to her hair so that it once again fell in ringlets onto her shoulders. Mantee rummaged in the bag she was wearing and produced some jewellery. She hung a necklace around Daintry's neck. Even Daintry's arms received some bangles. When they had finished Mantee stood back, looking at Daintry, and clapped her hands. 'Now you really look like a Forest Girl!' she exclaimed, laughing.

Daintry was paraded in front of a smiling Aleena and Sharla for approval and then returned to her bench outside the cottage. Meeka and Mantee disappeared to carry out other duties. Daintry had to admit that she now looked and felt like a Forest Girl. Her transformation was complete.

Chapter 23

Daintry sat quietly in the sunshine taking in her surroundings. She was already beginning to feel very comfortable in her bright new clothes and jewellery. A little later Meeka reappeared, grinned at her friend and gazed admiringly at her recent handiwork. She laughed. 'Not even your own family would recognise you now.'

The mention of her family immediately made Daintry sad. What had happened at her home since she had been so harshly removed from it? How were her father and Mogo now? And Mela? The thought of Mela once again brought the misery of her new status rudely home to her. Underneath her pretty clothes, she was still a convicted witch. Though she had heard some news about Conrad, it was little consolation, for if he returned to his position helping administer the King's Purse, it would be impossible for him to marry her, a branded criminal. Perhaps he would take as his bride one of the women from Taslar more suited to his status. Then there was always Mela's interest in him to think about.

Meeka quickly interrupted Daintry's melancholy. 'I'll show you where we sleep,' she announced. As Daintry obediently stood up, Meeka whispered to her, 'You've been sleeping in Aleena's bed.'

Daintry had already wondered that, but she made no reply. She walked slowly beside Meeka, her ankle still a bit painful. She was glad to discover that they did not have far to go.

Daintry's new home was with Meeka in one of the canvas-covered wagons. It contained little more than two low beds, but after the conditions Daintry had endured at Katangar it was heaven. Meeka threw herself down on one of the beds. 'I could stay here forever,' she announced, grinning at Daintry. Daintry promptly followed Meeka's example and lay down on the other bed. She had so many questions to ask, and Meeka seemed to have many of the answers.

They chatted for quite a while. By the time they finished, Daintry had a much clearer picture of everything. She learned that giving shelter and sanctuary to Princess Aleena and Sharla had made this community very vulnerable to reprisals by those opposing this action, and as a result the camp had to be guarded day and night. Lookouts were posted at four corners of the settlement, and scouts like Karl patrolled the surrounding forest. The scouts also brought news of what was happening beyond their own territory, because they often had contact with people who lived outside the forest. Altogether, with the addition of the fugitives from Katangar, the community now numbered about seventy, of whom by far the majority were women and children.

It was another two days before Daintry's ankle was healed enough for her to walk comfortably. During this time she rested a good deal, supervised by Saltima and cosseted by Meeka. She had frequent visitors, including Aleena. Although if it rained she remained in the wagon, she spent as much time as possible sitting outside in the sunshine. Incapacitated as she was, this gave her the opportunity to view the daily life of the people who had so kindly given her shelter.

Daintry quickly absorbed herself into the community of the Forest People, thanks to Meeka's support. Eventually she was fully able to take an active part. She joined Meeka in helping the other women in the day-to-day jobs needed for the smooth running of the community. She helped with the cooking and tended the fire, and when her ankle was strong enough she went with some of the other women to collect wood in the surrounding forest.

The fire was the focal point in the centre of the huge clearing. Here the cooking was done and food eaten. It was also the area where, in the evening, music was played and stories were told. Occasionally some of the women would dance, nimble on bare feet. As a child, Daintry had always been intrigued by seeing the barefoot Forest Women in the market at Toomer. She had even envied slightly the children they always had with them, perhaps because going barefoot was something she and Mela rarely had the opportunity to do. After her arrest, the condition had been forced upon her, and she had worn no shoes since, so it was no longer strange or new to her.

One day one of the women asked Daintry if she would like to learn how to make baskets. Daintry was an enthusiastic pupil and enjoyed sitting mastering the craft and listening to the women talking and occasionally singing at their work. After a while she became quite proficient, much to the approval of her teachers.

On another occasion, some of the women introduced Daintry and Meeka to the skill and joy of their dances. It was an uplifting experience for both girls to find their free expression in the movement of their bodies to the simple music.

Immersed in the everyday life of the Forest People, Daintry did not have so much contact with Aleena. Though Aleena stopped and chatted to her occasionally, Daintry quickly observed that both Aleena and Sharla tended to be a little remote from the rest of the group. Aleena was very much treated as the princess she was, although she was never addressed as such by the Forest People. Occasionally, she and Sharla helped with some of the tasks the camp women performed, and they ate with the others and joined the group around the fire in the evenings, but there was a noticeable deference in the attitude of the rest of the group to the occupants of the cottage.

Tomaz rode into the camp from time to time, and it was clear that Aleena looked forward to his visits and news of what was happening in Taslar. One day Daintry managed to talk to him and ask him about Conrad. Tomaz smiled. Perhaps he already knew why she was enquiring.

'Conrad Accker is a fine commander. Since the fighting force of the rebels was split into two commands, one under Conrad and the other under Elgar Rigor, their success has been unrelenting. They quickly eliminated the feeble opposition from the king's forces as they marched south towards Taslar. Conrad in particular is a courageous leader. Many are rushing to serve under him.'

Tomaz paused for a second. Then he grinned at Daintry. 'And many a maiden throws her bonnet at him.'

Daintry did not reply. It was not something she wanted to hear. Tomaz seemed to enjoy relating Conrad's romantic attraction for women. 'When he was in the palace at Taslar, many of the Court women showed an interest in him.' Tomaz laughed as he finished speaking.

Daintry changed the subject. 'Will the rebels capture Taslar?' she asked.

Tomaz nodded. 'Undoubtedly. It is only a matter of time before the city falls,' he replied.

'And what will happen then to the king?'

Tomaz shrugged his shoulders. He looked towards the cottage. 'There are those who say Princess Aleena should replace him.'

Then, perhaps because he felt uncomfortable discussing such serious matters with a young girl, Tomaz took his leave of her.

The news about Conrad saddened Daintry. While she was glad of his apparent success as a military commander, what Tomaz had related about Conrad's being wooed by other women increased her misery when she thought of what might have been.

How could Conrad, after glorying in such apparent admiration, ever consider marrying her? As a convicted witch, she would be despised and shunned by many. Perhaps even Mela would stand no chance of getting her claws into Conrad, seemingly surrounded as he was by many female admirers. Yet this thought gave Daintry little comfort.

Daintry's sadness must have reached the ears of Tazak, the white-haired leader of the ruling council, the group of elders who oversaw the affairs of the Forest People. His wisdom and insight were respected throughout the community. One day when Daintry was passing his wagon, he was sitting outside smoking his wooden pipe. He beckoned her over.

Daintry immediately obeyed. She liked Tazak and he always seemed to be friendly towards her.

He indicated to her to sit down, and took another puff of his pipe. He spoke kindly.

'You are sad, I think.'

Daintry nodded and gave a slight smile. 'Sometimes,' she replied.

Tazak concentrated on his pipe for a few seconds, as if he were mulling something over. 'I think you miss the man in your life.'

Daintry found it hard to form a reply. She had not realised how much Tazak knew about her background. Finally the words came out. 'He is far away and he will never marry me now.'

'But is he not in love with you?'

'We were to be married.'

'And why not now?'

Tazak's question almost brought tears to Daintry. The thought of what might have been was still painful. Her reply was emotional. 'Conrad could not marry me now, a convicted witch who carries the mark of Katangar on her body. Of late, he has found fame as a military commander, and many women admire him. It will be better for him to choose one of them, rather than me who would degrade him.'

After she finished speaking, Daintry became lost in her thoughts. Tazak puffed at his pipe again and was quiet, as if he too were thinking. Eventually he looked at Daintry and gave a little smile. 'The path of destiny can often cause us pain.'

Daintry knew there must be more. She waited for him to continue.

'Quite often what we perceive as an end becomes a new beginning,' Tazak observed quietly.

Daintry did not react. Tazak's words did not dispel her unhappiness.

Tazak appeared not to notice. 'There are many other young men besides Conrad Accker seeking a wife.'

This was not what Daintry wanted to hear. She remained silent.

Tazak gave a wave of his hand as if to encompass the rest of the camp. 'Here amongst the Forest People there are many eligible young men,' he suggested.

Daintry responded with a little smile. She was aware of the attentive looks she had been receiving from some of the unmarried men in the camp, but her heart lay elsewhere.

Tazak seemed to take her smile to indicate an interest in his proposition.

'Karl is a fine young man,' he observed.

Daintry was almost alarmed at the suggestion. At present she had no wish to throw her bonnet at another man. The suggestion that she take an interest in Karl was not a good idea. Though Karl had been her saviour, she knew that Saltima was very much attracted to him.

Her conversation with Tazak was interrupted by the return of two of the scouts who had been out and about in the forest. As they made their way towards Tazak's wagon, Daintry saw this as an opportunity to take her leave of the old man. The scouts would want to relate to him what they had learnt from their wanderings. With a smile and a 'thank you', she slipped away from what for her had been a very difficult conversation.

A few days later Daintry had an encounter that left her feeling extremely uneasy. One afternoon, while she was fetching some wood for the cooking fire, she found her way barred by Simon.

Simon was one of the younger men in the camp. He was not of the Forest People, but was a foundling rescued as a baby by Tazak, and he had been brought up by the community. Daintry had noticed him looking at her, but she had deliberately not offered any encouragement. Simon was not very highly regarded among the other women in the camp, as he tended to be arrogant and at times uncouth. As he stood there looking at her, Daintry felt very nervous. No one else seemed to be around.

Simon gave her an imitation of a friendly grin. 'You're a pretty one.' He continued to stare at her.

Daintry spoke as pleasantly as possible. 'Please let me pass. They are waiting for this firewood.'

She moved to walk past him, but Simon was too quick for her. He grabbed her arm. Daintry was becoming alarmed. Simon was known for his violent nature. He had a firm hold of her.

'What's the hurry?' he asked. 'The women have plenty of wood.'

Daintry tried to remain calm. 'But I need to get back,' she insisted.

Simon still held her arm. He grinned again. 'You need a man in your life,' he remarked unexpectedly.

Daintry was puzzled at his words. She did her best to smile as she replied. 'I have a man in my life.' She knew she had to break away from Simon. 'I must go now,' she insisted.

Simon held her fast. He shook his head. 'He is far away. I am here. I think you should be my woman.'

Daintry was even more alarmed. She had had no idea that Simon was desirous of her. She knew it was going to be difficult to dissuade him. She shook her head. 'That is not possible.'

Simon showed the first indication of determination with her. 'Why not?' he demanded. Before she could answer he almost cooed at her, 'I could teach you about love, better than your man now.'

Daintry shook her head again. She tried to break free. 'No. Please let me go.'

Simon's face began to cloud over and show his displeasure. He pulled her towards him. 'You think I'm not as good as your man,' he retorted angrily. 'Or perhaps I'm not as rich.'

Daintry did not know what to say. She struggled to extricate herself from his grip.

'Leave her alone.' Daintry had not seen three of the other firewood collectors creep up silently and unnoticed.

Simon looked at them for a full second, and then he angrily let go of Daintry and stood back from the path. 'You'll see,' he sneered as he turned to leave. He stomped off, cursing.

The three women did their best to console and calm Daintry, who was distressed and shaking.

Almost in a dream she picked up the firewood she had dropped during her encounter with Simon. She allowed the women to lead her gently back to the camp.

Despite Daintry's wish for silence, the incident became the gossip of the community. Later that day she saw Tazak lecturing Simon. It was abundantly clear that Simon resented being admonished. For the next few days he was sullen and angry. Several times Daintry found him staring at her from a distance. It made her feel uncomfortable.

Change came with Tomaz's next visit. He had his usual session with Aleena and then started his return journey. Later it was discovered that Simon had disappeared shortly afterwards and had taken one of the horses with him. Tazak despatched scouts to try and locate the fugitive, but they returned empty-handed. Worried, Tazak doubled the guard on the camp.

Chapter 24

The sound of shots being fired, followed by intense shouting, woke Daintry and Meeka. As they tried to comprehend what was happening, the canvas door of their wagon was pulled aside and a man's voice shouted, 'Outside! The camp is under attack!'

The two girls struggled into their clothes and emerged from the wagon to a scene of chaos. People were running here and there, the shouting was continuing and there was still an occasional gunshot. Daintry and Meeka stood petrified and bewildered, not knowing what to do. Karl came hurrying past, a still-smoking gun in his hands, and called to them to hide under the wagon. They immediately obeyed and crawled underneath the wooden floor. They could see most of the other women taking cover beneath their own wagons.

They were uncertain how long they lay there, trying to make sense of the commotion. It was still early morning and not completely daylight.

'Who is attacking us?' whispered Meeka.

The answer to her question appeared almost immediately. From their place of concealment they could see armed men in uniform emerging from the trees. The soldiers began to form a ring around the camp, spacing themselves equally apart.

'They are from the King's Guard,' Daintry whispered, recognising the bright uniform jackets.

As she finished speaking, a commanding voice rang out

somewhere in the area. 'You are completely surrounded and outnumbered. Surrender your weapons.'

Scarcely believing what they were witnessing, the two girls watched as the men of the camp emerged from the shadows and threw their guns into a pile. In response to another order, they formed two rows, their hands on their heads. Daintry could see Karl and Tazak among them. Suddenly a soldier banged on the wheels of the wagon where she and Meeka were cowering. 'Get out, and line up,' he ordered.

Silently they obeyed, joining the other women and children of the community, who were being assembled none too politely into a line by a young soldier. Some of the women were in tears or shouting abuse at the invaders. Several children were crying.

An officer, clearly in charge of events, was standing in front of the group of men. A soldier approached him. 'Captain, the camp is secure,' he announced. 'All the occupants we can find are here.'

The officer nodded. 'Good. Post sentries. We cannot take any chances; there may be a few still lurking about intent on no good.'

The soldier saluted, turned, and barked out some orders.

The captain turned to face the group of male prisoners. 'Who is in charge here?' he asked.

Tazak stepped forward from the front row. 'I am. I demand to know the meaning of this attack. We are a peace-loving community and we have done no harm to anybody.'

'You have also harboured escaped criminals and others convicted of treason,' the captain retorted. Abruptly he demanded, 'Where is Princess Aleena?'

'I am Princess Aleena,' answered a clear voice.

Accompanied by Sharla, Princess Aleena approached the assembly. She walked proudly, upright and commanding.

The captain turned to face her. He bowed slightly but did not salute. He addressed her. 'I am instructed to transport you to Geeva castle.'

'On whose orders?' Princess Aleena asked quietly.

'On the personal orders of King Henri. Do you wish to see my authorisation?' The captain patted his pocket.

'That will not be necessary,' Princess Aleena replied, rather coldly.

The captain turned to the prisoners again. 'Where are the escaped prisoners from Katangar? Show yourselves. I have no time to waste,' he demanded curtly.

Daintry stepped forward. Meeka followed her. Any other course of action seemed useless.

The captain glanced at them briefly. Then he barked, 'And the witch Saltima. You are also on the list.'

Saltima emerged from the rear group of women and joined Daintry and Meeka.

The captain faced the assembled Forest People. He spoke abruptly, partly to them and also by way of instruction to several of his men, who stood close by awaiting his command. 'We will leave immediately. Six men and six women will accompany us to Geeva castle as hostages. The escaped prisoners will be returned to Katangar.'

Tazak reacted angrily. 'You cannot do this. These men and women have done nothing.'

'Do not tell me, old man, what I can do and not do!' bellowed the captain. 'You are under arrest.'

'On what charge?' demanded Tazak.

'Concealing fugitives from the law is a capital offence. You will hang for it.' As he finished speaking, the captain turned to one of his officers. 'Ensure this man comes with us. Hurry. We leave immediately.'

Chaos prevailed among the group as the soldiers chose their hostages. The air was shattered by the screams and wailing of the women and shouts and protests from the men. At last calm prevailed as those selected resigned themselves to their fate.

Daintry, Meeka and Saltima had been standing miserably watching the proceedings. When she heard the captain announce that they would be returned to Katangar, a feeling of hopelessness and despair had overtaken Daintry. While she had been in the company of the Forest People, Katangar had seemed far away, in another world. Now she was to be sent back to a life of toil and misery. She had observed the fate of recaptured prisoners and knew that similar treatment awaited her. In her case there was also the question of The Beast. If she had killed him, they would hang her. If he was alive, she could not even begin to imagine the punishment he would inflict on her.

A sudden disturbance at the edge of the camp jerked Daintry out of her misery. Two soldiers were leading Simon towards the captain. The young man looked extremely uncomfortable to be there. 'Let me alone! I'm not a prisoner!' he shouted.

There was muttering among the assembled crowd as he was brought before the captain.

'I've done my job. I want my money.' Simon looked anxiously around as he spoke.

The captain did not respond immediately to him. Instead he addressed Tazak. 'One of yours, I believe.'

'That is so,' Tazak retorted, looking puzzled.

The captain smiled. 'And a traitor into the bargain, it would seem. You should choose your co-conspirators more carefully. Without his help we would not have found this den of opposition to the king's cause.'

At the captain's words there were shouts of 'traitor' and 'scoundrel' from the assembled crowd. Tazak said nothing, but there were tears in his eyes.

'Pay me. I've done my job. I want my money,' Simon growled.

The captain addressed his second-in-command again. 'Pay this man and send him on his way.' He added, almost to himself, 'I have little regard for those who turn against those they serve, even if it is the wrong side to uphold.'

The soldier disappeared for a few minutes. He returned with a sombre-faced individual dressed in a smart suit of clothes with a pouch at his belt. At a nod from the captain the man reached into the pouch, took out some coins and carefully counted them out into Simon's hand. 'Fifty gold pieces, as agreed,' he said.

As soon as the transaction was completed, Simon looked around furtively and then scuttled away, amid abuse hurled at him by the onlookers. As he disappeared from view, he shouted over his shoulder, 'You are all wrong! You will all die! The King's Guard will be victorious!'

The captain had remained impassive throughout. As soon as Simon had disappeared he issued the order to leave. 'We must depart immediately if we are to be clear of the forest by nightfall. Secure the prisoners and get the rest ready to march.'

The captain's men sprang into action. Those members of the community who were to accompany them as hostages were pushed protesting into two columns, while Princess Aleena and Sharla, Daintry, Meeka and Saltima watched. Daintry began to wonder what was planned for her and her companions. She was soon to find out. Suddenly a covered wagon, similar to the one she and Meeka slept in, emerged from the forest and drew to a halt close by. From its interior emerged a burly, red-faced man. What he carried struck fear into Daintry. Chains. They were to be shackled just like the recaptured prisoner she had seen at Katangar.

The man approached Princess Aleena. 'I fear I have to confine you, Your Highness.'

Princess Aleena made no reply. She calmly stretched out both her hands. The man did not waste time: methodically, he placed the cuffs around her slim wrists and hammered them into place. Sharla received the same treatment, and then the man came to Daintry. 'Now, pretty one, it's your turn.'

Daintry had been expecting to have her ankles shackled, as she had seen at Katangar, but the man ignored her worried glance down at her feet and merely grabbed her arm. Daintry soon had a metal cuff around each wrist, her hands linked by a short length of chain. The bonds were heavy and restricted her hand movements, but she was thankful that her ankles were unfettered. The man worked swiftly, and soon Meeka and Saltima were also confined.

Orders were shouted out and the group quickly assembled to leave the clearing. It was quite clear that the captain and his men did not want to stay in the forest one minute longer than they had to.

The covered wagon the troops had brought with them was quickly drawn up. The captain approached Princess Aleena, who was still standing with Sharma and the other prisoners. With a brief bow, he addressed her. 'Captain Parlak at your service, Your Highness. May I request that you join your carriage?' Without replying, Princess Aleena and Sharma climbed with some difficulty into the wagon.

Daintry vainly hoped that she, Meeka and Saltima might also be offered the dubious comfort of the wagon, but it was not to be. They found themselves pushed into position behind it, followed by the rest of the prisoners, who walked in their two columns. The soldiers, most of them on horseback, travelled alongside and at the rear of the procession.

With Captain Parlak at its head, the cavalcade moved off. It made slow progress, because it was limited to the pace of the walking prisoners, and at times the wagon had difficulty in finding a path through the dense forest.

Several hours later, the captain called a halt. The prisoners were glad of a rest. Of all of them, Daintry and Meeka perhaps fared the best, partly because they were accustomed to walking long distances, having endured a similar experience before, but they, too, were relieved to have a break. A pitcher of water was passed down the line, but there was barely a mouthful for each person. After a short time, the procession set off again.

Most of the prisoners walked in silence, lost in thought. Towards evening it became clear that even though the edge of the forest was close, the group would not be out of the trees before darkness fell. Captain Parlak gave the order to pitch camp. Sentries would be posted and fires kept burning all night. The decision did not please the soldiers, who were fearful of being in the forest.

'Why have we got to stop here?' one asked irritably.

'Another hour, and we would have been clear of this dismal place,' grumbled another.

Under the watchful eye of the guards, Daintry sank down gratefully, her back against a tree. Meeka followed her example. Saltima began examining the foliage close by.

'What will happen to us when we are taken back to Katangar?' whispered Meeka.

Meeka's question brought back the turmoil of Daintry's own plight. She knew well enough what would befall them. Meeka had not witnessed the scene with the recaptured prisoner.

'They will beat us,' she replied simply.

In a way Daintry envied Meeka. Meeka would be treated as just an escaped prisoner who had been brought back to the mines. Daintry knew that she was in a different position. Her encounter with The Beast had established her fate. She knew that they would most likely hang her. She hoped they would do it quickly and not beat her beforehand.

Saltima sat down with her two companions. 'I have been looking for the leaves of the darga plant,' she explained, 'but I could not find any here.'

'Why do you want them?' asked Meeka.

'Eat them, and they produce a sleep and then death,' Saltima announced calmly. She suddenly added, 'I am not going to be convicted as a witch and then burnt or hanged.'

'Find some for me as well,' replied Meeka.

Daintry remained silent. She was surprised at her friend's request. She had already made her mind up. She would not take her own life. She would face whatever was in store for her. She just hoped that she would have the strength to endure whatever lay ahead.

Chapter 25

The High Council of Altaria had dwindled drastically in number. As King Henri sat leaning on the table, he faced but three of its former members: Andor Durek, his close ally; Kurt Lassen, the new head of the King's Guard; and the youthful Erik Vasin, who had taken over the duties of Assem Rokar, now under house arrest.

King Henri was not pleased. 'Where are the rest of the members?' His question was directed at Andor Durek.

Andor knew well enough why the number of members had decreased. Most, fearing the outcome of the current situation in the country, had discreetly disappeared from view, intent on their own survival. Andor had a ready answer.

'Your Majesty, they have proved to be lacking in support for our cause. Their object now is to save their miserable skins.'

'If they are caught, have them tried for treason and executed,' the king retorted angrily.

Andor was quick to acquiesce. 'That will of course be done,' he replied.

The king turned to Kurt Lassen. 'Kurt, it has come to my attention that the town of Raker has fallen to the rebels. You failed to inform me. Why?'

'What you have heard is true, Your Majesty. But its fall was partly the fault of one of our commanders in the area.'

'What do you mean? I know nothing of this. Explain yourself.' The king's displeasure was evident.

Kurt had been dreading this meeting with the king. He and Andor had discussed the incident and how best to deal with the king's anger. The best solution, they had decided, would be to blame somebody else. Kurt had come up with a suitable answer.

'Your Majesty, unfortunately one of our commanders failed to recognise a prisoner he had captured as Elgar Rigor, the leader of the rebels in the area. He let the dog go free, which allowed a surprise attack on our forces to take place. Raker was already a stronghold of the rebels.'

The king's face clouded over in anger. He banged his fist on the table. 'You are employing incompetent commanders in the King's Guard. Who is this man?'

'He is one of the officers recruited from the palace staff, Your Majesty. His name is Conrad Accker.'

'Accker?' The king thought for a second. 'Is that not the young man who was assistant to Assem?'

Kurt nodded. 'Indeed it is, Your Majesty.'

'Where is he now?'

Kurt took a deep breath before answering. 'He was captured by the rebels and has joined them. He is now one of their commanders.'

'What? Are you completely incompetent? Your commanders are defeated at Raker, and one of them joins the rebels? You have been hiding things from me. That amounts to treason.'

Kurt squirmed under the onslaught of the king's wrath. Andor Durek came to his aid. 'Your Majesty, all is not as it seems. It is true that Raker was lost, but we can use the rebels' belief in their might to our advantage.'

'Explain,' snapped the king.

Kurt was more confident with the support of Andor. He had his answer ready. 'The loss of Raker is of little importance in military terms. The rebels are now marching south in two groups, one headed by the rebel leader Elgar Rigor, and the other by the traitor Conrad Accker. Their plan is to join together and then march on Taslar, but they have overstretched themselves, and their over-confidence is their weakness.'

'How do you know all this?' the king asked irritably.

Kurt smiled. 'We have reliable spies among their ranks.'

'And what do you propose to do? Sit and wait for them to attack the city?'

'I can assure you, Your Majesty, that the entire rebel force will be destroyed before it gets anywhere near Taslar.'

'What if you fail to stop them? I hope you have a plan for when they are knocking on the doors,' sneered the king.

'They will never enter Taslar, Your Majesty. The city is impregnable.'

'You try to tell me that you can eliminate the rebel forces and safeguard any threat to Taslar, yet the forces under your command, in spite of being strengthened by the increase in fighting men you requested, has so far failed to defeat this rabble.'

'It has been a difficult task so far, Your Majesty,' replied Kurt, 'but I have no doubt that with our new plans we can put an end to this rebellion within weeks.'

'And how do you intend to do that?' The king was clearly sceptical.

Kurt hesitated. He knew he was about to propose a debatable solution. He strived to sound confident. 'The rebels' belief in their ability to win will be their undoing,' he announced.

'How?'

'They are moving south with the intention of grouping in the Doocan Valley and eventually marching on and attacking Taslar as one force. We will lure them into a confrontation in the Doocan Valley. Our forces will be waiting for them.'

'What is their strength?'

'The last number we have is a thousand foot soldiers and a few mounted commanders.'

'And our numbers?'

'We have slightly over five hundred men.'

The king was aghast. 'What? We are outnumbered two to one!'

Kurt remained unperturbed. 'That is true. But our troops are well trained and the rebels have no such training. Also, we have a secret weapon.'

The king was intrigued now. He softened slightly. 'Tell me more.'

Kurt delivered his explanation. 'We have purchased three cannons and ammunition from Forancer.'

The king was silent for a few seconds, deep in thought. At last he spoke. 'I see. That's a clever move, Kurt. Most likely at the first shot the rebels will scatter like frightened rabbits.'

Kurt beamed. He had not expected his plan to have instant approval from the king. 'That's what I think, Your Majesty.'

Next the king turned to Erik Vasin, the new Keeper of the King's Purse, who had been sitting in silence listening to the conversation. 'What is the state of the Purse, Erik?'

A flustered Erik rose to the occasion. 'The situation is improving, Your Majesty. Money is now coming in from the sale of ore from the mines at Katangar, and soon we will have the income from this year's grain crop.'

The king nodded. 'Excellent,' he replied. He turned to Andor. 'So our strategy to clear the prisons and send the convicts to Katangar has worked.'

'Indeed it has. Every few weeks a fresh batch of prisoners is sent there. Men and women.'

The king again nodded his approval. 'Make sure this continues. Those who commit crimes can expect such an outcome.'

Andor was pleased. In spite of the original order to transport only prisoners sentenced to death to Katangar, he had also, without the king's knowledge, been sending prisoners convicted of minor crimes to the mines to boost the numbers and increase the income received from the ore extracted. He knew that his next proposal required royal assent. He cleared his throat. 'Your

Majesty…' he began. The king looked at him enquiringly. Encouraged, Andor continued. 'Your Majesty…' he began again. He hesitated, and then resumed. 'I propose that the women prisoners also be made to work underground at Katangar.'

The king shrugged his shoulders. 'If you consider it necessary, Andor, I will sign the order.'

Andor could not believe that everything had gone so easily. Now he had to deliver his prime bit of news to the king.

'Your Majesty, Princess Aleena has been recaptured.'

'What?' The king was beaming now. 'How?' he asked.

'She was found hiding among the Forest People.'

'That is excellent news,' enthused the king. 'Have her brought here and shown to people as the traitress she is.'

'That will be done, Your Majesty.'

The king suddenly thought of something else. He turned to Kurt Lassen. 'Kurt, try to ensure that the traitor Conrad Accker is captured alive. He must be made an example of and pay for his treacherous crimes against the state by public execution.'

Kurt readily agreed. 'I will issue instructions to our chief commander, Miklo Janack, that this is to be done, Your Majesty.'

The meeting rambled on for a short while and then it was evident that as far as the king was concerned there was nothing more to discuss. The three other men were relieved to be finally dismissed.

A short time later Andor and Kurt met up again.

'Are you sure your plan is going to work?' asked Andor.

'Absolutely,' replied Kurt. He added confidently, 'At the first cannon shot the rebels will turn and run.'

Andor was not so sure. 'Well, you convinced the king. Let's hope you are correct.' He smiled briefly. 'If not, you and I will be hanging from a rope, like that traitor Conrad Accker when he is caught.'

Chapter 26

Conrad Accker rode at the head of his men. The march south was almost completed and they were within ten miles of the Doocan Valley. Soon they would meet up with the band of rebels led by Elgar Rigor and there would be a united assault on Taslar. Conrad's comrades were jubilant with the success they had had so far and were confident that their mission to defeat the king and his henchmen would soon be complete.

Conrad had mixed feelings. When he had first agreed to join the ranks of the rebel movement, encouraged by Elgar, it had been a decision made in misery. In his mind the defeat of the King's Guard at Raker had been aided by his weakness as an officer. Had he arrested Elgar and his woman when the opportunity had been there, the outcome could have been different. He knew that Miklo held him in contempt, and doubtless he would have eventually received a severe reprimand for his error of judgement.

When he had been taken prisoner, he had been full of self-reproach. He desperately wished he had been killed in the fighting. When Elgar had asked him to change sides and join the rebel movement, it had stirred something else in him. He suddenly knew that his heart belonged to the rebel movement and not to the corrupt king and his followers. The feeling had been lying dormant all the time he had served in the King's Guard, and suddenly it had burst upon him. It occurred to him that it was better to die fighting for a just cause than for one with false and unjust values.

Conrad's rise to command under the watchful eye of Elgar had been rapid. In the few skirmishes the rebel movement had encountered during their march south, Conrad had shown himself to be completely fearless. Driven on by his self-criticism concerning past events, he was always in the thick of the fighting, secretly hoping that he would not survive. At the same time, his leadership qualities had blossomed. When the decision had been taken to split the force in two, he had been the obvious choice to take one of the commands.

Now it seemed the rebels' mission was drawing to a close, and this too was causing Conrad some concern, for it was clear that once the battle had been won there would be nobody to replace the king and rule the country wisely. In the rapid explosion of the rebel movement, it seemed that this had never been considered.

Conrad rarely thought about his own future. It seemed too distant and obscure. He had heard that Assem Rokar had been arrested, and it seemed doubtful that the old man would ever return to his former duties. Conrad's fate had been sealed the instant he had joined the rebel movement. He was now a traitor with a price on his head. If the rebels failed in their mission and he was captured, the outcome would be clear: he would be executed. If the rebels prevailed, his future was still uncertain. It seemed unlikely that he would be able to return to his former palace duties. He held no hope now of being able to offer marriage to Daintry and carry her as his bride to Taslar. There had been no contact between them since he had been enlisted in the King's Guard. He had often thought of her and their future together, but of late it had become a bitter thought of what might have been.

Two days later, Conrad and his men reached their destination, where they joined up with Elgar Rigor's men. When the two commanders met, Elgar was in a jubilant mood. He threw his arms round Conrad, grinning broadly. 'Greetings, my friend!' he exclaimed. 'It is good to welcome you here.'

'I am pleased we have made it here without too much resistance,' Conrad replied.

Elgar slapped him on the back. 'Your exploits as a commander are well known and respected. You have become a much talked-about figure. The women of Taslar will be throwing their bonnets at you.' He laughed as he finished speaking.

Conrad did not reply. He knew that he had become popular among his men, and on a few occasions his party had been cheered by the people as they marched through a village. But he shied away from being some sort of hero. What he had done had been an act of necessity and an attempt to regain his own self-respect, not a question of seeking glory and fame.

Elgar assumed Conrad's silence to be down to fatigue. He voiced his thoughts. 'Come, my friend. You have been on the march for a few days. See to your own and your men's comfort, and then join me for a glass of wine and a morsel to eat.'

Conrad welcomed the suggestion. The past days had not been easy, and now he was glad to be no longer on the alert, ready for any eventuality. However, by the time he had organised his men and cleaned up his appearance, over an hour had elapsed. As he entered Elgar's tent, he was surprised to see a second person there. A tall, slim figure, dressed entirely in black, rose from a stool to greet him. Steel-grey eyes regarded him.

Elgar rushed to introduce Conrad to the stranger. 'Commander Rojak, this is our second group leader, Conrad Accker.'

The stranger smiled. 'Conrad Accker, your reputation has preceded you. It is a pleasure to greet you. You have done well in securing the north of Altaria to our cause.' As he finished speaking he waved Conrad to a seat.

'I am glad to be here,' Conrad replied politely, taking the goblet of wine Elgar offered.

Conrad was surprised to see the instigator and acknowledged leader of the rebel movement. For all his popularity, Vasil Rojak remained a mysterious figure. He had never taken part in any of the fighting, but instead had directed strategy from a secret location, for he was Altaria's most wanted man. Few people seemed to know his background. Some claimed that he was a scholar; others, that he had held high office in Taslar under the previous king. To Conrad, his appearance here, away from hiding, indicated the confidence gained from the current strength of the rebel movement.

Vasil Rojak raised his glass. 'Gentlemen, I propose a toast. To our success in the final battle.'

'And to an end to a corrupt administration,' added Elgar.

Elgar and Conrad waited for their commander-in-chief to continue the conversation. It was clear to both of them that he considered it vitally important to emerge from obscurity to brief them personally.

Looking at his two commanders, Vasil smiled briefly. 'So, my friends, are we ready for the final onslaught?'

'We have worked and fought for this moment. We are ready,' Elgar replied. He continued. 'Is the plan still the same? To group here in the Doocan Valley and let the enemy come to us?'

Vasil nodded. 'Yes. But there are now some complications.' He paused briefly, looked from one to the other and then announced, 'I have it on good authority that the King's Guard have acquired three cannons.'

Conrad and Elgar were shocked at this news.

'How did they get them?' asked Conrad. 'There are no foundries in Altaria capable of producing them.'

'That puts us in a very different situation.' Elgar was clearly most concerned.

Vasil remained calm and took another sip of wine.

'The High Council purchased the cannons from Forancer and were supplied with three gunners as part of the deal,' he replied calmly.

'Does that mean that Forancer are supporting the king and his corrupt government?' Conrad asked.

Vasil shook his head. 'On the contrary, they support our cause entirely.'

The two commanders looked at their leader, seeking an explanation.

Vasil gave a grin of assurance before he replied. 'The powder supplied with the cannons has been tampered with. It will not fire the shot. The gunners have been chosen well and are aware of this.'

Exclamations of relief came from Elgar and Conrad. Landlocked as it was in central Europe, Altaria had always enjoyed good and amicable relations with its neighbour Forancer. It had seemed unbelievable that Forancer would meddle in Altaria's affairs.

Vasil produced a map of Altaria and spread it on the table.

'Now, gentlemen, let us review the current situation.' He indicated a section of the map. 'That's ours. Thanks to both your efforts, there is no longer any opposition in the north of the country. It now remains to eliminate the last of the King's Guard and then march on Taslar.'

'What resistance is there in the south of the country?' Conrad asked.

Vasil shook his head. 'Practically no support for the king. The farming communities of the south are fed up with the high taxes imposed on them.'

'And what about the central area, here?' Elgar pointed a finger on the map, drawing attention to the band of forest that almost divided the north and south of Altaria.

Vasil had a ready answer. 'The Forest People support us, as do the few hunters who live there.'

It was Elgar who asked the next question. 'What is your strategy for the revised battle plan?'

Vasil turned his attention to the map again. 'You, Elgar, with your men, will stand firm here in the Doocan Valley and resist the enemy head on.' He turned to Conrad. 'Conrad, your job is to circle round and attack the enemy from the rear. They will thus be trapped between two forces.'

Vasil grinned at Conrad. 'You have the difficult job, Conrad, but also the glory that goes with it.'

Conrad simply smiled in response. It was true. He would have the most difficult and dangerous job to do. Making his way unseen through territory patrolled by the King's Guard was going to be difficult in itself. Then to attack the rear of the enemy would place his force in a precarious position. He would either succeed in the mission or be wiped out with most of his men. Somehow, he no longer cared which it was.

Chapter 27

The party in the forest had spent a restless night. Daintry, Meeka and Saltima huddled together close to one of the fires that burned continuously. During the evening Princess Aleena had asked one of the guards if the three girls could join her and Sharla in the covered wagon, but he had harshly refused her request.

As the first glimpse of daylight started to appear, the camp broke into activity. There was barely enough water to go round, and it was quite clear that the party was short of food. Some of the soldiers grumbled that they had to share what was available with the prisoners. Princess Aleena gave her ration to another woman, pointing out with a smile that she was riding in a carriage whilst the other prisoners were walking.

The soldiers were anxious to leave the forest, and very soon the party set off again. As the sun rose higher in the sky, walking became more and more uncomfortable. There were frequent complaints from the mounted soldiers that the pace was kept so slow by the prisoners on foot. Some of the women collapsed from exertion and lack of sustenance. Whenever this happened, the hapless prisoner would be roughly hauled up by one of the soldiers onto his horse, where she would be forced to occupy an uncomfortable position lying in front of him and viewing the ground as it passed beneath her.

At around midday the party stopped at a crossroads close to some trees, which provided some welcome shade. Again there was little food, but one of the soldiers found a spring, which provided some badly needed and refreshing water.

It seemed as if the group were spending longer than usual having a break. Daintry heard one of the soldiers close to her grumbling that they were wasting too much time there. It was clear that Captain Parlak was expecting somebody or something,

'What do you think we're waiting for?' Meeka whispered to Daintry. Daintry did not have time to answer: at that moment a column of people appeared on the road, coming towards them.

When Daintry saw the new arrivals, her heart sank. It was a party of convicts. At the head of the column rode a King's Guard lieutenant. Behind him walked five men and three women, their faces clouded with fatigue and despair. Several guards accompanied them.

Captain Parlak held up his hand to the officer to halt the column. 'Where are you bound, lieutenant?' he asked.

The officer reined in his horse. 'Katangar,' he replied.

Captain Parlak nodded in the direction of Daintry and Meeka. 'I have two escaped prisoners from there. They will have to join your party,' he announced.

The lieutenant appeared none too pleased. 'We've scarcely enough food as it is,' he complained.

'Nevertheless, you will have to add these two to your consignment.'

The lieutenant shouted an order to one of his men. Two of them hauled Daintry and Meeka roughly to their feet. They were pushed towards the second party and shoved to the back of the column. Princess Aleena and Saltima, both in tears, wanted to say goodbye to them, but were prevented from doing so by the soldiers.

It was at this point that Daintry recognised one of the guards from Katangar.

'Well, who have we got here?' he sneered. He grinned at her. 'I wouldn't be in your shoes when you get back to Katangar. Karrick has plans for you.'

His words struck fear into Daintry. She realised that he was talking about The Beast. So she hadn't killed him that night. She knew he would take a terrible revenge on her.

The Katangar group lost little time in continuing their journey. At a gruff command from the lieutenant, the prisoners started walking again, watched miserably by Daintry and Meeka's former fellow captives. Saltima was being comforted by Princess Aleena. She had been unable to find any of the daga plant she had been seeking, and now she seemed to be resigned to her fate.

The column made slow progress in the hot afternoon sun. There was little talk among either the prisoners or the guards minding them. Daintry and Meeka walked side by side behind their new companions. In just a little over twenty-four hours their world had yet again been turned upside down. Now history was repeating itself as they were being transported once more to the hell of Katangar. Their hands had been released from the wretched manacles, but that seemed to be of little significance as they plodded steadily on.

It was well into the evening when the party halted close to a village. The male prisoners were marched off somewhere and the women were locked in a barn with a guard at the door. They sank down onto the straw, tired, footsore and hungry. A little later, their hunger was appeased when two older women from the village arrived carrying rather stale bread with some sort of fat on it, together with a pitcher of water, which they distributed under the watchful eyes of two of the guards.

Once the prisoners had eaten, there was some conversation among them. Aware that Daintry and Meeka had experience of Katangar, the other women were anxious to know what awaited them there. It was Meeka who gave most of the answers. Daintry knew that she would have a different fate.

At first light the following day, the prisoners were roused and given some bread and water, and then the whole party set off again. After their night of rest, despite the long journey ahead of them and fear of what might await them at their destination, their spirits were a little higher, and they occasionally talked to each other. The guards, too, appeared to be more relaxed.

It was mid-morning when the lieutenant called a halt. The prisoners were pushed to the side of the road. The necessity for this action was soon apparent. A large contingent of soldiers from the King's Guard appeared.

'Off to the big battle for Taslar,' one of the guards close to Daintry muttered.

As the column drew near, the officer at its head held up his hand and shouted an order. The soldiers halted. The officer dismounted and walked towards the lieutenant in charge of the Katangar group. They chatted for several minutes. Then they walked towards the prisoners, who were standing in a line at the edge of the road. As they drew closer, Daintry received a shock. The officer was none other than her childhood playmate Miklo Janack. She had not seen him for several years, but she recognised him immediately. Suddenly hope rose within her. Surely her old friend would help her.

Miklo glanced casually at the prisoners, as if indifferent to their existence. Suddenly his eyes lighted on Daintry. Some sort of recognition must have dawned, because he walked across to her. He scrutinised her for a second, but it was Daintry who spoke. One word broke from her lips. 'Miklo.'

A hint of a smile swept across Miklo's face, but it was not one of friendship. 'Daintry Brouka,' he sneered.

Visions of salvation rose within Daintry. 'Miklo, please help me,' she begged, almost in a whisper.

Miklo smirked at her. 'It appears to me that you are a prisoner bound for Katangar,' he replied casually.

'It's all a mistake. I can explain everything,' Daintry pleaded.

'Even the peasant clothing you are wearing?' Miklo looked her up and down, taking in her Forest Woman's garb, now tatty and dirty from the last few days of travel. His eyes rested a second on her bare feet, and then he grinned at her. 'It suits you.'

'Miklo, please help me, for old times' sake. Remember when we played together. I am innocent. I swear it.' Daintry hoped upon hope that he would help her.

Miklo stared at her coldly. 'That was a long time ago. War changes everything, including friendships.'

'But we were all friends. You, me, Mela and Conrad.'

He sneered again. 'Conrad is a traitor to his king and the cause he once swore to serve. He carries a price on his head and will hang from a rope when he's captured.'

Daintry was aghast. 'What do you mean?'

Miklo stared at her for a few seconds. Daintry feared that he might not answer, but suddenly he spoke again. 'The man you threw your bonnet at was a rising officer in the King's Guard. He abandoned all that to join the rebels. When he is caught, he will be tried for treason and executed.'

'It can't be true,' Daintry gasped.

Miklo laughed. 'I can assure you that it is true – and you can be the key to his capture.'

'What do you mean?' Daintry asked, puzzled at the remark.

Miklo moved closer to her. 'You will be held as a hostage. If Conrad's love for you is as strong as he claims it is, he will sacrifice his life for yours.'

Daintry shook her head. 'I would not wish him to do that.'

'Then you will die in his place,' Miklo retorted coldly.

It was too much for Daintry. She grabbed the lapels of Miklo's uniform. 'Miklo,' she cried out, 'you have become cruel and hateful!' She was now in tears.

Her outburst was of short duration. Two of the soldiers seized her and threw her heavily to the ground, where she lay sobbing.

Daintry heard Miklo giving orders. The next instant she was hauled to her feet. She found herself standing between two guardsmen, in front of Miklo.

Miklo addressed the two men. 'Geeva castle is not far away. Take this woman there. Tell the officer there to guard her well. If she dies or escapes, he will be executed. The same goes for you two. If the prisoner is molested in any way while she is in your care, I will have you both flogged until you drop. When you have delivered her, make your way back to this unit.'

The next few minutes were a sea of misery for Daintry. She found it hard to comprehend what was happening to her. She saw Meeka looking at her despairingly with tears in her eyes. One of her guards hurried off, grumbling, to obtain provisions for their journey. The other man followed, pushing Daintry in front of him. Suddenly he pulled her arms behind her back and tied her hands. 'You'll not escape while I'm in charge of you,' he growled.

Within minutes Daintry was forced to march between the two guardsmen. As they passed the rest of the prisoners, she could see Meeka sobbing. Tears were streaming down her own face. Everything had happened so suddenly, and to be forcibly dragged away from Meeka, with whom she had experienced and shared so much, was almost too much to bear. The sudden shock of the separation affected her badly. She no longer cared what happened to her. She knew well enough that if she had been returned to Katangar The Beast would have whipped her until she became senseless and that it was unlikely that she would have recovered from his punishment. Now she was still a prisoner, but with a different fate ahead of her. She had little doubt that eventually she would face execution, whatever happened.

Daintry's two guards hurried along at such a speed that their former colleagues and Daintry's fellow prisoners were soon lost to view. The pace was too much for Daintry.

'Please,' she gasped. 'I cannot walk so fast.' Reluctantly her two keepers slowed down, much to her relief. It was difficult walking with bound hands, but she knew she would receive no sympathy.

It was clear that the two men would rather be somewhere different. They complained almost continuously about their lot.

'Why did we have to fall for this trek?' one of them grumbled.

'Agreed,' replied the other. 'We could have been in Taslar tonight, sampling its wares.'

At around midday the two guardsmen decided to stop for a rest and a bite to eat. They chose a clump of trees close to the road.

Daintry was thankful for the break from walking and the respite from the hot sun. She sank down beneath a tree. She pleaded with her captors.

'Please untie me.'

One of the men looked at her for a second, as if undecided what action to take. Then he released her hands. The freedom was short-lived. The next instant he had looped the rope around one of her wrists and pulled it behind the tree. He wrapped the free end of the rope several times around the trunk, fastening Daintry securely. He stood back and looked her up and down. 'That'll stop you from wandering off,' he remarked. With that he wandered off to his companion, who was already relaxing in the shade.

Daintry enjoyed the brief reprieve. True, she was bound to the tree and one hand was out of action and uncomfortable, but at least she was able to sit down and rest.

She watched the two men as they consumed some food. She had not eaten very much that day, and now she felt the pangs of hunger. Eventually one of the men came over to her and deposited some stale bread and dried meat beside her. He held a canteen of water to her dry and cracked lips and allowed her to drink from it.

She managed to whisper, 'Thank you.'

The man grunted. 'I don't want you to die on me before I can get you to Geeva castle.'

'When will we be there?' Daintry asked wearily.

'Tonight, hopefully. Then I can get rid of the responsibility of you.'

All afternoon the small party trudged slowly along. Daintry was almost exhausted by the time they entered a small forest area. Perhaps because the end of the journey was drawing closer, the two men were less harsh towards her. They even heeded her when she complained that her hands were tied too tightly, and immediately loosened the rope a little.

They had been walking only a short time in the forest when the trees thinned and they came to a large clearing. Geeva castle stood before them.

Daintry's heart sank. The building looked dark and forbidding. She wondered what new ordeal awaited her in this awful place.

Chapter 28

The three surveyed the scene in front of them.

One of Daintry's minders heaved a sigh of relief. He turned to Daintry. 'At last. Now we can get rid of you.'

Daintry did not respond.

'God-abandoned place,' muttered the other guard, looking at the grim building ahead of them.

Geeva castle had an air of desolation and decay about it. Some of the walls were already visibly crumbling. They walked across the bridge over the dried-up moat. The timbers of the structure were showing signs of age. The door in front of them was in no better condition.

One of Daintry's guards picked up a stone and used it to hammer on the heavy wooden door. It seemed an age before a small flap in the door was opened and a face looked out at them.

'What do you want?'

'Prisoner for you.'

The flap was slammed shut and there was the noise of a small door in the main structure being opened. Daintry and her two guards stepped through. A grey-haired man dressed in a shabby and faded King's Guard uniform and carrying a bunch of rusty keys stood looking at them.

'Another one? I don't know where we're going to put her.' As he spoke, the man regarded Daintry with a look of irritation.

'You're to guard this one well,' instructed one of Daintry's minders. 'Confine her securely and keep her alive. If she escapes or is harmed in any way, it's a hanging offence.'

Daintry looked about her. They were standing in a large quadrangle surrounded by the outer castle walls. Crumbling turrets dominated the scene. Several guardsmen lounged around a well, enjoying the evening sunshine and watching the new arrivals with interest.

'This way.' The man with the keys grabbed Daintry's arm and started to lead her away. With a brief glance in her direction, Daintry's two minders quickly abandoned her and moved over to chat with the other guardsmen.

Daintry did not have to walk far. Her new guard opened a rusty metal door at the base of a turret and propelled her down some uneven stone stairs into a small dungeon. 'You'll have to stay here until I can find something different,' the man muttered as he began to free her hands.

Daintry took in everything with a glance. The cell was dark, and it stank. Water seeped from the walls and collected on the stone floor. As her captor untied her hands, the horror of the place overcame her. Panic took hold. As the man turned to retreat up the steps, Daintry rushed after him. As he reached the door she threw herself at him and grabbed his legs.

'No, no, NO!' she shrieked. 'Please don't leave me here. I won't try to escape. I promise.'

Her entreaties fell on deaf ears. Without a word, her captor flung her off him and slammed the door shut. She heard a lock being operated.

Daintry pounded on the door with her hands. Desperate words escaped from her. 'No! Don't leave me here! Please let me out.'

How long her attempts lasted she had no idea, but eventually, exhausted by the effort, she sank down in a heap close to the door. Uncontrollable sobs burst from her. After all she had been through, this was too much to bear. She wished with all her might that they would kill her quickly now, and free her from this torture.

She lay listening to the occasional sounds of human activity that filtered in through the small metal grille in the door: activity that was remote from her miserable world. Gradually, as the darkness increased, the sounds ceased, and only the noises of the night reached her ears. Occasionally, she heard scuffling and squeaking, which could only be rats, emanating from the darkness at the bottom of the steps. She lay there, fearful of moving and racked with hunger.

Somehow, late into the night, her weariness overtook her, and sleep gave her some relief from her ordeal. A chink of daylight was already piercing the grille when she awoke stiff and cold. She sat up, leaned her back against the wall, and waited. Somewhere she could hear the noise of hammering on metal. It seemed a long time before the door was flung open and bright sunshine flooded over her.

The guard who had placed her in the overnight prison stood there, keys in hand. He grinned at her. 'Sleep well?' he asked. Daintry did not reply. Prompted by a nod from her captor, she stepped out of her prison.

She found herself being led across the castle quadrangle towards the sound of the hammering. She felt weak and light-headed from lack of food, but it was a joy to feel the rays of the sun warming her body. The fear of where she had just spent the night made her plead with her captor, 'Please don't put me in there again.'

He grunted a reply. 'I've got something else arranged for you.'

With Daintry wondering in trepidation what might be in store for her, they made their way slowly across the quadrangle. For the first time, Daintry noticed that her captor walked with a limp. They passed the well, where several soldiers dressed in the uniform of the King's Guard were lounging. A group of women were laughing and frolicking with them.

Several of the women looked at Daintry and laughed. 'Come and join us, Forest Girl!' one of them shouted. Eyes down, Daintry continued walking. Her captor muttered something incoherent.

He led her into another building. It took a few seconds for her eyes to become accustomed to the gloom. They were in a large workshop, in the centre of which a fire was burning, blown into an intense heat by a young man operating a pair of bellows. Pieces of metal lay around on the floor and against the walls. Dominating the floor area was a metal cage, being worked upon by a huge man wearing a leather apron. This was the source of the hammering. The man looked up as Daintry and her guard entered. 'What now?' he asked, dropping his hammer.

'Fix this one up for the middle tower,' Daintry's guard replied, with a nod towards her.

The man glanced at Daintry, muttered something and then beckoned to her. 'Come here, girl.'

Trembling with fear, Daintry stepped forward.

'Put your foot there,' the man instructed.

Daintry placed her foot on the anvil he had indicated. The metal was cold beneath her bare skin. She trembled as she waited to see what the blacksmith was going to do. He was rummaging at the back of his workshop. When he came back towards her, he was carrying something attached to a chain, which dragged along the floor.

Daintry became alarmed. Remembering the sight of the recaptured prisoner at Katangar and her own experience when she left the Forest People's camp, she knew at once what was in store for her. She shook her head. 'No. Please. Don't chain me,' she begged.

Her plea was ignored as the blacksmith grabbed hold of her foot and closed the metal band around her ankle. It was far too big, and with a curse he searched for a smaller one. After several attempts, a band was found that fitted. 'Keep still, girl,' he growled, as he wielded his hammer. A few strokes, and the job was done. The heavy chain was now secured to her ankle.

Tearfully she wondered what was going to happen next. The smith picked up the balance of the chain and carried it over his arm. With a hammer still in his hand, he headed for the door. Daintry, attached to the other end of the chain, had no alternative but to trot after him. The guard followed.

Once again Daintry was led across the castle quadrangle.

As they passed the soldiers and their women companions, one of the women jeered at her, 'Look at you! Been a naughty girl, have we?' Some of the others laughed.

'Those women here again,' the guard grunted, almost to himself.

As they were crossing the yard, Daintry heard a voice calling her name. At first she could not determine where it came from. Then, high up in one of the turrets, she spied a familiar face looking down and waving through the iron grille. It was Princess Aleena.

Daintry would have waved and called back, but there was a tug on the chain and she almost stumbled. This could not stop her spirits rising. Suddenly she felt better. The thought that somebody she knew was close at hand made all the difference. She wondered what had happened to the other prisoners. Were they here too? Would she be able to have any contact with Princess Aleena?

They reached another turret. The guard opened a narrow door and they started to climb a stone stairway, which spiralled its way upward. It seemed a long way to the top; another creaking door was pushed open, and Daintry was led into a circular room. The blacksmith looked around and found what he wanted: an iron ring fastened to the stonework. A few blows with the hammer, and Daintry was firmly attached to the castle wall.

The guard had been watching the proceedings from the doorway. 'That'll stop any little bird from flying away,' he smirked.

With that, he and the blacksmith left, closing the door behind them.

Daintry glanced around her new prison. At least it seemed a bit better than the foul dungeon in which she had spent the night. An open window high up on the wall allowed a reasonable amount of light in, and a ray of sunshine was making its way through the barred aperture. There was even some furniture: a rough table, a chair and, best of all, a bed. It was this that attracted Daintry's attention. Dragging the chain after her, she walked across and sank down onto the rough boards that served instead of a mattress. She tried to comprehend what was happening to her. Nothing seemed to make sense any more. How long would she be kept here? When would she have to face the execution she was sure would take place at some point?

The sound of the door opening woke her up from a doze. At some point in her pondering she had curled up on the bed, exhausted from the discomfort of the previous night, and had dropped off to sleep. She was alert immediately, and sat up.

A boy with a mop of sandy hair, perhaps a few years younger than Daintry, entered the room. He carried a plate of food and a pitcher of water. He set his burden down on the table and glanced around, taking in Daintry and the chain attached to her leg.

'Some food for you.' His voice was not unkind.

'Thank you,' replied Daintry.

The boy turned to go, but Daintry was anxious to ask him some questions.

'What is your name?'

The boy hesitated. 'Rufin,' he replied. Then after a pause he added quietly, 'I'm not supposed to talk to you.'

Daintry smiled at him. 'Nobody will know.'

The remark seemed to pacify him. He hesitated before leaving. Daintry took advantage of the ground gained. 'Where do you live?' she asked.

'In the village,' Rufin replied, with a nod towards one of the walls as if to indicate the direction of the village.

'Are there many prisoners here?'

Rufin started to count half aloud. 'One, two, three… Fourteen,' he announced eventually.

'And Princess Aleena is one of them?' Daintry asked.

Rufin seemed surprised at her question. 'Yes,' he answered.

'Are there a lot of soldiers here?'

'Only three normally, but six are here to take the princess away.'

'Where are they taking her?'

Rufin shook his head. 'Don't know.'

Daintry was determined to gain as much information as possible from him.

'Who are the women I saw in the courtyard?' she asked.

Rufin's face clouded to a look of disgust as he answered. 'They're from the village. The soldiers bring them here. Samon gets angry about it.'

'Who is Samon?'

'He's the gaoler, and he looks after this place with his wife.' Rufin suddenly blurted out, 'He beats me sometimes.'

'Oh, that's awful,' Daintry sympathised.

She was about to ask more questions, but suddenly a voice shouted close at hand. 'Rufin! RUFIN!'

Rapidly Rufin sped away, scarcely closing the door behind him.

Daintry felt sorry for him and hoped that by asking questions she had not earnt him a beating, but her immediate need was to consume the food he had brought. She ate every morsel and quenched her thirst from the pitcher of water. Her hunger temporarily appeased, she explored the confines of her prison. There was little to it other than the bare stone walls and the meagre furniture. She soon discovered why she was chained to the wall: the lock on the door was clearly broken. As she looked up at the light penetrating the window, an idea suddenly occurred to her. She climbed onto the chair and stood upon it on tip-toe. She could just reach the window, and by pulling herself up with her arms she was able to look down and see a section of the quadrangle. Unfortunately the turret window from which Princess Aleena had greeted her was out of sight.

Several days passed, and some sort of routine filtered into Daintry's life. Her existence was now controlled by the stone walls that confined her. Boredom was an increasing burden. With nobody to talk to, the days were long. Her only visitors were either Rufin or – more often now – Samon, bringing her food. After the first encounter, Rufin seemed less inclined to talk to her, and she was unable to obtain any answers from Samon. Her only distraction was to occasionally stand on the chair and look out onto the courtyard. It was this occupation that was to bring a new fear to her. For some time she had been conscious of hearing sawing and hammering. Intrigued, she once again looked out of the window. At first she could see nothing, but then, pushing her face against the bars, she saw a scene that struck terror into every bone in her body.

Two workmen were erecting a gallows.

Chapter 29

'Well, gentlemen, are we ready for the final conflict?'

It was Vasil Rojak, supreme commander of the rebel movement, who spoke. He stood before his ten or so commanders, including Elgar Rigor and Conrad Accker, who were seated around the table in his tent.

Glasses were raised and there was a chorus of assurance. There was a calm but confident mood among the assembled company. Their plans had been made, and on the following day they would engage the enemy for the decisive battle.

'Commander Rojak, have we any new intelligence filtering through from the enemy?' asked one of the group leaders.

Vasil smiled. 'The good news is that more members of the King's Guard are deserting.'

'Then that is surely in our favour,' observed Elgar, who was sitting beside him.

'Indeed it is,' replied Vasil. His face took on a more sombre note. 'Unfortunately, I have just heard more disturbing news. Princess Aleena has been recaptured.'

'What?'

'How?'

Voices of concern came from around the table.

Vasil was more subdued as he answered. 'From the information I have received, she is again held at Geeva castle.'

'But how was she recaptured?' asked one of the commanders.

'It is understood that the Forest People were hiding her and she was betrayed by an informer,' replied Vasil.

Before any of the group could ask further questions, he spoke again. 'My friends, this latest news is unfortunate. With Princess Aleena in the hands of the enemy, it is possible that she will be used as a bargaining tool. It makes the need for a good outcome tomorrow even more important.'

There were murmurings of agreement from around the table.

Conrad sat silent and studious. It was true that the rebel forces were now in a superior position. The two forces were separated by just a short distance and were not yet within sight of each other, but they were close enough for the grand battle to commence. He knew that he would have one of the most difficult tasks. To have to circle round the enemy unseen and then lead an attack from the rear was not going to be easy. There was an element of luck in the strategy. This latest news was disturbing.

There was a commotion outside the tent. A guard pulled aside the canvas door and a lieutenant stepped in and saluted. He addressed Vasil. 'Commander, a member of the King's Guard has been stopped trying to cross our lines. He claims to be an emissary from their commander.'

'Very well. Bring him in,' ordered Vasil.

Two minutes later the lieutenant returned with two guards. Between them was a lieutenant dressed in a shabby uniform of the King's Guard. He looked around at the assembled company.

'State your business,' demanded Vasil.

The lieutenant stood erect. 'I have a message from our commander, Miklo Janack, for Conrad Accker.'

'Very well. Deliver your message,' Vasil replied curtly.

'By the authority of our commander Miklo Janack, I am to inform Conrad Accker that the woman Daintry Brouka is being held as a hostage at Geeva castle and that unless the deserter Conrad Accker surrenders and gives himself up to our commander within twenty-four hours, the woman will be executed as a convicted criminal.'

The lieutenant paused and reached into the leather pouch at his belt. 'I have a signed document to prove my message.' It was clear that he recognised Conrad as he finished speaking. One of the guards took the folded paper and handed it to Conrad.

Conrad read the demand through blurred eyes. Miklo had exercised a cruel revenge for his switch of loyalty. How was Daintry involved in all this? Why was she described as a convicted criminal? He now had an impossible decision to make. He bitterly regretted confiding in Miklo his fondness for Daintry. All eyes were on him as he sat temporarily stunned by the news he had just received.

It was Vasil who broke the silence. He turned to Conrad. 'Do you know this woman, Conrad?'

Conrad managed to find his voice. 'She wears our betrothal ring,' he replied softly.

There were mutterings of sympathy from the assembled company. Each man recognised the turmoil Conrad was going through.

The emissary addressed Conrad. 'Commander Accker, do you not remember me? I was with you at Raker.'

Conrad forced a brief smile. 'I remember you, lieutenant.'

'I would like to serve under you again. I wish to desert to your company.'

'No,' interjected Vasil. 'That cannot happen, lieutenant. You must return to your commander and confirm that you have completed your mission.'

The lieutenant turned to him and nodded slowly. 'I understand,' he replied. He paused. 'But I have to tell you something more.'

'Very well,' Vasil prompted.

The lieutenant hesitated again. He looked around the table and eventually fixed his eyes on Conrad again. 'Commander, even if you surrender, Commander Janack has no intention of letting this unfortunate woman go free. He intends to execute her. He has already indicated this. He has despatched the executioner to Geeva castle to carry out the task.'

The lieutenant's statement produced uproar from around the table. Expressions of astonishment and indignation filled the tent.

'Impossible!'

'An innocent hostage cannot be executed without the captors giving an opportunity for their demands to be met.'

Vasil held up his hand for silence. He addressed the emissary. 'Explain yourself, lieutenant.'

The lieutenant looked anxiously around as he replied. 'It is my understanding that the woman concerned is a convicted witch who has also escaped from the mines of Katangar.'

Again, comments and exclamations of disbelief circulated around the table.

Vasil took control again. He nodded in the direction of the emissary. 'Lieutenant, you have delivered your message. That will now be all. You may return to your unit. You will be given safe escort through our lines.'

The lieutenant saluted and withdrew from the tent.

Conversation broke out around the table. It was clear that there was both sympathy for and puzzlement concerning Conrad. Any questions were immediately halted by Vasil. 'Gentlemen, we have a big day ahead of us tomorrow. Let us rest and prepare.'

It was the signal for the dispersal of the group. Only Vasil, Elgar and an emotionally shattered Conrad remained behind.

Vasil placed his hand on Conrad's arm. 'I feel for you receiving this news prior to what lies ahead of us tomorrow. Do you still wish to command your side of the attack?'

Conrad nodded. 'Yes. I am still committed to it. The news I have received tonight will not affect my ability to carry out the mission.' In spite of everything, he knew that he was honour bound not to back out.

'I thank you for your allegiance and your commitment. I know that you will complete this difficult mission, but I also know that you will be doing it with a heavy heart. I would like to ask you a personal question.' Vasil regarded Conrad closely.

'Of course. Please do.'

Vasil hesitated a second, as if in thought, before he responded. When he spoke, there was softness in his voice. 'Conrad, may I ask you, are you in love with this woman who is held hostage?'

'Yes, very much. I wish to marry her.' Conrad was emphatic.

Vasil smiled. 'Such a marriage would not be easy. Do not forget that she is branded a criminal and will be scorned and rejected by many.'

'That makes no difference to how I feel about her,' replied Conrad.

Vasil nodded. 'I admire your loyalty, Conrad.' He paused. 'Once we have victory in our hands tomorrow, you have my permission to go to Geeva castle and rescue her.'

Conrad was almost overwhelmed. 'Commander, I will be eternally grateful.'

'Your mission will be twofold,' added Vasil. He gave a hint of a smile. 'It will also be to rescue Princess Aleena.'

'Princess Aleena!' Conrad's response was one of shock.

Vasil continued. 'Yes. Take as many men as you think you will need. I am reliably informed that there are no more than a dozen soldiers guarding her. Once the rescue is complete, hold the castle and safeguard the princess until I send you word.'

'But will I not be needed for the assault on Taslar?' asked Conrad. The plan had been for Conrad and Elgar, following a decisive win on the following day, to advance on the city, which would be the last obstacle to complete victory for the rebel movement throughout the country.

Vasil shook his head. 'No. Your task is more important, Conrad. You are charged with the safety of the two women held at Geeva castle.'

Conrad nodded. 'I understand and accept the responsibility. Once the castle is secured, I will defend it and its occupants with my life.'

Vasil ended the conversation. 'Now, my friends, let us get some rest before tomorrow's engagement. Good night, gentlemen.'

With that the trio dispersed.

Dawn was only just breaking as Conrad and his men moved stealthily through the forest. Since leaving the camp, their progress had been without incident. As they drew closer to the enemy, things became more difficult. Here the slightest sound might give them away as they waited for the first sounds of battle ahead of them. That would be the signal that the main offensive had been launched and for Conrad to lead the attack on the enemy's rear.

Conrad moved forward with a heavy heart. The news he had received the previous evening both puzzled and worried him. He kept asking himself the same questions. How had Daintry arrived at the position she was now apparently in? Would he survive the battle to carry out his mission to rescue her? He feared that the conflict would be severe and bloody. He tried to put his personal problems out of his thoughts and concentrate on the task in hand.

Suddenly one of the scouts he had sent ahead emerged from the gloom. He looked excited as he approached Conrad and saluted.

'Commander, a party of about twenty of the enemy is advancing towards us.'

Conrad was immediately ready. Turning to his second-in-command, who had also heard the scout's report, he issued his instructions. 'Commel, have the men stand at full alert and wait for instructions. We don't want any action until we hear that Commander Rigor and his men have engaged the enemy.'

The lieutenant nodded and departed to pass the instructions along the line. They waited, each man listening out for any sound and peering into the darkness.

Suddenly a group of soldiers dressed in the uniform of the King's Guard emerged from the shadows. As soon as they realised that they had weapons trained upon them, they threw their own guns upon the ground and raised their hands above their heads. Conrad recognised the leader as the emissary of the night before. The man spoke immediately. 'Commander Accker, I and my men surrender our weapons to you.'

'Your surrender is accepted. How many are you?'

'My men account for twenty-two, but I can assure you that many more will follow. A great number of the King's Guard are tired of serving under a worthless monarch. We want nothing more than to be rid of his arrogant and selfish rule, and we now wish to support the rebel movement.'

Conrad nodded. 'Very well, lieutenant. You and your men will be placed under guard until the outcome of the battle is decided. Any act of treachery on your part will result in the immediate execution of the culprit.'

Conrad turned to Commel. 'Place these men under guard.'

The prisoners were led off, seemingly happy with the outcome of their desertion. Conrad was wary. He feared that this might be a trap.

It was over an hour later that the first shots sounded clearly in the morning air. By now daylight was making everything easier for the scouts and for Conrad's main party. The shooting seemed to briefly gather intensity and then to slow into spasmodic shots. Puzzled, Conrad awaited news from his scouts. It did not take long for one to appear. His report of what was happening on the battlefield was startling.

'The enemy's forces appear to be in complete disarray. Swathes of the soldiers are surrendering and many more are throwing down their weapons and fleeing.'

219

'Are you sure about this?'

'Absolutely, commander. It looks as if there is precious little fighting for us to do.'

Conrad found it hard to believe what he had heard, but when the other two scouts returned a few minutes later with a similar story, he decided to implement the strategy already decided on and advance towards the rear of the enemy's position.

As they moved forward, it became clear that the three scouts had been completely accurate. Enemy soldiers were leaving the battle zone and casting down their weapons. They were immediately taken prisoner. It occurred to Conrad that if this continued, he would have more of his troops guarding prisoners than were left to fight.

Conrad and his men reached the main battlefield without firing a single shot. The scene in front of them was one of calm and closure. Small groups of former King's Guard soldiers stood idly waiting for instructions, guarded by members of the rebel forces. Several tents had been set on fire and were now burning fiercely, the acrid smoke blowing around the site. Out of the haze a smiling Elgar Rigor advanced towards Conrad.

'Welcome to victory,' he announced, throwing his arms around Conrad and embracing him.

'But what happened?' asked Conrad, as they drew apart. He was still puzzled by the turn of events.

Elgar grinned at him. 'More or less what we expected. The cannons failed to fire and it seems that the army of the King's Guard had little appetite for a fight. More of them surrendered than fought us. Scores more simply fled the battlefield.'

'We encountered some of them on the way here.'

Elgar slapped Conrad on the back. 'Taking Taslar will be a simple matter after this.' He laughed. 'And then, my friend, our task will be finished.'

'And what happens after that?'

Elgar shrugged his shoulders. 'Who knows? Our job will be done.'

Conrad did not reply. He knew his concerns for the future were not shared by Elgar. The rise of the rebel movement and the increase in support had been swift and successful, but now that their victory was almost complete and perhaps the king forced to abdicate, who was going to sort things out and regain some form of stability in the country?

His pondering was abruptly halted. Elgar spoke again in a lower voice. 'There has been one notable casualty. Commander Janack has sustained a serious injury.'

Conrad was shocked. 'Is he alive?'

Elgar nodded. 'Barely. I am on my way there now.'

'I will accompany you,' Conrad replied. It was not news that he had expected to hear. Though they now had different views, he and Miklo had shared a great deal.

As they entered the tent where Miklo lay, the orderly who had been bending over the commander stood back to let Elgar and Conrad see him.

Miklo lay on a makeshift couch, his chest covered with blood. He was deathly pale and his eyes were closed. However, they flickered open at the brief noise of Elgar and Conrad's arrival. He stared at the two commanders for a second, and then spoke softly. 'So the victors arrive.'

It was Elgar who responded. 'You are injured. I have an excellent surgeon under my command. I will have him attend to you directly.'

Miklo gave a slight smile and shook his head. 'I fear it will be of little use. I am mortally wounded. I stopped a stray shot.'

'Stick with us, Miklo, for old times' sake.' It was Conrad who spoke.

Miklo's eyes rested on him for a second. 'Conrad, my friend of old, it is sad that war placed us on opposing sides.'

Conrad was about to reply, but Miklo suddenly became more

alert. 'Conrad, Daintry Brouka, do you still desire her?' He closed his eyes again.

'Yes, I do,' Conrad replied softly.

Miklo's eyes jerked open again. His voice was fading now. 'Then you must hasten to Geeva castle. I gave orders for her execution. She may already…' His voice trailed off.

Before Conrad could answer, his old friend fell back dead.

Conrad rode hard, forcing the pace. Behind him were the troops chosen for the assault on Geeva castle. The size of his contingent had been dictated by the number of horses and competent riders available. He had wasted little time after victory, but had immediately set about the task of selecting comrades for the task ahead.

Most of the men were in good spirits. The complete collapse of the king's army had been a big boost to morale. A few of the party were disappointed that they would not be able to share the march into Taslar and the fall of this final objective.

Conrad had a heavy heart. The surprisingly easy victory had come at a great price – the loss of his childhood friend. Though the recent conflict had divided them, for most of their lives they had shared the same values. Miklo's death had cast a deep shadow over him. On top of that he was desperately worried that he might not be in time to rescue his beloved Daintry from the gallows. Even if she was still alive, there was always the threat that she and Princess Aleena might be used as hostages to prevent the castle being taken.

As evening approached, Conrad's second-in-command drew alongside him. 'Commander, the men and horses are tired. It will be impossible to reach the castle before dark.'

Conrad nodded. 'Very well, Commel. We will camp here in the forest for the night.'

A relieved Commel gave the order to halt and dismount. All the riders were grateful. Conrad had driven them relentlessly all afternoon, intent on reaching the castle as soon as possible. However, he knew that an attack in the dark was impossible. They would have to wait until the morning.

Conrad spent a restless and sleepless night. Always his thoughts were on what might lie ahead. By daylight he had his men mounted again and on the move.

The morning was already well advanced when the party came within sight of the castle. They approached carefully, expecting some sort of opposition. It did not come. Conrad despatched a scout to try and ascertain what the position was.

When the man came back, he was excited. 'The castle door is wide open,' he announced.

'It may be a trap,' Conrad advised.

They waited, but still nothing happened. Eventually Conrad chose six men and gave the order to advance into the castle. Slowly and with great care they passed across the bridge and through the great door. The quadrangle was deserted, but the first thing Conrad saw was the gallows with its rope hanging down. His heart sank. Had this gruesome instrument already been used on Daintry?

'Search the castle thoroughly,' he ordered.

It did not take long for his men to reappear. 'There are no prisoners here,' they announced.

'Are you sure?' insisted Conrad.

'We have searched everywhere. The castle is deserted.'

Chapter 30

From her restricted view, Daintry gazed at the scene far below her. The sight of the gallows being erected filled her with a paralysing fear. Instinctively she felt she knew who that wretched instrument was being prepared for. After taking one last look, she curled up on the bed, consumed by misery.

She was still in that position when Rufin arrived with some food. This time she remained on the bed. Rufin stared at her but said nothing.

As he turned to leave, Daintry asked in a subdued voice, 'Why are they building a gallows?'

Rufin stared at her again for a second before answering, as if he did not know what to say. He gave a shrug of his shoulders.

'Samon says they're going to hang somebody.' His voice was non-committal and she guessed he knew more.

'Who?'

'Dunno.'

With that he disappeared. Daintry knew that he had knowledge that he did not want to convey to her. It only made the fear that gripped her more intense. She picked at the food he had brought, but with little appetite. Again she lay on the bed, now fearful to look out of the cell window. She went over and over again the misery of what had befallen her during such a short period of time. At one time she would have thought it impossible. Her thoughts turned to the people she loved most: her father, Mela and Mogo. Would they know what had happened to her? When she thought about Conrad, she was filled with sadness and regret. She would never marry him now. Perhaps he would wed Mela after all, or one of the fine ladies from the Court.

She slept fitfully that night, continually waking up gripped with misery and anguish. When would the execution take place? Would they give her any warning? Perhaps Rufin or Samon would relent and tell her what was going to happen.

It was broad daylight when she woke up with a jerk to the sound of the door of her prison being pushed open. She found herself suddenly engulfed in sickening dread. She feared she was about to be taken away to meet her fate, but when she forced herself to look it was only Rufin who stood there, with her food. He seemed agitated.

'They're taking Princess Aleena away in a cage.' His voice conveyed his excitement.

Daintry could hear a commotion outside in the courtyard. Watched by Rufin, she rushed to the chair she had left beneath the window. Once again standing on the tips of her toes, she looked at the scene below. A four-wheeled open wagon pulled by two horses had been drawn into a central position. A steel cage just about big enough for one person had been erected on it. Daintry immediately recognised it as the structure the blacksmith had been working on when he chained her.

As she watched, Daintry spied Princess Aleena being led out by Samon and another guard. The princess carried herself with an air of dignity as she walked towards the wagon, barefoot and still dressed as a Forest Woman. Faithful Sharla, similarly garbed, followed. A door was opened on the cage and after what appeared to be a brief discussion the guards helped Princess Aleena to climb onto the wagon. She stepped into the cage, and the door was closed and locked. Sharla was then allowed to climb onto the wagon and sit beside the cage and her mistress.

Daintry watched in horror as the wagon with its royal occupant moved off, surrounded by what seemed to be a lot of soldiers. The sight of Princess Aleena being treated in such a cruel fashion was a sharp foretaste of the treatment Daintry was likely to receive as a mere commoner. She jumped down from the chair and faced Rufin.

'Where are they taking Princess Aleena?' she asked.

'One of the soldiers told me they were going to Taslar,' Rufin remarked casually. Then he added, 'I wish I was going as well.'

Daintry made no reply, and Rufin left her to her thoughts.

That day passed, and the next. Everything now seemed to be strangely quiet outside Daintry's prison. Gone were the sounds of hammering on metal and wood. The misery of waiting for something to happen was broken only by visits from Samon, who simply left Daintry's food and refused to be drawn into conversation with her.

On the morning of the third day, it was Rufin who brought her food. Daintry was anxious to find out her fate. Before Rufin could leave, she asked the question that was uppermost in her mind. 'What's going to happen to me?'

Rufin was clearly taken off guard. He stared at the floor for a second or two and then looked up at her, his face flushed.

'I've heard that they're going to hang you.'

Even though she had already guessed, hearing the words filled Daintry with trepidation. She wanted to know more.

'When?' she asked.

Rufin shook his head. 'I don't know.'

Daintry took a deep breath. 'If you hear, will you tell me?' she pleaded in a soft voice.

He looked at her sadly, nodded and quickly disappeared.

Later that day Rufin visited her again. Hearing him approach and knowing it was not the time for him to bring food, she feared the worst and braced herself for what he had to say. When he burst into her cell, his face was flushed with excitement.

'There's been a big battle, and the king's army have been defeated.' He could scarcely contain his exhilaration.

Daintry did not at first comprehend the true meaning of his words. She knew that the rebel forces had been successful throughout the country, but she knew nothing about the significance of a battle.

'My father says it means the king may have to abdicate,' Rufin tried to explain to her.

'But who will be king then?' Daintry asked, still puzzled.

Rufin shrugged his shoulders. 'My father thinks it will be a good thing,' he remarked. Still excited, he continued. 'I want to go to Taslar. That's where the next battle will be.'

'What will you do there?' Daintry asked.

'Join the rebels.'

'What's going to happen to me?' Daintry asked, obviously more concerned about herself than what was going to happen in Taslar.

Her question seemed to calm Rufin a little. When he replied, his voice was less agitated.

'Nearly everybody has left the castle. All the soldiers, the blacksmith...' He paused. 'And the hangman,' he added hurriedly.

That was good news, Daintry thought. At least it appeared that her fate had been put on hold.

Rufin left her soon afterwards, seemingly consumed with all the excitement of what was happening. Alone, Daintry tried to make sense of everything. When she was living with the Forest People, Princess Aleena had told her about the treatment her brother, Henri, had meted out to her, and Daintry was also aware of the rise of the rebel movement throughout the country, but the idea that the king would be deposed seemed to be far-fetched. Even if that did happen, who would replace him?

Towards evening, Daintry heard the sound of someone climbing the stone stairs to her prison. She hoped it would be Rufin again, so that she could ask him some more questions. Instead it turned out to be Samon. This time she was determined to find out what was happening. As the gaoler put what looked like decidedly stale bread and rotten cheese on the table, she tackled him.

'What's going to happen to me?'

'When I know, I'll tell you,' he growled.

'But all the soldiers have gone,' Daintry stressed.

Samon's face turned into a scowl. 'How do you know that? Was it Rufin? I'll beat the life out of him.'

Cursing under his breath, he turned and hurried from the room, closing the dilapidated door with a crash.

Daintry felt sad and worried. She feared what might happen to Rufin. She turned her attention to the food Samon had brought, but the taste confirmed its appearance: it was not fit to eat. She took a few sips of water and left it at that, accepting hunger as the only alternative.

As she lay on the bed a little later, she was alerted to some sort of commotion in the courtyard. She leapt up and hurried to her viewpoint. The light was fading, but by pressing her face close to the bars and craning her head she could just make out what was happening. She found it hard to believe what she was seeing. About a dozen men and women were moving excitedly in the direction of the main door of the castle. When she realised who they were, Daintry became excited in turn. It was her friends from the Forest People who had been taken as hostages. She was able to recognise them all in the approaching darkness. Tazak was amongst them. They were all escaping – but how?

Daintry did not care. She was determined to join her friends. She shouted at the top of her voice, 'Tazak, I'm here! It's Daintry. Wait for me!'

She called out again and again, but in their eagerness to leave the castle they were unaware of her shouts. She waited in vain, desperately hoping that one of them would hear her voice and turn towards her tiny cell window, but none of them did. Even when the sound of their departure had died away, she prayed that somebody might just have heard her and would come to her aid, but no one appeared.

Sobbing with disappointment, she desperately tugged at her chain, hoping that by some miracle it would dislodge from the wall, but it stayed firm. Eventually she curled up on the bed, hungry and miserable, wondering how all her friends had achieved release from their captivity, and watching the room dissolve into darkness.

Throughout the night Daintry alternated between periods of dozing and wakefulness. Only as the first signs of light were beginning to appear did she fall into a heavier sleep.

The sound of footsteps on the stairs woke her from her troubled rest. She remained where she was as Rufin appeared in the door. He appeared to be unharmed, which came as a relief to Daintry, as she had been concerned that her admission to Samon might result in punishment for the young man.

Rufin appeared to be quite elated. 'All the prisoners have escaped,' he announced excitedly. 'Samon is in a terrible state about it.'

Daintry sat up. 'How did they get out?'

'Samon is the only guard here now. The other soldiers fled when they heard about the defeat of the King's Guard. The prisoners ambushed Samon when he came to bring them food. They grabbed his keys and locked him in the cell. I found the keys where they'd dropped them and I let him out when I was sure they'd got away. He is talking about leaving as well. He fears what will happen to him.'

Daintry was silent, absorbing the information she had just received. She was glad that her friends had managed to escape, but she was still a prisoner.

'What will happen to me?' she asked eventually.

'I don't know,' replied the young man. 'Samon won't want you to get away. You're special,' he added thoughtfully.

This was not information Daintry wanted to hear. She wondered whether Rufin would help her to escape? It was worth a try.

'If you help me get out of here and take me home to Toomer, my father will reward you.'

He shook his head. 'I cannot. I am going to Taslar with my father. We are leaving right away. I just came to say goodbye.'

His words shocked Daintry. How could he go away and leave her chained up like an animal?

She made no reply. A few seconds later Rufin left the cell and she heard him descending the stone steps.

Daintry lay back on the bed. She was left alone for what seemed a long time. After a while, a new and frightening thought came to her. Surely she was not going to be left here to starve to death… The prospect of that was too awful. Besides, Rufin had emphasised that Samon considered her special. Whatever plans were in store for her, they presumably did not include starvation.

She was soon to find out. Her thoughts were interrupted by the sound of somebody slowly climbing the steps to her cell. Samon appeared in the doorway, a hammer in his hand. He barely glanced at her lying on the bed. Instead he got to work on the chain, where it was attached to the wall. A few blows of the hammer, and he held the loose end in his hand.

He turned to Daintry. 'Get up. You're coming with me.' As if to give emphasis to the demand, he gave a tug on the chain.

Daintry jumped up. 'Where are you taking me?' she asked.

Her question was greeted with anger. Samon raised his hand, and for a second she thought he was going to strike her. Instead he growled, 'Hold your tongue, girl, or it will be the worse for you.'

He slung the end of the chain over his shoulder and led Daintry out of the cell and down the steps.

She was astonished by the sight that greeted her. A cart was standing in the courtyard loaded up with chattels. A scruffy-looking woman waited beside it, and five dirty children scampered around.

The woman, clearly Samon's wife, regarded Daintry with some contempt. 'What are we taking that slut with us for?' she demanded.

'Be quiet, woman,' snapped Samon. 'She could be useful to us.'

Samon lifted Daintry onto the cart, where she was forced to crouch down in an extremely cramped position amongst the sacks and bundles and cooking pots. Samon dumped the rest of the chain beside her and fastened the free end onto the side of the cart. She was still a confined prisoner.

Samon urged the horse forward, and amid the commotion of his complaining wife and the shrieking and squealing children, who were forced to walk alongside, the cart moved off through the castle doorway.

Once again, Daintry was being taken away to an uncertain future.

Chapter 31

The wagon carrying Princess Aleena toiled slowly up the hill to Taslar. All of the party were weary after two days of travel in hot, dusty conditions. Princess Aleena had endured it all with calm dignity, travelling in the steel cage, her faithful Sharla close by. The party had spent the night at an empty hunting lodge owned by King Henri, and it had been a welcome rest for everybody, in particular the two captives, who were at last able to sleep in a proper bed, although guards had been posted at the door and window of their room.

Now, as the second day was nearing its end, the majestic walled city of Taslar stood ahead of them.

'Your journey is almost over, Your Highness.' The captain in charge of the party, riding alongside, addressed Princess Aleena.

She smiled at him. 'I am sorry that you and your men have had to endure such an arduous journey on my account,' she replied.

The captain nodded, but said nothing. Throughout the journey he had treated the princess with as much courtesy as possible, even at one stage providing a cloth over the roof of her cage to protect her from the rays of the sun.

As they drew near to the gates of the city, Princess Aleena turned to the captain again. 'Captain, where are you taking me?'

The captain's face was grim as he replied. 'Your Highness, I have orders to conduct you to the Castalon.' A notorious place of confinement, the Castalon was now only used for special prisoners.

'I see. Thank you,' Princess Aleena replied quietly.

The captain hurried ahead of the party to the closed gates. 'Open up, in the name of King Henri!' he shouted.

As if by magic the giant doors swung open.

The wagon trundled through the opening and entered the city.

The streets were crowded with people, for they had been alerted to the arrival of the princess by the town crier on the orders of King Henri. For the most part, the people lining the streets stood in silence, witnessing an event they were not in tune with.

The wagon made its way through the crowd. Suddenly it was forced to draw to a halt. A line of soldiers from the King's Guard blocked its path.

Andor Durek, finely dressed for the occasion and wearing his chain of office, was standing on a hastily erected platform. He addressed the crowd.

'Citizens of Taslar, observe the traitress Princess Aleena being returned to the scene of her crimes.' He pointed to the silent and white-faced princess, who was standing holding onto the bars of her cage.

There were mutterings among the spectators. Some openly expressed disgust, but it was a lone voice from the crowd that spurred a change in events.

'Down with King Henri! Princess Aleena for Queen!'

The cry was taken up by the crowd. Shouts of 'Queen Aleena' and 'Princess Aleena for queen' rang out. A number of people climbed onto the platform, and Andor Durek screamed as he was toppled to the ground. The crowd surged forward, surrounding the wagon. There were frantic efforts to open the cage and release Princess Aleena and help her and Sharla to safety. The captain and the few soldiers guarding them drew their swords, but in seconds they were overwhelmed by the crowd. Women and men alike began to vent their feelings on the soldiers. The captain was beaten to the ground, and a group of men ripped the keys from his waist and made for the wagon. Fights were now breaking out all around between citizens and soldiers.

Princess Aleena found her voice. 'Stop! Stop this violence.'

Her intervention appeared to have some effect; the crowd appeared to quieten down on hearing her speak.

Suddenly the crowd parted and a figure walked slowly towards the wagon. White-haired, but still proud and erect, Assem Rokar commanded respect from those assembled who recognised him. This was the majority, for his years in office had made him a familiar face to the people of Taslar. The commotion died to near silence.

Assem's voice was calm but authoritative. 'Who is in charge here?'

The captain struggled free from the two men holding him. 'I am. Captain Doco at your service, sir.'

Assem spoke again, 'Captain, please release Princess Aleena.'

Captain Doco made his way to the wagon. Removing the keys from the hand of the man who had snatched them from him, he unlocked the door of the cage. Holding his hand out, he helped Princess Aleena down from the wagon. Sharla followed.

Assem moved towards the princess. He bowed as he addressed her. 'Your Highness, it will give me great pleasure if you will accept the hospitality of my home until other arrangements can be made for you.'

Princess Aleena held out her hand as she replied. 'I accept your offer, Assem Rokar.'

Assem bowed again and touched her hand with his lips. He turned to Captain Doco. 'Captain, please escort Princess Aleena to my house.'

The captain reacted quickly. Retrieving his sword from the ground, he faced Princess Aleena, the hilt of his sword pointing towards her. He bowed. 'Your Royal Highness, I pledge my sword at your disposal.'

Princess Aleena smiled at him. She held out her hand for his lips as she replied calmly, 'Your pledge of allegiance is accepted.'

One of the soldiers who had been under Captain Doco's command shouted out, 'I will also pledge my sword for the Princess!'

'I, too!' shouted another.

Further pledges of support from the other soldiers rang out.

Princess Aleena smiled at Captain Doco. 'It seems that we have a ready escort, captain.'

For the first time, Captain Doco was smiling. 'That we have,' he agreed. He saluted and turned to shout orders.

The cage was lifted off the wagon and abandoned. Some form of seating was quickly arranged on the wagon, and Princess Aleena, Sharla and Assem Rokar were helped up onto it. Slowly the party moved off. Almost all the soldiers who had once guarded the princess as her captors now accompanied her as an escort. The departure of the princess was accompanied by the cheers and shouts of support from the crowds moving at the same pace as the wagon.

'Fools. Idiots! I am surrounded by them!' King Henri screamed at Andor Durek.

Andor had just returned to the palace, battered and bruised from his ordeal at the hands of the crowd. His fine clothes were torn and dirty and he had lost his chain of office. In spite of that he considered himself fortunate to have escaped worse treatment. His first task on returning to the palace had been to inform the king of the events in the streets below. Understandably, his report had not been well received.

'I have been misled by you all!' the king shouted.

Andor did his best to recover his position. 'Your Majesty, we could not foresee the change in the mood of the people.'

'The King's Guard have failed. They should have been able to contain the situation,' the king retorted, now angrily pacing the room. 'Where are Kurt Lassen and the rest of the council?' he demanded suddenly.

'They seem to have disappeared,' Andor replied glumly.

'Cowards! They are all cowards!' yelled the king.

Andor did not reply. All the other members of the council had left in order to save their own skins. He alone had remained faithful to the king.

'It was your idea to bring Princess Aleena back to Taslar and expose her to the people. Now you crawl back to me and tell me it was a complete failure!' the king shouted angrily.

Andor had no time to reply before more of the king's fury was hurled at him.

'Why is Kurt Lassen not here? He is in charge of the Guard. They should have arrested the troublemakers.'

'Your Majesty, the situation has changed completely. No one can be held responsible for the way things have gone. Who could have anticipated the rise and popularity of the rebel movement?'

'The guardsmen should have been able to beat down the rebels. We increased their numbers. It all comes down to Kurt Lassen's leadership. He has failed. Order his arrest.'

Andor tried to remain calm. 'It is not Kurt's fault. He could do nothing. Many of the guardsmen have either deserted or joined the rebel movement.'

'The leaders of the rebels should have been arrested and tried as traitors months ago,' retorted the king. 'I have been let down.'

As he paced the room he suddenly thought of something else to berate Andor with. 'You tell me that that old fool Assem Rokar was in the square today. How did he escape his guards?'

'I don't know,' Anton replied miserably.

'You're as big a fool as he is,' snorted the king.

Andor did not reply. He knew that what he had to say next would make the king have another fit of anger. He waited as the king paced the room ranting and raving. At last there appeared to be an opportunity. He cleared his throat.

'Your Majesty, we have to accept that the situation in Altaria is now beyond our control. The King's Guard is no longer an effective guard for you, and the mood of the people no longer supports you. In effect, the rebels have won. They are in control of all of the country.'

The king drew near to Andor, his face distorted with disbelief.

'Are you telling me that I have to abdicate?'

'I fear so, Your Majesty.'

'Never! It is unheard of. How dare you suggest such a thing? You must be mad. It has never happened before.'

The king paced up and down, waving his arms wildly.

'Who would rule the country? I am the victim of an incompetent administration. My people love me. It is only a band of hooligans who have been allowed to twist the minds of a few people.'

Andor waited patiently for the opportunity to reply. It came at last as the king stopped pacing and stood looking at the model of the palace he had intended to build.

Andor cleared his throat again.

'Your Majesty, things are extremely bad. The people of Altaria no longer want you as their king.'

Henri swung round sharply to face him. 'What are you saying?'

Andor plucked up as much courage as he could. He was fearful of making his next statement. He hesitated while the king stared at him waiting for an answer. He found his voice at last.

'In the square this afternoon, the people were calling for Princess Aleena.'

'What! She is a convicted traitress!' The king almost screamed a response.

Andor remained silent as the king continued to rant.

Eventually the king subsided into almost talking to himself. 'Such a thing cannot happen. A woman cannot rule Altaria.'

Andor plucked up courage to make an important suggestion. 'We have to leave Taslar.'

'Leave? Leave? I am staying here. I am the king.'

Andor spoke again.

'Your Majesty, the whole country is shouting out support for the rebels. Very soon the rebel army will arrive in Taslar. There is no one to stop them. It is only a matter of time before they attack the palace.'

For the first time the king appeared fearful. 'What will happen to me?' he asked in alarm.

'I fear for your safety, Your Majesty,' replied Andor. 'We have to leave while there is still time.'

The king appeared to be slowly accepting the situation. 'Where will I go?' he asked.

Andor had already made plans in case of this eventuality. 'I have a coach and some loyal servants who will take us south to a mountain retreat.'

'Well, if it is only temporary,' the king mused.

Andor silently breathed a sigh of relief. At last the king appeared to acknowledge the situation.

'When shall we leave?' asked the king.

'I can have everything ready for tonight, Your Majesty.'

The king nodded. Then with a sigh he agreed. 'Very well. Send my servant to me.'

Andor took a deep breath. 'Your servant has fled, Your Majesty.'

Anger streamed into the king once more. 'You are all disloyal to me! I cannot trust anybody!' he screamed. He turned on his heel, lifted up the table and with one sharp movement hurled the model of the proposed palace to the floor. 'I should have had more support. It could have been built if I had not been let down by fools and cowards.'

Andor waited for him to calm down. Then he outlined his plans for their departure from the city.

The king listened, now looking bewildered and confused. He merely nodded at Andor's proposals. The fact that his world had collapsed around him now appeared to have registered with him. Andor eventually left him slumped in a chair.

Darkness had already enveloped the palace when a coach drew up at a rear entrance. Andor had somehow found eight servants, including a coach driver who, on being offered a substantial bribe, had agreed to make the journey.

Andor had being making plans for several weeks. As soon as it had become clear that the rebels would eventually defeat the army, he had started to develop a strategy. He would journey with the king to one of the royal lodges hidden away in the mountains in the south of Altaria on the country's border with Forancer. It was a sparsely inhabited stretch of land, and for generations there had been discussion between Altaria and Forancer about which country actually owned the area.

Once he had left the king in relative safety, Andor's plan was to return in secret to Taslar and set to work to organise those still loyal to the king to create public demand for his return to the throne and the revival of stability. Then Andor would personally select new members for the High Council, men he could manipulate. To him it was simple and foolproof. All he had to do was get the king safely away, and keep him hidden while he carried out his intentions.

The road through the mountains was rough, rocky and dangerous. Sitting beside Andor, the king was a mass of grumbles. 'We are going too slowly,' he growled. 'At this rate we will never get there.'

He leaned out of the window and shouted out to the driver. 'Drive faster, you fool!'

The driver whipped up the horses, and the coach picked up speed. It was a fatal move. They were entering a precipitous section of the road. On one side of the narrow ledge rose a steep cliff, and on the other lay a sheer drop. Suddenly one of the wheels struck a deep culvert in the road. The coach swayed for an instant and then veered towards the edge of the road as the frightened horses panicked. It was all over in seconds. The coach and its occupants crashed over the edge in clouds of dust.

The incident was watched in horror by those following. They gazed in disbelief as the coach plummeted onto the rocky slope and smashed into pieces. The wagon following, which was laden with the king's possessions, drew to a halt. In silence the escorts dismounted and slowly made their way down the slippery mountainside. The remains of the coach had come to rest against a giant rock. Grimly they picked their way amongst the scattered wreckage. There were no survivors. King Henri, Andor Durek and the coach driver were dead.

Chapter 32

Crouching in her cramped position on the wagon, Daintry felt every bump as the wheels travelled over the rough road. One of the worst aspects of the journey was the frequent mischievous taunts and attention she received from some of the older children. One boy took to poking at her with a stick, until Samon spotted him and cuffed him around the head. It was also clear that Samon's wife resented Daintry's presence and as a result treated her with complete contempt. When they stopped for a meal, Daintry had to wait until Samon and his family had finished eating. All she was given was the scraps left by the children.

Towards the evening, after repeated grumbling and complaints from his wife, Samon reluctantly agreed to stop for the night. He helped Daintry roughly down from the wagon and pushed her towards a stout young tree at the edge of the clearing they had drawn up in. The loose end of her chain was wound around the tree and secured firmly. She was still a prisoner, but at least she could now stretch her limbs. A fire was lit and Samon's wife prepared some food. The smell of the cooking tantalised Daintry. She was now ravenous, but once again she was almost ignored and just fed the leftovers, which she consumed greedily.

Night began to fall, and Samon and his family bedded down. Daintry remained awake, her back against the tree, watching the darkness increase. She wondered where Samon and his family were bound. It seemed they were fleeing for their safety after all the prisoners had escaped from the castle under Samon's watch.

Their progress during the day had been slow, and she guessed they had not travelled very far. She could not understand why she had been taken along. Was she some kind of hostage?

Sleep did not come to her. She sat listening to the sounds of the night and contemplating her situation. Samon and his wife had not treated her kindly during the day, and she was still hungry. She knew that if they continued to feed her as little as they had during the last twenty-four hours, she would eventually die of starvation. Somehow she had to escape their clutches, but how? The heavy chain that held her fast was preventing her from fleeing.

Suddenly an idea struck her. The shackle on her leg was actually quite loose. She remembered that the blacksmith had had a job to find one that would fit her slim ankle. Could she manage to prise it off? Slowly and methodically she set to work. Her first efforts were not successful. Her heel refused to pass through the ring. She tried to lubricate the area with saliva, but that did not help. Frustrated and disappointed, she rested a few minutes before trying again. Her eyes spied the plate Samon's wife had given her food on. Slowly, and trying her best to be as quiet as possible, she managed to scrape some grease off the plate with her finger. She applied this to her heel and the inside of the ring. It's now or never, she thought as she attempted once again to force the stubborn flesh through its bond. She pushed with all her might on the steel band. The metal dug into her instep, causing her almost to cry out in pain, but she gritted her teeth and continued to try to work it over her foot. Just as it seemed she would be defeated, slowly the steel started to slip over her heel. Seconds later she succeeded in squeezing the rest of her foot through the band. She was free!

Her instant reaction was one of shock that she had freed herself from her confinement, coupled with the pain from her foot where the steel had dug into the flesh during the exercise. She quietly rubbed the area to obtain some relief. Slowly she assessed the situation. She knew that she had to be wary of making any noise. Samon's wife appeared to sleep lightly, and several times she had woken up and gazed around before dropping off again. Samon had got up once to relieve himself, and on his return had glanced in her direction before settling down again. If that happened again while she was making her escape, all would be lost.

She waited until everything seemed quiet, and then slowly and carefully she stood up. With a brief reassuring glance at the sleeping family, she silently slipped away into the gloom. She picked her way among the trees, trying to avoid the clumps of bushes that grew here and there. A twig snapped beneath her foot, and in the still of the night it sounded frighteningly loud. It made her freeze for an instant, but it provoked no sound from behind her.

For most of the night Daintry made her way through the forest. It was close to dawn when fatigue finally overtook her. She sank down beneath a tree for a brief rest. The next thing she knew was that it was daylight. She leapt up in a panic. She was sure that Samon must be looking for her by now. Uncertain how far she had walked through the darkness from the place where the family had camped for the night, and scolding herself for falling asleep for so long, she set off again.

Her progress was now much slower. For one thing, she had no idea which way to go: the forest appeared to be so big, and there was no indication of the route she should take. On top of this, she was now suffering the effects of not having had adequate food for several days. Pangs of hunger gripped her constantly, and at times she felt light-headed. She found a few bushes bearing edible berries, but the meagre amount she was able to consume did little to alleviate the feeling of emptiness.

She had been walking for about an hour when without warning she suddenly came face to face with another human being. For a second or two they stared at each other, both overcome with astonishment. In those split seconds Daintry formed a picture of the other. He was a man of about her own age or perhaps younger. He carried a gun and had several dead rabbits hung over his shoulder.

It was the young man who spoke first. 'Who are you?'

Her predicament flung any caution Daintry might have had far away. She needed help, and unless she received it she would die of hunger in the forest.

'I am lost. Please help me.'

'What are you doing wandering in the forest? Who is with you?' The young man seemed anxious, as if on his guard.

Daintry could sense his fear. She knew that in order to gain his trust she would needed to elaborate, in spite of the risk such a confession would entail.

'I am alone. I was at Geeva castle, but there is no one there now. I have walked for a long time and I am starving. Please help me. I wish you no harm.'

The young man studied her for a second, and then he seemed to reach a decision. 'Come with me,' he invited. 'My mother will give you something to eat.'

Daintry could have wept with relief. At least he sounded friendly, and there was the prospect of food. 'Thank you,' she replied quickly. Then, as they started to walk, she added, 'I am Daintry Brouka from Toomer.'

'I am Marat, son of Tolek.'

'Do you live in the forest?' Daintry asked.

Marat nodded. 'Yes. With my father and mother, but my father is away fighting the rebels.'

They continued in silence and Daintry wondered whether she should relate the news she had received from Rufin about the recent battle between the rebels and the King's Guard, but after a very short while they reached their destination. Daintry was surprised how close she must have been to it.

They had entered a large clearing in which stood a cottage. Smoke spiralled upwards from the chimney. Several animals pottered about outside, and Daintry could see that there were a few cultivated fields behind the dwelling.

As they approached, a muscular woman, who could only be Marat's mother, emerged from the cottage. She stared at the two of them with a mixture of curiosity and displeasure.

'Who is this?' she demanded, with a nod in the direction of Daintry.

'I found her wandering lost in the forest. She says she is from Geeva castle,' Marat explained.

'Why did you bring her here?' the woman asked angrily. It was clear Daintry was not welcome.

Marat looked uncomfortable, and his mother turned to Daintry. 'Have you lost your voice, girl?'

Daintry shook her head, 'No. I am Daintry Brouka from Toomer. I was wrongfully convicted and held against my will at Geeva castle.'

The woman spat on the ground. 'A likely story,' she retorted.

Suddenly she grabbed Daintry by the hair, making her scream. Daintry found herself gripped in a hand of steel. Her blouse was pulled down from her shoulder, exposing the Katangar mark.

The woman snorted. 'I thought so. She is an escaped prisoner from the mines. See, she is marked.'

Daintry's hair was released and she stood there rooted to the spot, unable to speak as fear coursed through her veins. Marat and his mother stood looking at her. Seconds passed that seemed like minutes. Then the woman, looking at Daintry with contempt, issued an order.

'Bind her arms and lock her in the barn. They'll be looking for her. There could even be a reward.'

Marat made a move as if to carry out his mother's order, but at that instant Daintry found her voice.

'No! Please, not that! I am innocent and no one is looking for me. Please let me go. I just want some food and to return home.'

Marat's mother continued to stare at her, as if contemplating Daintry's plea.

Desperately Daintry cried out again. 'Please! Please let me go! I have done no harm to anybody. Imagine how it would be if I were your daughter.'

Her words at last had some effect. The woman turned to her son. 'Take her to the road and leave her there.'

Within a few minutes Daintry found herself walking beside Marat again, clutching and ravenously eating a crust of stale bread his mother had reluctantly given her.

Marat led her through the forest for several hours. He told her that he had grown up there and that his father was a Forest Guard. Daintry knew that the Forest Guards were an elite group of men charged with keeping law and order in the forest. Marat explained that his father had received the command to join with the King's Guard in their fight against the rebels. Since he had left, Marat and his mother had not heard from him.

Eventually they reached a stony, dusty road. Marat pointed out the direction Daintry needed to take to get to Toomer. He gave her some food from his bag, for which she was exceedingly grateful. She was sorry to lose her companion, but she knew that he could go no further. When it came to saying goodbye she had tears in her eyes. She stood watching him retreat into the forest, and then with a final wave he was gone. Once again she was on her own.

Wearily she started walking on the uncomfortable surface. It was hot, and she was parched from lack of water. She was glad when the road crossed over a narrow river and she was able to have a cool drink and soak her tortured feet in the water. While she was doing this she heard the unmistakable sound of horses' hoofs. In the distance she could see a group of riders approaching. They were riding hard, as if intent on some purpose, creating clouds of dust. Fearfully she hid from view as they passed. She stole a peep as they rode away from her. She could see that they were heavily armed. They were not dressed as King's Guard soldiers and she wondered whether they were part of the rebel movement.

Poor Daintry was not to know that the rider leading the group was her beloved Conrad returning from Geeva castle after his unsuccessful attempt to rescue her.

For the rest of the day she trudged on, weak and footsore. She consumed the food Marak had given her, and supplemented the meagre portion with a few berries she had managed to find, but it was insufficient to quell the hunger she felt. She knew that unless she had enough to eat soon, she would be unable to continue walking. Several times riders passed her, but they were all men, and she feared to make herself known to them. Each time, she concealed herself, hoping that the next people she saw would include some women who might help her.

Towards evening, when she was already looking for somewhere to rest for the night, Daintry's fortunes changed. Close to a clump of trees she spied several gaily coloured wagons drawn up at the side of the road. Horses grazed nearby. A fire burned brightly and a group of people sat around it, chatting, eating and drinking. Children ran about here and there. Daintry knew at once that she would be among friends. This was a temporary camp of Forest People.

As she drew near to them, they all regarded her with interest. Though her clothes were dirty, tattered and torn, she was still dressed as a Forest Girl.

One of the men greeted her. 'Why, 'tis a Forest Maiden all alone.'

Hunger and fatigue made talking difficult for Daintry. All she could gasp out was, 'Please help me. I am trying to get to Toomer.'

The group of three men and five women crowded around her. The same man spoke again. 'But where are your people?'

'I am not of the Forest People,' Daintry tried to explain.

'You say you are not of our people, yet you dress as a Forest Maiden,' remarked one of the other men.

'I was innocent, but I was convicted of a crime and sent to the mines at Katangar. I managed to escape into the forest. I was injured, and the Forest People found me and cared for me. Then we were betrayed, and our camp was raided by the King's Guard. Some of us were taken to Geeva castle. I have been walking all day and I am very weary.' As she finished speaking, the smell of the nearby food made her gasp, 'I am so hungry.'

One of the women sprang into action. She scolded the man who had been questioning Daintry. 'Can you not see that the poor girl is exhausted?' She turned to Daintry and pointed to the ground close to the fire. 'Sit there, child, and have some food.'

Daintry was soon huddled by the fire, a bowl of rabbit stew on her knees. Never had anything tasted so good.

The man who had originally questioned her sat down beside her. He spoke kindly.

'What you say was confirmed to us yesterday. Tazak and eleven others passed by our camp on their way to their own people after fleeing from the castle.'

The news excited Daintry. 'Tazak and the others were here yesterday?' she asked.

The man nodded. 'Indeed they were. We were able to help them on their way.'

Before Daintry could reply, the man introduced himself. 'I am Barco, leader of this family. We are travelling to Taslar.' He smiled at her. 'But I would like to hear more of your story.'

Feeling safe and protected for the first time in many days, and with her hunger now satisfied, Daintry told the group about her family and who she was. She related the events that had resulted in her being sent to Katangar, and how she had escaped and found refuge with Tazak and the others.

When she had finished, Barco nodded in sympathy. 'You

have endured more than any maiden should. We will help you get to Toomer.'

His words brought tears to Daintry's eyes. Here at last was somebody who would be glad to help her. She was no longer alone and struggling with adversity. She managed to gasp, 'Thank you.'

Sitting with her new friends that evening, Daintry found a contentment she had not experienced since being forcibly removed from her previous time with the Forest People. She was introduced to the rest of the group, and everybody was friendly. There was singing, during which she struggled to keep awake as the tiredness from her day tried to overtake her. Eventually she was found a place to sleep in one of the wagons.

Chapter 33

'You wish to speak with me, Your Highness?' Assem Rokar asked, as he entered his parlour, where Princess Aleena awaited him.

The princess smiled at him. She had known the aged member of her late father's council ever since she was a child, and a kind of bond existed between them. As a little girl she had been a frequent visitor to his place of work in the palace and he had often told her stories. On a few occasions she had visited his house, in which she was now safely housed. She knew that he was one of the few people she could confide in.

'I seek your wise counsel, Assem.'

The old man nodded and sat down on a nearby chair.

The princess paused for a few seconds, formulating the question she wished to ask. 'What is going to happen to the country now? My brother is dead and there is nobody to lead the people.'

'And no High Council to administrate,' added Assem.

'Do the people know that there is no High Council?'

Assem shook his head. 'I believe not, though unless something happens soon they will certainly find out. That is what I fear.'

'Why?'

Assem pondered the question. 'Most of the people have supported the rebels in what they have done, but there are those who will seek to take advantage of the situation for their own desires once it is known that there is no effective control at the top.'

Princess Aleena looked at him thoughtfully. She had a quick grasp of what he was indicating. 'You mean there are people who might attempt to gain power?'

Assem nodded. 'I do,' he replied.

'What then can we do?'

Assem smiled at her. 'You have heard the demands of the people. They call for Queen Aleena.'

'But a woman cannot rule Altaria,' the princess pointed out.

'It can happen if the High Council desires it. The law can be changed.'

Both were silent for a few minutes. In the few days since Assem had instigated the princess's rescue, she had recovered from her ordeal well. With the tatty garb she had worn when he had first seen her imprisoned in a cage replaced by an elegant gown, and now well groomed again, she looked every bit a queen. Clearing his throat, he raised the question that concerned him most.

'It seems to me, Your Highness, that the main issue is whether you wish to be queen.'

Princess Aleena sat in silence, deep in thought. When she replied she chose her words carefully.

'It is something I never considered. I grew up knowing that according to the law of the land my brother would be king and I would just be a princess, married off to somebody. My brother was not a good king and many suffered under his rule, including me. When I was removed from the palace and accused of treason, I came to know a different way of life. I began to understand the people of Altaria, their worries and their problems.' The princess paused for a moment, reflecting. Then she continued in a quiet voice filled with emotion. 'When I was taken to Katangar, my own brother effectively sentenced me to a slow death. I experienced the horror of that place. No woman – or man – should be sent there.'

She fell silent again as she remembered her recent ordeal.

Assem waited patiently, giving her time. He knew that she had more to say to him. When she eventually did speak again, her voice was calmer and had regained power.

'Perhaps now I have the opportunity to rectify some of the wrongs that have taken place, but I feel that I am in a position where I am aware of what is expected of me but do not know how to carry it out.'

She continued to look at Assem, seeking answers.

Assem had expected this reaction from the princess. He already given a lot of thought to the current situation in Altaria.

'I think what is needed initially is a High Council and a First Minister.'

Princess Aleena smiled. 'I believe there is a First Minister here in this room.'

'You do me a great honour, Your Highness, but a Keeper of the Purse is also required.'

The princess thought for a second, and an idea came to her. 'What about the young man you had as an assistant – Conrad Accker? Would he not be suitable?'

'He would be more than able, and a younger pair of eyes than mine are needed for the job. However, Conrad Accker has made quite a name for himself as a leader in the rebel movement. Perhaps he may wish to continue in a different role from that of figures.'

'We must contact him and find out. Where can he be found?'

'I believe he is in Taslar, but he is from Toomer and has spoken for a maiden there.'

Princess Aleena looked at him curiously. 'Daintry Brouka?' she queried.

Assem was surprised. 'You know of her?'

Princess Aleena smiled. 'She was with me when I was hiding with the Forest People. She is an attractive and sensible young woman. She too was at Katangar and has suffered much. She was imprisoned at Geeva castle when I was there and was still held there when I left, but I know not where she is now.'

The princess was quiet for a second or two. Assem knew she was recalling those difficult and dangerous times. His respect and admiration for her were growing steadily. She had suffered greatly at the hands of her brother, but today she was very much a queen in waiting and was already making decisions and giving suggestions as one. He was determined to stand by her and assist her in any way he could. His confidence was amplified by her next question.

'How can a new High Council be formed?' she asked.

Assem had already considered the problem.

'Perhaps it will be possible to reinstate some of the previous members of the council who can be trusted. I am willing to try to contact some of them,' he suggested.

'I think we should do that,' the princess agreed.

'I will set about it immediately,' asserted Assem.

'What about the leaders of the rebels? Should they not be part of the council?' asked the princess.

This was something Assem had also thought about. He voiced his thoughts. 'There are only two who need to be considered, and they are Elgar Rigor and Vasil Rojak.'

Princess Aleena voiced her surprise at the mention of one of the names. 'Vasil Rojak? I remember seeing him when I was a tiny girl. He was part of my father's council many years ago.'

Assem nodded. 'He has a great love of Altaria and has commanded the rebel movement throughout the uprising, organising the resistance and placing spies and agents. I think he and Elgar Rigor should be offered seats on the council.'

Princess Aleena had another question. 'How many members must the High Council have in order to operate legally?'

'Eight members, plus the reigning monarch. However, we need to ensure that the new council is well balanced.'

'In what way?'

Assem smiled as he explained. 'We need stability in the country now, not revolution. The rebel movement has served its purpose. It is now time to lay it to rest.'

The princess laughed. 'You are very far-seeing, Assem.'

Assem made no reply. There was still one important item needing the approval of the princess. His voice took on a sombre note as he addressed her once again.

'Your Highness, there is one more thing to discuss, and that is the funeral of your brother. His body has now been brought back to Taslar.' He looked at her enquiringly.

She was quick to answer.

'My brother was not a popular king, but he is of the royal line of Altaria. He will be buried as all the members of the royal family are, in the cathedral of Taslar. It will not be a state funeral like my father's, but just a simple ceremony.'

Assem nodded. 'I will make the arrangements,' he replied.

Assem left the princess soon after that. He was well pleased with the outcome of their meeting. His love for and devotion to the country of Altaria had made him anxious and concerned about the future. During his discussion with the princess, his fears had quickly dispelled. He now knew that she was more than ready to be queen. She was already making queenly decisions, and he could detect the wisdom of her father in her thinking. He would now make contact with the former members of the High Council who had been so ruthlessly removed from office by King Henri, and persuade them to return. Once they had been reinstated, the High Council could amend the ruling and approve Princess Aleena as the ruling monarch, and she could be presented to the public as the queen of Altaria. His next problem would be to try to locate Conrad Accker.

Finding Conrad proved in the end to be the easiest of Assem's tasks. After their failed attempt to reach Geeva castle in time to rescue Princess Aleena, Conrad and his party had returned to the main rebel army, ready to join the assault on Taslar. This had turned out to be an unnecessary exercise. They had arrived at the city to find the doors wide open and welcoming following the return of Princess Aleena. The soldiers of the rebel movement found themselves treated as heroes, and celebrations of victory over the former corrupt administration were widespread.

It was in the aftermath of the festivities that the reality of the situation began to filter through to the population. While the rebel movement had achieved its goal of liberating the country from the oppressive control of the king, it was clear that Altaria was now at a crossroads, with no effective administration.

Feeling that their mission had been completed, many of those who had fought for the rebel movement had returned home to their previous lives once the exhilaration of victory had subsided. For Conrad the situation was different. Up until his enforced enlistment in the King's Guard, Taslar had been his home. After the last of the fighting, feeling that his commitment to the military was finished and that an uncertain future awaited him, he had returned to the city and taken up residence there again, renting a small house close to the city centre. It was here that Assem Rokar found him.

Conrad was overjoyed to see the old man once again and was anxious to learn about the new developments that were taking place, many of which had been initiated and were being led by his former mentor.

When Assem Rokar suggested that he become Keeper of the Purse, Conrad at first expressed concern that he was not qualified for the job, but Assem insisted that he had enough experience to be proficient in the position and that he himself would be on hand to offer guidance and suggestions if needed. Conrad Accker thus became the second appointment to the new queen's administration.

Chapter 34

Daintry had now spent five days with her new Forest People friends. While they treated her as an honoured guest, Daintry was slightly frustrated with the length of time it was taking them to reach Taslar. The small group had made slow progress, taking a day of rest here and there. Daintry was anxious to get home to her family, and every delay seemed to be time wasted. However, when she suggested that she continue alone from Taslar to Toomer, Barco was horrified, pointing out to her the dangers of a young woman undertaking such a journey alone and on foot. He advised her that it would be much more sensible, when they reached Taslar, to seek out a wagon that was going to Toomer, which would offer her security. Reluctantly Daintry agreed. Her proposal to make her way alone seemed to have some effect, because the following day Barco announced that they would be proceeding to Taslar without further delay.

Daintry was excited to arrive in Taslar. In her short life she had never been to the city, and she listened with interest to the descriptions the women gave of all the exciting things she would see there.

The group encamped on the outskirts of Taslar, and the next day Daintry went into the city with three of the women, helping them to carry the baskets they had made to sell in the market.

As they made their way through the giant gates and started to walk through the narrow streets, Daintry felt almost overwhelmed by the crowds of people. She gazed in wonderment at beggars in their rags, women dressed in elegant gowns, and men with their smart clothes. When they reached the market area, she was fascinated by the range of goods for sale in comparison to those in the tiny market she was accustomed to in Toomer. There were fruits and vegetables she had never seen before, and goods of every description. The noise was constant, as the vendors shouted out to passers-by to come and buy their wares.

The Forest Women managed to find a vacant spot and set down their baskets. Then they too joined in the shouting. Daintry watched everything with interest.

It was there that Conrad found her.

As he left his house and strode through the crowds on the way to the palace, he was deep in thought. He had only been in his new post as Keeper of the Purse for a few days, and it had become clear that the finances of Altaria were in a pitiful state. The Purse was all but empty. Ahead of him were two objectives. One was to ease the burden of taxation on the citizens of Altaria, and the other was to be prudent on spending until the situation improved. It was what to spend the meagre money available on, balanced against the sacrifices he would have to make, that was occupying him that morning.

A cursory glance around him shattered his train of thought. At first he was unable to comprehend what he was seeing. He stared in disbelief at the slim, fair-haired young woman sitting on the ground surrounded by baskets. Surely it was Daintry, but not the Daintry he knew. At the same instant Daintry recognised him. She almost recoiled in horror, and one word escaped from her lips: 'Conrad.'

Conrad was in front of her in an instant. Questions flooded into his mystified thinking. 'Daintry!' he exclaimed. 'What are you doing here?' His eyes were drawn to the colourful, though tatty and torn clothing she was wearing, and her grubby feet 'Why are you dressed like this?' he asked. He could see that the three smiling women she was with were clearly Forest People.

Misery overtook Daintry. The last thing that she had wanted to happen was for Conrad to see her like this. There were tears in her eyes as she struggled to find an answer. All she could muster was, 'So much has happened to me since we last saw each other.'

Conrad mistook her reaction for excited delight at seeing him. But her story could wait. He was full of his own important news. His admiration for her steadily began to creep back.

'My precious Daintry, so much has also happened to me, but the most exciting news I have for you is that Princess Aleena is to be crowned our queen, and I have been made the new Keeper of the Purse.'

He gazed at her with pride, waiting for her response. His excitement made him ignore her silent reaction and her misery. 'Don't you understand?' he continued. 'It means we can be married at once and live in a fine house.'

The reality of his words hit Daintry full on. She shook her head violently, tears now starting to flow down her face.

'No, no. I cannot marry you. It would be wrong.'

'But why not?' Conrad persisted, puzzled at her reply.

Daintry continued to shake her head as she struggled to find words. Eventually all she could repeat hoarsely was, 'No. It would be wrong.'

Conrad persisted. 'I'll go and see your father. We can be married right away.'

Miserably Daintry tried to dampen his enthusiasm. She shook her head yet again to emphasise her words. 'No. I can never marry you. I am not the Daintry you once knew. You must find somebody else.'

'But I want you,' Conrad insisted.

He reached out to touch her. This was too much for Daintry. She shrieked, 'No! Leave me!' With that she leapt to her feet and ran away into the crowd.

Conrad reacted quickly. 'Stop! Please come back!' he called after her as he turned to pursue her.

Daintry sped away blindly on nimble feet. Conrad ran after her, but she had a head start and quickly became lost in the mass of people thronging the area. He searched in vain for her, but she seemed to have disappeared.

Tears streaming down her face, Daintry became the object of curiosity as she pushed her way through the crowd. Some, having seen what happened, cheered her on. Others laughed or simply stared. Eventually she had to stop to catch her breath. A wrinkled old woman sitting outside a booth beckoned to her. 'Come here, girlie,' she called. Desperate to escape from the crowds, Daintry accepted her invitation to enter the booth. Here she was at least out of sight. The old woman followed her and indicated a seat.

'Sit there,' she invited, not unkindly.

The woman sat down opposite Daintry. She looked closely at her as she spoke. 'Why do you run away from your lover?'

'He wants to marry me, and I cannot do that.' Daintry's voice was sad and subdued.

'The problem you envisage is a minor one,' the woman answered.

Daintry was silent.

'Shall Karrella tell you what she sees?' asked the woman.

Looking around her, Daintry realised that the old woman was a fortune-teller.

'I have no money,' she whispered.

'Have I asked for money?' Karrella answered.

Daintry did not reply. Karrella placed a crystal globe on the table in front of her and gazed at it intently.

'I see you have had much torment in the past. But that is over. I see you dressed in a fine gown and living in a grand house, but that will not happen immediately.'

Daintry listened, intrigued. She had never had her fortune told before.

Karrella continued. 'You will be told something important soon.'

'What will I be told?' Daintry almost whispered the question.

Karrella shook her head. 'I see nothing more,' she announced, putting an end to the forecast.

Daintry was surprised and shocked. Clearly the old woman was not going to tell her anything else, and what she had related was more of a mystery than a help. She felt a sudden urge to leave.

'I must go now,' she announced, rising from her seat.

Karrella shrugged her shoulders. 'As you wish,' she muttered.

Daintry left the booth, puzzled and wondering whether she had really learnt anything important. At the same time it occurred to her that Karrella might not be all that she appeared to be.

Once again she pushed her way through the crowds, unsure of where to go and all the time conscious that Conrad was most likely still searching for her. Suddenly she found herself back at the gates she and the other Forest Women had entered by earlier in the day. A covered wagon drawing near to the gates attracted her attention. She recognised it immediately. It was Adler the carrier. He must be on his way to Toomer. A thought came to her immediately. He could take her home.

The wagon was almost at the gates. 'Adler! ADLER!' she shouted desperately as she ran towards it.

Hearing his name, the carrier reined in his horses. He stared around and his gaze fixed on the young Forest Girl now running alongside his wagon. He waited, mystified. He had no business with the Forest People.

Almost out of breath, Daintry reached Adler's side. She looked up at him. 'Adler, it's Daintry Brouka. Do you not recognise me?'

He stared at her in disbelief. Then recognition dawned. 'That it is!' he exclaimed. Then, still puzzled, he muttered, 'But I thought you would be dead by now.'

'I'm not. I'm here!' Daintry almost shouted. Then she pleaded desperately, 'Adler, please take me home.'

Adler continued to stare at her for a few seconds, and then her request filtered through. He suddenly became alert.

'That I will, and gladly!' he exclaimed cheerfully. He reached down to her. 'Step up,' he invited.

Daintry found herself being hauled up onto the wagon. She sat down on the bench beside Adler.

As they passed through the gates of the city, Daintry suddenly remembered her abrupt departure from the market and the basket-sellers. She could not leave Taslar without saying goodbye and thanking the Forest People for all their kindness and for looking after her. She pleaded with Adler to divert to the area where the Forest People had parked their wagons. A little reluctantly, Adler obliged, though he advised Daintry that he was already late leaving Taslar and they could not stop for long.

Things did not quite work out as Adler had hoped. Once at the camp, Daintry was surrounded by her friends, all anxious to make her parting from them cheerful and friendly. Barco came up to her, looked at her rather sadly and took her hands as he spoke. 'Remember that there is always a place for you with the Forest People.' His words brought tears to Daintry's eyes. She felt overwhelmed by all the kindness.

It was seeing Adler glancing up at the now descending sun that suddenly reminded Daintry that they had to leave. Amid waving, calls of good wishes and many tears, she and Adler left the group for the journey to Toomer.

Perched up beside the carrier, as the wagon took the road leading to Toomer, a feeling of calm and joy came over Daintry. After all the danger and torment she had experienced in the last few months, she was at last returning home. She would see her father, Mela and Mogo again.

The thought reminded her of something she had been wanting to ask Adler ever since she had encountered him in Taslar. Interrupting a brief silence between them, she asked her question. 'How are things at my home?'

She did not expect the response she received. Adler was silent for a few seconds, and then he turned to her, looking grave. 'I wish I could be the bearer of better news,' he replied sadly.

Chapter 35

The shock of Adler's reply stunned Daintry. It took her a few seconds to take in what he had said. She eventually found her voice.

'What's happened?' she asked anxiously. 'Is my father still ill?'

Adler stared at the road ahead. He shook his head as he replied. 'No. He recovered from the fever soon after they arrested you.'

'But what's happened?' Daintry desperately wanted to know more.

Adler took his time in answering. He turned to her briefly as he spoke again. 'It was after you were taken. It affected him badly. He was like a man possessed. Though he was still weak, he insisted on searching for you. He went to the Round Tower, but you were no longer there.'

At the mention of the Round Tower, the memories of that awful time flooded back to Daintry. She was just glad that her father had not seen her there. Adler's next sentence dispelled that brief moment of comfort.

'When your father was told that you had been taken to the mines at Katangar, he became consumed by a desire to rescue you.'

'What did he do?' Daintry asked hoarsely.

Adler sighed. 'He pleaded with me to accompany him to Katangar. He somehow had this notion that he could pay for your release.'

'You took my father to Katangar?' Daintry asked in horror.

Adler nodded. 'I did. And the experience changed him.'

'What happened?' Daintry was becoming more and more upset at Adler's revelations.

Adler paused to collect his thoughts. 'When we got to the mines, we were met by the commandant, a pig of a man. He took us to see you at work, but he would not let us get close to you or speak to you.'

'My father saw me at Katangar?' The thought sickened and horrified Daintry. Somehow she needed confirmation of what she had just heard.

Adler appeared unmoved. He continued his narrative. 'The sight of you working at the capstan drove your father frantic. He pleaded for you to be spared the ordeal. He offered the commandant one hundred gold pieces for your release.'

'And was that refused?' Daintry already knew what the answer would be.

'That it was. The commandant laughed in his face and told him that if he wanted his daughter back he would need to find five hundred gold pieces.'

'What did my father say?'

'He told the commandant one hundred pieces was all the money he had. And the commandant just replied, "Then you have no daughter," and walked away.'

Adler turned to Daintry again. He looked sad. 'That was what finished your father. He fell down as if dead and I had to carry him to my wagon and bring him home.'

'Is he still like that?' The news she had just heard saddened Daintry to the core.

'No. He recovered soon enough, but he is a changed man. He just sits in his room and broods. He has no interest in anything – not even the mill. Andrei the miller runs it almost on his own. I believe it produces enough to keep your family and supply the baker, but that is all.'

Daintry was silent for a while. What Adler had related troubled her immensely. The thought of her father seeing her slaving at Katangar was not a pleasant one. It brought back her memories of that time in vivid detail. It also impressed upon her that she was still a convicted person who had escaped punishment. Would they come and take her again? It was a grim thought, but it was overshadowed by what Adler had told her about her family. It was clear that since her departure the family fortunes had diminished, and with her father no longer the dynamic person he had hitherto been, the future looked decidedly grim. An overbearing part of her thinking was that the suffering of those close to her had been brought about by her own action in visiting Saltima for a potion to help her father.

It was some time before she was able to ask further questions of Adler. When she did it was about those dear to her. 'How are Mela and Mogo?' she asked quietly.

'Mela is well enough, but she had a difficult time looking after your father and Mogo.'

'And Mogo?' Daintry queried.

'It seems she fell when the men came to take you away. She broke her leg and was laid up for a while. She walks with a limp now.'

Again Daintry received Adler's words in silence. With each bit of news he related it seemed as if things got worse. Now she just wanted to reach Toomer and see her family for herself.

For the rest of the journey it was Adler who did most of the talking. At one stage he pulled into the side of the road to give the horses a rest and prepare a meal for himself and Daintry. But Daintry had no appetite. She sat beside the fire Adler had built and pecked at the food. She was glad when they were once more on the road heading for Toomer and home.

It was dark when they at last entered the town. Familiar sights began to appear in the gloom. Daintry could hardly wait for Adler to stop his wagon at the end of the street where the

Brouka house stood. Adler merely nodded and smiled when she thanked him. Then he watched as she made her way the short distance to the familiar door.

She pounded on the door with both hands. It seemed a long time before it was opened a crack.

On the other side of the door Peena stood peering through the gap. She gazed in amazement at Daintry. Then, as recognition dawned, she let out a shriek and turned partly away from the door. 'Mistress Daintry is here!'

Within seconds Daintry heard the commanding voice of Mogo.

'Let her in, you stupid girl.'

Peena opened the door wide. As Daintry stepped through, Mogo appeared, leaning on a stick, followed by a white-faced Mela. Mogo immediately took charge and issued her instructions. 'Peena, go and tell the master, and then prepare Mistress Daintry's bed. Mela, heat up some soup.'

Peena hurried away, and within a minute Anton Brouka appeared. He stared in disbelief at the sight of Daintry standing in the kitchen. As reality registered, he let out a cry. 'My daughter! Daintry!' With tears in his eyes he rushed towards her and took her in his arms, repeating the words, 'My daughter, my daughter. You have returned to me. You are home.' The tears flowed down Daintry's cheeks. Somehow she was speechless.

Father and daughter continued to hug each other, and it was Mogo who eventually broke up the encounter. 'Master Brouka, Daintry needs a bath and some food. Look at the state of her. Thin, dirty and dressed like a ragged Forest Girl.'

Anton stepped back from Daintry, though he continued to hold one of her hands and gaze at her fondly. As Mela reappeared, Mogo ushered Anton out of the room with another instruction. 'Explanations can wait. Daintry needs a good wash.' She turned to Peena, who had just reappeared, and barked out another command. 'Peena, prepare a bath for the mistress.'

After that everything happened in a whirl. Daintry was almost force-fed some soup by Mogo and then led to the bath. Surrounded by Mogo, Mela and Peena, she was divested of her clothing and immersed in the water. There was little talking as they scrubbed her and washed her hair. It was Mela who noticed the mark on her shoulder. She recoiled in horror as her eyes fixed on it. No words came from her. Daintry was found a nightshirt to put on, and Mogo applied salve to the cuts on her feet caused by sharp stones. Then she was escorted to her bed and laid down to sleep.

The following morning, Daintry awoke from a deep and refreshing slumber. It was a long time since she had felt the softness of her own bed, and she lay there relishing its comfort. Now, in familiar surroundings, the reality of her situation became more apparent to her. In the eyes of many people she was still a convicted criminal, subject to the demands of the law. Would the constable's men come and take her away again? The thought troubled her, but she received some comfort from the fact that Princess Aleena, who had been in a similar predicament, was now to be queen of Altaria. It was an odd situation.

Her musings were broken by the appearance of Mogo. 'Time you got up,' she announced. 'Your father is waiting to hear what happened to you and how you escaped from the mines.'

Daintry allowed herself to be pampered as Mogo, treating her like a little girl again, found her a shift and a dress to wear. Daintry obeyed each command, though she had some difficulty putting on footwear. Her feet, which had been bare for months, felt very uncomfortable when she forced them into shoes.

After eating some breakfast, she made her way to her father's workroom. She had observed the previous evening how weary he looked. His appearance had confirmed Adler's account of what had happened to the family since she had been away. Now she desperately wanted to talk to him and find out the true state of affairs. When she arrived at his workroom the door was open. Anton was sitting at his table waiting. He had been up early, anxious to talk to his daughter, though he had forbidden Mogo to wake her until later. When he saw her standing in the doorway, he smiled at her and beckoned her to enter and sit opposite him.

She greeted him cheerfully. 'Good morning, Father.'

'Good morning, my child. How are you feeling? Last night you looked so tired.'

'I feel much better today, thank you, Father.'

Anton scrutinised Daintry. There was much he did not understand. He had recovered from the previous night's shock at seeing his beloved daughter, whom he had thought lost forever, standing dirty and bedraggled in front of him. Now he wanted to know her story.

'I want to hear about everything that happened to you from the moment you were taken from this house.'

As best she could, Daintry related the events of the previous few months, omitting to tell him about the more violent aspects of her ordeal. She did not mention that her arrest had come about as the result of Mela informing on her, and Anton never did learn about her sister's involvement.

Her father listened intently, remaining silent until she had finished, and absorbing every detail of her narrative. For a few moments he said little. Then he brought up the subject she had been avoiding. Still observing her closely, he asked, 'When you were in Taslar, did you see Conrad?'

The question instantly brought misery to Daintry. Her voice was almost a whisper as she answered.

'Yes, Father, I did.'

'And what did he say?'

Daintry could feel tears forming as she replied softly, 'He wanted to marry me, very soon.'

'And you accepted his proposal?'

Daintry shook her head. 'I refused his offer of marriage.'

'You refused?' Anton showed a reaction for the first time.

Daintry found it hard to answer. Already the tears were in her eyes. She was choked with emotion as she responded. 'I cannot marry him. He is to be the Keeper of the Purse.'

She paused, finding it hard to speak the words. Eventually they came. 'I am a convicted criminal. I have been to Katangar. I carry its mark. Marrying me would degrade him.'

The mention of Katangar brought up once again the other fear Daintry carried. While her father was digesting her last statement, she suddenly burst forth with the terror that had begun to haunt her.

'Father, will they come for me again? I could not bear being sent back there.'

Since his daughter's arrival the previous evening, the problem had been occupying Anton's thoughts. Ever since he had seen Daintry in that awful place, he had carried the terrible memory of what he had witnessed. He had already made up his mind that Daintry would never be sent there again, and had worked out what needed to happen to avoid her arrest. He addressed her again.

'How many people know you are here?'

Daintry was surprised by the sudden question. 'Only Adler the carrier, as far as I know,' she replied thoughtfully.

Anton nodded. 'Daintry, you must not leave the house and the garden under any circumstances. Is that clear?'

'Yes, Father.'

Then she asked anxiously, 'But what will happen if they do come for me? They will take me away again.'

Anton shook his head. 'I promise you that nobody will force you from this house without my consent.'

The words were of little comfort to Daintry. Even in the security of her own home the fear was constant. She did not reply. She wondered how her father could prevent her from being taken. Perhaps he had plans to hide her somewhere.

Before her father dismissed her, Daintry wanted to know how the family fortunes were. She changed the subject abruptly and asked the question that had been lurking in her mind since Adler's report.

'Father, how are things at the mill?'

Anton was surprised – almost shocked – at the question. He was not in the habit of discussing his business with the women in his household unless a development was going to affect them directly. However, when he saw the concerned look on Daintry's face, he decided to tell her the truth.

He sighed slightly. 'The heavy burden of taxation has almost crippled me. The one mill produces enough flour to keep us in food and a house to live in, but we are as paupers compared with before.'

'Perhaps the economic situation will improve when Princess Aleena becomes queen and Conrad is Keeper of the Purse,' Daintry suggested.

Anton merely shrugged his shoulders. As far as he could see, that was a possibility for the future: he had to deal with the day-to-day situation now. He regretted bitterly that Daintry was no longer able to marry Conrad. It would have been good to have a daughter married into such society. However, he was wise enough to realise that such a match was impossible and would make Conrad the object of ridicule and scorn. But where would he now find a willing husband for Daintry?

Chapter 36

Daintry did her best to adjust to her new situation. She helped Mogo and Peena in the kitchen whenever she could, but the limitations of being confined to the house soon began to tell. She longed for the space and companionship she had experienced with the Forest People. The loss of Conrad remained with her, and tears were never far from her eyes when she thought about what might have been.

For the first few days, Mogo pampered her like a long-lost daughter, but gradually she reverted to the Mogo Daintry knew best, ruling both her and Mela with a firm hand, yet at the same time hiding a tender love for both girls. Her recovery from the injury she had suffered during Daintry's arrest had been slow, and being obliged to walk with a stick was a source of much frustration for her.

Mela had been badly affected by her sister's return to Toomer. The guilt she experienced for initiating Daintry's arrest had troubled her greatly ever since Daintry had been taken away. When she had spoken to the pastor about Daintry's action in obtaining a potion to help their father's illness, she had been filled with the desire to create in secret an element of revenge against her young sister and teach her a lesson for taking Conrad from her. Perhaps, she thought, the pastor would send for Daintry and order her to do some sort of public penance. That would be utterly humiliating for Daintry and would cause loss of face for Conrad, who would most probably no longer wish to marry her.

Never had she imagined that the kindly old pastor she had known since she was a tiny girl would inform the Witch Prosecutor what Daintry had done. When Daintry had been taken away by the constable and his men, she had become eaten up with the realisation that her actions had caused not only degradation and danger to Daintry, but also trauma and distress for her family.

With only Peena to help her after Daintry's arrest, Mela had been almost overwhelmed by the workload of looking after both her sick father and a laid-up and complaining Mogo. She had been kept going with the vain notion that perhaps after a few days of punishment Daintry would be released from the Round House. When the news had trickled through that Daintry had been sent to the mines at Katangar, the true reality of her actions had hit Mela hard. She knew well enough that she would most likely never see her sister again. She had thought of taking her own life, but she had lacked the courage to carry it out. Instead she had spent sleepless nights and gone about her work silently and eaten up with remorse.

Even the eventual return to relative health of her father, and Mogo's recovering sufficiently to hobble about with a stick did not help. She had remained full of guilt and self-reproach, speaking only when she was spoken to. When Daintry had appeared on the doorstep of the family home, in rags and exhausted, Mela had been both relieved and frightened. What would Daintry say to her? Would she now become despised and hated as it became clear what foul deed she had performed against her own sister to satisfy her pride? Surely, she thought, Daintry would demand some sort of retribution.

But Daintry did not confront or accuse her, and this puzzled her. How could Daintry have suffered so much and yet not want to point the finger at the very person who had been the cause of all her misery? In the end Mela could stand it no more. She had to talk to Daintry and confess her crime. One day she followed her sister into the garden and blocked her way on the path.

Surprised, Daintry looked at her and asked with a concerned smile, 'Mela, is something wrong?'

Mela stared at her in disbelief. How could Daintry be so calm and placid? She hesitated and then spoke very quietly. 'You must hate me every minute of the day.'

Daintry was surprised. 'Hate you? Why?'

'I caused all your problems. I am responsible for the downfall of the family.'

'You? How can you be responsible?' Daintry was astonished at her sister's claim.

'You don't understand,' Mela replied wretchedly. She knew she had to reveal the truth to Daintry, but it was hard. She searched for the right words.

'I reported you to Pastor Kartov for giving our father the potion from Saltima, the witch. That's why they arrested you and accused you of witchcraft. Please believe me: I never dreamed they would do that.'

Mela dissolved into tears as Daintry tried to get a grasp of what she had just admitted.

'But… But I don't understand.'

Mela's voice had reduced almost to a whisper. 'I went to the pastor. I thought he might order you to do penance, but instead he informed the Witch Prosecutor of what you had done.'

Daintry pondered what Mela had just related. She suddenly remembered what Pastor Kartov had told her when he had visited her in the Round Tower. At the time the pastor's revelation had not completely sunk in, so concerned had she been about her predicament, and later she had all but forgotten the incident. Now it became clear how her ordeal had been initiated. It was odd that her own sister had been the direct cause of her arrest. She needed to know more.

Before Daintry could reply, Mela spoke again. 'I feel so wretched. The guilt hangs over me. I don't know what to do. You must hate me so.'

A wave of compassion swept over Daintry. Suddenly she hugged her sister. 'My dear sister, how can I hate you? I wish you had not done what you did, but I do not hate you for it. You must understand that.'

Mela looked at Daintry through her tears. 'I was so angry with you for taking Conrad away from me. I wanted to have revenge.'

The mention of Conrad brought Daintry's own misery to the forefront. She spoke in a soft, sad voice. 'You can marry Conrad now, for I cannot.'

'Why not?' Mela demanded, puzzled at her sister's statement.

'I carry the mark of Katangar – the mark of a criminal. Conrad has achieved high office. If he married me, he would be despised and ridiculed by those around him. People would point the finger of condemnation and contempt at me.'

'But—' Mela started to say something but was halted by the shrill voice of Mogo.

'Mela, Daintry, where are you?'

It was the end of their discussion. Knowing Mogo of old, both girls hurried in the direction of the voice, Daintry calling out, 'Coming,' as they hurried into the house.

Her confession to Daintry did little to alleviate Mela's misery. The guilt of her betrayal stayed with her, and it seemed that she was unable to free herself from its clutches. On the third day after Daintry's return, she made her way to the market to purchase some food for the family. On the way she passed the church. Suddenly she was overcome by a desire to venture into it. She entered its silent interior. She was the only occupant, and she sank down into one of the pews. She rested there, desperately trying to seek some sort of comfort. The tears that were never far away slowly began to flow. An occasional sob escaped from her lips.

'You are troubled, my child.' A gentle voice spoke behind her.

Mela had not heard the soft footsteps of Pastor Kartov coming up to her.

Mela found herself saying, 'I have sinned greatly.'

'We are all sinners,' the pastor replied softly.

'My sin weighs heavily on me,' Mela whispered.

'Tell me about it.'

'I accused my sister of being a witch.'

The pastor placed his hand on Mela's forehead as he spoke. 'In the eyes of the church you have committed no sin.'

Mela made no reply.

Eventually the pastor removed his hand, at the same time speaking again. 'Go forth from this place, joyful that any sin you may have committed is forgiven.'

Slowly, Mela stood up from the pew. 'Thank you,' she whispered.

Pastor Kartov smiled kindly at her as he posed the question that was concerning him greatly. 'It is rumoured that your sinful sister has returned to Toomer. Is that correct?'

Mela was caught unprepared. She knew that she could not lie to the pastor. She wished she could be struck dumb and be unable to answer. She barely whispered, 'Yes.'

As she hurried away from the church, a new concern pressed upon Mela. Would the pastor keep the secret of Daintry's escape from the mines and her return home? She prayed that he would.

She saw a large crowd gathering as she approached the town square. What could be the reason? It had to be something important. She soon found out. A woman told her that the town crier was about to make an announcement.

The woman had hardly finished speaking when the portly figure of the town crier appeared. He rang his bell loudly as he walked. Advancing into the thick of the crowd, he stood up on a platform and regarded his audience as he unrolled the document he was carrying. With a loud voice he read out the contents.

'Now hear this. The High Council of Altaria has unanimously agreed that as there is no male descendant available at this time to rule the country, Princess Aleena, daughter of the late King Oliff, shall henceforth be accepted as the new monarch. Long live Queen Aleena!'

Having delivered his message, the town crier stepped down from his perch. He was besieged by citizens of the town who wanted to know more, but he had no further information to give them. Meanwhile the news was being discussed among the rest of the crowd. Some were greatly in favour of the High Council's decision, while a few others raised concerns about being ruled by a woman, but the majority treated the news as just another event that would not make their lives any easier.

Mela hurried home, anxious to bring the news to her father and tell Mogo and Daintry. The thought of Daintry once again brought her misery to the surface. Rather than lighten her guilt, her interview with Pastor Kartov had made things worse as a result of her admission that Daintry was at home again.

Mela's fear that the pastor would act on the information turned out to be justified. That evening he made his way to the Round Tower and the house of the constable. He did so with a heavy heart. He had known the Brouka family for many years, and Anton Brouka was a stalwart and upstanding citizen of Toomer. Nevertheless, as a man of the cloth he knew where his duty lay. Witchcraft was a scourge that had to be condemned, and those found practising it had to be punished as a warning to others.

Chapter 37

Anton Brouka had had a productive day. The fine, sunny weather had spurred him on to make the journey to see his one remaining mill and also to visit his sister Marna, whose husband, Rac, farmed some land further on from the mill.

He rarely saw Marna, because they had little in common and they did not get on well with each other. Now, however, circumstances were forcing him to ask her for help. Ever since Daintry had come home, he had feared for her safety. He also feared Adler's loose tongue. It would only be a matter of time before the secret was circulated that Daintry, having escaped from justice, was once again living under his roof. His plan was simple: he would send Daintry to stay with Marna and Rac. There on the isolated farm she would be safe.

Anton's suggestion did not meet with any enthusiasm from Marna. Why, she demanded, should she keep and feed Daintry for nothing? In the end Anton had been forced to give her a few silver coins from his now meagre savings and agree that Daintry would help with various household tasks. The arrangement was not perfect, but it was the best solution he could come up with to try to ensure Daintry's safety.

Before leaving Toomer, he had discussed the situation and his proposal with Daintry. Daintry was not keen to spend any time with her aunt, whom she could remember from her childhood as being cold and strict. She had pleaded with her father to be allowed to return to the Forest People, but he had firmly refused.

The sight of her returning home in the tattered and dirty clothes of a Forest Girl had saddened him. He had a deep fear that if he allowed her to return to the Forest People, his beloved daughter would be lost to him forever.

Having reached an agreement with his sister, Anton made his way to the mill. Since the loss of his second mill in the fire, this had been the only source of flour in the area. His miller, Andrei, had worked hard keeping the output of the mill going while Anton was ill, and Anton had formed a respect and admiration for the way he had run things in his absence. It now occurred to him that if there were no son-in-law to oversee the mill when he was no longer around, Andrei would be a most suitable candidate for the post. Unfortunately, his one mill did not produce sufficient flour to meet the demand, and the shortage of bread had been a constant worry for the people of Toomer and elsewhere.

Andrei was expecting him. As Anton rode up, he emerged from the mill and led the horse to a mounting block.

'Greetings, Master.' He held out a floury hand.

'Greetings, Andrei. Do things go well?'

Andrei looked up at the sky and grinned. 'I could do with more wind,' he announced.

Anton nodded in agreement as they made their way into the mill, its sails stationary in the still air.

Comar, Andrei's assistant, greeted his employer before scuttling away to a task in a different part of the mill.

For over an hour Anton and Andrei discussed the current situation. It was clear that in spite of Andrei's efforts the mill could never meet the demand placed upon it. The obligation to sell grain to Forancer had made things even worse.

After a while, Andrei brought up an interesting suggestion. Having satisfied himself that all the current business was completed, he raised the subject that had been occupying his thoughts for some months.

'Master, Comar and I have been looking at the new mill. We believe we could get it working.'

'What? Do you think so? Finishing it would require a lot of work, materials and equipment, and I have no money to spare now.'

Andrei thought for a moment, collecting his words to reply.

'The millstones are in place, as you know, as is the wheel. The roof needs more work, it is true, and we shall need a drive shaft, but we think we can salvage some items from the other mill.' He paused for a second and then added, 'We shall have to dig out the mill race again.'

Anton was warming to the idea. 'You really think all this is possible?' he asked.

Andrei nodded. 'I do.'

Anton was considering the practicalities. 'I don't know how much a new drive shaft would cost now,' he remarked, almost to himself. 'It was going to be twenty gold coins originally.'

He was beginning to feel optimistic about the possibility of opening the new mill. If Andrei could get it finished, it would solve a lot of problems. A watermill could grind corn day and night and would not be dependent on the wind. If only he could afford the drive shaft... All the money he had in the world was seventy gold coins.

'Comar and I can finish digging out the mill race in our spare time,' Andrei volunteered, looking at his employer hopefully.

'I will enquire about a drive shaft,' announced Anton firmly, his own passion for the watermill beginning to return.

The two chatted for a long time over the possible resurrection of Anton's dream. In the end they made a visit to the site, Andrei anxious to show Anton his ideas. Evening was approaching when Anton arrived home. It had, he decided, been a good day, and for the first time his enthusiasm and his interest in his business were beginning to return.

Darkness had already descended when there was a loud knocking at the door. Concerned, Anton rose from the supper table and made his way to open the door. The town constable stood there.

'What business do you have here?' Anton enquired none too politely, realising that what was happening was the thing he had feared most.

The constable cleared his throat. 'I have it on good authority that the convicted wench Daintry Brouka is living here once more.'

'What of it? How does that concern you?' Anton retorted.

'She is a criminal who has escaped justice. It is my job to ensure that she is confined again.'

The constable's words angered Anton. He glanced at the manacles the constable carried. Never would they be placed on his daughter. Memories of seeing her slaving at Katangar came back to him. He faced up to the constable.

'If you dare take my daughter, I swear I will put my sword through you.'

Anton's words appeared to deter the constable, who stood there in silence for a few seconds. Then he muttered, 'Rest assured: I will return with help,' and with that he turned on his heel and disappeared into the night.

Anton slammed the door and turned to face the women of the house, who on hearing the commotion had suddenly appeared behind him. Daintry had overheard the constable's words, and they struck fear into her. She realised that she was no longer safe in her father's house. Her previous experience of the Round Tower and Katangar flooded back to her. No, she decided: she would not go back there. She would kill herself rather than endure all that over again.

Anton acted swiftly. He knew that he had little time to get Daintry safely away. He issued his orders.

'Mogo, get Daintry ready. She must be dressed as a boy. Mela and Peena, help her. Daintry, prepare yourself for the journey. I am taking you to your aunt.'

Things happened quickly after that. Anton rushed off to obtain horses, and Daintry became the centre of attention. She was divested of her pretty dress and stood idle while some form of alternative clothing was found for her. There was nothing in the house in her size that would comply with Anton's instructions. In the end Daintry found herself dressed in one of her father's old shirts and a pair of his britches, both far too large for her. Her hair was bundled up under a hat, and an old pair of Mogo's boots was placed on her feet. The boots were much too big, and there was a danger of them slipping off as she walked.

'It's the best we can do in the time available,' grumbled a concerned Mogo.

The transformation of Daintry was barely complete before Anton returned. Daintry watched her father buckle on his sword and place two loaded pistols into his belt in preparation for the journey ahead of them.

Goodbyes were brief as Daintry, with tears in her eyes, was led outside to where two horses now stood waiting. Anton helped her up onto one of them. She had never ridden a horse before and was terrified at the prospect.

Father and daughter rode through the darkness. Few people were abroad, and they managed to leave the town without any problem.

Perched high on the horse, Daintry clung on desperately, fearful of falling. Fortunately her mount was placid and they proceeded slowly and steadily. They passed no other travellers.

It took them nearly two hours to travel to their destination. The isolated farm was already in darkness. Anton dismounted and pounded on the door with his fist. It was some time before a light appeared in one of the windows. The door opened slightly and Rac appeared, dressed in his nightshirt. There was no time for conversation before the door was wrenched from Rac's grasp and flung open wide. Marna stood there glaring at her brother.

Her voice expressed her displeasure. 'Anton! What is the meaning of this? We are a working house. We need our rest.'

Anton was apologetic. 'Marna, I am deeply sorry to arrive at this late hour, but it was dangerous for Daintry to remain in Toomer any longer.'

Marna appeared to accept her brother's explanation. 'Very well,' she said grudgingly. 'You're here now.' She turned to her husband. 'Rac, get the girl down off the horse.'

Rac jumped into action. He was a man of slim build, unlike his wife, who was large and muscular. He lifted Daintry off the horse and set her down on the ground.

Goodbyes were brief. Anton hardly had time to embrace his daughter and tell her to do all she can to help her aunt, before Marna cut him short. 'Very well, Anton. You have delivered the girl. There is no need for you to linger. We need some more sleep.'

With that Anton had little alternative other than to remount his horse and with a final wave start his return journey.

Marna immediately turned to Daintry. 'Don't just stand there. Into the house, girl.' She grabbed Daintry's arm and shoved her through the door.

The cottage appeared to be small. By the light of the candle Rac carried Daintry could see that she was in the kitchen. Marna nodded in the direction of the stove. 'You can sleep there.' She grabbed a blanket from somewhere and flung it onto the floor. Then she and Rac retreated through a door, leaving Daintry with no light except for the dim red glow from the embers that still burned in the stove. Daintry had little option other than to curl up on the blanket in front of it.

Daintry spent a restless night. It was difficult for her to adjust to the hardness of her bed and her sudden removal once again from familiar surroundings. Within hours she had been plucked from a comfortable, amenable environment to one that appeared to be quite hostile. In the past she had had little contact with her aunt, but she had formed the opinion that Marna was very different from her brother.

A nudge from a booted foot woke her. Aunt Marna stood over her. 'You lazy girl,' she snapped. 'You should have had the stove lit by now. You must work here to earn your keep.'

Daintry scrambled to her feet. She had hardly slept at all, and only towards the latter part of the night had she had any rest. She hurriedly started to light the fire in the stove under Marna's critical gaze.

It was when Rac appeared for breakfast that the first stirrings of fear of her aunt crept into Daintry. During sleep she had abandoned the cap she had been wearing to conceal her hair, and her curls now fell loose about her shoulders.

Suddenly Marna declared, 'That hair of yours will have to be shorn off. It will get in the way of your work.'

To give action to her words she picked up a knife from the table.

Daintry's reaction was to let out a shriek. 'No! NO! Please, not my hair. I'll keep it under the cap.'

Her protest failed to deter her aunt, who advanced towards her menacingly. Daintry was now backing away, shouting at the top of her voice, 'No! No!'

It was her uncle who came to her rescue. 'Let the girl be, Marna,' he growled.

His words seemed to have an impact. Marna flung the knife down with the remark, 'Very well. But if it gets in the way of your work, it's off.'

From then on, this was a constant fear for Daintry, as the threat was issued by her aunt on several occasions in the following days.

It soon became abundantly clear to Daintry that she was regarded as nothing more than a servant. Marna kept her busy from early morning until late at night. When she was not working for her complaining aunt, she was expected to help her uncle in the fields, often being obliged to undertake tasks that were hard and too heavy for her. It was also quite obvious that in the relationship between her aunt and uncle it was her aunt who ruled the roost. Rac spent most of the day outside, away from the cottage. He appeared to be a man of few words, and on the occasions Daintry was working with him he said little, merely showing or telling her what to do.

The same could not be said of Marna. Complaints and grumbling rained down on Daintry as she struggled with the workload she was allotted. It was a constant flow of abuse. She was lazy. She was slow. She had not been brought up properly.

She had been staying with her aunt and uncle for almost a week when it happened.

On that particular morning Marna was busy doing the washing, and it was Daintry's task to fetch water from the well, which was a couple of minutes' walk away. Having only the boots that were far too big for her, Daintry struggled to carry the heavy pails of water. The water had to be drawn from the well by a bucket, and the windlass used to lift the full bucket was extremely hard to turn. Every time Daintry returned to the cottage, Marna grumbled and berated her for being so slow.

'But it's so hard to get the water up from the well,' Daintry pleaded, to no avail.

She had just returned with another load of water when Marna suddenly lunged at her. 'You lazy girl!' she shouted in Daintry's ear. 'You need a sharp lesson.'

She took hold of Daintry's arm and marched her towards a nearby barn. Daintry did her best to struggle free, but Marna was much bigger and stronger than she was, and she held Daintry's arm securely. Daintry was suddenly aware that her aunt had a switch in her other hand.

Daintry was pushed face downward over a bale of straw and held down firmly. The next instant her shirt was lifted up and blows started to rain down on her back. She started to scream and beg at the top of her voice, but her pleas were ignored. She lost count of the number of strokes her aunt delivered.

Eventually the hand holding her down released its grip and the punishment ended.

'Let that be a lesson to you,' her aunt commanded. With that she was gone, leaving a sobbing Daintry slumped over the bale.

Daintry's back burned, and for what seemed a long time she just remained where she was. Eventually, still in a state of shock, she stood up slowly and gingerly and carefully pulled down her shirt. She stumbled out of the barn into the sunlight. There was nobody in sight. Her aunt had returned to her washing.

Almost automatically, Daintry started walking, still in a daze and with no idea which direction to take. She had a compelling urge to get away from the place where she had been so brutally treated. She tried to run, but her boots hampered her progress, so she returned to walking again. It did not take long for her to reach the road down which her father had brought her a few days previously. She started to follow it, with no destination in mind. She was unprepared for what happened next. Rounding a blind bend, she suddenly came face to face with her uncle. There was nowhere to hide or run.

He was as surprised as she was. 'What are you doing here, girl?' he demanded.

Daintry shook her head. Words would not come.

Rac grabbed her arm and forced her to walk beside him. Within a few minutes they were back at the farmstead. Marna stood in the doorway of the cottage, observing them as they approached.

Her uncle grinned. 'Look who I found on the road.'

His remark rekindled Marna's wrath. 'You ungrateful girl! How dare you run away!' As she spat out the words, she seized hold of her niece. Daintry found herself being propelled towards the woodshed in her aunt's steel grip. The door of the shed was opened, Daintry was pushed inside, and the door was closed and secured with a bar.

Her aunt's voice sounded again. 'You'll stay there until suppertime.' With that she was gone.

Daintry sank onto the floor of her prison. It was all too much. How could she be treated so cruelly by her own family? When would her life return to normal?

Chapter 38

Assem Rokar was slightly apprehensive. He was on his way to the second meeting of the new High Council of Altaria. In the last few weeks the burden on him had been heavy. First had been the installation of Conrad Accker as Keeper of the Purse, and then arrangements had to be made for the crowning ceremony of Queen Aleena, a simple affair without the glamour and pomp such occasions usually demanded. Before this event could take place, however, the High Council had to approve the appointment of Altaria's first queen.

Assem had painstakingly made contact with some of the old members of the council, people he knew could be trusted to conduct themselves for the good of the country. Sadly, his progress had been hampered when one of them turned his invitation down, refusing to serve under a woman. Elgar Rigor, the former commander of the rebel army, had willingly accepted a place on the council. Vasil Rojak, the instigator of the insurrection, had declined. As far as he was concerned the job was done and others could take over, and he retreated back into obscurity. Eventually Assem had managed to secure sufficient members for the High Council to operate legitimately.

Assem had skilfully masterminded the process, breaking a few rules here and there. At the first meeting the installation of the new council members and the appointment of ministers, followed by the council's official approval of Princess Aleena as the country's first queen, had gone reasonably smoothly, mainly due to Assem's behind-the-scenes efforts. It had been unanimously agreed by all present that Assem would be the council's new First Minister.

Now a second meeting was to be held to get down to the task of running the country and regaining the stability so abused during King Henri's brief reign.

When Assem entered the council chamber, most of the rest of the members were already sitting around the table, waiting for the arrival of Queen Aleena, who had recently left Assem's house and moved back into the palace. Assem took his place close to the head of the table. Conrad Accker, as Keeper of the Queen's Purse, sat opposite him.

Queen Aleena entered and the group rose from their chairs.

The queen greeted the assembly with a pleasant smile and a cheery 'Good day, gentlemen.'

After that it was down to business in earnest. Ministers wanted to know the state of the country's finances, and Conrad had to admit that they were not good. The country was desperately short of money to pay its way.

One minister raised his concern at the lawlessness that had crept into the country under the administration of the previous council and the rule of King Henri. This prompted a question from another minister, who asked how many guardsmen were now available.

Pagar Yarrow, who was once again in control of the renamed Queen's Guard, responded. 'At present the number is one hundred and fifty loyal men.'

'Can we not recruit more?' Elgar Rigor asked. 'There must be many able and willing men who saw service in the rebel movement.'

'I propose that we try to do that,' replied Assem. Then he added, 'I also propose that a small number remain here to guard the palace and the city of Taslar and the rest be temporarily deployed throughout the kingdom to help the constables keep law and order.'

'I think that is an excellent idea,' the queen remarked thoughtfully.

Echoes of agreement sounded around the table.

Slowly the council worked its way through the agenda, looking at and dealing with the various areas of administration that had been neglected by its predecessor. As the meeting drew to a close there was a general feeling of satisfaction and optimism with the way it had been proceeding.

Up until this point Queen Aleena had taken a supporting role, giving encouragement here and there but remaining conscious that she was a woman in a hitherto male-dominated area. Now she had something to say to her ministers.

'Gentlemen,' she began, 'I beg your attention, for I have a personal request to make, which I hope you will approve.' She paused, gathering her thoughts.

All those present waited in silence for her to continue. They did not have to wait long for her to elaborate.

'I wish to discontinue the employment of women in the mines at Katangar.' There were a few expressions of surprise from around the table. But the queen had not finished. 'I also want to issue a royal pardon for all those women who have been incarcerated there, whatever their crimes.'

This proposal received a mixed reception.

'I believe that this change should take place,' announced Assem.

'I too, believe this should happen,' declared Conrad.

'But if we do that we will lose production, and in turn income from the mines,' pointed out one of the original members of the council.

'These women are criminals. They should stay where they are,' asserted another.

Queen Aleena turned to him. 'I was at Katangar. Would you have the country ruled by a queen who carries the mark of Katangar – a criminal?' she asked.

The man looked uncomfortable and made no reply.

The queen had more to add. 'Many of the women at Katangar have committed no crime at all. Some are innocent young girls, who could be your daughters.'

Her words seemed to have a dramatic effect. In the end the proposal was unanimously agreed to. It was left to Assem to raise a Royal Command announcing the changes.

The meeting broke up. It had been a long session, and much had been discussed and plans put in place to deal with the problems that faced the kingdom.

As the queen was leaving the chamber, Assem addressed her.

'Your Majesty, I would request some of your time to show you something of vital importance.'

Queen Aleena consented immediately. She had a certain fondness for the white-haired Assem and relied on his wisdom very much at this present time. A suitable time was arranged, and then the queen departed.

Assem and Conrad were left alone in the chamber. Assem caught Conrad by the arm. 'You must also attend the meeting with the queen,' he emphasised. 'I have important news to impart.'

Intrigued, Conrad would have liked to ask for more information, but Assem immediately changed the subject. He smiled at the younger man. 'Are you not overjoyed by the queen's proposal?' he asked.

Conrad regarded Assem for a second, his look questioning.

Assem elaborated. 'If a royal pardon is given to all the women who were at Katangar, then that will include the fair maiden you have an interest in. You will be able to take her as your wife.'

'If she still wants to be my wife,' Conrad replied sadly.

Assem did not reply. He had been concerned about the melancholy that had enveloped Conrad since his brief meeting with Daintry in the marketplace of Taslar, but there had been little he could do other than offer sympathy when needed.

When Daintry had run away from him, Conrad had spent hours frantically searching for her, but his efforts had been in vain: she seemed to have disappeared into thin air. Word of Conrad's dilemma had reached the ears of Queen Aleena, who had been anxious when she received the news of Daintry's disappearance. She had sent one of her servants to assist Conrad in his search, but no trace of Daintry had been discovered in Taslar. Conrad had sacrificed time from his work to make a quick journey to Toomer and a visit to the Brouka household. There he had learnt from Anton that Daintry was living with her aunt for safety. Anton had refused to tell him where Daintry was, and Conrad had returned to Taslar deeply disappointed. He had subsequently immersed himself in his role as Keeper of the Purse.

It was later on the day of the meeting of the High Council that Conrad, Queen Aleena and Sharla joined Assem for what he explained to them was to be a visit to a part of the palace that contained a secret. Assem led the group down to the lower floors of the palace by the light of the lanterns he and Conrad carried. This was an area that was rarely visited, and the steep stone stairways and dark corridors were full of dust and dirt. Conrad was intrigued to learn what Assem had to show them, but Queen Aleena was clearly puzzled as to why her trusted Assem had insisted that she accompany him to such an awful place. Sharla showed obvious signs of discomfort and fear.

They walked for what seemed to Assem's three companions to be a long time along the narrow corridors, the two women holding up their skirts to avoid the dusty floor. At last Assem stopped in front of a door that was covered in spiders' webs. He took a large key out of his pocket and fitted it into the lock. He had trouble operating the mechanism, and he and Conrad wrestled with it for several minutes. At last Conrad managed to turn the key. The heavy door grated on the floor, and Conrad had to help Assem push it open so that they could all enter.

The light from the lanterns revealed a small room, devoid of anything apart from two chests, which were covered in dust. Assem produced two more keys and then addressed Queen Aleena.

'Your Majesty, your father was a careful and a thinking man. He cared passionately for Altaria and was always concerned about its future. It was under his direction that these chests were started. It was his security in case difficult times came to Altaria.'

As he finished speaking, Assem turned his attention to one of the chests. The key turned easily in the lock, and he lifted the lid to reveal a large number of canvas bags, the neck of each carefully fastened with a cord. Assem untied one of the cords and tipped the contents of the bag onto the lid of the chest. Gold coins spilled out. Turning to his astonished watchers, he announced with a smile, 'Every bag is full of gold coins, and the other chest contains the same.'

For the first time, Queen Aleena spoke. 'Assem, there must be a fortune here!'

Assem nodded. 'There is.'

'Can this money be used by the Purse?' asked Conrad.

'It can indeed,' Assem assured him. 'That was King Oliff's intention.'

The reality of the situation began to take shape for both the queen and Conrad.

'That means we can cut the burden of taxation on the people,' Conrad observed excitedly.

'The mines at Katangar need no longer employ convicts. They can be changed to employ only skilled free men who will work there willingly for good recompense,' Queen Aleena said thoughtfully.

'We need no longer sell our precious grain stocks to Forancer to get an income,' added Conrad.

Queen Aleena wanted to know more. 'How did you learn about this money?' she asked Assem.

Assem explained. 'Your father entrusted me with his secret and gave the keys to me shortly before his death, begging me to keep the money safe for the future.'

'And you never told my brother?' the queen queried with a slight smile.

Assem shook his head. 'No,' he replied.

The queen regarded him sternly for few seconds. 'That was an act of treason, Assem,' she remarked casually, but she was smiling, almost laughing, at the same time.

'I felt it was my duty to safeguard the secret until there was a real need,' Assem replied.

'And the need is certainly now,' agreed the queen. Then she turned to Conrad. 'You will have quite a task counting all this money, Conrad.'

Conrad smiled. 'Your Majesty, it will be my pleasure,' he replied.

'Let me know how much there is,' the queen announced with a smile. Then she addressed her First Minister again. 'Assem, give the keys to the Keeper of the Purse.'

Assem readily obliged. Locking the chest, he smiled and handed Conrad the keys.

Chapter 39

Anton Brouka was in a more positive frame of mind. Changes were taking place in the country. There was now an air of hope and expectation in Toomer. The town crier appeared more often on his plinth in the market square, and each time he seemed to be the bearer of good news for the townspeople. While in some quarters there had been a critical and scornful reaction to the announcement that the kingdom was to have its first queen, now that concerns about the event had settled down it seemed that the change had given rise to a new optimism. First had been the news that the burden of taxes on the population was to be reduced. Then had been the appearance of members of the now renamed Queen's Guard who had been drafted in to keep law and order. This had created a feeling of security and stability in the kingdom.

On a personal level Anton was beginning to feel much more confident about the future of his mills. He had been impressed by the hard work of Andrei and his assistant in managing to finish building the new watermill. He had witnessed with admiration Andrei's dedication and was now beginning to look upon the young miller as someone who could safeguard the future of his mills. Anton had managed to have a drive shaft prepared, and it had been a momentous day when the giant watermill had first started turning, backed by the availability of the first grain from the country's harvest. It was now generally known that grain was no longer being sent to Forancer. This all meant a brighter future for Anton and his family.

Anton's brighter mood was however dampened by the situation regarding Daintry. When she had reappeared dirty and dishevelled on the doorstep he had been overjoyed, but he had also been aware of the danger she was in. When the constable had appeared a few days later to arrest her yet again, his fears had been confirmed. He had bitterly regretted having to take Daintry to his sister, because he knew well enough his sister's hard and unyielding character. Yet he had felt that their farm was the only place where Daintry would be safe. Since taking her there, he had not even visited her, fearful that his movements might be watched by those wanting to make mischief.

When Conrad had appeared in Toomer in search of Daintry, Anton had found himself in a dilemma. While he had eventually looked with favour on Conrad's interest in his younger daughter, he now knew that this interest was misplaced. He resented bitterly the fact that Daintry was now a marked woman and would carry that stigma for the rest of her life, and he had been forced to remonstrate with Conrad that it was no longer possible for him to marry Daintry. He had felt sad at having to send Conrad back to Taslar so downhearted, but he felt that it was for the best. If Conrad, who now held one of the highest and most important positions in the country, were to marry Daintry, he would find his position undermined. Anton had even suggested that Mela might be a better proposition as a bride, but the idea had not gone down well with Conrad. Anton was conscious that Mela should already be married, but so far the candidates he had selected for consideration as bridegrooms had been met with scorn by her. He was acutely aware that eventually he would have to overrule Mela's opposition and decide for her.

Anton was completely unaware of the present state of Mela's mind. After Daintry's arrest, she had become overcome by remorse at the result of her actions. She had kept the secret to herself, but it had caused her many sleepless nights. When Daintry had reappeared and related the brutal treatment she had received, Mela had been affected very badly. Sometimes the idea had even come to her to commit some sort of crime that would result in her been sent to Katangar so that she would suffer equally to Daintry, but the thought of what she would have to endure had stifled her bravery.

When in her misery she had ventured into the church and been comforted by Pastor Kartov, she had been seeking freedom from her guilt and unhappiness, but she had not been prepared for being almost forced into admitting that her sister was free again. As the reality of her admission began to sink in, she had been once again overcome with anxiety and guilt, and when the constable had appeared a few hours later to arrest Daintry, Mela had been thrown into an even deeper state of remorse. Twice she had denounced her sister, the first time out of petty jealousy and the second through innocently seeking her own absolution. Overwhelmed by guilt, she had silently helped Mogo prepare Daintry for the journey to Aunt Marna's farm. In the days following Daintry's departure she had become quiet and withdrawn. She helped Mogo and Peena with the household jobs and then retreated to her room, tormented with shame.

One morning early, after yet another a sleepless night, she made up her mind. As if in a dream she left the house and walked through the streets, her head swathed in a shawl. Nobody recognised her as she purposefully made her way to a stone bridge just outside the town. Here the river flowed swiftly and was deep. She knew it was a favourite place for those seeking escape through death.

As she approached the bridge, her pace quickened, action initiated by the fear that at the last minute she would change her mind. Still determined, she hurriedly glanced around to see if anybody was watching. There was nobody in sight. Quickly she climbed onto the low wall at the side of the bridge. She sat there for a second or two, staring into the fast-flowing water swollen by recent rain; then with a slight effort she hurled herself forward.

She seemed to fall for a long time and then she hit the water. It enveloped her as she sank, seeping into every part of her. She desperately hoped that the end would be quick as the water entered her nose and mouth, causing her to splutter and choke. She found herself instinctively struggling in the water. Suddenly she felt a firm surface beneath her. The fast flow of the river had carried her away from the deep section and into a shallow area. With her soaked clothing she was lying face down in a foot of water, choking on its intrusion into her body. Suddenly she felt herself being lifted by a strong pair of arms and dragged out of the river. She was laid gently on the ground, coughing and trying to regain her breath. She was aware of a voice and somebody near her.

Strong hands turned her over. She found herself looking into the bluest eyes she had ever seen. The owner was talking to her. 'Are you all right? Can you speak?'

Somehow she managed to reply. 'Yes. Thank you.'

He spoke again, his tone warm and caring. 'You fell into the river. I was passing and I pulled you out.'

Mela struggled to sit up. She tried to assess what was happening to her. A young man dressed in the uniform of the Queen's Guard was bending over her. His arm was around her shoulders, partly supporting her. His face had a look of concern as he spoke again. 'Do you feel you are injured? Do you think you can walk?

'I do not think I have injured myself.' As if to give an emphasis to the statement, Mela made a move to stand up. Her rescuer helped her, with a firm arm around her.

Mela stood wet and dripping water in front of the young man. She suddenly felt embarrassed. She almost blushed as she thanked her saviour. 'I am most grateful, sir, for your assistance, but I fear I have disrupted your journey.'

The blue eyes were focused on her as the young man replied. 'It has been my pleasure. It was fortunate that I was passing this way and able to assist you.'

Mela suddenly shivered in the cool air.

Her rescuer noticed immediately. 'I will accompany you to your home. Do you live near here?' he asked.

'I am Mela Brouka, of this town.' As she spoke, Mela glanced briefly behind her in the direction of Toomer.

'I am Tomaz Razner, the Queen's Messenger, and I am on my way to the town of Toomer. It will be my privilege to escort you to your home.' He had hardly finished when Mela started to shiver uncontrollably. He immediately removed his uniform coat and placed it around her shoulders.

'Thank you,' Mela whispered, her eyes now firmly focused on Tomaz. She was beginning to be quite intrigued by her rescuer.

'Come, we must get you home at once, before you die of cold.'

Again he placed his arm around her shoulders. 'Can you walk?' he asked again.

Mela looked up at him. She gave a slight smile. 'Yes, I think so,' she replied.

Tomaz gently encouraged her to take a few steps. For the first time Mela noticed another man, also in uniform, standing holding two horses a short distance away.

Mela glanced at her feet. 'I have lost my shoes,' she exclaimed, almost embarrassed.

They had reached the horses. Tomaz took hold of the reins and instructed the other man, whose name was Marcu, to search for Mela's lost shoes. He waded into the river but found only one. Its companion had disappeared.

'A maiden cannot walk the streets without shoes,' Tomaz remarked, smiling at Mela. With strong hands he lifted her up onto one of the horses.

Slowly they made their way to the town, Mela perched high up on the horse led by Tomaz. She directed them to her father's house.

Once they were there, frantic activity took place, Mogo at first scolding Mela for falling into the river and then despatching her with Peena to get out of her wet clothes. Anton appeared and immediately ordered some refreshment for Mela's rescuers.

Gradually things settled down. Over a meal Tomaz explained that as the newly appointed Queen's Messenger he was now employed transferring information to the town criers for them to announce to the citizens the new laws and changes that would affect them. The family listened intently as he related how he had risen to the rank of captain in the old King's Guard and had been the messenger who, in secret, had regularly brought news to Princess Aleena when she had been in hiding with the Forest People.

Anton was immediately alert on hearing this piece of information. 'My younger daughter, Daintry, was also looked after by the Forest People,' he interjected.

Tomaz stared at him for a second and then exclaimed, 'Daintry? I remember the maiden there! She was cared for by Princess Aleena.'

Anton smiled. 'That is true,' he agreed.

'But where is she now?' Tomaz queried, looking around the table.

Anton looked grave. 'I ask you to hold a secret. She is in hiding.'

As Tomaz looked at him, seeking more information, Anton added miserably, 'She was at Katangar. Alas, as a marked criminal, she is now a fugitive.'

Anton's statement alerted Tomaz to his present mission. Excitedly opening the pouch at his belt, he held up a document. 'But no more!' he exclaimed. 'Here is a document signed by Queen Aleena, which I am taking to the town crier. It grants a royal pardon to all the women who were at Katangar, whatever their crimes.'

'What?' Anton could hardly believe the good news. Addressing Tomaz, he exclaimed, 'You have brought welcome tidings to our house!'

Tomaz's news changed many things. For the first time, Anton felt happier for his younger daughter. As soon as he considered that she would be completely safe he would bring her home, away from his domineering sister.

Anton was not the only person inspired by Tomaz's announcement. For Mela, the news was even more dramatic. For the first time, the cloud of misery was starting to lift. It was almost as if she were being released from her guilt and remorse. She now realised the feeble stupidity of her attempt to drown herself. It was a miracle that Tomaz had been at the spot to rescue her. Thankfully, there appeared to be a general acceptance from those present that she had simply fallen into the river. No one had enquired how she had come to do so – not even Mogo.

Something else was beginning to lift Mela's gloom. Ever since she had first set her gaze on Tomaz's blue eyes she had been attracted to him. He had acted so gallantly towards her, and he was so handsome in his uniform. She had listened with interest to his stories of life in Taslar, which had no comparison to the life she led in Toomer. When he conveyed during the course of the conversation that he was not married, she decided he was a suitable candidate for her consideration.

Mela's fascination had not gone unnoticed by Tomaz. Later, when he and Anton were conversing, Tomaz brought up the subject that had been developing ever since he had pulled Mela from the river. It was Anton who gave him the opportunity to ask the question that was uppermost in his mind.

'I am indebted to you, sir, for rescuing my daughter.'

'I consider it to be my good fortune. She is a comely maiden,' Tomaz replied politely.

He was determined to ask his next question.

'I would like to ask if she is yet spoken for in terms of marriage.'

Anton was not surprised at the question. He had observed the attraction developing between the young man and Mela. 'As yet, no man has offered her his cap,' he affirmed.

Tomaz was elated. 'Then I pray you, sir, allow me to offer Mela my hand in marriage.'

Anton nodded and smiled. 'You have my permission to ask her,' he replied.

Chapter 40

Daintry's life with her aunt and uncle did not improve. After Marna had cruelly beaten her, and Rac had foiled her attempt to run away, she squatted on the floor of the woodshed, sunk in misery, a sore back reminding her of her aunt's punishment as she wondered what lay in store for her.

When she was released from her prison several hours later, Marna was completely unrelenting.

'Let that be a lesson for you. And don't be so lazy in future,' she snapped, as a sorrowful Daintry emerged from her captivity.

'I will try harder, but please do not beat me again. If you do I will run away,' Daintry replied miserably.

Her aunt made no reply, but perhaps Daintry's threat had some effect, because the punishment was not repeated. Unfortunately, incarceration in the woodshed for some misdemeanour or other did take place from time to time.

Change came one day when Daintry was ordered to help her uncle Rac with a most unpleasant task. She found herself shovelling animal manure into large baskets, to be carried out to the fields. It was a back-breaking job and extremely dirty. Very soon she was covered in the filth. It splattered all over her, and the stench was equally hard to cope with. Her uncle had just departed, taking a load to the fields, and she was filling another, when she suddenly became aware of a familiar voice calling her name.

She looked in the direction of the sound. A wagon had stopped at the edge of the yard and her father was descending from it. The faces of Mela and Peena were peering out from the canvas-covered wagon.

Daintry uttered a cry of anguish. 'Father!' She dropped the shovel and stood there wretched and dirty, tears beginning to stream down her face.

At that instant, alerted to the noise, Marna emerged from the cottage.

Anton looked at Daintry and then rounded angrily on his sister. 'Marna, what is the meaning of this? Am I to understand that this is the daughter I placed in your care?' As he finished speaking he nodded in the direction of Daintry.

Marna went white. 'W-we agreed she would work her keep,' she stuttered in reply. At that moment Rac reappeared.

Anton took control. 'Marna, Rac, come with me. I want to talk to you.' As he made a move towards the cottage, he addressed Mela and Peena, who were still on the wagon gazing in disbelief at the dishevelled Daintry. 'Mela, Peena, get Daintry cleaned up.'

Anton, his sister and her husband disappeared into the cottage. Mela and Peena set to work on Daintry. They could do little more than lead her to the well, help her out of her soiled garments and try to eliminate most of the dirt and smell with cold water. They produced the clothes they had brought with them and helped her into them.

Daintry was at first bewildered by the sudden change in her situation and the speed of events. 'What is happening?' she asked. 'Why are you and Father here?'

Mela grinned at her. 'We've come to take you home.'

Daintry was still puzzled. 'But why? The constable will come for me again.'

Mela smiled again. 'I don't think so – not now,' she replied.

Daintry wanted to know more, but at that instant her father emerged from the cottage, still looking angry, followed by a subdued Marna. Rac accompanied his wife, but quickly disappeared.

'Is Daintry ready to travel?' Anton asked Mela. He was clearly in a hurry to leave.

'Yes, Father.'

Silently Anton ushered the three young women into the wagon. He flicked the reins of the horses and the party moved off. His sister, who stood watching in silence, was ignored by all four occupants of the wagon.

There was little conversation on the journey back to Toomer. Daintry was still perplexed by what had happened, but neither Mela nor Peena appeared inclined to talk. She was left to ponder in silence why she was being allowed to return home.

As soon as they were back in the Brouka household, Moga took charge. Staring at Daintry, she suddenly held her nose. 'Daintry, you stink.' Turning to Mela and Peena, she issued her commands. 'Peena, prepare a bath for Daintry. Mela, don't just stand there. Help your sister.'

Daintry found herself being scrubbed clean, closely supervised by the critical Mogo. It felt wonderful to be dressed in the comfort of her own clothing again.

When she was alone with her sister shortly afterwards, she again asked the question that was bothering her. 'Why has Father brought me home? What has changed?'

Mela smiled. 'It's good news. Queen Aleena has granted a royal pardon for all the women who were at Katangar.'

Daintry tried to let Mela's words sink in. It all seemed too good to be true. She felt as if a huge burden had been lifted from her. Perhaps she would no longer need to fear the arrival of the constable. She wanted to ask more questions, but Mela had another piece of news to relate.

'I'm going to be married,' she announced, grinning broadly.

'Oh! Who are you going to marry?' asked Daintry.

'Somebody you know,' Mela replied, still smiling.

'Somebody I know…?' Daintry repeated, dreading the answer, for in her mind it could only be Conrad.

But she was wrong. Clearly excited by the prospect, Mela was eager to relate her new status to her sister. 'I'm going to marry Tomaz Razner, the Queen's Messenger. He asked me to marry him, and I accepted. Father has agreed as well. We'll live in a fine house in Taslar.'

It took Daintry a second or two to recall the handsome young man who had regularly visited Princess Aleena when they had been living with the Forest People.

'I remember Tomaz,' she recalled quietly. Then she hugged her sister. 'I hope you will be very happy. He is a fine young man.'

Mela suddenly broke away. She regarded Daintry anxiously. 'Can you really forgive me for what I did to you?'

Daintry hugged her again. 'Dear Mela! Of course I forgive you.'

In the short time that she had been reunited with her sister, Daintry had noticed the change in her. She was no longer the sulky, brooding Mela, but instead was exhibiting a cheerful radiance that was new. Daintry was glad for her.

Before she could ask Mela anything else, Peena appeared. She spoke to Daintry. 'Mistress, the master has asked me to find you and tell you he wants to see you.'

Daintry hurried to her father's workroom. She was anxious to learn more from him about her new status.

Her father jumped up as she entered. He walked towards her and suddenly embraced her.

'My precious daughter, can you ever forgive me for sending you to Aunt Marna?' he asked sadly.

There were tears in Daintry's eyes as she replied. 'Please don't ever send me there again, Father. I'd a thousand times rather go and hide with the Forest People.'

'Neither will be necessary now,' her father replied, as he sat down again at his table. He waved towards a chair. 'Come and sit down and I will explain.'

Daintry obeyed.

Anton regarded her for an instant. Clasping his hands on the table, he recalled events.

'Shortly after I took you to Aunt Marna, the constable returned with some men from the Guard. They were angry to find that you were no longer here and they made numerous threats against me.' He paused for a second. 'But there was little they could do.'

Daintry made no reply. The night the constable had come to arrest her was still a vivid memory. She wanted to ask her father more about the change to her situation, but she could see he had more to relate. His face became angry for a second as he continued.

'I deeply regret sending you to your aunt. I knew she was strict and had a cruel streak in her, but I never dreamed she would treat you the way she did.' He suddenly looked closely at Daintry. 'Mogo tells me that you were whipped. Is that true?'

Mogo had seen the fading marks on Daintry's back while her sister and Peena were bathing her, and she had asked her about them.

Daintry nodded and whispered, 'Yes.'

'It will never happen again. I cannot forgive my sister for that,' Anton exclaimed angrily.

Daintry was still anxious to learn more about her current circumstances. She steered the conversation by asking another question.

'Father, what will happen to me now? Mela told me that the women who were at Katangar have all been pardoned.'

Anton almost had tears in his eyes as he replied.

'It's true. It's the best news ever. The new queen has granted a royal pardon to all the women who were at Katangar. God bless Queen Aleena.'

Daintry was slowly coming to terms with her new status. 'Does that mean that I am free and the constable will not come for me again?' she asked cautiously.

Her father looked at her. He was smiling. 'Of course. That is what it means.'

'I am so glad,' Daintry whispered. The load she had been carrying was slowly lifting.

'And your sister is to be married. Tomaz Razner will make a fine husband for her.'

Daintry did not reply immediately. Her father spoke again.

'I have asked Tomaz to wait a while, as I did with you and Conrad, so that I can furnish you both with a proper dowry.'

At the mention of Conrad, Daintry was suddenly sad. What would happen now? She had assured him that she could not marry him.

Anton could see that his younger daughter's silence reflected a concern. 'Do you still want to marry Conrad?' he asked quietly.

'I do, Father, but I fear he may not wish to marry me now. I told him to find somebody else, because I bear the mark of Katangar.' Daintry was close to tears as she expressed her doubts.

Anton smiled lovingly at her. 'I think he does wish to marry you. When you were with Aunt Marna he came seeking you, but I could not tell him where you were.'

Daintry looked at her father. This new information alleviated her anxiety slightly. Would Conrad come again and ask her to marry him? Or would her conduct in Taslar and his inability to make contact with her have made him change his mind? She prayed that this had not happened, but all she could do was wait and hope.

Chapter 41

For the first few days after her homecoming Daintry tried very hard to return to the life she had led before her ordeal. She helped Mogo and did her share of the housework and endeavoured to return to some sort of normality. At first she was reluctant to venture out of the security of the house. In spite of the reassurances she had received, past events were still very much part of her life and she still feared that something might change and the constable would appear again to arrest her. The thought was a constant companion.

Her first outing since returning home was when Anton took her and Mela to see the new mill in operation. Mainly as a result of the efforts of Andrei and his assistant, the great wheel of the mill had begun to turn on a regular basis and produce much-needed flour. Both girls knew that this would greatly improve the family's fortunes, and they had witnessed the more cheerful bearing of their father. Mela in particular was keenly interested in the new mill, because if all went well with it her father would soon have sufficient money to provide for her dowry, and then she could marry Tomaz, which at this time was all she could think about.

The visit was a happy one. A number of people from the nearby village came to watch the great wheel turning. A celebration meal was laid out on a table beside the mill, with most of the food paid for by Anton and prepared by Mogo, Mela and Daintry. The village women also contributed some food, for their community had an interest in the mill and the prosperity it would bring. Already Anton had employed two men from the village to work there. The celebration went on for a long time, as people enjoyed themselves in the pleasant autumn sunshine. In the evening there was music and dancing. It was late when Anton and his two daughters left the scene. Daintry was pleased to see her father looking much happier again. Only her constant underlying worry about Conrad cast a shadow on the day for her.

Mela in particular had appeared to enjoy herself to the full, and on the way home she chatted freely to Daintry. Now that she was betrothed to Tomaz, relations between the two sisters had improved greatly. They talked together, their differences swept aside. Daintry listened and responded, but beneath her outwardly happy demeanour her misery was increasing. She had not heard from Conrad since her return from Aunt Marna, and as each day passed she became more and more convinced that her action in the market at Taslar had driven him away. For the most part she kept her sadness to herself, just doing her work and from time to time listening to Mela relate her ambitions for the future.

An unexpected visit from Tomaz was a highlight in the Brouka household, particularly for Mela, for it was clear that the main reason for it was to see her.

Once again Tomaz was invited to dine with the family, and Mogo, Mela and Daintry prepared a sumptuous meal. As they ate, Tomaz described the events that were happening in Taslar. He was particularly pleased to relate that he had been invited by the queen to have a place on the High Council, and he was looking forward to his new role.

It was inevitable that Mela took up as much of Tomaz's attention as possible, and Daintry found it difficult to ask the question that was uppermost in her mind. Eventually things went her way and she found herself more or less alone with him, with only Peena close by.

It was Tomaz who spoke first. Smiling at Daintry, he remarked, 'I am pleased to see that you are now home and looking so well after your ordeal.'

Daintry felt herself blushing as she remembered how she must have appeared to Tomaz during his visits to the camp of the Forest People. She replied quietly, 'Thank you. I am well now.'

Tomaz smiled at her again. He had almost been unable to recognise her at first, because she looked so different from his memories of her. Now that she was wearing a pretty dress, her curls falling around her shoulders, he realised what an attractive young woman she was.

'I will tell Queen Aleena you are safe and well,' he offered. 'She will be pleased to have news of you.'

'Thank you,' replied Daintry. Finally she had the chance to ask her question. 'How is Conrad?'

'He is well, but he is working very hard in his new role,' explained Tomaz.

Daintry was keen to know more, but at that moment Mela returned and once again Tomaz's attention was occupied. Daintry had to be content with the meagre news she had received.

Eventually Mela persuaded Daintry to accompany her to the market to buy food. Still slightly reluctant, Daintry overcame her fear and walked into the town with her sister. At first she was afraid that people would stare at her and point her out as a woman of shame, but she was surprised at how few people looked at her in a strange way. A few people even greeted her in a friendly manner, as if they were unaware of what had happened to her.

Two incidents marred an otherwise pleasant venture out into the public eye. The first of these happened as Daintry and Mela were leaving the market.

Mela suddenly clutched her sister's arm, pointed and exclaimed, 'Look!'

Daintry directed her attention to the area Mela was indicating. What she saw made tremors of fear flood through her body. The constable, accompanied by a soldier from the Queen's Guard, was leading a prisoner in the direction of the Round Tower. The scene in front of her brought back vivid memories of when she had been in a similar situation. She felt pangs of compassion for the man being led away and knew what he must be experiencing, whatever his crime.

As the three approached, Daintry was tempted to flee, but she seemed to be held rigidly to the spot. Would the constable recognise her? What would he do if he did? Every second seemed like hours as she watched them get closer. Suddenly they were in front of her. The constable glanced in her direction, and recognition seemed to dawn, but then he appeared to shrug his shoulders as the group went on its way. Some sort of relief came to Daintry.

Mela had watched the whole incident with curious interest. When the prisoner and his escorts had disappeared from view, she whispered to Daintry, 'I know what he did,' clearly referring to the prisoner.

Daintry made no reply. Her thoughts were still full of the events of the last few minutes.

Her silence did not deter Mela from elaborating. 'He stole a loaf of bread from the baker. Peena told me.'

Daintry remained silent. Mela had never been in the same position as she and the poor prisoner they had just seen.

The second incident that day was equally distressing for Daintry. For some reason Mela decided to return home via a route that took them past the church. Daintry made no objection, but as they started to walk down the lane more unhappy memories surfaced. It was here that she had been dragged with bound arms to face the Witch Prosecutor and a predicted fate. She hardly heard Mela's unceasing chatter as the memories came flooding back to her.

Suddenly, when they were close to the church, Pastor Kartov emerged from a side gate. He glanced at the two girls, who were still a few steps away. For a moment his look centred on Daintry, and then in an instant he turned around to re-enter the gate, crossing himself as he did so. By the time the two girls reached the spot he had disappeared from view.

'Well, he was in a hurry,' Mela remarked casually.

Daintry said nothing. She was thinking of the last time she had seen the old pastor, when he had visited her in the stinking cell at the Round House. It was not a pleasant memory, and it was one she could not share with her sister. She was relieved when they reached their own street and the security of their home.

The next excursion was a more cheerful event for Daintry. After her first visit to the market with Mela, she had fought with herself to venture out again. Eventually logic took over. Nothing had happened after the first visit, and it seemed she would have to learn to live with the occasional incident that brought back unpleasant memories.

This time it was Peena who accompanied her. Nothing happened until they were leaving the market, loaded with provisions. It was then that she spied a group of Forest Women selling their baskets. She had barely had a chance to take in the spectacle when she realised that one of the women was calling her name.

She suddenly recognised the owner of the voice.

'Meeka!' she cried out, dropping her load and rushing over to her friend.

Meeka threw her arms around her. 'Daintry! I was hoping upon hope that I might encounter you today!'

'It's so good to see you, Meeka.' Daintry was close to tears. She stood back and viewed her friend. 'But what happened to you? The last time I saw you they were taking you back to Katangar.'

Meeka laughed. 'I never got there. We were rescued by men from the Forest People, and the guards didn't care any more anyway. But look at you! Dressed like a lady again.' She eyed Daintry up and down and grinned.

More composed, Daintry briefly related her tribulations since she had last seen Meeka.

Even Meeka was subdued at her revelations. 'I guess I got off lucky,' she remarked quietly.

Daintry scrutinised her friend. 'But what about you?' she asked.

Meeka grinned. 'I'm a real Forest Girl now.' She glanced down at her gaily coloured clothes and bare feet. Then quite coyly she added, 'And I'm going to marry Gerik.'

Daintry remembered Gerik. He was one of those who had faithfully guarded the camp. An attractive young man, he had been eyed by many of the other eligible young women in the camp. She was happy for her friend. 'Good for you!' she replied laughingly.

Meeka had more news to relate. 'Saltima is also in our camp still. She is going to marry Karl.'

'Oh! I'm so pleased for her!' Daintry exclaimed.

Meeka's next remark brought pangs of wistfulness to Daintry. 'Why don't you come and join us again?' she asked.

Daintry smiled at her. 'I wish I could, but my destiny lies elsewhere,' she replied, her voice tinged with sadness.

Meeka's suggestion made Daintry anxious again. Where did her destiny lie? She was unsure. It was so tempting to return to the Forest People when she thought of all the happy days she had spent with them, free from care and close to nature.

The two young women chatted for a long time, while a patient Peena waited for her mistress so that they could continue with their mission. In the end Daintry had to take her leave from her old friend. There were tears in her eyes as she waved goodbye.

It was a subdued Daintry who walked back to her father's house. Her fate now seemed to be so uncertain that she had been almost inclined to accept Meeka's offer and return to the Forest People and the simple joys she had experienced living with them. But she knew that such a decision would hurt her father terribly. No, she had to remain where she was and accept what the future had in store for her. But if Conrad no longer wanted her as his wife, what would that be?

Chapter 42

'I feel that we are making good progress.'

It was Assem Rokar who spoke, as he took a seat opposite Queen Aleena. He was responding to a question she had asked him soon after he had entered her workroom.

'In what way?' the queen asked.

Assem paused as he took the goblet of refreshment offered by Sharla. Taking a sip of the liquid, he elaborated. 'I believe that there is more stability in the kingdom now, and the efforts of Conrad Accker are beginning to show. He is proving to be an excellent Keeper of the Purse.'

'I am very pleased to hear that,' replied the queen. Then, with concern in her voice, she asked, 'Assem, do you think the people of Altaria have accepted me? I mean, accepted having a queen for the first time?'

Assem knew that she had been anxious in her new role, ever since she had ascended to the throne. To him she was still the little princess who had visited his house and been anxious to do the right things. Now that she was queen of Altaria, he was once again her confidant, somebody she could release her fears to. He knew he had to reassure her once again. 'I think they have,' he replied.

'I am glad,' Queen Aleena replied softly.

Assem gave a hint of a smile as he spoke again. 'Your Majesty, if I may presume to say it, all you need to do now is choose a suitable consort.'

The queen reacted quickly. Only Assem would make such a remark to her, but she knew what he was referring to.

'You mean Prince Alon?' she asked, looking at him coyly.

Assem nodded. 'I do.'

The queen regarded him with a mixture of curiosity and reproach.

'I have heard from Prince Alon since my return to Taslar.' She paused for a second, as if considering what to say next. Then she added, 'We may meet sometime, but it is early days, and neither of us is in any hurry.'

'I am happy for you. Prince Alon would make a good consort.'

The queen's response was only a shy smile.

Both were silent for a few seconds. Assem knew that the queen had received a letter from Prince Alon: he had seen a messenger dressed in the livery of the Forancean Court arrive at the palace. Since, as First Minister, he had not duly received any communication concerning the messenger's presence, he had rightly assumed that the visit was for Queen Aleena.

He was pleased for the young queen. The two royal families of Altaria and Forancer had always been close and made summer visits to each other. He had observed the childhood friendship between Princess Aleena and Prince Alon. They had often played together, and as they grew up they had spent time together on various pursuits. Prince Alon was the fourth son of King Garton of Forancer and was known to be more interested in the arts than in any matters of state. Before her incarceration, Assem had been expecting Princess Aleena to announce her betrothal to the handsome young prince, but that situation had been abruptly terminated. Now he was delighted that clearly their friendship had been revived.

The queen broke into Assem's brief musing with a question changing the subject.

'Conrad still appears to be very sad. Has he not renewed his agreement with Daintry Brouka?'

'It is my understanding, Your Majesty, that the lady in question has refused his hand in marriage.'

'Do you know why?' the queen asked, though she believed she already knew the answer.

'She was convicted as a witch and sent to Katangar.'

'But that situation has changed, since she now has a royal pardon,' the queen pointed out quickly.

'That is so,' Assem agreed, 'but who knows what happened to her at Katangar?'

There was sadness in her voice as the queen spoke quietly again. 'My own brother had me sent to Katangar on a false charge, just like Daintry Brouka. Only those who have been there can understand the horror of the place. As long as I am queen no more women will be sent there.' She paused. 'And eventually, I hope, no men either.'

'But an escape was arranged for you, and the Forest People gave you sanctuary,' Assem interjected.

The queen nodded. 'That is true, but Daintry had a more traumatic time than I and Sharla. When she came to the Forest People she was exhausted and sick. She would not have lasted much longer on her own.'

She paused for a second, deep in thought. 'Daintry Brouka is a sweet, gentle girl, but also very resourceful. She will make an excellent wife for Conrad.'

'But it seems that is not to be,' Assem pointed out.

Queen Aleena smiled at him.

'I will talk to Conrad. He needs a woman's advice,' she remarked.

A few hours later Conrad followed the page to the queen's workroom. Queen Aleena was busy writing at her desk as he entered, but she immediately rose to greet him.

'Good day, Your Majesty.' Conrad bowed slightly.

The queen smiled. 'Good day, Conrad. What news from the Purse have you for me?' As she spoke, she chose a nearby chair to sit on and indicated one opposite for Conrad.

317

Conrad sat down. He was getting used to the almost casual manner in which his meetings with the queen took place. They were so different from the formal and uncomfortable brief sessions with King Henri. He was eager to answer the queen's questions and to relate his good news.

'Your Majesty, all the money from the palace cellar has now been transported to the Purse's vault and been counted. It was quite a task for my assistant, Wilner, and me.'

'How much value is there?' the queen asked anxiously.

Conrad quickly glanced at the document he held. 'At the worst assessment there is over three years' normal income for Altaria.'

The queen suddenly broke into smiles and clapped her hands.

'Conrad, that's splendid news!' she exclaimed excitedly.

'It is indeed,' Conrad agreed. 'It can solve so many problems.'

'Lower taxes for the people of Altaria,' Queen Aleena suggested with a smile.

'That has already been arranged, and we can pay the Guard regularly now,' replied Conrad.

'That would be a good thing. Under my brother they were never paid on time,' the queen remarked thoughtfully.

Suddenly she regarded Conrad with a look of concern. She voiced her thoughts.

'You have worked very hard, Conrad, since you became my Keeper of the Purse. But you also need to make some time for yourself.'

'I will do my best,' Conrad replied.

The queen regarded him in silence for a moment. 'Tomaz came to see me earlier. He has just returned from Toomer. He is to marry Mela, the sister of Daintry Brouka.'

'Yes, I heard the news on the way here today. I am pleased for both Tomaz and Mela.'

Seizing the opportunity provided and scrutinising Conrad closely, the queen asked, 'And what of Daintry? Were you not betrothed to her?'

A sad countenance overcame Conrad. 'As you know, I met Daintry in Taslar a little while ago, and she told me she could no longer marry me. Then she ran away and could not be found.'

'But you went to Toomer after that to look for her.'

Conrad nodded. 'Yes, but she was not there. I saw her father and he would not tell me where she was. He said that she was in hiding.'

The queen was silent again for a few seconds. Then she spoke in a soft voice.

'Conrad, do you know what really happened to Daintry?'

Conrad shook his head. 'Just what Master Brouka told me: that she had been convicted of witchcraft and sent to the mines at Katangar.'

Queen Aleena nodded. 'That is true. She obtained a herbal potion to cure her father of the fever and for that she was accused of being a witch. If she had not been sent to Katangar, she would have been executed.'

After a brief pause, she continued. 'I met many women like Daintry at Katangar. Women completely innocent of any crime, forced to endure the most awful treatment, slaving for many hours each day at a capstan to lift buckets of ore from deep underground to the surface, all to satisfy my brother's greed. Fortunately Daintry managed to escape and was rescued by the Forest People. I got to know her while she was being cared for by them.' The queen gave a little sigh. 'Then we were both recaptured and taken to Geeva castle.'

Conrad sat in shocked silence, absorbing what he had just heard. He found himself almost choked with emotion. He could remember seeing the group of prisoners being led to Katangar. How could gentle Daintry have been treated like that? Eventually he would obtain more detail, but for the present all he could feel was pride and admiration that she had experienced all that and somehow survived.

Queen Aleena respected his silence, but she spoke again.

'And what now, Conrad? Are you going to abandon Daintry?'

Conrad shook his head. 'No. After what you have told me, I love her more than ever, but I am puzzled why she said she could not marry me and ran away from me.'

The queen looked at him closely and lowered her voice as she replied.

'I think I know why. All the women who went to Katangar were branded like animals with a hot iron, the mark of a criminal and one of shame. When Daintry refused to marry you, she was thinking of you. She did not want to degrade you and have you humiliated as her husband because of what had happened to her.'

Conrad found himself unable to speak. In the last few minutes his love for Daintry had soared to new heights. When he had met her in Taslar and she had refused to marry him, it was to protect him: she had not been thinking of herself. All he could bring himself to say was, 'I understand everything now.'

Queen Aleena smiled at him. 'You must go to her without further delay.'

Conrad nodded, but he still harboured doubt. 'But she may still not wish to marry me, after all she has been through.'

'I think she does,' the queen replied, with a little smile. She suddenly added, 'And I think she will, now that she has a pardon and is released from the stigma of bearing a mark.'

Conrad was deep in thought. He wished he had known all that the queen had just related when he had encountered Daintry in the market at Taslar. It would have explained a lot. Now he just wanted to see Daintry again as soon as possible.

The queen interrupted his thoughts. 'Take a horse from the Royal Stables, and two guardsmen to accompany you, and hasten to Toomer without delay. You must put the poor girl out of her misery and not let her suffer any longer.'

'Yes, thank you, Your Majesty. I will journey there first thing tomorrow morning.'

'That will be good. And tell Daintry that her queen would like to see her again soon.'

'I will do that, Your Majesty.'

As Conrad rose to take his leave, Queen Aleena suddenly thought of something else. Before he went on his way, she announced quite firmly, 'With my Messenger marrying Mela Brouka and my Keeper of the Purse marrying Daintry Brouka, I hope to see a double wedding here in Taslar. Don't forget!'

'I won't, Your Majesty,' Conrad replied, grinning slightly as he adopted the queen's more light-hearted approach.

As he was leaving the queen's company, she called after him. 'Remember, do not return until you have received a promise of marriage from Daintry. That's a Royal Command, Conrad.'

She was laughing as she spoke.

Chapter 43

Conrad rode into Toomer, accompanied by the two soldiers from the Queen's Guard. One of them had been to Toomer previously with him, and as they drew nearer to the town he described in some detail to his companion the delights and pleasure that could be found in the drinking houses there.

Conrad was silent. All his thinking was directed to what he might experience in Toomer and how Daintry would react to his visit. His heart had gone out to her when he heard from Queen Aleena about the ordeal she must have experienced. When Daintry had needed him most, he had been unable to be there. How must she have felt? It was a miracle that she had escaped from Katangar: few who went there were so lucky. Now he desperately wanted to see her again, to take her in his arms and tell her how much he loved her. But would she still want to marry him? The question nagged at him.

Once the party arrived in Toomer, Conrad directed his two companions to see to the stabling of the horses and then, leaving them to their anticipated pleasures, he made his way to his old home. His parents were overjoyed to see him again and kept his attention longer than he had intended. As he was telling them about recent events in Taslar, his heart and thoughts were with Daintry.

It was his father who noticed his subdued mood. During a brief lull in the conversation, he regarded Conrad with a twinkle in his eye. 'But I think, my boy,' he remarked, 'that your visit to Toomer concerns something of greater importance.'

Conrad nodded. 'Yes, Father. I wish to see Daintry again, and I hope that she will agree to be my wife.'

His father took him by the arm. 'Then I urge you to talk to her without delay.'

'Yes, you must,' interjected Conrad's mother, 'for Daintry is a sad young lady these days.'

Conrad left his parents' house soon after that and made his way next door, to Anton Brouka's residence.

He knocked loudly on the door. It was opened by Peena, who greeted him courteously and held it open for him.

As Conrad stepped into the house, Anton appeared. Immediately he embraced his guest.

'It is good to see you again, Conrad.'

'It is good to be here, Master Brouka.'

'Come.' With a wave of his hand Anton indicated the direction of his workroom. 'Peena, a glass of wine for our guest.'

Anton settled into his chair, and Conrad took a seat on the opposite side of the table. He regarded his host. Anton appeared to be more relaxed and cheerful than on his previous visit.

It was Anton who spoke first.

'All the women have gone to the dressmaker, I suspect to purchase material for Mela's wedding dress.' He winked at Conrad.

Conrad changed the subject. 'How are your affairs now? Are things improving for you now that taxes have been reduced?'

'Yes, indeed,' replied Anton. 'I am optimistic again for the future. The new mill is performing well.'

'That is indeed good news,' enthused Conrad.

Anton chuckled. 'At least I can afford a dowry for my daughters now, which of course pleases Mela no end.'

Shortly afterwards Peena appeared with the wine. This small break in the conversation gave Conrad the opportunity to bring up the subject that had been dominating his thoughts.

'Master Brouka, I have come to see Daintry and ask her to be my wife.'

Anton was silent for a few seconds. He spoke gravely. 'You have my permission, of course, but my understanding is that Daintry had no wish for such a marriage when you met her in Taslar.'

'But that is all changed now that she has a royal pardon.'

'That is true. But Daintry has experienced much since her arrest. She is quiet and subdued now.'

'I will make her happy again.'

Anton smiled. 'I am sure you will, but I fear Daintry's heart may lie elsewhere.' He paused, collecting his thoughts. 'Only recently, she begged me to allow her to return to the Forest People.'

Conrad was shocked by this disclosure.

'I must talk to her!' he exclaimed.

'Of course,' agreed Anton, taking a sip of his wine.

There was a short silence between the two men. Conrad was alarmed at Anton's news. He had not even considered such an eventuality, though he had been puzzled to see Daintry dressed as a Forest Girl.

It was Anton who renewed the conversation. He appeared deep in thought, as he spoke in a subdued voice.

'Daintry has had to endure more than any other girl of her age should. The ghastly conditions she experienced at Katangar were unspeakable. I saw her there, and the memory haunts me still.'

Anton fell silent, scanning Conrad's face for a reaction. It was not long in coming.

'I feel for Daintry and I deeply regret that I was not in a position to rescue her from such an ordeal. Queen Aleena was also sent to Katangar, and she has told me of some of the horrors. Fortunately they were both rescued by the Forest People.'

Anton nodded and with a slight smile remarked, 'Perhaps Daintry met another there who wished for her hand in marriage.'

Conrad had been contemplating such a situation. Before he could reply, there was the unmistakable sound of the women returning. Anton sprang into action with a hurried command.

'Quickly. Go into the garden. I will send Daintry to you.'

Conrad needed no urging. He escaped through an adjoining door into the familiar territory of his childhood. As he left he heard Anton summoning Mogo.

As the three women re-entered the house, Mela chatted gaily about their visit to the dressmaker. She had spent a long time choosing material and items for her dowry and now she was well pleased with the result of her outing.

Daintry, though happy to help her sister, had watched the proceedings with some sadness. Would she ever be in Mela's position now? It seemed unlikely. Most of the time she had been keeping her feelings to herself: everything was too painful to talk about, even to her sister. Several times since she had seen Meeka in the marketplace the idea of returning to the Forest People had loomed up again in her thinking. Perhaps she could persuade her father to allow her to go back to them, but she hesitated to bring up the subject again with him just yet. She would wait until Mela was married.

It was Mogo returning from being summoned by Anton that disrupted Daintry's musing and Mela's exuberance.

Grabbing a basket, Mogo handed it to Daintry. 'Take this, Daintry, and go and collect some berries from the garden.'

In silence Daintry started to obey.

'I'll come with you and help you,' announced an excited Mela.

'You stay here,' snapped Mogo. 'I have another job for you.'

Surprised at Mogo's sudden change of tone, Daintry meekly took the basket and left for the garden. She liked its secluded and peaceful atmosphere. It was a place where she had spent many happy moments.

As she walked down the path towards the place where the berries Mogo had requested grew in abundance she suddenly became aware that she was not alone. When she realised who was standing there, she dropped the basket and broke into a run. One word escaped her lips. 'Conrad!'

The next instant she was in his arms.

'My precious Daintry,' he whispered, 'can you forgive me for not being here sooner?'

Daintry lifted her head and looked into his eyes. She spoke quietly. 'It is I who must ask your forgiveness for running away from you in Taslar.'

Placing his arm around her, Conrad slowly led her to the seat where all that time ago he had first pronounced his love for her. They sat there together, holding hands.

It was Conrad who broke the silence.

'I have spoken with Queen Aleena and your father. They have told me what you have endured. I am proud of you, but sad that I did not come to your aid.'

'It is past now,' murmured Daintry, leaning her head on his shoulder.

'How could such a thing happen to you?' Conrad retorted, almost angrily.

'I try not to think about it any more,' Daintry replied softly.

There was a brief silence between them, past events rekindled for Daintry. This prompted her next remark. 'And now Mela is to marry Tomaz Razner, the Queen's Messenger.'

'Tomaz is a fine man. They will make an excellent marriage,' Conrad observed thoughtfully.

'And Princess… I mean Queen Aleena: how is she now?' asked Daintry.

'She is a good and considerate queen,' Conrad announced. Then he added, 'She sends you her greetings and wants to see you again soon.'

That would be nice, Daintry thought, remembering the care she had received from Aleena.

'I would like that,' she said simply. Then, remembering her time with the Forest People, she added, 'Princess... Queen Aleena looked after me when I first came to the Forest People. I was sick and weak. She even allowed me to sleep in her bed.' Still deep in recollection, she continued in a quiet voice. 'The Forest People were so kind to us. They fed us and gave us clothing and shelter and asked nothing in return.'

'But what of us, my love?' asked Conrad. 'I have come to renew my hopes and ask you to marry me. Tell me you will. It will make me very happy.'

Daintry lifted her head from his shoulder and looked into his eyes again. The tears were not far away as she replied, 'It is what I want more than anything else, but I feel I am not worthy of you.'

'Hush. Do not say such things.' Conrad slowly kissed her on the lips.

Daintry broke away from him. She looked at him anxiously. 'But I have been to Katangar. I carry its mark. People would despise you if I married you, and then you would hate me.'

Conrad shook his head. 'That is not so. Queen Aleena has decreed that this is not to happen. Women who have been to Katangar have a royal pardon now.'

Daintry was floating between happiness and anxiety. All of a sudden she thought of something else. 'My betrothal ring!' she cried out. 'They stole it from me in the Round Tower.'

Conrad gave a little laugh as he replied. 'Fear not, my love. I will buy you another, even better one.'

'I've still got your stone!' Daintry exclaimed. Hurriedly she extracted it from her bodice. Throughout all her suffering it had hung around her neck, regarded as worthless by all who had seen it.

Conrad looked at it as it nestled in Daintry's hand. He smiled. 'Perhaps it protected you,' he said softly.

'I would like to think so,' Daintry whispered.

She fingered the stone as it now hung outside her dress. It made her recall the past. 'When I was a prisoner, sometimes without hope, I used to clutch it and think of you.'

'When the fighting was over, I came to Geeva castle to rescue you, but you were no longer there,' Conrad remarked sadly.

'I saw you. I was so close to you. I was hiding when you passed on the road to Geeva castle, but I did not realise it was you,' Daintry replied softly.

'If only I had known…' Conrad thought back to his desperate ride to the castle.

There was silence again for a few seconds, the two of them content in each other's company. It was again Conrad who broke the stillness of the moment. Taking one of Daintry's hands, he held it to his lips. He spoke again.

'And what now, my love? Will you marry me now?'

Daintry breathed her reply. 'All I want now is to be your wife.'

Conrad suddenly smiled, remembering something. 'I have been instructed by Queen Aleena that I am not to return to Taslar without a promise of marriage. It is a Royal Command,' he announced.

'In that case, how can I refuse?' Daintry replied, laughing.

The next instant they were in each other's arms and kissing passionately, oblivious to the world around them.